SPIRITS, TALES & A BODY BY THE BALES

SPIRITS, TALES & A BODY BY THE BALES

A MOTHER/DAUGHTER COZY MYSTERY

LILY & CASSIE BY THE SEA MYSTERIES
BOOK TWO

NELLIE H. STEELE

This is a work of fiction. Names, characters, places, and incidents either are the product of the author's imagination or are used fictitiously. Any resemblance to actual persons, living or dead, events, or locales is entirely coincidental.

Cover design by Stephanie A. Sovak.

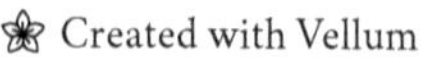 Created with Vellum

CHAPTER 1

Cassie raced down the darkened hall and into the cool fall night air. She gasped as she doubled over, glancing behind her into the building. The screaming face of a suspended specter sped toward her at an alarming rate. Its shrieking filled the air as it approached.

Cassie gulped in another breath. Her hair escaped at every angle from her tight ponytail and she smoothed it back as best she could.

"Well?" Lily's voice questioned.

Cassie leapt, pressing her hand against her chest and spinning to face her mother. She twisted to glance into the hall again.

The ghost retreated, taking its shrieks with it.

Cassie shook her head and waved her hand in the air. "It's still moving way too fast. People won't even get the full effect of the decorations with that thing zipping around."

Cassie motioned emphatically toward the floating ghost, already on its return journey, racing toward them with its frightening face. She tugged her fabric ponytail holder from her hair before finger-combing it back into a sleek high ponytail.

Lily tapped her pencil to her lips. "Maybe we should trim his line and let him speed up and down a smaller section of the hall. Or can we loop him and let him run in a circle?"

Cassie pointed a finger at her. "Oh, there's an idea. Though I'm not sure how scary a ghost flying around in circles will be."

"You're right, not effective. Well, we'll either need to find a way to slow him down or reroute him."

Lily tugged a folded paper from her cardigan pocket, jotting a note on the paper in an unused margin. "Just another thing added to the list."

She shoved the paper into her pocket and slid the pencil into the messy bun at the nape of her neck.

"That list is longer than the time we have left," Cassie groaned.

Lily glanced at her watch. "It's already after seven. Maybe we should do one last run-through and call it a night. I'm tired, sore, and starving."

Cassie's shoulders slumped as she considered another walk-through. With a sigh, she said, "Okay." She tugged a headlamp onto her forehead and flicked on the light. "Here we go."

"Ladies! Ladies! Yoo-hoo!" a familiar voice called. Cassie swung her head in the direction of the shout. The svelte form of Mayor Tinsley Thompson hurried toward them, wobbling on her suede mocha heels that matched her tan and mocha skirt suit.

Tinsley winced, covering her eyes as Cassie's headlamp shined brightly at her.

"Sorry, Mayor Thompson," Cassie said, clicking off her headlamp. "We were just about to head back in for a final run-through tonight."

Tinsley let out a chuckle as she closed the gap between them, lowering her hand and showcasing her broad grin. "And how is it looking?"

"Well," Lily said tapping the paper in her pocket, "we've got a list of things that we'd like to adjust. We're going to take one last look tonight before we head home and discuss everything over dinner."

Tinsley gazed past their shoulders into the barn. "Any chance for a sneak peek?"

"You're welcome to head through the hay bale maze portion, but no previews of the interior just yet," Lily said.

Tinsley's smile faltered a bit before she answered. She rubbed her palms back and forth as she tensed her jaw. "Not even a little one for the mayor?"

"Not yet," Lily answered.

Tinsley waved a finger in the air. "You do realize the festival is Friday."

Lily bobbed her head up and down. "We are aware of that, yes. We'll have it ready. If you come by the day before we can give you a pre-festival preview."

Tinsley's eyebrows rose toward her hairline. "I suppose that'll have to work. I'm just dying to see what you've done."

"And you shall," Lily promised. "After we've made the adjustments."

"Well," Tinsley said with a forlorn glance into the building, "I suppose I'll let you get back to it." She took one final glance around Cassie, craning her neck to stare into the darkened hall before she sashayed away.

"We'll never finish this Halloween maze with all the interruptions," Lily murmured as she tugged her headlamp onto her forehead and clicked it on.

"At least we have interest," Cassie said as they rounded the building to the front.

Lily pulled open one of the doors to the abandoned barn

set in a large field at the edge of town. "I can't believe there's this much."

"I can't believe we have to lock this place up every night so the paparazzi don't sneak in for advanced photos!" Cassie said as she tugged the door shut behind them, plunging the interior into semi-darkness, lit only by their headlamps and the eerie lightning they'd spent days perfecting.

With plastic sheeting hung from the rafters, the mother-daughter duo had divvied up the large barn space into hallways, rooms, and dead-ends, designed to entertain the seaside town of Hideaway Bay's residents and visitors during the Halloween season.

Those brave enough to enter the haunted carnival-themed maze would encounter animated props, spooky standing decor, and have the chance to collect a prize. A game, also designed along with the maze by the two women, asked festival-goers to solve riddles, retrieve pictures of objects, and fill in questions for a chance to win gift cards to several participating Main Street shops.

Lily and Cassie's own shop, Buy the Sea, headlined the generous package, aimed at giving residents the chance to shop, dine, and enjoy everything the town offered.

Cassie flicked off her headlamp trying to gauge the opening scene as visitors would see it.

Lily checked her note sheet before she clicked hers off. "Okay, lightning looks good, but I still think this needs a little extra something."

"Do you think we could pull off the life-sized jack-in-the-box with that creepy clown I saw at the Spooks'N'Specters store in Misty Hollow?"

Lily cocked her head and sighed. "I'm beginning to think you're right. It would be effective, though I hate to have you driving two towns over for a three-foot clown. And then you have to build a box for him."

"We have the budget, though, and I already found a box. I've got the metallic wrapping paper. I could do a really cute job of making it. We'd just need to think about how to make him pop up."

"Spring motor? Listen, let's head over there tomorrow morning. I'd like to take a last look at what they have."

Cassie shot her a glance, flicking on her headlamp.

"Ah," Lily squeaked as she shielded her eyes. "Cassie!"

Cassie jabbed a finger toward her mother. "You want to go and look at that severed clown head again, admit it!"

"I will not!" Lily said as they followed the hallway created by the sheeting, past a vampire that hissed.

"You've been after that creepy clown head for weeks."

"I think it's effective. We'll create a blackout in the ceiling and make it look like it's popping through."

"Ugh, I'll avoid that room."

The ladies completed their walkthrough, noting several things to adjust, fix or change before they stepped into the evening air. Cassie pulled the doors closed behind them and locked the barn with a chain and padlock.

"I'm beat," Lily grumbled as she climbed into Cassie's Wrangler, peeling her headlamp off her sweaty forehead and dumping it in her tote.

"I'll be glad for the trip to Misty Hollow tomorrow. It'll be just the break we need before we start putting the final touches on the maze."

"Final touches," Lily said, her head slamming into the headrest behind her. "I feel like we'll never get to those words."

Cassie fired the engine and gave her head a shake. "One way or another, we'll get there."

"Did you call in the order?" Lily asked as Cassie eased the car away from the barn.

Cassie chuckled as she answered, glancing back and forth

before pulling onto the road. "No one calls things in anymore, Mom. I ordered on the app."

"Well, whatever, as long as I've got an order of stuffed shells and a bowl of soup waiting for me, I don't care which way you did it."

With wide eyes, Cassie shot a surprised glance at her mother. "Oh, you wanted stuffed shells?"

"Cass! Tell me you didn't get the wrong order. I specifically said stuffed shells. I've been talking about it all day."

Cassie's face broke into a wide grin. "I know, I know. I got your shells."

Lily shook her head and gave her daughter a playful smack on the arm. "Don't do that to your old mother. It's been too long of a day."

"You're not *that* old," Cassie said, pulling into the parking lot of the Italian restaurant on the edge of town. After tapping around on her phone, a woman in a crisp white shirt and black pants dashed from the restaurant, a take-out bag in hand.

"Put it in the back, Cassie?" she called as she circled the car.

"Yep!" Cassie answered.

The girl swung the hatch open and slid the bag inside. "Enjoy. Can't wait to see the maze!" She slammed the tailgate shut before she offered a wave as she hurried back into the confines of the eatery.

"I'm starting to get the jitters with this maze. We may have oversold it," Lily said.

"I can't believe how excited everyone is." Cassie pulled onto Ocean Drive, cruising past the seaside estates toward their infamous home.

The lone light they'd left on earlier glowed through the living room window as Cassie's tires crunched the gravel of their driveway. The dark form of Whispering Manor rose in front of them, obliterating the rising moon.

Cassie eased the car to a stop, tugging on her emergency break before she swung her door open and collected her tote bag from the back. "I'm going to need the pain relievers tonight," she called, her muscles protesting when she pulled the take-out bag from the rear.

Lily climbed the stairs to their wide wooden porch, squinting down at the alarm keyfob in her hands.

"I never can see which one of these is the unlock button," she complained, turning the fob toward the light streaming from the living room window.

Cassie mounted the first wooden step. "It's the right."

"Are you sure?" Lily inquired, her thumb hovering over the small key on the right.

"Yes...ish," Cassie said as her sneakers hit the porch's floorboards.

"The last time you were only kind of sure, we had Wyatt out here, weapons hot," Lily said as she pressed the right button and strained for the electronic voice inside to announce the alarm system had been disabled.

A crisp British accent mumbled unintelligible words from their foyer.

"Ha, it's off. I was right," Cassie said with a triumphant smile.

Lily swung the screen door open and shoved her key into the lock.

Cassie arched her eyebrows upward. "And I beg to differ. Wyatt wasn't weapons hot, as you put it. But he did use the siren."

"And the lights and he screeched to a halt and nearly tripped himself getting out of the car."

The front door swung open on creaky hinges and the women stepped into the Victorian rambler. A one-eyed tuxedo cat raced down the stairs, pausing as he reached one of the pair of carved wooden angel statues at the bottom. He rubbed his whiskers against the angel's robes before he sashayed across the foyer to Lily and Cassie.

"Hey, buddy," Cassie said, squatting down and giving him a swipe down his back. "Did you miss us?"

"I bet you're starved, Willy," Lily said to the cat. "I know I am."

He swung his single eye toward her and offered a meow before he spun back to rub against Cassie's outstretched fingers.

"We'll get you some food before I change, and we settle down to eat."

"Don't be too long, I'm as hungry as he is!" Lily called as she trudged up the squeaky staircase, heading for her room at the top.

"Come on, buddy," Cassie said, hefting the take-out bag up as she led her one-eyed feline to the kitchen. She dumped the bag on the table near the bay window and grabbed a can of cat food from the pantry.

Another meow escaped the dapper cat's mouth as the can popped open and the fishy aroma of Sea Captain's Choice filled the air. Willy stalked back and forth, tossing his body against Cassie's legs until she set his bowl down.

With another stroke down his back, which the cat ignored as he chowed down, Cassie hurried from the kitchen and up the stairs to her bedroom.

She wound the carousel that sat on her dresser as she peeled off her t-shirt and jeans, swapping them for a pair of pajamas, a plush robe, and a pair of fluffy cat slippers. Cassie gave the carousel a final glance before she left her room, smiling at it. After their theft a month earlier, she thought she'd lost the item. They were lucky to have it retrieved, found in the culprit's hotel room torn apart but undamaged, overall.

Cassie shuffled down the stairs and swung around toward the kitchen. Plates clattered from within, and the microwave revved.

"Cold?" Cassie inquired as she scooped Willy's bowl from the floor.

Lily switched the plates, pressing a few buttons before the microwave sprang to life again. "Not hot."

Cassie laid two napkins and silverware on the table.

Lily retrieved two potholders and waved a finger in the air. "Uh-uh. I'm eating on the couch."

Cassie wiggled her eyebrows in approval and swiped the items off the table. After retrieving two sodas from the refrigerator, she followed her mother to the living room.

They settled on the couch, Willy leaping up between them, for their meal. A small brown leather journal lay on the coffee table in front of them.

Cassie eyed it as she propped her feet on top. "I don't think you'll ever get to read that journal."

Lily puckered her lips as she blew on her potato soup. "I'd be surprised if I got to it before the maze opens. And it's driving me crazy!"

"I'm really glad we got it back with the carousel. At least you'll be able to finish it at some point."

Lily waved her empty spoon toward it as the warm soup slid down her throat. "A week's delay is far too much. I'm really interested to see what else Henrietta has to say."

"Well, we know she hid the treasure right here," Cassie answered, referencing the hidden treasure of the pirate, Black Jack, that she and her mother found only a month earlier after moving into the most talked-about house in Hideaway Bay.

"Yes, and then became so despondent she threw herself to

her death." Lily shook her head. "It just doesn't make sense to me. I'm interested to see if her writing becomes disturbed."

"Maybe her brother died first. Didn't Wyatt say he died young? Maybe that made her so forlorn that she killed herself."

"We should look up the date of his death. You could be on to something."

"I'll try to find some information tomorrow after our trip."

"Oh, ambitious of you," Lily said, her eyebrows raised. "I doubt we'll have a minute tomorrow after our trip."

Cassie pulled her lips to the side in a display of thought before she palmed her phone in one hand and tapped around on it. "There!" She dumped the phone on the cushion next to her. "Done!"

"When did he die?" Lily inquired as she snapped the lid onto her now-empty soup container.

"I don't know. I sent a text to Pearl and asked her if she could find the information."

"Passing the buck, huh?" Lily said with a wink.

Cassie raised her chin and smiled. "Delegating, like Daddy taught me."

Lily bit her lower lip, her eyes turning misty as she reached out to clutch Cassie's hand. "He'd be so proud of you."

Cassie firmed her lower lip as memories of her late father flooded into her mind. She swallowed hard as she fought to keep the memory of the phone call announcing the plane crash that robbed her of both her father and husband from dancing across her mind.

The chime of her phone pulled both women back to reality. Cassie glanced at her lit display. "Pearl says she's on it. She'll let us know tomorrow."

Lily closed her take-out container with half the stuffed

shells remaining in the Styrofoam rectangle. "Whew, I'm stuffed *and* exhausted."

Cassie blew out a long breath. "Me too. I'm too tired to even finish my chicken parm. I'll save it for tomorrow." She closed the lid, snapping the tabs into place to secure it.

"I'm heading up," Lily announced as she stood from the couch. "As soon as I drop this off in the fridge."

"I'll take it," Cassie offered, waving her hand at her mother for the container.

"I'm not going to make you ask twice." Lily passed the containers to her daughter.

With everything balanced between her two hands, Cassie scurried from the room.

Lily stretched and yawned before taking a step toward the foyer. The small brown journal caught her eye as she circled the coffee table. With pursed lips, she swiped the book from the wooden top and shoved it in her robe's pocket.

She winced as she climbed the creaky staircase, her muscles protesting each movement. "I'm getting too old for this," she murmured as she passed through her bedroom to her en-suite bathroom and downed two over-the-counter pain relievers.

She shuffled over the hardwood floor, padding onto her area rug and plopping onto her bed. After tugging the journal from her pocket and setting it on the nightstand, she peeled the robe off and tossed it at the foot of the bed.

With another groan, she slid between the sheets and stretched her tired muscles before flicking off her light.

The room plunged into darkness. After a moment, Lily's eyes adjusted to the dim light of the waxing gibbous moon gleaming through her window. She squeezed her eyes closed, hoping the pain reliever let her drift off to sleep.

With a sigh, she realized it wouldn't happen. Design ideas,

modifications, and new item placements floated through her head. In her mind, she constructed the clown head popping from the ceiling display. With the mechanics approved by her brain, she moved on to adjusting the too-quick ghost. After coming up with a few ideas to try, she rolled onto her side.

She'd never sleep if this continued. Her mind would never stop adjusting, fixing, and creating. Lily heaved in a deep breath as she hauled herself up to sit and flicked on her bedside lamp.

The light shined down on the worn leather book.

"All right, Henrietta, let's see what you have to say."

She flicked open the journal, paging to find where she'd left off before it was stolen. After sliding on her reading glasses, she settled in to read the last of Henrietta Blanchard's tragic tale.

Her eyes scanned the first few words, discussing their plans to prepare for the arrival of the treasure. After reading two sentences detailing the modification of the library book-shelf and digging of a tunnel, Lily froze.

Her forehead crinkled and her eyes flicked away from the handwritten page. She stared into space, trying to place what had distracted her.

Her stomach dropped and a chill raced up her spine as the noise sounded again. Footsteps creaked across the floor-boards outside her room. They paced back and forth, hitting a squeaky floorboard just outside her door over and over.

Lily arched an eyebrow. Someone or something hovered outside her door.

CHAPTER 2

*L*ily tugged her glasses from her face, staring at her door. The creak sounded again as footsteps paraded back and forth.

"Cassie?"

The footsteps stopped the moment her voice sounded. "Cass, is that you?"

No answer. She shook her head. "You must be hearing things, old girl," she murmured as she slid her glasses back on.

Lily rolled her neck, relieving her tired muscles before she let her head fall on the pillow behind her. She must have heard Cassie climbing the stairs. Her overtired mind probably assumed she'd heard the floorboard creaking outside her room when in reality it had been Cassie heading for bed.

"All right, Henrietta, let's see what happens after you get the treasure settled."

Lily sucked in a breath and eyed the scripty handwriting filling the page.

. . .

I have ordered a locking mechanism be installed in the bookcase at the rear of the library. The lock is controlled by six tumblers. I have created a keyword unknown to everyone outside of myself and Clif.
I–

The protest of the creaky floorboard resounded again. Lily let the book fall into her lap as her shoulders slumped.

"Again?" She raised her voice and shouted at the door. "Quit fooling around, Cass!"

She shook her head, a frown forming on her lips. The floorboard squeaked again.

Lily slammed the journal closed. "That's it!"

She whipped the covers back and swung her legs over the bed. "Cassie, if that's you, I'm gonna swat you on the rear. And Willy, if it's you, same!"

She stormed across the room and flung the door open. A burst of icy air rushed past her as she stared into the empty corridor. Her eyes searched the area. Across the house, warm light glowed from Cassie's open door.

"Cass!" Lily called. Perhaps she had been here moments ago. Or her cat, Willy.

"Yeah?" Cassie's voice called from downstairs.

Lily's eyes widened and she stepped to the railing overlooking the foyer, treading across the squeaky floorboard. With a hard swallow, she leaned over and searched downstairs.

Cassie's blonde head poked from the library seconds later. "Mom?"

Lily's forehead crinkled. "Were you up here a few seconds ago?"

"No. I've been down here the whole time. I didn't think I could sleep, so I figured I'd grab a book." Cassie waved a small book clutched in her hand.

"What about—" Lily began when a furry critter pranced into the foyer from the library.

"What about what?"

"Was Willy up here poking at my door?"

"No. He's been with me the entire time."

"Are you sure?"

Cassie dropped her hand to her side, her shoulders slumping. "Yes, I'm sure." Cassie stared up at her mother. "Why?"

Lily twisted to stare at her door. "Nothing."

"Are you sure?"

"Yeah. Must have heard you banging around downstairs. Figured it was your cat looking for sanctuary."

Cassie flicked the lights off in the library and began her climb of the stairs. Willy raced ahead of her, rubbing against the railing as he turned the corner to head to Cassie's room.

"Did you find something to read?"

Cassie screwed up her face. "More or less."

"What's that mean?"

Cassie waved the book in the air. "I went with one of Henrietta's books. I hope I can get through it."

"If her journal's any indication, she's not a bad writer."

Cassie reached the top of the stairs and paused before heading toward her room. "I meant with the language barrier. I'm sure this isn't a modern-day cozy mystery."

"Which one did you pick?"

"*The Adventures of Black Jack.*"

Lily's eyes shot wide and her jaw fell open. "Aww, I'm jealous! I wanted to read that one."

"Too late, I swiped it. I'll let you know if it's any good."

"Don't stay up too late reading about my man, Clif."

Cassie shuffled away from Lily, her fingers grazing the railing as she chuckled. "Your man, huh?"

"You'll see," Lily called to her daughter. "You're going to fall in love with that rogue!"

"We'll see!" Cassie called as she shuffled into her room and swung the door shut.

Lily giggled as she retreated to her bedroom. Her foot trod across the squeaky board again and she hesitated, swallowing hard. Who or what had been hovering outside her bedroom moments earlier?

* * *

Cassie tugged her top over her head as bright fall sunshine streamed into her window, glinting off the calm ocean waters outside. As the bright pink cotton slipped past her eyes, she flicked her gaze to the book on her nightstand. She hadn't read it last night after all.

She swallowed hard as she considered how she'd selected it. As she had browsed for a novel across the room, Willy had approached the bookshelf that hid the secret passage. She'd ignored him. He always had a fascination with that bookcase since it led to a sea cave. She figured he'd gotten a whiff of something floating on the wind behind it.

After swishing his tail across the floor several times, he'd leapt to his feet, his ears flattening against his head. His one eye glowered at some unknown object.

"What is it, buddy?" Cassie asked him.

A low growl emanated from the cat, and he arched his back high in the air. His mouth opened in a hiss, his red tongue curling inside, and his tail bristled like a bottle cleaning brush. Cassie crinkled her nose at his odd behavior. What had he gotten a whiff of that had disturbed him so much?

Moments later, the book now laying on her nightstand had flown from the shelf. It shot several feet in the air before slamming into the hardwood floor and sliding to a stop against the area rug under the sofa.

Willy raced across the room, slinking low to the ground, his ears flattened. He leapt onto the window seat and crouched against the cushion, his one eye peering warily around the room.

Cassie swallowed hard as she stood in stunned silence. Her eyes swiveled to the bookcase, focusing on the hole where the book had been. Something must have caused it to fly from the shelf.

"Probably a gust of wind from that tunnel," she said aloud, her voice quavering as she sought to convince both herself and the furry creature across the room.

She shoved the novel in her hands back into its slot, and wandered across the room to retrieve the wayward book. She gasped as she discovered the author. None other than Henrietta Blanchard, rumored to haunt Whispering Manor, had penned the tome.

She thought they'd put the haunting rumors to rest when they'd discovered most of the disturbances were from treasure hunters breaking into the house to search for clues. This, however, added a new layer to the tale.

She'd not thought about it much longer. Her mother's voice called to her from upstairs. She, too, had experienced an odd incident. The second occurrence had left her with chills, but she preferred not to discuss it before bed. She wondered if she'd prefer not to discuss it at all.

Before she could contemplate it any further, her mother's voice broke into her thoughts.

"Cass? You ready yet?"

"Almost!" Cassie called, slipping her feet into her slip-on sneakers.

Her mother appeared at her open door, peering around the jamb. "What are you doing? Come on!"

Cassie wrinkled her nose as she rose from the bed and grabbed her purse. With a quick pat on Willy's furry head and a promise not to be too long, they stepped into the cool fall morning air. The ocean lapped at the shores behind the house, its gently rolling waves creating a rhythmic harmony that blended with the seagulls' cries overhead.

The sun shone brightly in the cloudless, azure sky, glinting off the windshield of Cassie's pink Wrangler. Lily shielded her eyes as she shook the arms of her sunglasses open and slid them onto her face.

Cassie climbed into the driver's seat with Lily joining her moments later after arming the alarm system.

"Okay, let's get going!" her mother said.

"Wow," Cassie said as she slid the shifter into drive. "You're in a hurry."

Her tires crunched over the driveway's gravel as they approached Ocean Drive. She swung right, heading north toward the neighboring town of Misty Hollow.

"I don't want anyone else to get that clown's head! It said they only had one remaining in stock last night."

Cassie rolled her eyes as she sped down the road. "They've probably always had one in stock. I can't imagine anyone would have bought that creepy thing."

"I'd wager it's going to be one of our most effective scenes," Lily said as the fall leaves flew past her window.

Red, orange, and yellow leaves fluttered from the canopy of trees on the two-lane road. They swirled high as Cassie blazed past them.

"Speaking of creepy," Cassie said, adjusting her sunglasses as she spoke, "did you figure out what happened with your midnight visitor?"

Lily shrugged as she tugged her seatbelt away from her neck. "Must have just been a random noise I heard."

Cassie side-eyed her. "You seemed pretty sure it was someone outside your door last night."

She kept her eyes trained on the scenery outside her window. "So, I was wrong. Wouldn't be the first time."

"Hmm," Cassie murmured.

"Why are you suddenly so interested? You didn't seem to be last night."

Cassie's fingers tightened around her steering wheel, and she winced before she bit her lower lip. "Didn't want to scare myself before bed."

Lily flicked her gaze over to Cassie. "Oh, right. I forgot you believe in ghosts."

Cassie rolled her eyes as the sign for Misty Hollow welcomed them to the small burg. "I was having my own issues with creepy stuff last night. I couldn't handle yours."

Lily's features pinched as she considered Cassie's statement. "Do tell."

"Mind if I tell you over some hot chocolate?"

"No, though I don't want to be late to the store."

"We'll get it to go," Cassie said, flicking on her turn signal and easing the car off the road and into the parking lot for *The Misty Marshmallow* whose sign boasted the best donuts for dipping.

Lily slipped her seatbelt off as Cassie shoved the shifter into park. "I'll run in, it'll be quicker."

"I want a donut," Lily said, flinging her door open.

"What about the store opening?"

"I'll eat fast. Come on."

After placing their order, they carried steaming hot to-go cups of deluxe hot chocolate and two still-warm, gooey donuts wrapped in wax paper to a small table in the back corner.

"Ohhh, mmmm," Lily murmured as she bit into the sticky glazed donut.

"It's good," Cassie agreed with a mouth full of donut. After swallowing her first bite, she ate a spoonful of whipped cream from the top of her frothy concoction before blowing on it.

"So," Lily said as she tested the hot chocolate then returned to blowing on it, "what was your frightening ghost encounter? Was Ri wandering around in the library bugging you about reading her books?"

Cassie shot her mother a wry glance. "I'm not going to tell you if you're going to make fun of me."

"I'm not making fun of you. But I can't imagine what was so creepy down in the library with the lights on."

Cassie sipped at her hot chocolate before she turned her attention to the half-eaten donut in front of her. She puckered her lips as she spun the paper around.

"Cass?" Lily prodded. "Come on, I was only joking. What happened?"

Cassie licked her lips and flicked her gaze to her mother's face. She swallowed hard. "While I was looking for a book, Henrietta's book flew off the shelf and across the room. It landed near the sofa."

Lily froze mid-bite, her eyebrows raising to her hairline. "What?"

Cassie lifted a shoulder as she wrapped her fingers around her warm beverage. "Willy was at the bookcase leading to the secret passage. I figured he caught a whiff of something. But then he scurried away, his tail was huge, and his ears were flat against his head. He hissed at something and then the book flew off the shelf and across the room."

"Did he catch it with his claw? Maybe it hurt his foot and it flung off the shelf when he tugged his paw away."

Cassie shook her head and bit her lower lip, her eyes rising to meet her mother's. "He was already away from the bookcase *without* a book attached when the book flew from the shelf."

"Well, there has to be some explanation," Lily said.

"Same as for your phantom visitor."

Lily sipped at her still-steaming hot chocolate. "Yes, I'm sure there is! Must have been a creak somewhere else that sounded like it was outside my door."

"But that doesn't explain how a book flew off the shelf."

"Gust of wind from behind the bookcase?" Lily proposed before she slid her last bite of donut onto her tongue.

Cassie gave her a stony glance. "Really? A gust of wind blew a single book–no, not a single book, a particular book– off the shelf and across the room?"

Lily chuckled as Cassie chewed her last bit of donut. "What are you suggesting, Cass? That Henrietta really is haunting Whispering Manor?"

"If the shoe fits," Cassie answered, wide-eyed as she wiped her hands on a wad of napkins.

Lily rolled her eyes and rose to stand. "Oh, come on. You can't be serious."

Cassie offered a shrug, balling her napkins up and tossing them in the nearby trashcan before she clicked the to-go lid onto her cup.

They exited into the bright morning sunshine and strode to Cassie's SUV. As they slid into their seats, Lily said, "Let's get to that Halloween shop. I'm sure they've got way more ghosts than we do."

"At least theirs are fake," Cassie retorted.

* * *

Cassie clutched the three-foot-high clown closer to her as she stared at the video playing on the display. A white-clad wisp of a woman wandered across a dilapidated room. After a moment, the video skipped, streaks of white fuzz skittering across the screen. When it corrected, the woman stood staring at the viewer with unblinking eyes and a grimace on her pale lips.

"Watching Henrietta haunt someone else?" Lily questioned from behind her.

Cassie leapt, pressing her hand against her chest and squeezing her eyes shut as she blew out a breath. "Stop scaring me like that."

"Oh, Cassie, there are no such things as ghosts," Lily said.

"We'll see," Cassie murmured as she wandered away from the display.

"I saw an Ouiji board over there if you want to grab it for a quick conversation with her."

"Very funny," Cassie said. "Though I'd prefer to start with a medium. Maybe Henrietta's angry that we found her treasure and removed it. The hauntings didn't start until after that."

"How do you know?" Lily questioned, eyeing a doll with a broken face that screamed when she touched it. "Maybe some of the disturbances we had when we first moved in were ghostly."

"Maybe. I thought all that would die down once we found the treasure. I really thought everything we experienced was a direct result of the treasure hunters but now…" Cassie's voice trailed off as she offered a slight shrug.

"I guess time will tell. Though I still maintain everything has an explanation."

Cassie stopped in the middle of the aisle and fixed her gaze on her mother. "And what if that explanation is a ghost?"

"Then I guess we'll have to figure out a way to deal with her. Or him."

"Him?" Cassie questioned.

"What if it's Clif?"

Cassie pulled her lips back in an overemphasized wince. "Yikes. That's even worse."

"How is it worse if it's her brother?"

"He was a ruthless pirate. Who knows what he'll do to us! I had a nightmare when we first moved in that he shot me."

Lily puckered her lips as she stacked another two red-colored strobe lights into her basket next to her creepy hanging clown head. "I'd prefer Clif to Ri. He seemed quite friendly. Henrietta is a bit less forgiving."

Cassie crinkled her nose at her mother's assessment. "A guy who killed every member of a ship's crew except one seems 'friendly'? I'll stick with crabby Henrietta, I think."

"If we even have ghosts." Lily halted mid-aisle and pressed a hand to her forehead. "Okay, stop this nonsense talk, and let's think before we leave. Is there *anything* else we need? Lights, props, spinning motors. Anything?"

"Well, you got your creepy clown head, and I got my three-foot jack-in-the-box clown which is what we came for."

"Yeah, but I don't want to get back to the maze and think 'Oh, we should have gotten blank!'"

Cassie's eyes scanned the store in search of anything that triggered an idea. Her eyes settled on her mother. "How much budget do we have left?"

Lily's eyebrows raised and she cocked her head. "What did you have in mind?"

Cassie raced around the store, adding items to their cart before they approached the cashier.

She spilled her armload of items onto the counter as Lily unloaded her basket. She flicked her gaze to her daughter, reaching up to give Cassie's ponytail a playful tug. "How did I know you'd want a dozen more things if given the chance?"

Cassie's lips formed an amused grin as she studied the

book with the feather quill that moved on its own, the automated ouija board, the creepy woman on a swing, and the animated fortune teller's ball.

She stuck her hand on her hip. "I like the electronic stuff. And since we had some money left over, I figured we'd splurge on a few items. Plus, a few of these are coming out of my own pocket for Whispering Manor."

Lily arched an eyebrow at her.

Cassie went back to sorting items, shrugging. "I thought the animated books would be fun on the bookcase."

"We already have those, remember? Courtesy of our resident ghost."

"And I liked the creepy Victorian doll that walks around."

"Uh-huh. You could have made one of those with your old Walking Wendy and a Roomba."

"Maybe I'll make her a friend next year. But she'll be mute."

"Stick an Echo Dot on her and then she can talk and even sing."

Cassie offered her mother a wry glance. "Looks like you'll be helping me with this project."

"If we ever finish this maze," Lily said with a grumble.

The cashier rang out their purchases, bagging the smaller items and wishing them a spooky holiday season. Cassie pushed their cartload out to the parking lot. With a quick tug, she rolled her backseat forward, making room for their bounty.

"Let's stop by the maze site and drop off the stuff that's going there," Lily said as she shoved another bag into the tiny trunk.

Cassie ran the cart back to the store front before she nodded in agreement. "Okay, but my clown needs to go with me so I can work on his box at home."

Lily clicked her seatbelt and adjusted the shoulder strap. "Right and your little resident doll."

"Yep. Oh," Cassie answered as she fired the Jeep's engine, "by the time we're finished unloading, it'll be lunchtime."

"May as well eat out!"

Cassie backed from the spot in the nearly empty lot. "How's pizza? I'd like something quick so we can get back to work."

"As long as I don't have to cook it, I don't care what it is," Lily said as Cassie pulled the car onto the road.

Within thirty minutes, they were easing to a stop outside of the barn. The women climbed out of the car and stretched before Cassie wandered to her trunk and tugged open the door. She fiddled with her keys, approaching the barn doors as Lily grabbed a bag.

Cassie lifted the lock in her hands, its steel glinting off the late morning sun. She lined the key up with the keyhole before drawing her chin back toward her chest. Her nose wrinkled and she dropped the key to her side.

"Hey, Mom!" she called over her shoulder.

"What?"

"Come here for a second." Cassie puckered her lips as she studied the lock.

Lily trundled up the ramp with a bag in each hand. "What is it?"

"Look at this lock."

Lily dumped the bags next to her and leaned over to study the metal object. She grabbed it from Cassie's hand and peered at it again. "Wait," she grumbled, digging in her purse for a pair of reading glasses.

After palming her sunglasses and sliding the readers on her face, she studied the lock again. "Scratches."

"Those weren't there yesterday."

"Are you sure? It could be from using the key repeatedly."

"This is not a scratch from using the key. This is a gouge."

Lily straightened and stared at her daughter. "What are you saying, Cass?"

"That someone's been tampering with this lock."

"Whatever for?" Lily inquired as she gathered the bags again.

Cassie slid the key into the lock and turned it. "I can't believe they're so desperate for a sneak peek that they'd try to pick the lock."

"I guess it's big news around here."

"This is a little extreme." Cassie tugged the big barn door open. Heat wafted from inside the large space. As she retrieved a bag to carry it inside, she froze. "OMG!"

"What?" Lily inquired, still fiddling with shoving her reading glasses back into her purse as the two bags of purchases dangled from her arm.

"Look!" Cassie exclaimed, waving her arm at the barn's interior.

A few walls hung limply from the rafters, torn down from several holders. Decorations had been tossed from their original locations in a heap. All their hard work had been trashed and the almost-built Halloween maze stood in ruin before them.

CHAPTER 3

*L*ily's shoulders slumped as she stared at the mess. "Are you kidding me? We were already behind and now we'll have to double-time it to get this up and running."

Cassie nodded as she pressed her cell phone to her ear. The line trilled on the other end before the now-familiar voice of Sheriff Wyatt Cooper answered.

"Hey, Wyatt," Cassie said. "Sorry to call you on a Saturday but…" She paused to sigh. "We've had a bit of trouble again."

"At the house?" his voice questioned.

"No, at the maze. The lock's been tampered with, and someone trashed the inside."

Cassie heard him grumble as his chair protested his rising from it. "Don't go inside. I'll be right there."

She ended the call with a word of thanks before she stuffed the phone into her back pocket. "Wyatt says to wait out here until he gets here."

Lily sighed and tossed the bags to the side. "This is really getting old. There's no treasure left and still, we're being hounded by these jokesters."

Cassie's lips formed a frustrated frown. "I wouldn't call them jokesters. This goes way beyond a prank." She leaned back against the barn's side, her arms crossed tightly over her chest.

Lily's shoulders slumped and she wrapped an arm around Cassie's shoulders. "It'll be okay, Cass. We'll fix it. And it'll be better than it was before."

Cassie rubbed her palm against her forehead. "It's not that. Well, okay, it kind of is. But it's also that we're constantly targets here. First the house, now the maze."

"Better the maze than the house," Lily said.

"Good point," Cassie answered with a chuckle. She glanced in at the wrecked decorations. "I guess it'll force us to work faster."

"Lily? Cassie?" a new voice called.

The women spun to face the new person. "Lucy?" Cassie inquired.

The blonde waved as she adjusted her scarf. "Yep, it's me! Just taking a stroll and thought I'd say hello."

"Lovely day for it," Lily answered.

Lucy smiled and stared up at the blue sky before wandering up the ramp toward the barn door. "Do you ladies need any help?"

Lily slid the barn door slightly closed before she answered. "Trying for a sneak peek?"

Lucy held up her hands in defeat. "You caught me." She giggled nervously. "I can't wait to see it! We're all dying to get a sneak peek."

"I'll bet," Lily answered as the police car trundled down the dirt road toward them.

Sheriff Wyatt Cooper eased the car to a stop before he climbed from behind the wheel. "Morning, ladies. Oh, Lucy, didn't expect to see you."

"I was just passing through," Lucy said. "Hey, you didn't promise Wyatt a sneak peek, did you?"

"Ah," Cassie said, hesitating as she selected a path forward.

Her hesitance led Lucy to speculate on another reason. "You aren't still having trouble, are you?"

Lily sighed. "The truth is, yes. Someone broke in and made quite a mess."

"Oh no!" Lucy exclaimed, her lips turning down into a frown. "That's terrible."

Wyatt wove between the women and eyed the lock. "And you say this was tampered with?"

"Yes," Cassie answered. "See the scratches."

"Well, if you need any help cleaning up and restoring the place, let me know," Lucy said to Lily. "I'd be happy to help you."

"Thanks, Lucy. I think we'll be okay."

"I doubt that," Wyatt answered.

Cassie snapped her gaze to him. "What do you mean?"

Wyatt hung his hands from his belt with his thumbs. "This is a crime scene. I'll have to go over the entire place. Search for evidence. Have forensics out. This won't be touched anytime soon."

Lily's jaw fell open. "Aww, no. Wyatt, come on. I'm fine with you having a look inside and making sure it's safe for us to go back in, but you can't stop us from rebuilding it. The whole town's been so excited, and we've put a lot of time and effort into this."

Wyatt's head fell to the side as he winced. "Well..."

"Come on, Wyatt," Cassie whined, a pout on her lips.

"Yeah, Wyatt, you'll disappoint the whole town," Lucy chimed in.

Wyatt squashed his lips together and shook his head.

Lily raised her eyebrows and lifted her shoulders. "The real crime will be if the town doesn't have its maze thanks to what was likely a high school prank."

Wyatt chewed the inside of his cheek and shook his head. "Well, with all of you ganging up on me, I don't have much choice." He wagged a finger at them. "But no one's going inside before I check the place out, all right?"

Lily held up her hands. "You got it, chief."

"Uh-huh. And that's sheriff, not chief. Two different things."

Lily offered a chuckle and a grin at his correction.

He motioned to Cassie's Wrangler. "Why don't you wait in the Jeep? Just in case."

The women retreated back toward the SUV as Wyatt slid the door open.

"We're okay, Lucy, I'd hate to keep you," Lily said as they regrouped at the Jeep's open tailgate.

"Oh, it's no trouble," Lucy said with a wave of her hand, leaning against the tailgate.

Lily offered a polite smile as she scratched her forehead. "The thing is as soon as Wyatt gives us the all-clear, we'd like to get right to it. We've got some ground to make up in addition to all the other things that were still on our list."

Lucy nodded before realization hit her. Her face twisted into a knowing mask. "Ohhh, right. I gotcha." She winked and smiled. "Third wheel."

"Not really that," Cassie claimed. "But we've got to hit the ground running as soon as we can, or we'll never make it for the grand opening."

"Right, sure. Well, like I said, if you need help rehanging the walls or whatever, just let me know. I'm happy to pitch in."

"Thanks, Lucy. Much appreciated," Lily said. "And sorry to kick you out, but–"

"No, no. Don't give it another thought. I understand. Have a great day, ladies!" She eyed the items still laying in Cassie's car before she flicked her gaze up to them. "Can't wait to see what you have in store."

Cassie and Lily waved as Lucy strode away toward town.

"I didn't think she was going to leave," Cassie admitted as she disappeared down the road.

"I can't believe she was here," Lily answered as she grabbed two more bags from the back.

"Me either. This town really is obsessed with this maze. Why did you tell her what happened?"

Lily waved her hand at Cassie. "Oh, it'll get out soon enough."

"Do you think Wyatt will tell?"

"I think Wyatt has to write a report and I think more than only his eyes will see it. And I think Lucy will say she saw him here, and someone will tell someone else and before you know it the whole town will have the place torn apart board by board."

"Good point," Cassie said, recalling how quickly and easily news traveled in the small town of Hideaway Bay.

The women unloaded the rest of the items for the maze before they plopped into the space they'd cleared at the rear of the car. Their legs dangled as they waited for the all-clear.

Lily leapt from the car to the ground after a few moments. "Here he comes."

Cassie followed her, and they strode toward Wyatt, meeting him halfway to the barn.

Lily shielded her eyes from the sun glinting off the barn roof. "Well?"

Wyatt shrugged and flicked his gaze around the field. "Well, I don't like it, but you haven't given me much choice."

"So, we're clear to go in?" Lily asked.

Wyatt pursed his lips before nodding. "Yeah, yeah, you're

clear. I didn't see anything dangerous. No one still on the premises. But if you come across anything–"

"We'll call you first thing," Lily promised.

"We won't even touch it," Cassie added.

"Good. I don't want any vigilante justice." He paused and flicked his gaze at Lily. "Like people running around with baseball bats."

"That happened once," Lily said in defense. "And the esteemed descendent of Redbeard was nosing through the trash on our porch!"

"Once was enough," Wyatt warned. "Don't do anything foolish." He paused for a second. "And just to be sure, I'm sending a deputy out here while you are on site. Give him your schedule so we make sure we have someone posted here while you're here."

Lily glanced toward the barn. "It seems more dangerous when we're not."

"Good point," Wyatt answered. "I'll have someone patrol regularly."

"Thanks, Wyatt," Lily said. "We appreciate that."

He nodded as he stepped back toward the patrol car. "Call me if there's even a whiff of trouble."

The two women smiled and waved as he turned the car around and pulled away, dust trailing behind him.

Cassie blew out a long breath. "Well, I guess we'd better get to it."

"Mmm-hmm," Lily murmured, "we've got a lot of ground to cover."

They grabbed more of the items from Cassie's vehicle before they climbed the ramp and entered the barn.

Cassie grabbed the other two bags Lily had discarded at the barn door earlier. "I hope we don't have to make new walls."

"I'm with you. I hate the wall-making."

They carried their purchases inside, and Cassie tossed the bags into a corner before she wandered over to assess one of the partially torn-down walls. She studied the top. "I think we can fix it. Looks like they just came off their hooks rather than tore."

"Perfect," Lily said as she sorted through the decorations heaped in a pile.

"I'll grab a ladder and rehang these and then we can replace the decorations and set up the new ones."

"Looks like they got the lights, too," Lily said with a sigh. "I'll try to reset those while you're hanging from the rafters."

"Very funny," Cassie grunted as she dragged her ladder to the room's center.

Through a working lunch, the ladies sorted through the mess, restoring everything to its rightful place. By dinner time, they were ready to add new items to the mix.

"Whew," Lily said, slumping to sit on the makeshift stage for their skeleton band, *The Rolling Bones*. She adjusted the hat on the lead singer, whose bony little hand clutched a microphone. "I'm beat."

"Me too," Cassie admitted as she strung the lit letters behind the band. "I thought we'd actually get something done today, but we're right back where we started."

"At least we got that far. Maybe we can come back tomorrow if the girls will cover at the store."

Cassie nodded as she swiped at her sweaty forehead with her wrist. "Yeah, maybe we can duck out early. I think only Amber's in at noon, but Chloe should be there by two."

"We can do a few hours here. Set up the new stuff."

Cassie leapt down to the wooden floor below. It groaned under her weight as she shuffled across and eyed the words. "Look okay?"

Lily twisted and glanced up at the colorful letters. "Looks good. Let's go home. Your cat is probably starved."

"And so am I." Cassie clicked off the light display and set the remote down on the stage. She tugged her mother up to stand.

"I'm too tired to even get take-out. Let's go straight home."

Cassie wrinkled her nose. "What are we going to eat? I'm *not* cooking."

"I'll eat cereal," Lily said with a groan. "That's all I have the energy for."

They gathered their things, locked the barn, and headed to the car. In the distance, a patrol car sat near the corn maze. They waved as Cassie eased the car toward the road.

"I hope there's no more trouble," Lily said as the tires climbed onto the pavement.

"Me too. I do *not* want to rebuild that again."

"No, we've got our own house to decorate with your creepy little finds."

"My creepy finds?" Cassie exclaimed. "I didn't buy a severed clown head!"

"You're never going to let that go, are you? Meanwhile, we'll have a creepy life-sized doll roaming around the house."

Within minutes, Cassie was tugging the emergency brake on, and they slid out of the car. "I'll grab the stuff from the back."

"Leave it until morning," Lily said with a tired wave.

"There's not much. Besides, I don't want to leave Bessie in the car."

Lily squinted down at the alarm key fob. "Bessie?"

Cassie swung the tailgate open. "The doll."

"You named her?"

Cassie loaded the box under her arm and lined the bags up her other arm. She kicked the tailgate shut and waddled to the house. "Yeah. She needs a name. We can't call her creepy doll all the time."

Lily slid the key into the lock and twisted. "We could. It seems appropriate." She swung the door open. A screeching scream filled the air.

CHAPTER 4

Cassie winced, her eyes closing to slits at the wailing. She hurried into the house as Lily pressed any and every button on her keyfob.

Cassie dumped the bags and doll's box on the floor.

"Turn it off!" Lily shouted over the din.

"I'm trying!" Cassie hollered. She tapped digits on the keypad. The alarm finally quieted. "Didn't you turn it off?"

"I thought I did. I can't see these buttons."

"I think I got it–" Cassie's words were interrupted by the ringing of her cell phone. She tugged it from her pocket and swiped to answer. "Hello?" She paused. "Yes, just a false alarm. Thank you for checking." After passing along a code word, she ended the call.

A siren screamed in the evening air. Within seconds, red and blue lights painted their porch.

"Guess they didn't cancel the alarm in time," Lily said with a sigh.

The patrol car screeched to a halt, spraying gravel everywhere. Wyatt flew from behind the wheel, weapon drawn.

"Lily! Cassie! You okay?"

Lily waved him down. "We're fine. False alarm."

His chest heaved as he slowed to a stop on the porch. With his weapon holstered, he bent over, his hands resting on his thighs as he gulped in air. "You ladies have got to stop scaring me like that."

"Sorry," Lily said. "I can't see the darn buttons."

Wyatt offered a weak chuckle and a nod.

"Why don't you come in for a minute? I'll get you a glass of water."

"I've got it," Cassie said, bounding to the kitchen.

Wyatt righted himself and stepped inside the foyer. "For what it's worth, I can't see the buttons either. Set the alarm off at the station at least once a month. After a while, Ruby taped green paper over the unlock and red over the lock. Now I only set it off every couple of months."

Lily chuckled at his ineptitude with technology. "That may be an idea for me. I can't be bothered to get out my reading glasses."

Cassie returned with a large glass of water. "Here you go."

"Thanks, Cassie," Wyatt answered, raising the glass as he accepted it. He took a sip. "Any trouble at the maze?"

"None while we were there," Lily answered. "You want to sit down?"

"No," Wyatt said with a shake of his head. "Looks like you just got home. I don't want to intrude."

"You're not intruding," Cassie said.

"Not at all. And if you'd like to stay for dinner, we're having cereal."

Wyatt crinkled his brow at the statement. "As tempting as that sounds, I think I'll pass."

"We've got the kind with marshmallows," Cassie said, cocking her head.

"Chocolate or plain?"

"Chocolate," the women answered together.

"Oh, well, if you can spare a bowl, maybe I'll stay."

Lily chuckled and waved him toward the kitchen as she closed the door. "It's the least we can do considering you've worked harder than you ever have in your life since we moved to town."

Wyatt poked his thumb toward the porch. "Give me a second to close the patrol car's door. I think I left it open."

"We'll be in the kitchen. Come on back when you're finished."

Lily and Cassie made their way to the kitchen at the back of the house. "How embarrassing," Lily muttered as she tugged open the pantry.

Cassie fished three bowls from a cupboard and three spoons from a drawer. "At least we know we have good police protection."

She set the table with the limited items they'd need for their meager dinner before retrieving milk from the refrigerator. As she placed it on the table next to the Choco-Count cereal, Wyatt returned.

"Help yourself," Lily said, motioning to the table as she filled glasses of water.

Willy wandered into the kitchen, murmuring a hello to Wyatt before he stalked to Cassie and rubbed at her legs, meowing loudly.

"Yes, I will get your dinner first," Cassie promised the vocal kitty.

Lily delivered the waters and sank into a chair across from Wyatt. Cereal clinked against the ceramic bowl as he shook the box before sliding it toward Lily and splashing milk over the brown bits and chocolatey marshmallows.

Cassie cracked a can of cat food and spilled it into Willy's red bowl, placing the feast in front of the cat. As he chowed down on the fishy food, Cassie circled the table and eased into the chair near the window, reaching for the cereal box.

"Sorry about the misunderstanding again," Lily said as she passed the milk to Cassie.

"No problem. The cereal more than makes up for it."

Lily chuckled at the statement. "I'm not sure that's true."

Wyatt offered a shrug as he chomped on the sweet cereal. "It was this or a Hungry Man steak."

"And you picked this?" Cassie inquired.

"Steak is a kind word for what you get in that package."

The women chuckled at the sentiment. "So," Cassie said, "what made you change your mind? You were about to pass up this wonderful offer."

"The chocolate," Wyatt mumbled between spoonfuls of cereal. "I thought you ladies would have some healthy cereal that tastes like cardboard."

"Definitely not," Cassie said. "We always keep a sugary cereal in the house."

They fell into silence for a few moments, each of them enjoying their small meal.

Wyatt helped himself to a second bowl. "So, did you get everything set up at the barn?"

"We did," Lily answered.

"And tomorrow," Cassie added, "we'll be adding the things we were supposed to add today. Assuming the girls can handle the store and we can sneak out early."

"Will you finish in time for the grand opening?"

"Gosh, I hope so," Lily said.

Cassie chased a marshmallow around her bowl. "Did you find any clues as to who could have done this?"

Wyatt shook his head as he fished a few marshmallows from his milk. "Didn't see a thing. Did either of you?"

"Nothing," Lily admitted. "Who would do something like this?"

"The O'Rourke guy is still in jail, right?" Cassie inquired, shooting a wide-eyed glance at Wyatt.

"Mmm-hmm, yep. I checked as soon as I got back to the station. Serving a very long term upstate."

"Well, that rules him out," Lily said.

Wyatt's head bobbed up and down and he loaded his spoon with more cereal. "Maybe it's the curse."

"The curse?" Cassie asked as she snapped her gaze to him.

"Mmm-hmm," Wyatt murmured as he munched on the cereal.

Lily widened her eyes. "Another curse? Or the same curse? Isn't this house cursed? Are we carrying it with us or are there two?"

"Another one. Barn's cursed."

"You're kidding," Lily said with her shoulders slumping.

"Mmm-mmm, nope. Whispering Manor is haunted. Well, supposedly was, but we seemed to have solved that. But the barn is cursed."

"How did it get cursed?" Lily inquired.

"Farmer built it on an ancient Indian burial ground. Weird stuff happens there all the time."

"Such as?" Cassie prompted.

"Things out of place, animals acting strangely, fires, deaths."

Cassie blinked her eyes and shook her head in disbelief. "Wow, this town is full of strange tales."

"You can't actually attribute anything that happened to an Indian curse, right?" Lily inquired.

Wyatt shot her a dubious glance without answering.

"Oh, Wyatt, come on," Lily pressed.

"There are unexplained happenings. Things I can't attribute to anything else."

"Like unexplained deaths?" Cassie asked.

"Sort of," Wyatt answered, standing with his bowl in hand and crossing to place it in the sink. "Old Farmer Brown died on that property. Right in that barn. Trampled to death by his own horse."

"Well, that's explainable," Lily answered. "The horse trampled him."

"But why?" Wyatt asked, sinking back into his chair. "What spooked the horse?"

Lily shrugged and let her spoon fall into her empty bowl. "Could have been anything. Rat in the barn, some kind of ailment."

"Or the curse."

Cassie slumped in her chair as she listened to the conversation unfold around her. "Was this house built on an Indian burial ground?"

"No," Wyatt answered. "This one was cursed by that pirate gold. But we solved that."

Cassie gathered up her bowl and her mother's. "Or did we?"

Wyatt twisted in his chair to follow her across the kitchen. "What do you mean?"

Cassie shot a glance over her shoulder as she rinsed their bowls and dumped them into the dishwasher before scooping up her cat and settling at the table. "We've had a few... incidents."

Lily rolled her eyes.

Wyatt tapped his fingers on the table and cocked his head. "Incidents?"

"She's being overly dramatic."

Wyatt's gaze flicked between the two women before settling on Cassie who continued to stroked Willy's tuxedo fur.

She offered a slight shrug. "Mom heard someone walking outside her room, but no one was there."

"Random groan of the house," Lily said.

Cassie shot her a glance. "How do you explain the book, then?"

"Book?" Wyatt inquired.

"Henrietta's book flew off the bookshelf and across the room when I was in there last night."

Wyatt's eyes went wide, and he shook his head. "I told you when you moved here the house was haunted. And cursed."

"Curses don't exist. And neither do ghosts. This is ridiculous," Lily said.

Wyatt shrugged again. "Is it? Unexplained things here. Unexplained things at the barn."

"Bull," Lily said, slapping her hand against the table. "Everything has an explanation. Everything. And I'm not going to accept that our incident at the barn was ghosts or an old Indian curse. Some real, live human being did that."

Wyatt's lips turned down at the corners and he lifted his shoulders in a shrug.

"I'm not letting you off the hook that easy," Lily said to him, her eyebrows raised. "Someone did this and I'd like to know who. We worked hard on that maze and to have someone trash it… well, it stinks."

"That much we agree on," Wyatt answered. "And I'll do everything I can. But you may need to accept that not everything that happens in Hideaway Bay is explainable."

Cassie shivered as she stroked Willy's fur.

"Well, I hope whoever did it doesn't do it again before we open. We won't survive another trashing of the place," Lily said.

Wyatt rose from his chair with a nod. "I'll have someone at the site twenty-four-seven. So, we'll do our best. In the meantime, if you have any other… incidents here," he said, his gaze flicking to Cassie as he said the words, "let me know, okay?"

Lily stood and nodded. "We will. Thanks for getting here so quickly and again, sorry for the false alarm."

"No problem, the cereal was well worth it."

"I'll walk you out," Lily offered.

Their footsteps receded to the front door and their murmured goodnights reached Cassie's ears. Lily returned to the kitchen and plopped into the chair next to Cassie. She sank her chin into her palm and gazed at her daughter.

"Well, what do you say, kid?"

Cassie sucked in a deep breath as she let the cat slip to the ground and stalk away. With a shrug, she grasped the chair, tapping its bottom with her fingernails. "I'm tired but not ready for bed."

"I feel the same, but I'm not sure I want to do anything except stretch out in bed."

"Looks like you can spend some time with your journal."

The corners of Lily's mouth turned up as she bobbed her head up and down. "I'm interested to keep reading it. Are you heading up to read Ri's book?"

Cassie mashed her lips together and gave a slight shake of her head. "No, I think I'll play with my new toys first."

Lily rose from her seat and kissed the top of Cassie's head. "Don't stay up too late."

She shuffled from the room and, after checking the front door's lock again, she climbed to the second floor. She sank onto the edge of her bed with a groan and tugged off her shoes. They rolled across the floor as she tossed them down and flopped backward into the satin duvet.

"Ugh," she moaned as her eyes threatened to close. She pulled herself up and pushed herself to rise and change into her pajamas. She finished her nightly routine and flicked off the bathroom light as she shambled back into her bedroom.

Her gaze flicked outside, and she caught sight of a figure. She approached the window and leaned closer, her eyes scanning the landscape outside. She squinted into the darkness, unable to locate the figure she'd just spotted.

With a confused sigh, she left the window behind and slid between the sheets. After plumping her pillows behind her, she slid reading glasses onto her nose and pulled the little brown journal onto her lap.

"Okay, Henrietta, what happened to you?" she questioned.

A creak responded and Lily's muscles stiffened. She bit her lower lip as she scanned the room over her half-glasses. With a shake of her head, she muttered, "You're being ridiculous, Lily."

She wiggled her shoulders and settled back into her pillows, tugging the cover open on the book and paging to her spot.

I have ordered a locking mechanism be installed in the bookcase at the rear of the library. The lock is controlled by six tumblers. I have created a keyword unknown to everyone outside of myself and Clif.

I set the tumblers myself so not even the builder is aware of the word. Clif found the prospect of me performing manual labor amusing. He stumbled upon me working to set the lock, a dirty smudge on my cheek as I toiled.

"Well, Ri, you look a bit worse for wear," he said as his thumb rubbed at the dirty spot on my face. The cheeky grin on his lips betrayed his faux concern.

With a roll of my eyes, I shoved his hand away. "I am working."

"You? Working?" he said, his voice taking on an incredulous tone. "And I assumed miracles to be fake."

"Really, Clif, if your pirating does not pan out, perhaps you could tell your jokes at the local pub for donations."

Clif offered me another cheeky grin, his teeth gleaming in the candlelight that flickered in the room.

"I am quite serious," I informed him. "I dismissed the staff for

the evening and am finishing the locking mechanism myself. You see, I have set the code so that only you and I shall know it."

"Well, I am pleased to see you taking such an active role in our joint venture."

I popped the brass plate back onto the rear of the mechanism and pounded it in with a hammer, then raised my hand for him to pull me to stand. "Did you expect anything less?"

"Certainly not," he answered as he righted me. "Which is the sole reason I hired you."

"And I am worth every piece of gold you shall pay me."

"I have no doubt."

I pushed the bookcase shut. The satisfying click of the locking mechanism echoed throughout the room. Clif wandered toward the shelf and tugged on it. I arched my eyebrow at him.

"You did not expect it to open, did you?"

"Of course not," he answered smartly. "What is the code?"

Our conversation was interrupted by the opening of the manor's front door.

"Hello?" Mother's voice called into the house.

My eyes threatened to roll in their sockets as a sigh escaped my lips. Clif drew his into a thin line, whispering, "Humor her, Ri. She does care for you."

"She cares for you far more," I retorted as Clif called to her.

"In the library, Mother!"

My wisp of a mother appeared at the doorway, clasping her hands in front of her as she eyed us. "Ah, there you both are. How lovely. I am so pleased to see my children reconciled rather than sniping at each other."

Father joined her, wrapping an arm around Mother's shoulder, and smiled at the scene. Carolina skirted around them, heading for the bookcase near the window seat to peruse the selection.

A pleasant expression played across Mother's features. "They say something good always comes from something bad and I believe we have found that."

I glanced down at the area rug beneath my feet as I called upon my best skills of deception. "Yes, I am quite pleased to have reconciled with Clif," I said, patting his arm. "Now he can provide me with news of William."

Mother's smile faltered and she flicked her gaze to Clif. He wiggled his eyebrows at her as though to suggest she humor me.

"Henrietta–" Mother began, rubbing her palms together.

"I am sorry, Ri, but I have no news," Clif interrupted.

"What a terrible shame," I said, flicking my gaze to my hands and sighing. "Well, I suppose I shall ready myself for bed after a walk on the roof walk. I do hope, despite you having no news, to spot William's ship returning." I shifted my gaze to the room's other occupants. "Unless there is something you require? Perhaps, Carolina, you would like assistance in selecting a book?"

"No, thank you," my snippy little sister said.

"You should try one of Ri's books, sister. I have always found them quite entertaining."

Carolina flicked her blue eyes toward us before returning them to the shelf. "Your loss," Clif said to her. "Ri, perhaps I could accompany you on a beach walk instead of you taking to your roof's parapet."

I pretended to weigh the request before slowly nodding. "All right. Together, we shall scan the seas for signs of William. Excuse me a moment, brother, whilst I fetch my shawl."

I flitted from the room, ever the hopeful wife, pausing a moment between the angels gracing the bottom of the staircase.

"Really, Clif, is it wise to indulge her?" I heard Mother say in a low voice.

I hurried up the stairs as I struggled to hold in a giggle. After fetching my royal blue wrap, I pounded down the stairs, calling to Clif.

"Clif? Clif! I am ready!"

"Coming, Ri." His voice lowered. "Really, Mother, it is nothing to worry yourself over. I have the matter well in hand."

Clifton strode from the confines of my library, meeting me in the foyer. I lifted my eyebrows at him, and he pressed a finger to his lips before responding in a loud voice, "Ready? I hope the walk proves pleasant and tires you enough to rest comfortably."

He slammed the door shut behind us as we exited to the porch beyond the door and descended the stairs, circling the house to the beach.

"You're laying it on rather thick, aren't you?"

"It was your idea," I reminded him as I adjusted my shawl around me.

"No one suspects you are acting. Mother is quite worried, in fact."

"I heard you assure her you have it handled. I trust that settled her frayed nerves. She trusts you implicitly."

He wiggled his eyebrows at me as the sun lowered behind us, painting the sky around it.

"Ironic, really. That she places her implicit trust in her son who is a pirate, but none in her firstborn daughter."

"Oh, Ri, don't hold too much against Mother. It is not her fault that you are a woman beyond your times."

"A woman beyond my time? What does that mean?"

"It means women in our society are constantly discounted. A ridiculous notion. I imagine one day women should have the same rights as men."

My eyes widened. "Perhaps Mother ought to question your judgment, Clif. If she heard talk like that from you, she may have you committed."

"You do not agree?"

I considered the question. A society where I, as a woman, could own property, make laws, and otherwise direct myself through life as a man does? It seemed fantastical. Yet, as I considered it, the notion appealed greatly to me. A smile spread across my lips.

"I suppose the idea of an equal society appeals to me, yes. I hope this is the case one day."

We walked along in silence for a few moments as the waters ebbed and flowed against the rocks and sand.

After a moment, I inquired, "Do you imagine we shall live to see that day?"

An eerie giggle interrupted any further reading. The high-pitched chuckle set Lily's nerves on edge. Her muscles stiffened and her heart skipped a beat. She raised her eyes from the yellowed pages, her gaze darting around.

The creepy laugh cut through the air again. Lily sucked in a sharp breath, her eyes widening. She leaned forward, snapping the book shut.

The floorboard outside of her bedroom door creaked. Her heart pounded against her chest and her mouth went dry.

CHAPTER 5

*L*ily stared at the door leading to the hall as the floorboard creaked again. Her throat closed, and her pulse raced. Heat washed through her body.

"Hello?" she squeaked out.

"Ready or not, here I come," a child's voice called. A ghoulish giggle floated through the air.

"Henrietta?" Lily whispered. "I-I'm sorry I read your diary! But it's so intcresting."

"There's no hiding from me!" the voice continued.

Lily slid the diary onto her nightstand and swung her legs over the bed's side. Her lips tugged back into a grimace and her gaze darted around the room in search of a hiding spot. Was there such a thing as a hiding spot from a ghost, she pondered?

The floorboard creaked again, calling her attention back to the door. A bang sounded and the door shook. Lily's heart stopped again, and she gulped. Another smack thudded into the door. The robe hanging on the back shook.

"Don't bother trying to run," the voice said. Lily's forehead crinkled as she frowned at the dire warning.

Another thud sounded, and the door creaked open. It slowly swung to reveal the voice's source. Dressed in a Victorian-style dress, with wild dark hair and glowing eyes, the specter floated across the threshold and into Lily's bedroom.

The ghost continued her movement toward Lily, a pale white hand outstretched in front.

"You'll never get out of here," she said, a chilling chuckle punctuating the statement.

Lily sucked in a deep breath, her head falling to the side as she rolled her eyes, mostly at herself. She blew out the breath she'd been holding and stood, approaching the ghost. As she closed the distance, the ghost veered off, changing directions and wandering toward the fireplace in the room.

She trundled along, her skirts sliding across the floor away from Lily. The ghost floated into the fireplace, bumping against it before she turned and wandered in another direction.

"Very funny, Cassie!" Lily called as she trailed behind it and snatched the envelope marked "Mom" taped to the animatronic ghost's chest.

Lily ripped it off the dress with a sigh as the ghost warned, "There's no hiding from me." It bumped into the bed and spun to roll across the room in another direction.

"Can't believe I thought you were Henrietta," she mumbled at the wild-haired doll.

"Ready or not, here I come!" the doll answered.

Lily lifted the ghost girl under her arm and toted it toward the door. She set it outside, the floorboard creaking as it began to wander away. "Keep your creepy ghosts on your side of the stairs!" Lily shouted before slamming her door shut.

She shuffled across the room and sank onto the bed, sliding her finger under the envelope's flap. She tore open the container and slipped a piece of paper from inside.

Cassie's script writing filled the page.

Clifton Nichols died September 18, 1802. Henrietta Blanchard died August 14, 1802. So, she died BEFORE Clif, not after... that blows our theory that she tossed herself from the Widow's Walk after his death.

Hope you find some answers in her diary!

Cass

P.S. How do you like my new friend? I changed her name to Ri.

The drawing of a winky face followed the note. With a wry smile, Lily swiped her phone from the charging disk, donned her readers, and sent a text to Cassie. *You could have delivered that information in so many other ways.*

As she swung her feet onto the mattress and under the covers, her phone chimed. The message from Cassie began with another winky face and continued: *But that was the most fun way. What do you think? She's creepy, right? She fits right in!*

Lily's thumbs tapped out a response: *Don't let Wyatt see her. He'll think she's real!*

She shook her head at the response. *So did you!* A tongue-sticking-out emoji followed. With a shake of her head, Lily texted a good night and slouched down on the mattress as she dumped her phone on the charger.

She eyed the brown journal, considering reading more. Instead, her mind did a little math. Henrietta and Clifton hid the treasure in 1798. They died about a month apart in 1802. Four years. For four years they'd had the treasure. For four years she'd known of her husband's death. Her brother had died second, not first.

Lily eased into the pillows and turned the light off. Moonlight gleamed from the window and Lily stared at the shadows on the ceiling as she pondered one burning question.

What had made Henrietta throw herself from the Widow's walk?

* * *

Cassie's fingers traced the dark grain in the circular wooden table as her mother shuffled from the room. She needed a distraction from the latest conversation. Maybe she'd spent too much time trying to figure out the best way to scare the pants off other Hideaway Bayers that she now searched for spooks and specters in every dark corner.

Or perhaps she'd watched too many scary movies. Or maybe she just wasn't quite as sure as her mother that other-worldly creatures didn't exist.

And she wasn't alone. Wyatt believed the house's curse explained their recent happenings. And there was a similar explanation for the trouble they'd experienced at the barn.

Cassie sucked in a breath. In any instance, they had no other explanation. And if she went to bed right now, she'd lay awake dwelling on it.

Instead, she'd let her mind relax by playing with her new toys. The corners of her mouth turned up as she rapped her knuckles against the table before she stalked from the room.

The pile of purchases still sat next to the front door. Cassie plopped onto the entryway mat cross-legged and pawed through the bags. A warm furball rubbed against her back, his purr vibrating against her spine.

She twisted a hand behind her, grasping his tail and swiping upward. "Hey, buddy."

Willy reversed his direction, a meow escaping from him.

Cassie wrangled open the box containing the magical books. "Did you miss me today?"

Another mewling cry answered her as she freed the animated item, tossing the box to the side and unwrapping the plastic and foam protecting the books.

Willy left her side to dive at the cardboard container, chasing it across the floor until he smashed it into the corner. He stuck his head inside, his tail swishing as he explored the box's interior.

Cassie smirked at his enthusiasm for the so-called toy. She flicked a gaze to the toy bin in the living room filled to the brim with items supposed to entertain a cat for hours. Instead, they sat untouched while Willy wandered around with a box on his head.

Cassie teased the plastic tab from the battery compartment and switched on the item. Books clattered back and forth as though they were alive. She climbed to her feet and shuffled into the library.

She scanned the space before she crossed to the bookshelf near the window seat. After clearing a spot, she squeezed the decoration between the other books on the shelf. As she stowed the removed books in the drawer at the bottom of the shelf, the animated decoration triggered. Books slid forward and back as if possessed by a spirit. Spooky noises floated through the air.

Cassie slid the drawer shut and eyed the contraption. Her smile faded as she recalled Henrietta's book flying off the shelf only last night. She swallowed hard and backed away from the bookcase.

"Maybe this wasn't the best choice," she mumbled.

Cassie shook her head and spun on her heel, returning to

the bags in the foyer. She rummaged through, finding the ghost-writer book she'd purchased. She wrinkled her nose, dumping it back in the bag.

"Why did I get so many ghostly book things?"

Her eyes flicked to the large box laying across the floor. An image of a ghostly woman in a Victorian dress stood with cobwebs hanging around her. Cassie tugged open the flap and flipped the box's top off.

A mass of curly black hair poked from the protective Styrofoam. The protective wrap squeaked against the sides as Cassie shimmied it up. She reached in and grabbed the ghost's bony shoulders, struggling as she wrapped her feet around the box to hold it on the ground.

After a fight, she wrangled the figure from the container, setting it down next to her. She slid the box into a corner and returned to the ghost woman. With a crumpled dress, the lady stood no taller than her waist, her hands pinned to her sides.

Cassie stared down at the figure before she grasped it and tugged it upward. The ghost woman flew toward the ceiling. Cassie made a face and tried again, this time keeping a foot on the ghost's base.

She pulled her up to normal height. The ghost's hazy white eyes stared blankly back at her. With parted gray lips, dark circles rimmed her eyes and gray veins decorated her delicate porcelain skin.

Cassie stared at her for a moment before she started to adjust her poseable arms. After twenty minutes of work, she settled on one hand hanging casually at her side and the other reaching toward her intended victim.

She fussed with her hair for a few moments, her eyes falling to the ghost's face again. With a lick of her lips, she pulled her phone from her back pocket. She pulled up her internet browser and ran a search on Clifton Nichols.

A Wikipedia article detailed a small amount about the infamous pirate. Cassie scanned the side panel, listing important dates. She found the date of death listed as September 18, 1802. With another gaze at the ghost, she ran a search on Henrietta Nichols Blanchard. After a few useless clicks, Cassie stumbled upon a website detailing the tragic life and death of Henrietta Blanchard, the ghost of Whispering Manor.

She skimmed through the more sensational details to find the date of death. August 14, 1802. Cassie crinkled her brow. Henrietta died before her brother. Her brother's death couldn't have been the reason she committed suicide then.

Cassie rested her chin against the top of the phone as she clicked off the display. In front of her, the ghost shuddered, its head lolling to the side, eyes staring forward at Cassie.

Cassie stumbled back a step, smacking into the foyer table. It screeched across the floor as her heart pounded at the movement.

Her breath caught in her throat, and she stared, her jaw hanging open and her eyes wide, at the ghost. She hadn't turned it on. It shouldn't have moved.

The fabric of her dress swished as she stuttered forward, hand outstretched to Cassie. The ghost teetered back and forth before toppling toward Cassie. Her hand grazed Cassie's face, landing hard on her shoulder.

Cassie's lower lip trembled as a terrified scream caught in her throat. With shaking hands, she flung the ghost backward. It collapsed backward, crashing onto the floor.

Willy scrambled from its path, racing up a few stairs and whipping around to stare at the wayward ghost.

Cassie slid her eyes closed and pressed a hand against her heart. "Willy!" she exclaimed. The details of the spooky incident became clear. The cat had rubbed against her inanimate friend, sending her careening toward Cassie.

It had not been a case of the doll becoming alive with a spirit, but just a clumsy cat. She chuckled at her own silliness as she shuffled over to the animatron and righted it, staring at the spooky eyes again.

"I think I'll rename you Ri after that."

Before heading upstairs, she jotted a note to her mother and taped it to Ri's chest. She hefted the doll up and climbed the stairs, setting her down at the top. She bent over and flicked on the ghost's switch.

The woman rumbled across the floor toward Lily's room, yammering spooky phrases as she went. Willy arched his back as the ghost trundled across the hardwood. After a moment, he spun and retreated into Cassie's room.

"I'm right behind you, buddy!"

Cassie gave one final glance to the ghost as she wandered toward her mom's room before she skirted the railing and disappeared into her bedroom.

With the carousel playing, Cassie tugged off her clothes and pulled on her cozy jammies.

She sprawled under her duvet and glanced at the clock. Given the hour, she grabbed her remote and toggled on the television across the room. She surfed through the channels, finding a horror movie, a TV program about witches, a haunted house film, and *The Exorcist* playing. She winced and emphatically pressed the power button to turn off the device. As she dumped the remote on the nightstand, her eyes fell to the small book she'd pulled from the shelves last night. Or rather, that had pulled itself from the shelves.

She ran her hand over the cover and swallowed hard. With a lick of her lips, she curled her fingers around it and tugged it onto her lap.

She eased the cover open, studying the writing inside.

The Adventures of Black Jack

Cassie ran her finger over the words before she flipped the page. A numeral graced the top.

She read the first words under the chapter indicator.

A massive wave slammed into Neptune's Servant, rolling her until her masts nearly kissed the ocean. Water sloshed over the deck, foaming and pooling as the ship threatened to capsize. Black sails, wet and whipping in the wind, sprayed water across the deck. High above the crow's nest, the Jolly Roger flew proudly, snapping in the wicked winds.

A man cowered in the corner, clinging desperately to the railing as he emptied his stomach's contents over the rail. Most others on the massive ship were tucked below deck, riding out the storm in the safety of the ship's bowels. All except for one man.

A bolt of lightning streaked through the night sky, illuminating him. He stood tall at the ship's wheel, guiding her expertly through the storm. Water poured from the brim of his worn tricorn hat as rain pounded around him.

Thunder boomed overhead, and the ship rolled again. The only other man above board clutched the railing as he dragged himself up to the helm area.

"Sir," he shouted over the rain hammering against the deck. "We'll never make it! We must turn back!"

The man narrowed his eyes and flicked his gaze sideways to his first mate. A sly grin crossed his rugged features. "Oh, we'll make it, Johnson. Or my name isn't Black Jack." A boom of thunder punctuated his statement.

A loud bang resounded, and Cassie snapped the book closed, jumping. Her eyes rose, wondering if a storm was blowing up the coast, similar to the one Henrietta detailed in her opening scene.

Her mother's voice floated through the air moments later. "Keep your creepy ghosts on your side of the stairs!"

A slam sounded, signaling the closing of Lily's door.

A sly grin creased Cassie's lips, and she crawled out from under the covers, discarding her reading material on the duvet.

In bare feet, she darted across the hardwood and into the hall, hurrying toward the specter she'd named Ri, and flicked the switch on her base. The ghost wound to a stop just past the stairs, her pale hand still outstretched, searching.

Cassie dragged her to the side out of the way, leaving her tucked facing the corner before darting back to her bedroom and closing her door.

She turned the key on her carousel and light music filled the air as she dove under the covers again. After a quick text exchange with her mother, Willy readjusted his position with his back pressed against her as she opened the book again, intent on learning more about Black Jack's Adventures.

"Sir, please! The storm is far too dangerous. We'll sink!" the man implored again.

"We won't," Black Jack assured him, his deep voice filled with confidence.

The first mate sighed. "Jack... you're blinded by ambition."

"And you by fear."

The man raised his chin, water dripping from his hat. "No, Johnson, we sail straight on."

"We will be crushed against the rocks!"

"We will not. And we will beat the others to the bounty. And sail happily away laden with treasure before the others ever even come close."

"By God, Jack, I hope you're right. There are over seventy-five souls aboard this ship. I would hate to see them all lost to the Locker."

"We will lose none of them to the Locker, Mr. Johnson. Though

we may lose some of them as they run with their tails between their legs after this adventure." Jack swung the wheel around and the ship dove to the side. "It takes a brave man to follow Black Jack. This should help weed out any who lacks the stomach."

With another twirl of the wheel, he sent the ship on a careful course, threading past dangerous rocks and undercurrents as the storm continued to batter them.

Mr. Johnson struggled to keep his footing.

"Find me five men with good stomachs. The next part will prove tricky."

A soft puff escaped Cassie's lips and the book slid face down on her chest. The carousel continued its whimsical tune as she slipped off to sleep, exhaustion overcoming her.

A hissing sound disturbed her. With her eyes still closed, she tapped the cat and mumbled, "Go to sleep, buddy."

She rolled to her side, the book clattering to the floor. Cassie's fingers dug into her pillow as she squeezed her eyes shut, choosing to leave the book until tomorrow.

"Cassie," a voice called to her.

"Huh?" she murmured, still half asleep.

"Cassie," the voice repeated. Tinkling music played behind the voice, sounding distorted and slow.

"What?" she questioned again in a slow, sleepy voice, her eyes still closed.

"Wake up, Cassandra. You must wake up. There is something you must do."

Cassie groaned and scrubbed her face.

"You must find the journals. Find the journals, Cassie, find the journals."

"Journals? What journals?" Cassie questioned as she rolled onto her back and forced her tired eyes open.

She blinked a few times as the room came into focus. A

figure stood at the end of her bed. As her vision sharpened, her eyes shot wide, and her jaw gaped open. She scurried back toward the wall as she stared at the source of the voice, her feet kicking at the covers furiously to raise herself to sit.

Standing in front of her, with an outstretched arm, was her animatronic ghost.

CHAPTER 6

Cassie shot up to sitting, her heart pounding. She sucked in a sharp breath as sweat beaded on her forehead. Her gaze scanned the room in search of the phantom.

She swallowed hard, her heart settling into a normal rhythm when she found her room devoid of the specter. She finger-combed her hair back, sitting in bed for another few moments to allow her breathing to slow.

Her brow furrowed as she considered the life-like incident. She must have been dreaming. Her mind must have melded together her recent purchase with her reading and her mother's fondness of Henrietta's journal.

Cassie swung her legs over the side of the bed and slid into her cat slippers as she pulled her robe around her shoulders. Still lounging on the bed, Willy's one eye popped open, and he stretched a paw out long in front of him before he rose to his feet, his back arching high.

After a gaping yawn, he strutted toward her and leapt off the bed, darting out the door and downstairs to demand his breakfast. Cassie followed behind him, peering over the railing as he raced down the wooden steps.

She passed the corner where her ghost stood as a silent sentinel and slowed to a stop. Her eyebrows smashed together again, and her pulse quickened as she stared at the animated contraption.

Cassie licked her lips as the ghostly eyes stared back at her. When she'd turned it off and dragged it over last night, she'd left the robotic woman facing the corner. Now, she faced out with her back pressed against the wall, not her face.

Cassie tilted her head as her mind sought any reasonable explanation that did not involve a haunting. Downstairs, pots and pans clanged in the kitchen. She flicked her gaze to the foyer below before sliding her eyes back to the ghost.

Her lower lip pressed upward as realization dawned on her. With a shake of her head and a smirk, she bypassed the creepy statue and snaked her way to the kitchen.

The sweet smell of French toast frying met her nostrils as she turned the corner into the room. In a frying pan, four slices of the eggy delight sizzled in melted butter. Maple syrup warmed in a pot of hot water near the sink.

"Mmm," Cassie said with a deep inhale, "smells delicious."

"I figured I'd treat you," Lily answered with a smile as she flipped the slices over revealing browned undersides. She shot a glance at her daughter. "Despite your mean trick on me last night."

Cassie offered her a wry glance as she set the table. "You paid me back good, though, thanks a lot."

"Oh, those texts really got to you, huh?" Lily inquired.

"Texts? No," Cassie said, setting two plates next to the pan as Lily checked the bottom of the toast for a golden-brown finish. "Your little ghost trick in the middle of the night."

Cassie bustled back to the table with the maple syrup wrapped in a tea towel to dry. "What I can't figure out, though, is how you got her to say all that stuff." She wiped the last beads of moisture off the bottle and set it on the table before slinging the towel over her shoulder. "Ohhh, never mind. You used the Echo."

Cassie waved her hand in the air as she plopped onto the chair with the mystery solved.

Lily waddled across the room with a plate in each hand, setting one in front of Cassie before she eased into the chair next to her. "What are you talking about?"

"Your trick with Ri last night. Who, by the way, I am renaming to Bessie after that because it was downright creepy."

"I don't know what you're talking about," Lily answered, pouring maple syrup over one slice of her French toast.

Cassie's shoulders slumped and she shot Lily a glance as she drizzled the syrup over her breakfast. "Oh, come on. Own up."

"To what?" Lily questioned.

"You sent my little ghost friend into my room last night to talk to me. Payback for the note she delivered to you earlier, huh?"

Lily ceased eating, a piece of French toast stuck through the tines of her fork and syrup dripping to her plate below as she eyed Cassie. "I did no such thing."

Cassie stared at her for a moment, a smile playing at the corners of her mouth. "Of course, you did. Who else would have done it?"

"Cassie, I did *not* send that contraption into your room in the middle of the night. I was out once I finally fell asleep. I don't think I got up once. I'm not sure I even moved!"

Cassie's brow crinkled again, and she recalled the ghost's new posture this morning. Someone had sent the thing into her room and then replaced it in its spot in the hall.

She swallowed hard, flicking her gaze to her mother. "If you didn't do it, then who did?"

Lily squashed her lips together and shook her head. "Oh, Cassie, are you being serious, or is this a joke?"

Cassie's eyes widened. "It's not a joke! Last night the ghost wandered into my room and spoke to me. When I opened my eyes, she, it was standing at the bottom of my bed. She told me something about a journal."

Cassie tapped her forehead with her fingertips as she tried to recall the exact words. Lily chuckled as she cut another piece of her meal and swirled it around in the syrup.

"It's not funny! That ghost came wandering into my room last night, yammering on about finding a journal."

Lily's eyebrows shot up, an amused expression on her lips. "Sure she did."

"I'm not kidding!" Cassie exclaimed.

"Well, if the thing just roams around at random, I'm sure she did wander into your room. I'm surprised she wasn't banging on my door again last night."

Cassie shook her head as she answered. "No, I turned her off after you tossed her out last night. And put her in the corner next to the wardrobe."

"Isn't that where she was this morning, too? You probably dreamed the whole thing."

Cassie shook her head, worry etching her features and shining in her blue eyes. "I put her facing the corner. This morning when I came past her, she was facing me."

Cassie shot her mother a terrified glance, swallowing hard as her fork clattered onto her plate. She let her eyes rise up to the floor above them as though she expected a ghost to descend through the ceiling.

"Cassie," Lily said, placing her hand on Cassie's and patting it, "you probably thought you put her that way, but you didn't. Or maybe you didn't turn it off and it shifted around."

"No!" Cassie said, her voice rising an octave higher. "No, I *know* I put her that way."

"Well–" Lily began as she searched her mind for an explanation.

"Which means she did wander into my room last night and speak to me."

"And then what? Put herself back in the corner before you woke up?"

"I guess!" Cassie insisted.

Lily pursed her lips and gave her head a slight shake. "Okay."

"Mom!" Cassie whined. "I saw her. I was asleep and I heard someone calling my name. The voice told me to wake up. And called me Cassandra. She told me there was some-thing I had to do and then told me I had to find the journals."

"And you saw the spirit doll thing when this happened? You're sure you didn't dream it?"

"I didn't dream it. I was half-asleep but when I opened my eyes, there she was standing at the end of the bed with that creepy white hand reaching for me."

"Then what? Did she wander away again? Or say anything else?"

"No," Cassie answered.

"So, how did she get back to her corner hangout? Don't tell me you went back to sleep with her in the room?"

"No," Cassie said, shaking her head. Her forehead wrin-kled. "I don't know. I don't remember. I woke up this morning and everything seemed normal but when I went past the ghost, she was facing a different direction. Are you sure you're not just messing with me?"

"I'm not messing with you, Cass. I didn't touch that thing. And even if I did, the way you and Wyatt are rambling on about curses at every turn, I wouldn't have sent it into your room."

Cassie bit her lower lip and shivered. "Oh, Cassie," Lily said with a roll of her eyes, "there are no such things as ghosts! You probably dreamt the entire thing."

Lily carried her plate to the sink and rinsed it before dumping it in the dishwasher. Cassie followed her, shoving the last piece of French toast in her mouth before running water over her sticky plate.

"Then how do you explain her position being moved?" she demanded as she set the plate and fork into the dishwasher.

"I'm telling you, you probably forgot that you put her facing that way. I can't see you facing her in the corner. Nobody puts Ri in the corner," Lily said, doing her best Patrick Swayze impression.

"Very funny. I know I put her that way."

"Let it go, Cass," Lily said, wrapping her arm around her daughter's shoulders as they stalked from the kitchen to the foyer, "there's a reasonable explanation for everything. We'll find it, eventually."

"Or we'll keep being haunted by Ri."

"How do you know it was Ri?" Lily asked, mounting the stairs. "We already found her journal so that makes no sense."

"Maybe there're more."

"Doubt it. She died in 1802 and this one goes up to that time. Thanks, by the way, for tracking that information down. It's interesting that she died before Clif, but that they died so close together."

Cassie mulled over the information, her thoughts turning to the death dates of her supposed specter and her brother. "Yeah, I'll be interested to see if there is any hint as to why she would commit suicide in her journal."

"We'll find out. Though likely not today. We'd better get a

move on if we want to open the shop on time. Your haunting nonsense cost us!"

"It's not nonsense," Cassie called as she swung right at the top of the stairs. She wrinkled her nose as she eyed the animatron in the corner, still frozen in the same position she'd left it in before breakfast.

"Yeah, yeah," Lily yelled as she disappeared into her room. "Just hurry up!"

* * *

Bright sunshine streamed through the shop windows. The quaint *Buy the Sea* logo with its choppy waves and sailboat for a "B" created unique shadows across the wood floor.

Cassie sprawled in the store's back storeroom with a variety of tools spread around her. She eyed the tall box in front of her as she planned how to transform it from a brown storage container into a whimsical jack-in-the-box.

With plastic spread across the floor under her, she took a deep breath and flipped over one of her metallic decorative sheets and sprayed it thoroughly with spray glue before positioning it on one of the box's sides.

She smoothed the blue sheet across the rectangular surface and spun the box, repeating the process with a new sheet in a different color. After she papered each of the four sides, she used smaller pieces to create diamond patterns on each side in contrasting colors.

After decorating the lid, she attached it with a piece of elastic. With a spring motor attached to her three-foot clown, she tucked him into the box. Only his wild orange hair peeked out over the top. She closed the lid and stepped on the step-pad trigger.

The lid popped open, and the clown sprung upward with his fingers stretched as though reaching for something. After a moment, the clown descended back into his box. The lid, however, remained open.

Cassie wrinkled her nose at it. That would need to be fixed. She brainstormed a way to close the lid on her new creation as she heard Chloe's bubbly voice wishing Lily a good morning.

"How's that maze coming?" she asked as she stowed her bag behind the register counter.

"Okay, I think," Lily answered. "Cassie's working on a new toy for it now. Hey, would you mind if we ducked out early today once Amber gets here? We'd like to work on it more, and we're behind schedule thanks to a mishap."

"Sure, no problem at all," Chloe said, waving Lily's concern away. "I heard about what happened from Uncle Wyatt."

Cassie poked her head out the door. "Thanks, Chloe!"

"That stinks! He said they don't have any idea who did it. Everyone's looking so forward to it, I can't even imagine who would do it."

The bell above the door jingled, announcing the arrival of newcomers.

"I come bearing gifts!" Meghan called.

Cassie stuck her head out of the door, spotting a drink caddy in Meghan's hands.

"Is that hot chocolate from *High Grounds*?" Cassie inquired, her lips turning up at the corners.

"It is!" Meghan announced.

Cassie scrambled to her feet and hurried to the register where Meghan plunked the drinks down.

Lily tugged one from the cardboard caddy. "Mmm, how much do we owe you?"

"On the house," Meghan said. "A perk of being the owner."

"Are you sure?" Cassie inquired as she freed a cup of the chocolatey concoction and sipped it.

"Absolutely!" Meghan pursed her lips before she let her gaze flit between the two women. "So…"

Her words were interrupted by the jingling of the bell. "Saw Meghan bringing hot chocolates and thought I'd pop in with some cookies." Genny, owner of the *Cake my Day* bakery next to *Buy the Sea*, waved a white box filled with goodies in the air.

"Aww, thanks, Genny," Chloe cooed as she tugged the box open and pulled a frosted cookie from within.

"Did you really bring the cookies to go with the hot chocolate?" Meghan asked.

Genny adjusted her tortoise-rimmed glasses and offered an uncertain chuckle. Meghan arched a perfectly made-up eyebrow over her heavily made-up eye. "Or were you hoping to get the scoop, too?"

"Scoop?" Lily inquired.

Meghan flicked her gaze to the woman, her features twisting into an amused expression. "We heard there was a ruckus at the maze sight."

"That it was trashed," Genny added.

Lily pulled one corner of her mouth back, balancing the chocolate drink against her shoulder as she shook her head. "There really are no secrets in this town, are there?"

"Well, there is one," Genny said. "Who trashed the infamous maze?"

Cassie nodded as she chomped on an oatmeal scotchie. "Yes, that one seems to not have any answers yet."

"So, how bad was it?" Meghan asked, biting her glossy ruby red lower lip.

Cassie swallowed another sip of hot chocolate, washing down the last bite of her cookie. "It wasn't a total loss, but we had some repairs to do. We spent yesterday getting everything back together."

Genny shoved her hands in her back pockets. "Will you still be ready in time to open?"

"I think so," Lily said. "We're getting close to finishing. Of course, we didn't expect to spend yesterday redoing things, but we'll just have to spend a little extra time over the next few days."

"Gosh, I hope it's ready. I can't wait to see it!" Chloe said.

"Me too!" Meghan squealed. "Half the reason I came over here wasn't to assess the damage but to make sure you'd still be opening."

Cassie took another sip of her hot chocolate and nodded. "Oh, we're still opening. Although, I'm not sure anyone will be all that excited."

"Everyone's excited," Genny said.

Meghan bobbed her head up and down. "Definitely. And with the drama of someone trashing the place, we're even more excited!"

"So, we've acquired some street cred with the mishap, huh?" Cassie inquired.

"Yep," Meghan said with another nod, "add the break-in on top of the barn being haunted and *everyone* is dying to see this!"

Cassie flicked her gaze to Lily who shook her head.

"We heard about the curse or whatever. I didn't realize that was widespread knowledge, though."

"Oh, sure," Meghan said with a wave of her hand, "*everyone* knows about the haunted Hunter barn."

"Haunted, huh?" Lily said. "Is *every* place in Hideaway Bay haunted?"

"Nah, just a handful of places," Chloe said. "The barn included."

"I thought it was cursed, not haunted," Cassie said.

Chloe shrugged as she freed a duster from under the

counter and waved it over the window display. "Cursed, haunted, same thing."

"Not really," Lily said.

"Well, I guess it's both," Genny answered, her hands shoved into her back pockets. "Tragic things happen there, hence the curse."

"And there's supposed to be a ghost running around there, too," Meghan said.

"Or more than one ghost," Chloe contended.

Meghan waved her hand at Chloe's statement. "Yeah, whatever. One ghost, bunches of ghosts, either way, haunted."

"Who are the ghosts there?" Cassie inquired.

Lily tugged the corner of her mouth back and shook her head at Cassie as Chloe detailed them.

"Well, there's the farmer who was trampled to death. He wanders inside the barn, not able to accept that his own horse killed him."

Meghan's eyes widened. "And the horse itself appears as a ghost, too. It re tramples him to death almost every night!"

Genny offered a shrug and faced Lily and Cassie. "When I moved, I heard a Native American roamed the place, cursing anyone who disturbed his rest."

Chloe moved on to dust the decorative lighthouses on the shelf. "I'm actually surprised you haven't had more trouble at the maze than just this."

Meghan leaned forward toward Lily and Cassie and lowered her voice. "Have you?"

"Have we what?" Lily questioned.

Meghan lifted her eyebrows. "Had more trouble?"

Chloe spun to face them. "Any ghost run-ins? Spooky stuff happening? Weird vibes?"

Genny lifted her shoulder in a partial shrug. "Spine-chilling screams from nowhere? Icy cold blasts of wind with no windows open?"

Lily crinkled her brow. "Ladies, ladies, the only spine-chilling screams in that barn are coming from the animatrons we've installed to scare the pants off our patrons."

Amber pushed through the door of the shop, studying the scene in front of her. "Aww, did I miss all the good scoop?"

Lily flicked her gaze to Amber. "There is no scoop to miss," she said. "We don't know who trashed the maze, but we are sure it is a living, breathing human. We also managed to repair the damage, and, with your help, we hope we'll finish in time."

"With my help?" Amber's eyes lit up. "Do I get to help decorate? Do I get to see it early?"

Lily chuckled at the girl's enthusiasm. "Sorry, no one's getting a sneak peek. But if you can hold down the fort here with Chloe, Cassie and I can duck out early and do some more work."

"Oh," Amber answered, her lips puckering in a deflated expression, "sure, I can do that much. Would have been way more exciting the other way, but I guess I can make this contribution."

Lily winked at her. "Thanks, Amber. And we wouldn't want to ruin the surprise for you! Everyone will get to see the inside soon."

"All right, ladies," Cassie said. "I hate to break up the party, but we'd better get going if we want to make any progress on the maze!"

Lily glanced at her watch. "Gosh, you're right! It's already almost one. We spent too much time talking about the fake haunting! I hope we'll have enough time to finish our own haunting."

Meghan and Genny wandered to the door, calling their

goodbyes and reminding the ladies how much they were anticipating being scared out of their wits at week's end.

"Give me a minute to load my little creation into the Wrangler and I'll be ready," Cassie said, darting into the storeroom.

Within ten minutes, she'd cleaned up her area and slid the new animated device into the back of her SUV. Lily climbed into the passenger's seat, twisting to eye the new animatron.

"How's he look?" she asked as Cassie slid behind the wheel.

"I think he's good. One final adjustment to make sure he pulls his lid closed when he retreats into the box, and he'll be all finished up."

Lily buckled her seat belt, adjusting the neck strap. "I can't wait to see him."

Cassie eased the car down the alley before pulling onto the main road. "I'm setting him up first thing when we get there."

"Okay, I'll work on my clown's head display."

"I think you should put a sign on that warning people it was your creation. I don't want to be blamed for people's nightmares."

"Very funny, Cassie," Lily said with a wry glance at her.

Cassie wove through the streets toward the outskirts of town, pulling onto the two-lane country road that led to the barn. As she swung the Wrangler onto the gravel path, her brows knit.

"Is that a car?"

"I see the police cruiser," Lily said, glancing out the window.

"No, over there." Cassie waved a finger to the left side of the barn.

"Oh, yeah," Lily said, craning her neck for a better view. "Wonder who that is and why they're here."

"Maybe Wyatt put double protection on the place."

Lily slid her seatbelt off as Cassie killed the engine. She stepped from the car and eyed the police cruiser. Empty. Where was the officer? Was there some trouble?

Cassie pulled her tailgate open and began tugging her jack-in-the-box from the SUV.

"Hey, Cass," Lily breathed.

"Yeah?" Cassie said, popping her head around the Wrangler to stare at her mother.

Lily lifted her chin and thrust it toward the police cruiser. Cassie twisted to glance at it before whipping her head to stare at her mother again.

Lily shrugged, palms up, and tapped a finger in the air toward the barn. Cassie tiptoed toward her mother, leaving her animated creation sticking halfway out of her trunk.

"Do you think there's trouble?" she whispered.

Lily shrugged again. "Only one way to find out."

CHAPTER 7

*C*assie took another look at the empty police cruiser before they began a slow creep toward the barn door. "Kind of weird if there is trouble again."

"Why?"

"It's a Sunday afternoon. Really? The criminal decided to spend Sunday afternoon trashing our maze again?"

"I'm not sure the criminal plans his or her days out that way, Cass. Did you think they'd prefer a lazy Sunday afternoon instead of mayhem?"

Cassie shot her mother a wry glance, puckering her lips and giving her a slight headshake. "No, I didn't mean the criminal took the weekend off. I mean it's broad daylight!"

They inched up the ramp toward the door.

"It's open a crack," Lily whispered.

"Yep," Cassie breathed.

A shriek sounded from within. Both women's eyes widened.

"Maybe we ought to wait in the car!" Cassie suggested.

Lily firmed her jaw, grabbing a broom from a witch

display near the door. She crept forward, brandishing the broom over her shoulder.

"Mom!" Cassie hissed.

"Enough is enough, Cassie. If someone broke in, I'm not going to stand for it."

Cassie hurried behind her. "Maybe we should wait for the officer to chase the person away."

"And maybe he needs a hand."

Lily reached for the barn door and wrapped her fingers around the handle. She shoved it open, raising the broom high as a cackle emerged.

Lily's posture stiffened and her eyes went wide at the scene inside. She squashed her lips together, letting the broom fall to her side.

Cassie's jaw dropped along with her shoulders.

Inside the space, a small group of people huddled, expressions of shock on their faces at being caught. In the center of the group, stood town mayor Tinsley Thomson. Next to her, flashlight drawn, Officer Whittaker. To his right, Seaside Cafe's owner, Ben. Penny Whitlock, Lucy, and a few other of the town's residents rounded out the group.

Tinsley pulled her lips back in an amused grimace. "Lily! Cassie!" she exclaimed, throwing her hands in the air in mock surprise before she ran her palms down her black leggings. Paired with a black turtleneck, boots, and a dark Halloween-themed vest, she appeared as though she'd dressed in a catsuit for her trespassing trip. "Fancy meeting you here!"

"Mayor Thompson?" Cassie questioned.

"Officer Whittaker?" Lily asked.

"Oh, uh, hi. We didn't expect you," the uniformed man answered.

"Clearly," Lily said with a raise of her eyebrows. "What's going on here?"

"Well," Tinsley said, drawing the word out as her eyes darted around, "we heard about the trouble and–"

"We twisted Officer Whittaker's arm to show us around because we couldn't stand the wait any longer," Penny burst, drawing in a ragged breath after and raking the back of her hand across her forehead with relief.

"Penny!" Tinsley squealed.

Lily and Cassie's eyebrows both shot up. Lily stuck her hands on her hips. "Really, ladies, it's only a few more days!" She flicked her gaze to the uniformed officer. "And Officer Whittaker, I'm surprised at you!"

The man winced as though his mother scolded him. "Technically, Mayor Thomson is my boss, so when she said to open it up, well, I opened it up."

Lily stood the broom against the barn's side and crossed her arms. "So, have you gone over it with a fine-toothed comb?"

Tinsley chuckled, waving her hand in the air. "Of course not. We barely saw anything!" She began leading the group from the barn into the autumn afternoon air. As she passed Lily and Cassie, she leaned closer to them, lowering her voice. "There were a few things, though, that looked off in the area with the band. Just in case you didn't know."

"Thanks, Mayor Thomson," Cassie said. "We didn't quite finish with our clean-up from the last incident, but we'll get there."

Tinsley offered a knowing nod and winked at her. The others filed past them. Penny offered a whispered and penitent "I'm sorry" as she passed.

Lily patted her arm and smiled at her. "It's okay. I hope you liked what you saw so far."

"Oh, it looks fabulous," Penny said. "I can't wait to see it all pulled together with the lights and effects."

"It really looks great, even not all lit up and working," Lucy said as she swiped one side of her hair behind her ear.

"Thank you," Cassie replied.

The group spoke for a few more moments, everyone expressing their excitement to see more before they shuffled off, some walking to their next destination, others piling into the car Lily had spotted earlier.

"Really sorry," Officer Whittaker said. "Mayor Thomson said–"

Lily held up her hand to stop his comments. "It's fine, Ted. I'm glad people are this excited to be honest, though I really just want to get some work done and finish this thing up so it's ready to open."

"Well, it looks great so far. And for what it's worth, they didn't see the whole thing. The group split up and everyone went in different directions so, they only each saw snippets."

Lily pressed her lips together and nodded. "Ah, good, well, at least there'll be something for them to be surprised by when we open."

Officer Whittaker smiled and nodded, glancing around the space for another few moments.

"Uh, Ted," Lily prompted after a minute.

"Yeah?"

"Could you maybe…" She flicked her fingers toward the police cruiser.

"Oh, right, what am I thinking? Let me get out of your hair and let you work." He stepped toward the door. "Oh, and by the way, outside of the unexpected visitors, no trouble."

"Good," Lily answered as Cassie returned to the car to retrieve her creation.

Officer Whittaker offered her a wave, sliding into the police cruiser as she lugged the oversized jack-in-the-box from her Wrangler.

Cassie hauled the item into the barn, setting it up to greet visitors as they stepped inside. "At least no one has seen this little masterpiece!"

She smiled down at it, squatting in front of it to hide the step pad under the welcome mat. "Give it a try!"

Lily studied the colorful box before she smacked her foot against the doormat. The grinning clown sprung from inside the shiny compartment, the lid flinging open as he leapt with his hands reaching toward Lily.

"Ohhh, nice," Lily said, commending her daughter on her creation. After a moment, the clown descended into the depths of his box, tugging the lid shut behind him.

"Very effective, Cass. Just like my clown's head will be."

"We'll see," Cassie said as they donned their work belts, filled with tools, notes, and their headlamps, and set off into separate areas to add final touches.

They spent the better part of the afternoon adding the new purchases, adjusting existing displays, and rearranging items, then called it quits.

Tired and sore, they headed home, stopping to pick up chicken salad on croissants from the Seaside Cafe. The two women slogged through their front door as the sun hung low in the sky.

Willy raced down the stairs to greet them. Cassie ruffled his fur. "Not too late this time, bud."

"And we didn't set the alarm off, either."

Cassie tossed her keys into the bowl by the door. "Thank goodness. I just want to change, eat and relax."

"And here I thought you enjoyed those surprise visits from a gun-waving Wyatt."

"I could do without the gun-wielding, siren-blaring parts."

"Well, I'm glad to have obliged you and not set off the alarm tonight."

"Meet you in ten," Cassie called as they parted ways at the top of the stairs.

She wandered past the animatronic ghost, still parked in the corner and staring out at her with blank eyes. Cassie squinted at the ghost as she skirted past. She twisted to stare over her shoulder at the fake woman, swearing those glassy eyes followed her passage.

Her footsteps faltered, grinding to a halt. Had the ghost moved? Cassie shook her head and pushed herself to continue to her bedroom. She was being ridiculous, of course.

If it had moved, she thought as she peeled off her sweaty t-shirt, it was likely a jerk of the mechanism, a burst of left-over power from the battery despite the switch being off.

Cassie tugged her pajama top over her head and wound her carousel. She chuckled at herself as she recalled thinking the ghost had wandered into her room and spoken with her while she slept.

Her mother was right. A ridiculous thought. She must have dreamt the whole thing. Cassie slid into her pants and donned her robe as the musical carousel played a jaunty tune. Across the room, the little horses bobbed up and down as the mechanism spun them around in a circle.

While she pulled on her slippers, though, the carousel wound down, the horses freezing in their positions.

Cassie sighed. "Again?" she called to it. "There can't be *another* piece of paper caught in your gears, can there?"

She shuffled across the room and wound the device again. It wouldn't budge. An icy cold gust of air blew past her as she leaned forward, hands on her thighs, to study the item. Cassie straightened and shivered, tugging her robe tighter around her.

Across the room, Willy narrowed his eyes at nothing. He issued a low-pitched growl and a hiss. Cassie swallowed hard as she spun to stare in the direction of the cat's gaze. She spotted nothing, but another shiver ran up her spine.

A second icy blast gusted past her. Was someone here with her? Had a spirit entered the room?

Cassie's pulse quickened and she flared her nostrils as she tried to slow her breathing.

"Hello?" she called.

No answer came. She bit her lower lip as she stepped back, inching away from some unknown threat.

Willy's ears flattened against his head, and he issued another hiss before slinking off the bed and hiding underneath it.

"Thanks for the backup," Cassie grumbled as she worried about what she'd do next.

Cold air caressed her cheeks again and ruffled her hair. Her heart skipped a beat as an unearthly groan tickled her ears.

"Cassie," a tinkling whisper voiced.

With a gasp, Cassie continued her trek backward, bumping into her window seat. Her knees hit it hard, buckling, and she collapsed onto her backside.

"Wh-who's there?" she squeaked.

This time her inquiry prompted a response from whatever had entered her room. The cold air disappeared as quickly as it came. Across the room, her door wobbled for a moment before slamming shut.

Cassie issued a yelp before she leapt from her seat and raced to the door. She grasped the doorknob and twisted it, tugging as she braced herself against the door jamb.

The door wouldn't budge. She was trapped. The question lingered in her mind as she spun, pressing her back against the door, was she alone, or was someone in here with her?

* * *

Lily waved behind her in silent acknowledgment of Cassie's statement to meet in ten minutes. She shambled into her bedroom with a deep sigh. The maze building took another toll today. Her muscles ached. She hoped she had the where-withal to finish the task and open the maze in a few days.

A few days, she reflected, as she shuffled across the room into her ensuite bathroom, kicking her shoes off. She hoped she could withstand another few days.

She tugged her champagne blonde locks back into a low ponytail before she swiped a cotton ball covered in astringent over her face. After slathering her skin with a generous amount of face cream, she tugged her top over her head and tossed it into her hamper.

She slipped her arms into her plaid pajama top, straightening the collar before she began buttoning it. Her eyes fell to the brown journal on her nightstand.

She eyed it as she recalled the story Cassie relayed to her this morning. The subtle but strange incident coupled with the odd story about Ri's book had even her questioning things. And then there was the creaking of her floorboard when no one was there.

Lily shook her head at herself as she tugged on her pajama bottoms. "You're getting as bad as Cassie. And you've got to be the one who stays grounded in reality."

As she shoved her feet into her slippers, a noise sounded outside her door. "Come on in, Willy!" she called. "Though I'm not feeding you. That's Cassie's job!"

The floorboard creaked under something or someone's weight.

"Come on, Willy!" Lily called again through the partially ajar door. "Just push it open."

The creak sounded again, but the door didn't budge. Lily pulled on her robe and tied it with a sigh, crossing the room.

She whipped the door open. "You're a lazy b–" Her voice

cut off mid-word. She searched the area outside of her room. No cat. Nothing. Not a soul. Or perhaps... No. Lily dismissed the thought with a shake of her head. There wasn't a ghost wandering around in front of her door.

As she settled her mind and her nerves, an icy blast of air smacked her in the face. The floorboard in front of her creaked again. But no one trod on it. No one was there. At least no one in physical form.

Lily swallowed hard as she retreated back a step, her eyes wide. She'd never believed in spirits, but she pondered if she was staring one right in the face at this very moment.

Another cold blast hit her before a whistling sound circled her. A rattling sound drew her attention behind her. She twisted to glance in its direction. The journal on her nightstand shook before the cover blew open. Pages whipped in the wind gust, flicking them from right to left.

The pages stopped moving, freezing the book open at a specific spot. Breathless, Lily inched toward the journal. With raised eyebrows, she eyed the writing scrawled across the page, though she could not make it out at this distance.

She crept closer until the three words written on the page came into focus as she squinted at them. They made her eyes widen.

Time for death.

She swallowed hard as the words rattled through her mind. Another gust of air blasted past her. Across the room, her bedroom door slammed shut.

Lily sucked in a sharp breath, her muscles tensing. She raced across the room and gripped the doorknob. She twisted it and tugged, fighting against the barrier that trapped her inside.

With a gasp, she spun to face her room, leaning against her door. She rubbed at the back of her neck wondering if the ghost had locked her in alone or if two souls occupied the space.

CHAPTER 8

$\mathcal{C}$assie fretted for another moment before she raced across her room, an idea forming in her mind. She swiped her phone from the charger on her nightstand. With trembling fingers, she toggled in her numeric passcode and navigated to her phone app.

She hurriedly scrolled through her list of contacts until she found the one she searched for: Mom. Her still shaking finger tapped the green call icon and she pressed the phone to her ear.

With a hard swallow, she waited for the familiar trill, indicating an outgoing call. It never came. Instead, a high-pitched set of three notes bleeped in her ear. A robotic voice announced the call could not be completed as dialed, encouraging her to check the number and try again.

"What?" Cassie cried as she stared at the phone clutched in her hands, a horrified expression on her face.

She tried the call again. "Come on!"

Another error message followed dead air. She stared at the phone. Four bars. She had service. Why wouldn't the call go through?

Panic laced her thoughts, and she sank onto the edge of her bed. With a labored breath, she tapped back into her phone, choosing the messaging app this time. Her fingers flew across the keyboard as she typed a message to her mother.

Mom... I'm trapped in my room. The door is stuck. I can't get out!

Cassie pressed the send button and waited, staring at the lit screen awaiting a response. After a moment, a red triangle with a white exclamation point appeared next to the message. Cassie pressed it.

Message failed to send.

Her heart fell as she stared at the failure report. A retry link shined in blue below it. Before she could tap it, letters paraded across the screen.

Cassie pulled her hand away, staring with wide eyes as her phone typed a message on its own. In the message box, words began to form. She swallowed hard as she realized what the letters spelled.

Find the journals, Cas

Before the final letters could appear, Cassie dropped the phone on the floor. It thudded against her fluffy area rug before clattering face down across the hardwood floor. Cassie kicked backward, climbing onto the bed and hugging her knees to her chest.

She didn't understand what was happening, but she felt certain that message had been typed by a ghost.

* * *

Lily whipped around and gave the door another angry tug.

"This is ridiculous," she muttered to herself. "I am not trapped in my own room because of a ghost."

With no progress on freeing herself, Lily tightened the tie on her robe and strode across the room. "There are no such things as ghosts."

She flicked the journal closed, dismissing the eerie message, and snatched her cell phone. After finding Cassie's name in her contact list, she pressed the call icon and waited.

Dead air filled the line. She tapped the end call button and tried again. Nothing. With a frustrated sigh, she tried a text message.

It did not send. She squashed her lips together in frustration as she tossed the phone on the duvet. "Useless."

She shuffled across the room and tried the door again. With it stuck fast, she hammered against it with her fist.

"Cassie!" she shouted. "Cassie! My door's stuck!"

She pressed her ear against the door, listening for any sounds of life. Silence filled the air.

She tried pounding again but to no avail. With a mumbled curse, she spun in search of another way out. She eyed the windows, starting with the one overlooking the ocean.

She peered out, wondering if she could shimmy down a drainpipe somewhere. The sheer drop to the deck below dashed her hopes. She tried the other window across the room. Nothing she could use to slow her descent.

"Shoot!" she breathed.

As she stared out at the night sky, considering opening the window and shouting for help, but unsure anyone would hear her, something caught her eye. She squinted into the distance, trying to make out a form half-hidden within the trees.

Was it a person? She unlocked the window, prepared to

slide it open and shout when a noise sent her leaping in the air.

She pressed her hand to her chest as she realized it was her cell phone ringing. Cassie must have gotten her text. Lily dove for the phone on the bed, swiping to answer it without looking at the display.

"Thank goodness!" she exclaimed. "I could use some help here!"

"Lily? Everything okay? Are you safe? Should I send a patrol car?"

Lily's eyebrows furrowed as she pulled the phone from her ear and stared down at the display. It read Wyatt Cooper.

"Wyatt?" she questioned, as though the phone lied.

"Yeah? Lily, what's going on? Is everything okay?"

"Well, yes and no. Sorry to panic you like that. I thought you were Cassie. And, no, you don't need to send a patrol car."

"Well, too late, I'm already on my way over."

Lily huffed out a breath as she collapsed onto the edge of the bed. "Well, it may not be a bad idea. Maybe you can help. I can't seem to get a hold of Cassie."

"Help with what?"

"My bedroom door is stuck. I'm trapped inside. I can't get a call out to Cassie or a text. Honestly, I'm surprised she's not wondering where I am, but I can't seem to get through to her. I've tried banging on the door and yelling for her. Nothing."

"I'll be right there. Don't move."

"You're in luck. I can't move."

Wyatt chuckled at the poor joke before hanging up.

Lily sucked in a breath and blew it out as she clutched the phone in her lap. Hopefully, Wyatt could jimmy the door open and free her. Then she'd have to find Cassie. Where was she?

As she toggled open the unsent message on her phone, a creak sounded behind her. She twisted to identify the source. Across the room, her door slowly inched open, its hinges creaking in protest.

* * *

A shiver shook Cassie as chills raced up her spine. She buried her head between her knees as she held her legs tight to her. After a moment of panic, she raised her eyes, peering over her pajama pants and scanning the room.

No movement. She lifted her head and glanced warily around. Her gaze fell to the phone, face down on the floorboards across the room. She grimaced at it, wondering if the ghost still typed a message on the screen.

Her breathing sped and her pulse raced as she pushed herself to find out. She inched to the edge of the bed, her eyes never leaving the phone. Slowly, she lowered one leg down, her toes pointed like a ballerina until they touched the floor.

With a fixed stare, she lowered the other leg and rose to stand. She took one step, then another until she hovered over the phone. She stared down at the object, a cold sweat forming across her shoulders.

With a firm jaw, she extended her fingers toward the phone. Just as her fingertips grazed the cool surface of the phone's case, she froze. Noise from across the room caught her attention.

Her heart skipped a beat and her eyes slowly rose from the floor to the door. It lazily crept open, its hinges creaking. As the door swung open, its hinges protesting, music filled the air. The carousel began to spin, its jaunty music resuming and its horses bobbing up and down as it circled.

Cassie's eyes widened and she darted for the opening,

praying it didn't slam shut as she reached it. She skidded as she slid through the door, clutching the door jamb to stop herself from hurling toward the railing and pitching head-first into the foyer below.

She sucked in breaths as she gave a glance back to her former prison. The little carousel still tinkled away.

Across the open space, a floorboard creaked. Cassie snapped her gaze in its direction. Her mother appeared from inside her bedroom, white as a sheet with wide eyes. She clutched her cell phone in her hands.

The two women locked eyes before they uttered the same words. "I think I just heard a ghost."

Cassie screwed up her face as her mother voiced an identical statement. "What?"

"Huh?" Lily answered from across the way.

Neither woman had the chance to answer before their front door burst open. Wyatt flew through the door, taking the steps two at a time. He spun toward Lily's room as he reached the top, and skidded to a stop.

"Lily?" he questioned.

Lily squeezed her lips together and nodded. "Yeah, sorry. The door popped open right as you hung up."

Cassie wandered toward them. "Your door just opened? You saw a ghost? And you called Wyatt? What is going on here?"

"You said the same thing!" Lily retorted, waving her hand at Cassie. "What's your story?"

Cassie flicked her gaze between her mother and Wyatt as she launched into her tale. "Okay, I was changing into my pajamas when my carousel stopped playing again. While I was checking it out, I felt a cold wind. Then Willy started growling and hissing and hid under the bed. Another gust of wind blew past me, and I swore I heard someone call my name. When I asked who was there, the door slammed shut and wouldn't open. I tried to call and text you, but nothing would go through. But when I was trying to resend the text to you, someone started typing on my phone. I got so scared that I dropped it on the floor and was just about to pick it up when my door opened. I made a run for it. That's when I found you in the hall."

Cassie jabbed a finger at Lily. "What happened to you?"

Lily's eyebrows shot up and she explained her earlier experience. "About the same. A cold blast of air, then my door slammed shut, and I couldn't get out. Couldn't call or text you. I was considering climbing out the window when Wyatt called. I told him I couldn't get out of the bedroom and couldn't get a hold of you. Then, suddenly, the door opened."

"Anything spooky while you were locked in?"

"Being locked in was the spooky part, Cass," Lily said.

"Anything else? Weird texts on your phone or a ghostly voice?"

"No. Though…"

"What?" Cassie prodded.

Lily frowned and waved her hand in the air, dismissing it. "It's nothing."

"What?" Cassie insisted.

"Just when the wind was blowing around, it blew the journal open. But that's it."

Cassie gasped, pressing her hand to her throat. "Did it say anything… weird on the page it opened to?"

Lily lifted a shoulder and shook her head. "Typical Henrietta stuff. Very dramatic."

Wyatt put his hands on his hips and narrowed his eyes. "What does that mean?"

Lily flung her arms out to the side. "It said 'Time for death,' okay?"

Cassie sucked in another breath.

Wyatt flicked his gaze to Cassie. "Is that what yours said? The weird phantom text messages?"

"No. Mine said 'Find the journals, Cas.' I don't know if there was anything else, I dropped my phone."

"Whoa," Wyatt answered. "This is getting creepy."

Cassie's head bobbed up and down.

Lily flicked her gaze between her daughter and Wyatt before her head lolled to the side in disbelief. "Oh, come on, you two. There has to be a reasonable explanation for this."

"A reasonable explanation?" Wyatt guffawed. "The reasonable explanation is the ghost!"

"Wyatt's right!" Cassie exclaimed. "Henrietta is the reasonable explanation."

Lily stuck her hands on her hips and shook her head at them. "Not that."

"Come on!" Cassie squealed. "How else can you explain the creepy message she opened the journal to?"

"I can explain that any page that the journal would have landed on would have likely contained some odd message that seems threatening."

"Okay, fine. Then how do you explain my message? It's the same message she gave me last night."

"Wait," Wyatt said as his gaze darted back and forth between the two women, "Henrietta visited you last night?"

"Yes," Cassie said with a nod as Lily said, "no."

Cassie cocked her head, a set expression on her features. "She did. She came into my room and told me to find the journals."

"What journals?"

Cassie flung her arms out to the sides. "I don't know, that's what she said!"

Lily wagged a finger at them. "No."

She poked her finger toward the doll standing in the corner. "That doll wandered into your room. Though I still think you dreamt it. Because the doll is still in the same spot you left her."

"But a different position," Cassie argued.

Wyatt glanced over at the ghost doll and winced. "What is that?"

Cassie stepped toward it and flicked the switch at the base. "An animatron. I bought it at Spooks'n'Specters over in Misty Hollow."

The ghost toddled around the landing, her arm outstretched as she wandered aimlessly. "There's no hiding from me!"

Wyatt screwed up his face as he followed the doll's roaming. "Why would you buy that?"

"I liked it. Look, there's an easy way to establish if Henrietta is trying to get a message to me. It should be on my phone."

"Well, let's see it then!" Lily exclaimed.

Cassie hesitated, chewing her lower lip.

"Well?" Lily prodded.

"If I get stuck in there again, break down the door." Cassie flicked a glance at Wyatt, who still followed the movement of the Victorian doll around the landing.

She pursed her lips as she skirted the railing and approached her room. She hovered in the doorway before she darted inside. She raced to her phone, swiped it from the floor, and ran back to the door, slowing to a normal pace as she crossed the threshold.

She approached the others and flicked on her phone's display. "It was on the screen with your text thread."

Cassie input her passcode and the display showed the last screen she'd seen. Her failed text message still sat at the bottom of the screen.

Underneath it, the message box where the ghostly text had paraded across the screen sat empty.

Cassie's eyes went wide as she stared at the screen. "What? No! It was right here!"

Lily tugged one corner of her lips back. "Sure it was, Cass."

"It was right here!" Cassie exclaimed, disappointment filling her voice.

"I believe you, Cassie," Wyatt said, wandering back to them after leaving the ghost girl roaming down the hall. He shot a glance at Lily.

"I didn't say I don't believe you. I believe you *think* you saw it there. But I also believe you were frightened, and your mind may have played tricks on you."

"It wasn't a trick. It was here. The letters appeared one by one. Find the journals. That's what it said."

Lily shrugged as she crossed her arms over her chest. "But what journals? We have Henrietta's journal."

"Could there be more than one?" Wyatt asked.

Across the room, the doll rammed into a wall and spun to wander in a new direction. "Ready or not, here I come!"

"No," Lily answered after the distraction. "This one goes up until her death."

"Hmm," he said, his finger rubbing his chin.

The doll rammed into another wall. Instead of pivoting, she continued to bang against the barrier. Her outstretched hand tapped the wall over and over.

Cassie rolled her eyes at the doll as she stalked to it and switched it off. She lifted the animatronic ghost from the floor and shuffled her back to the corner.

Lily let her hand slap her side. "I'm not sure what's going on here, but I'm starved."

"I guess I should get out of your hair and let you eat," Wyatt said. "Seems you have things under control for the moment."

"You're welcome to stay," Cassie answered, rejoining

them at the top of the stairs. "We picked up an extra chicken salad sandwich from the cafe."

Wyatt lifted his eyebrows as he considered it. "Well, if you have extra…"

"Come on," Lily said with a wave, "your Hungry Man will have to take another night off."

Wyatt followed them downstairs and into the kitchen. Cassie wandered to the pantry and retrieved a can of cat food. "Oh, I forgot, Willy's still upstairs hiding under the bed."

She cracked the lid open and emptied the food into his red bowl. "I'd better go–" Her words ceased when the cat darted into the room, drawn by the sound of the can popping open.

"That's Willy," Lily said as she unloaded the takeout from the bag. "A 'fraidy cat until there's food around."

Cassie set the dish in front of him and rubbed his fur. "Did you see a ghost, buddy?"

The cat ignored her, intent on chowing down on his Sea Captain's Choice.

"No, he didn't," Lily answered, taking a seat at the table next to Wyatt. "Because there are no such things as ghosts!"

"Then how do you explain what we just experienced?" Cassie inquired, sinking into a chair.

Wyatt pulled a Styrofoam container toward him and popped it open. "I'd like to hear more about everything that's been going on."

Lily sliced into her croissant, cutting it in half. "Nothing's been going on. A few minor things that seem unexplainable, but I'm sure all of it has a perfectly reasonable explanation."

"A book flying off the shelf isn't perfectly reasonable," Cassie retorted. "Especially when it's *her* book."

"Henrietta's book?" Wyatt asked.

Cassie stared down at her croissant and nodded. "Yeah.

The Adventures of Black Jack. A novel written by the widow's walk ghost herself. It can't be coincidence or just some casual occurrence with a reasonable explanation."

"It can when it flew off a shelf that leads to a secret passage."

"That's been sealed off," Cassie reminded her mother. "So, it wasn't a random gust of wind from the ocean or something that traveled all the way up through and just happened to blow *that* book off the shelf."

Wyatt polished off half of his chicken salad sandwich and wiped his fingers on a brown napkin from the takeout bag. "And wind seems to be the culprit with the door incident."

"Yes," Lily said. "We must have a draft problem in the house."

"Or a ghost problem," Cassie argued.

Lily tugged the corner of her mouth back and shot Cassie an unimpressed stare.

"What?" Cassie questioned, raising her palms. "Come on. A rogue gust of wind blows Henrietta Blanchard's book off a shelf. And then a phantom wind whips through the house and blows *both* of our doors shut, trapping us in our rooms at the same time."

"I'm sure it's possible," Lily argued. "A physics professor could probably argue about the wind currents in the house and how the placement of our rooms in opposite corners makes this plausible."

Wyatt wrinkled his nose. "I'm with Cassie on this one."

"You two always side with each other when it comes to ghosts. But I'm not willing to believe a spirit is roaming around these halls just yet."

"We could find out," Wyatt said after a momentary pause.

Cassie straightened in her seat, her eyes set on him with an expectant stare.

Lily arched an eyebrow. "I'm not even sure I want to ask how, but I guess I will. How?"

"Well, you know Ruby, my secretary, right?"

"Uh-huh," Cassie said with a nod.

"She's a medium of sorts. Maybe she can come in and, you know, see if she gets any weird vibes or anything."

Lily's expression conveyed her surprise at his suggestion.

"What do you think, Mom?" Cassie asked.

"I'm not even sure what to say," the woman admitted. "What do you mean she's a medium of sorts?"

Wyatt snapped the lid on his takeout container as he finished the last bites of his meal. "Well, you know, she gets feelings and vibes. It's not like she hosts seances or goes to graveyards and communes with the dead or anything, but she has a sixth sense."

Lily chewed the inside of her cheek as she attempted to formulate an answer that sounded rational but not dismissive. "We'll think about it."

"Has she ever been in Whispering Manor before?" Cassie asked.

Wyatt gave his head a firm shake. "No. Never set foot inside the house. Said she wasn't sure her nerves could handle it."

"So, what makes you think she'd want to try now?" Lily questioned.

"Well, I'm sure she'd brave it to help out a friend. If she thinks it'll help, she'd do it, I'll bet."

"Give us some time to think about it," Lily answered. "If we think we need her, we can ask then."

"All right. Well, I suppose I should–"

A loud bang cut off Wyatt's next words. All eyes rose to the ceiling above them. Cassie gulped. "What was that?"

Another boom echoed through the house in response to her question.

CHAPTER 9

Wyatt withdrew a small gun from the waistband of his jeans as he studied the ceiling.

"Don't move," he breathed, rising slowly and tiptoeing from the room.

Moments later, the ladies overheard him yell. "I've got a gun. So, whoever's up there, come out now with your hands up."

Lily rose from her seat and scurried toward the hall. "Mom! He said to wait here."

Lily waved the comment away as she continued. "I'm not letting Wyatt roam around the house if someone's here. He may need our help!"

Cassie heaved a sigh, but climbed from her seat and followed on her mother's heels. They stepped into the hall, finding Wyatt slowly climbing the staircase.

"Any answer?" Lily whispered.

"Get back!" Wyatt said, waving them away.

"No! What if you need backup?" Lily eased the bat from the umbrella stand and held it over her shoulder.

Wyatt squashed his lips together and shook his head at Lily. "Someone's up there!" he breathed.

"How do you know?" Cassie whispered, palming an umbrella for defense.

He motioned to Lily's door, then toward Cassie's room. "Doors are closed."

"Again?" Lily inquired.

Wyatt raised his voice, hollering up the stairs. "We know you're up there! Come out with your hands up. This is the sheriff."

Another loud bang resounded. Everyone jumped, wincing and ducking down.

"What was that?" Cassie whispered.

"I'm coming up!" Wyatt called. "I'll shoot first and ask questions later!"

"Really?" Cassie breathed.

"No, just–shh," Wyatt hushed her with a wave as he crept up another two steps.

"I'm coming with you. And I will swing first and ask questions later," Lily promised.

"Mom!" Cassie protested, but wandered up the stairs, trailing behind the others. She craned her neck to check her door. Closed. What was the intruder doing?

They crept up the last few stairs. Wyatt swept his weapon around the perimeter of the upstairs. He waved at them with a few unintelligible hand gestures, poking a finger at Lily, then waving it overhead toward her door before closing it in a fist.

"What?" Lily asked, dropping the bat to her side.

"I'm going to go to your room first."

"Why didn't you just say that," Lily inquired.

"I just did," Wyatt answered. "Shh. And stay back."

They inched toward Lily's door with Wyatt in the lead. He trod on the creaky floorboard as he wrapped his fingers around the knob and glanced over his shoulder at Lily and Cassie. With a nod, he shoved the door open and pointed his weapon inside.

Empty. Slowly, he crept into the room, his weapon still at the ready. He peeked behind the door before he whipped the closet door open, then glanced in the bathroom.

"Clear," he called.

"On to Cassie's room," Lily answered.

Wyatt squeezed past the women and into the hall. "Follow me." They wandered across the squeaky floorboard again, crossing to the opposite side of the house. As they rounded the corner toward Cassie's room, Cassie spotted her ghost woman. The animatron lay sprawled on the floor, her dark curls spread around her.

Cassie eased the prop up to standing and continued behind the others. They reached Cassie's door and Wyatt began his complicated signaling.

"Just say it, I can't understand that, Wyatt," Lily complained.

"I'm going to open the door, stay back."

Lily nodded but readied her bat. Wyatt lowered his chin to them as he wrapped his hand around the knob and pushed the door open. He waved the gun around the interior before he side-stepped into the room, peeking behind the door before he aimed the weapon at the bathroom. He checked the closet. Nothing.

"Empty," he called.

Lily lowered her bat and stepped inside along with Cassie. "We could try the office. There's also the spare bedroom over–"

Another loud bang resounded, and wind whipped through the room.

"Oh no," Cassie murmured.

Another gust blasted them, blowing her hair back from her face. The door slammed shut again.

Cassie raced toward it, grasping the knob and twisting as she tugged. "No!"

Wyatt stowed his gun in his waistband. "Let me try."

Cassie stepped back and allowed Wyatt to try the door. He pulled against it but couldn't budge the door.

"We're trapped!" Cassie exclaimed.

Lily wrapped her arm around Cassie's shoulders. "This is ridiculous. This can't be caused by a ghost."

Wyatt studied the door, his fingers following the edge. "Here's the problem."

"What?" Lily asked.

Wyatt grabbed the knob again and jiggled the door as he pulled. After a moment, he lifted upward then tugged. The door swung open. "Door was caught on the jamb. It must get stuck at an angle when it blows shut."

"Or when Henrietta pulls it."

Wyatt stepped out into the hall again. He stared across the space. "Lily, your door is closed again, too."

"There *has* to be a reasonable explanation."

Another clap sounded, followed by another burst of wind. Lily grabbed the door as it swung on its hinges, threatening to close again. "Not again."

Cassie scurried from the room.

"The breeze came from this way," Wyatt said, heading toward Lily's room. "Do you have a window open?"

"No," Lily said.

Wyatt pushed her door open, scanning the room again. "Then where–"

Another slam and another burst of air. Lily's shoulders slumped and she let the bat hit the floor as she lowered her arm. With a shake of her head, she swung it upward and pointed at the door leading to the widow's walk. "There's our issue. The dang door is unlatched."

All eyes floated to the door at the top of the narrow wooden stairs. It swung open then banged shut. A burst of wind swirled around them, and Lily's door banged shut again.

Wyatt yanked it open and emerged into the hall. Lily climbed the stairs and grabbed the door as it threatened to swing open again. She hooked the latch before she descended down to the others.

"Now, let's see if we have any more ghostly encounters."

"How did that get open?" Cassie inquired.

"You were the last one up there. Did you latch it when you came in?"

"Of course," Cassie said, crossing her arms over her chest defensively. "I think."

Lily matched her stance. "Do you think or do you know?"

"I think. Maybe I forgot." She flung her arms out. "I dunno!"

"Well, there you have it," Lily said, flicking her gaze to Wyatt. "The widow's walk is the culprit for the slamming and stuck doors. Cassie is our ghost."

Wyatt raised his eyebrows at the statement. "Well, I suppose that's one way of explaining it."

"That's the only way of explaining it," Lily countered. "Looks like Ruby is off the hook!"

"That doesn't explain the creepy words on my phone or the ghostly visit during my sleep."

"I really think those are just the product of an overstimulated mind, Cass," Lily said.

"I'm not making this up!"

"I didn't say you were! But we've been working day and night on the maze. There are lots of creepy things in there.

And then the weird happenings here. I think your mind is tricking you."

Cassie squashed her lips together as she considered her mother's words. The phone no longer contained the message she'd thought she'd seen. And the ghost girl had mysteriously returned to the same spot she'd been left in. Perhaps Cassie had imagined it all.

"I guess you're right," Cassie admitted.

"Well, I suppose with that solved, I should get out of your hair," Wyatt said.

"Thanks, Wyatt," Lily said as they descended the stairs. "Sorry for all the trouble."

"No problem. I've been eating better this week than I have in years. So, I can't complain."

Lily chuckled at the statement as Wyatt stepped onto the porch. "Have a good rest of your night."

"You too. Maybe you'll sleep a little better now."

"I hope so," Cassie said with a wave and a half-hearted smile. "Thanks."

They said their goodnights and Lily closed the door with a tired sigh.

"Well, that was an unexpected turn of events," Lily said.

"I'm starting to find life in Hideaway Bay is a series of unexpected events."

Lily stifled a yawn and stretched. "I think I'm going to head up to bed early. I'm wiped out and the latest odd incident didn't help any."

Cassie wrapped her arms around her midriff. "Okay, I guess I'll head up, too."

Lily eyed her for a moment. "You don't still believe this was a ghost, do you?"

Cassie blew out a breath as she pondered the question for a moment. "No, I guess not. You're right. Everything has a logical explanation. Though I'm not sure I want to read Ri's book."

"Why? It sounds fun!"

Cassie shrugged as they climbed the stairs. "I guess I'll keep going and see what Black Jack got himself up to after he rides out the storm his first mate swears will capsize them."

"Really?" Lily inquired, pausing at the top of the stairs.

"That's what he said. They wouldn't survive the storm. And Black Jack swears they will."

"I can't believe you don't want to keep reading!"

"I guess it's interesting enough. It's just the author that has me nervous."

"She's not haunting you, Cassie," Lily called as she shuffled to her bedroom.

Cassie rounded the railing and headed toward her room. "Remind me of that when I have another nightmare!"

She stepped into her room, finding Willy lounging in the center of the bed. She crossed to the carousel and wound it. As she set it back in its spot, she recalled the incident earlier.

"Just the wind," she murmured to herself. Willy offered a soft meow at Cassie's statement.

"Yeah, me too, Willy," she said. "The wind slammed the door shut and trapped us. But it also made the carousel stop working. And then as soon as the door opened, it played again."

She shambled across the room, slipping under the covers and stroking the cat's head.

"I didn't want to say anything to Mom. She thinks I'm crazy. But I don't think any of this was from that widow's walk door. And I could have sworn I latched it."

The cat peered at her with his single eye. After a moment, he leapt from his spot and stalked around the bed, his back arching as Cassie stroked it.

He climbed onto her chest and rubbed his head against her cheek.

"You don't think I'm crazy, do you?" she asked him.

In response, the cat climbed off her and laid a paw on Henrietta's book. He meowed and twisted to face Cassie.

She wrinkled her nose at him. "You're creeping me out, Willy."

With a swipe of his paw, he inched the book toward the nightstand's edge. Cassie snatched it before he could knock it to the floor.

"All right, all right. I'll read it."

Satisfied, the cat climbed back onto her chest and nestled down for a nap, a loud purring emanating from him.

Cassie pulled the book open and found the page she'd left off on.

Rain poured from the brim of Mr. Johnson's hat. "Sir, I'll never find even two men, let alone five."

"Are you saying I sail with cowards?"

"I'm saying, sir, no one will risk it in a storm like this. Their chances of survival below are slim enough, however, on the decks… why, they may be swept over!"

"Have them tie themselves to the mast."

"Sir!" Johnson shouted.

"We will make it, Mr. Johnson."

Johnson shook his head, flinging water in every direction.

Jack kept a steady hold of the wheel and eyed him. "We'll make it, or my name isn't Black Jack."

"Technically, sir, your name isn't Black Jack."

Jack twisted the ship's wheel, spinning it in a dizzying circle until she responded, pulling starboard. "Very funny, Mr. Johnson. But I assure you, we will make it."

"Sir, the sea is too angry."

"If we turn back, the angry sea may still swallow us," Jack shouted over the pouring rain pounding against the deck.

"Yes, but at least we should not be smashed against the rocks! The course you've set takes us dangerously close. Even in favorable weather, many a ship is lost there."

"Those ships do not have me as their captain."

Mr. Johnson clung to the railing, his head shaking in vehement disagreement.

"We shall come through it, Mr. Johnson," Jack assured him. "And afterward, we shall enjoy the spoils of being first to the Ruby Fly."

"There is a reason no one else dares to take this passage in a storm."

Jack's lips pulled back in a wicked grin. "I know. We must remember to wave at the ghosts of men who have gone before us with weaker captains as we pass them by."

The ship rolled to the side and Jack whipped the wheel again. "All right, forego the five, but find me three. Three men willing to tend the sails as needed. And for their bravery, they shall be offered a larger portion of the bounty."

"I'll try, sir. I'll try."

"You'd better do more than try, Johnson!" Jack shouted after him.

The man stumbled down the stairs, weaving his way across the deck until he disappeared below. Jack eyed the stormy horizon. The ship pitched and rolled, groaning as it fought to stay afloat in the turbulent waters.

He'd sailed these waters many times before. Treacherous, yes. Impossible, no. He'd taken ships, both larger and smaller, through the tricky passage in all manners of weather. And he'd do it again. Neptune's Servant would emerge victorious. And their bounty would be plentiful.

His lips formed another smile as four huddled forms climbed from below deck. Rain pelted their backs as they hurried to the *main mast, tethering themselves to it. The wiry body of his first mate, Johnson, hastened toward him, climbing the stairs while clutching the railing on each side.*

"I found them, sir."

"Who?" Jack inquired.

"Evans, Collins, and Harper."

"Excellent. Then Evans, Collins, and Harper shall be richer than the others. Now, when I give the signal, trim the sails back immediately. And then on my second command, let them out full."

"Yes, Captain," Mr. Johnson said. "I shall watch for your signal."

He wobbled down the stairs, fighting the violent rocking of the ship and crossing to the men who awaited orders. Jack eyed the dark horizon, searching for the point where he'd need to maneuver carefully.

A bolt of lightning lit the night sky, followed by a crack of thunder.

Thunder boomed overhead, causing Cassie to jump. Willy had long since abandoned his spot on her chest in favor of sprawling on his plaid blanket next to her. Cassie frowned as winds whipped wildly outside her window. The sound of whispers that typically haunted the house with even the slightest breeze turned to screams.

Cassie slouched down under her covers further as though they would protect her from the storm. She stared down at the book clutched in her hands, unable to focus on the words as lightning lit the night sky.

She bit her lower lip as thunder rumbled again. The light on her nightstand flickered. Cassie snapped her gaze to it.

"Please don't go off," she whispered.

A second later, the room plunged into darkness.

* * *

Lily wandered into her room, heading straight for the bed. She pulled her robe off and tossed it on the bench at the foot before she climbed under the covers. She piled pillows behind her and plumped them before settling back.

With a long, deep sigh, she eased into their forgiving firmness, letting her head fall back. Her mind wandered to her daughter, Cassie. Did she really believe a ghost haunted Whispering Manor? Then again, could Lily be sure they didn't?

Some of Cassie's story couldn't be explained. But perhaps her imagination had run away with her.

With a sigh, Lily grabbed Henrietta's journal and pulled it onto her lap. "Maybe you'll ease my nerves."

She paged it open, a shiver running up her spine as she recalled the words scrawled across the page when the journal had blown open earlier. *Time for death.*

What was it in reference to, she wondered? She found her page but stared blankly at the words written on it. Instead, she decided to find the page with those three words. They had stood alone. Why had they been written? What preceded them? What came after them?

"One way to find out," Lily muttered.

She flipped through the journal to the approximate location it had opened to earlier. Writing filled the pages. With her finger holding her place, she flipped forward, going to the last entry, without finding the words. She tried going back without finding it.

"Maybe it was after the last entry," she mused aloud.

Lily fanned the pages until she found the first blank one, then paged through one by one. She found no trace of the three words.

"This is ridiculous," she grumbled, returning to the first page of the journal.

Beginning with Henrietta's first entry, Lily went through page by page in search of the one with only the three haunting words. She reached the back cover without ever finding them.

Her throat went dry as she closed the book and sat it on her lap. Her mind questioned her own sanity. Had those been the words she'd seen earlier?

She couldn't have mistaken them, could she? But if she had seen them, where were they in the journal?

She gnawed on her lower lip as other ideas ran through her mind. Had Cassie been correct? Had they been visited by a ghost?

Her last thought was punctuated by a rumble of thunder. And then the room plunged into blackness.

CHAPTER 10

Cassie sat in the darkness. Only the sound of her own frightened breathing filled the gaps between rumbles of thunder. She blindly reached for her phone on the nightstand, knocking it onto the floor below.

It thumped onto her rug as Cassie issued a curse under her breath. With a grimace and a trembling lip, she hung from her bed, searching the area rug for the device.

Her fingers hit a cold, hard object and she snatched it, fiddling to find the power button so she could toggle on the flashlight. After flipping it around twice, she managed to light the screen.

Bluish light bloomed, casting the room in deep shadows. Cassie flicked her gaze to the window as thunder boomed again. Lightning flashed, revealing a figure standing in front of the glass, limned in the storm's light.

Cassie gasped, tossing her arms up in the air as her eyes widened. The phone flew from her hands, sailing across the room and slamming onto the hardwood floor.

She gave a frightened moan, wrapping her arms around herself as the room plunged into darkness again.

"Hello?" she called.

The winds whipped, drowning out any answer she may receive. A noise sounded across the room.

"Willy?" she whispered as she felt blindly next to her. Her fingers hit the furball. The cat still lay on the bed.

"What was that?" she breathed, realizing the noise she'd heard wasn't the cat.

She raised her voice and tried again. "Hello?"

"Cassie," a voice answered her, almost drowned out by the winds.

Cassie's lower lip trembled, and her features pinched as she clutched at her midriff. In the darkness, she could make out nothing. She had no idea who called her.

"Cassie," the voice called again, still muffled.

"What?" she cried out. "What do you want?"

Her door creaked open, and a bright light shined at her. She squinted against it, shielding her face with her hands.

"Cassie," her mother said. "Are you okay?"

"Huh? Oh, yeah," Cassie said with a shake of her head.

"I heard some banging. I thought maybe you fell or bumped into something in the dark."

"No, I dropped my stupid phone," Cassie said with a huff as she climbed from under the covers and slid her feet into her slippers.

"Oh. I'm heading down for a few flashlights. You want to come with me?"

Cassie waved her arm in the direction the phone had flown. "Yeah, just let me get the phone and see if it survived the fall. It's over there somewhere, shine your light toward the bathroom."

"Wow, Cass, how'd your phone get all the way over there."

"I told you I dropped it."

"Dropped it!" Lily exclaimed. "More like threw it."

Cassie hurried toward the object and snatched it from the floor. "I didn't throw it, it fell and rolled across the floor."

She toggled it on, finding the screen intact. "Seems no worse for the wear."

With a flick of her thumb, she turned on her own flashlight and they made their way downstairs in search of a more formidable light source.

They retrieved two lanterns from the pantry as the house groaned overhead, violent winds beating against its side.

"You want to hang out together in the living room?" Lily inquired.

"Sure, maybe until the storm dies down. I'll never sleep with this racket."

They shuffled into the living room and collapsed onto the couch.

Cassie slumped down, kicking her feet onto an ottoman. "I really wish the power was on so I could make a hot chocolate."

"I wonder how long we'll be out. This is the first time this has happened here."

The storm continued to rumble with gusty winds for another twenty minutes. They waited with only lanterns beating back the darkness for an hour before the electricity returned, its familiar hum filling the house.

"There we go," Lily said as she flicked on a lamp and turned off her lantern.

"That wasn't too long, at least," Cassie said. "Do you want a hot chocolate?"

Lily crinkled her brow as she perched on the edge of the couch. "Really? I was going to go to bed."

Cassie shrugged, twisting the ties on her robe together into a braid. "I'm wide awake now."

"All right," Lily said with a groan as she pulled herself to stand. "Let's go make one. But we'll probably regret this in the morning."

"I'll just lay awake up there, so it's not like I'm missing out on sleep."

"The storm's passed now," Lily answered as they shuffled toward the kitchen, "you still won't be able to sleep?"

Cassie shot her a sideways glance, pulling the milk from the refrigerator and pouring some into a pot. "No, I won't. I… thought I saw another ghost during the storm and that's how my phone got all the way across the room."

Lily cocked her head, pausing as she reached for the packets of hot chocolate. "Again? What did you do? Chuck the phone at it?"

"No, I was trying to turn my flashlight on after I knocked the phone onto the floor when the lights went out. I grabbed it from the rug but couldn't find the right button. Lightning lit up the room and I thought I saw a figure by the window. I jumped and the phone flew out of my hands. Then I heard a noise. And then I heard a voice. I'm pretty certain that was you calling me, but I couldn't make it out over the wind."

Cassie offered her mother a sheepish glance as she stirred the milk over the heat.

Lily shook the packets before ripping them open and dumping them into the pot. "Oh, Cassie, you've got to stop with this ghost nonsense. It's going to drive you crazy. You're seeing things at every turn."

"Sorry, I know! But I can't help it."

"I really thought all this ghost stuff would be over with once we found that treasure. And some of the notoriety of this house would vanish, but at this rate, the locals will have us tied with the Amityville house."

"Or worse," Cassie admitted. She poured the milk into two mugs. Lily topped them with marshmallows, whipped cream, and a drizzle of chocolate sauce.

Cassie pulled butterscotch cookies from the cupboard and shoved them under her arm before lifting the mug. "At least only Wyatt knows."

"If you keep it up, Ruby will know. And then everyone will know, and we'll be right back up there with the Winchester house."

"Oh, no," Cassie said as she settled into an armchair and pulled a blanket over her lap. "You don't think we'll have to keep building and building and building, do you?"

"I hope not. I almost went mad when your father and I had the bathroom remodeled. It's like living in chaos."

"Wasn't it the bathroom you never used?"

"Yes! I can't imagine what it would be like if it had been the one we actually used daily."

Lily grabbed a cookie from the package on the coffee table and bit into it. "You know," she said, still munching on the cookie, "I hate to say this and get you all riled up again, but…"

Cassie scooped some of the whipped topping from her mug and licked the spoon. "But what? You saw a ghost?"

"Nothing quite that dramatic," Lily assured her after a sip of her chocolatey drink. "But I did have something strange happen before the lights went out."

Cassie shifted in her seat, perching her mug on the arm as she leaned forward. "What happened?"

"Well, remember I said when I got locked in my bedroom earlier that the book blew open to a page with the words 'time for death?'"

"Yeah," Cassie said with a nod, reaching for another cookie.

"Well," Lily began, her eyes slowly raising to Cassie's. "I wanted to see what the words were in reference to, so I paged through the book to find them."

Cassie dunked her cookie into the whipped cream before biting off a piece. "And?"

"I couldn't find them."

Cassie froze, considering the statement. "Maybe you missed them."

Lily shook her head. "They were the only words on the page when I saw them earlier. I thought she was being dramatic. I went through every page of the book and found no pages with only those words."

"Are the words anywhere in the book? Maybe you thought they were the only words on the page."

Lily shook her head vehemently. "They were the *only* words, Cassie. Honestly, I can't believe you're telling me I mistook a blank page with three words for a page filled with them after you've been insisting something odd is going on here. Now I have experienced something odd and you're dismissing it."

"I'm not dismissing it," Cassie said. "I just can't believe it. This is even more definitive proof that something strange is going on here."

Lily slouched further down on the couch as she sipped at her hot chocolate. "Maybe I was mistaken. Maybe I panicked and thought I saw those words on the page."

"Just like, at almost the exact same moment, I panicked and thought I saw words on my cell phone?"

"Yes," Lily said with a nod.

"Don't you think that's just a little too coincidental?"

Lily drained the last sips of her hot chocolate. "I'm not sure, but I'm not ready to fully jump on the ghost bandwagon with you and Wyatt. I need something more than this to call Ruby in for a seance or whatever she's going to perform."

Cassie pulled her arms closer to her body as she shivered. "Gosh, I hope not a seance. That's creepy."

Lily climbed to her feet and offered a hand to pull Cassie

to stand. "Well, that's just another reason to stop telling Wyatt we have ghosts."

Cassie shook her head as they plodded to the kitchen to dump their mugs in the dishwasher. "Now I'll never sleep thinking about Ruby doing a seance here."

"Don't think about it," Lily suggested.

"Easier said than done."

"Want to sleep in my room again like when you were a kid and watched a scary movie?"

Cassie considered it as they climbed the stairs. "No, I'll try to sleep in my own room." She yawned and stretched. "Maybe I will fall asleep without any trouble."

Lily nodded and headed for her room as Cassie rounded the bend toward hers. She eyed the ghost standing in the hall as she passed it, jabbing a finger at it. "You stay out of my room tonight."

She plodded past, stopping just outside of her bedroom. Squashing her lips together, she strode back down the hall and hefted the doll under one arm.

"I'm not taking any chances with you, Ri," she said as she rounded the railing and descended the stairs. She tucked the animated prop into a corner of the living room. With her cell phone still in her robe's pocket, she snapped a picture of it.

"Just in case I have to prove you moved," she warned the doll.

The doll stared back with blank eyes. Cassie gave it one last glance before she headed upstairs. With the doll tucked safely away, she slipped between the sheets and dozed off for the night.

* * *

The alarm screamed through Cassie's odd dream about a pirate ship attached to a cinema. She opened her eyes to slits and peered at the offending device. With a slap, she silenced it and closed her eyes again before rolling onto her back.

With a heaving sigh, she forced her eyes open. Bright sunshine streamed in through the windows, a stark contrast to the stormy night they'd rode out. Cassie stretched as she contemplated the big day.

Her actions prompted a curious meow from her bedmate. Willy's one eye popped open as he stretched. He gazed at Cassie, trying to ascertain if he needed to leap up and prepare for his breakfast or if he still had time to lounge.

"A few more minutes, buddy," Cassie said as she stroked his fur. Her mind ran over the list of tasks she needed to complete. They'd taken the day off from the shop so they could focus on readying the maze for its first visitors.

Opening night jitters swept through her already. The build-up had been epic. Would the town be pleased with their efforts, or would the maze be a flop?

"What do you think, Willy?" Cassie asked as the cat groomed his face with a moistened paw. "Will we be invited back next year, or will everyone hate it?"

His eye flicked to her, and he offered a trilling sound in response. "Yeah, I guess we'll find out. Well, I'd better get going, I guess."

With another long stretch, Cassie shoved the covers off and tugged on her fluffy robe. She headed downstairs for a hearty breakfast before anything else.

Quietness filled the house. Her mother must still be sleeping, she assumed, as she tiptoed down the wooden stairs.

She reached the bottom, swinging toward the kitchen. After a moment's hesitation, she retreated across the foyer and into the living room.

The animated doll still stood where she'd placed it in the wee hours of the morning. Had it moved? She tried to recall the exact position it had been in when she'd left it. A curse escaped her lips as she realized she'd left her cell phone upstairs.

She waved a hand at the doll, trying to dismiss it. She'd likely not moved. And she could check on it later. As she shuffled from the room, she did a double take. Had the doll blinked its eyes?

CHAPTER 11

Cassie stepped back, warmth washing over her. Sweat beaded across her forehead as heat shot through her. She swallowed hard, staring at the face.

The doll stood motionless, its hand outstretched to her in a silent plea. Cassie wrinkled her nose at it before she heard movement on the stairs. She leaned back and glanced out the door, finding her mother shuffling down.

"Good morning. Are you ready for today?" Cassie inquired.

Lily stifled a yawn as she hit the wooden floor of the foyer. "I could have done without the power outage and midnight snack, but I think I'll pull through."

Cassie stepped into the foyer. "I was just about to make breakfast."

"You made a wrong turn."

"Yeah, I know. I brought the doll down here last night and I was just checking on her."

"Checking on her?" Lily inquired as she trailed after Cassie to the kitchen.

"Yeah. I took a picture of her last night when I put her in the living room. I wanted to see if she moved on her own."

"And did she?"

Cassie pulled an electric griddle from a cupboard and set it on the counter after settling Willy with his breakfast. "I'm not sure. I left my phone upstairs and didn't feel like trudging back up. I'll check after I've loaded up on pancakes."

Lily arched an eyebrow at her as she oiled the griddle before turning on the heat. She pulled a box of pancake mix from the cupboard overhead and started mixing the batter.

"What if she moved?"

Cassie shrugged, dunking a bottle of maple syrup into a hot water bath with a sigh. "I don't know."

Lily poured the batter onto the hot griddle. The silver dollar pancakes sizzled. "Why don't you go check the doll now?"

"Well…"

Lily shooed her daughter from the kitchen with a hand wave. "I've got the pancakes. Run up and grab your phone. Then if she moved, we can discuss it over breakfast."

"I'm not sure I want to know."

"You'll feel better if you check. Maybe she's stuck in the same spot and then we can move on."

Cassie sighed and sagged her shoulders. "Okay."

She disappeared from the kitchen as Lily flipped the pancakes. "Don't take too long!" Lily called after her.

She hurried to the foyer and darted up the stairs. She swiped her phone from the charger and tapped around to find the picture as she descended the stairs. She swung into the living room and held the camera up, comparing the current location of the doll to the one in the picture.

Her lips pulled to the side as she studied them, her gaze flicking back and forth between picture and object. It looked roughly the same. Was her head tilted a bit more? Maybe.

That could have been anything. It could have fallen after Cassie left it last night from being carried downstairs.

She bit her lower lip and continued to study it. Nothing definitive, she concluded with a sigh. She flicked the phone off and shuffled back to the kitchen. A plate of hot pancakes sat in front of her chair.

She pulled the syrup bottle from the warm water bath and toweled it dry before drizzling it over her pancakes. Her mother joined her moments later.

"Well?" she asked as she eased into a chair and poured syrup over her pancakes.

"Nothing major. Her head might be slightly different, but it could have fallen after I stuck her in the corner. She's the same, more or less."

"There, you see! The other night must have been a fluke. I bet you either forget which way you put her, or she wasn't completely switched off."

"I guess," Cassie said with a defeated sigh.

Lily eyed her as she took a bite of her syrup-laden pancake piece. "It's a good thing, too. We've got to focus today."

Cassie waved her fork in the air. "No room for error!"

"None. Although, I'm not sure if I'm hoping they love the maze or hate it."

Cassie offered her mother a wry glance as she chewed her pancake. "I know what you mean. I'm not certain I want to build another one next year, but I also don't want our hard work wasted."

"You and me both," Lily said as she lifted her empty plate from the table and dumped it in the dishwasher.

Cassie followed her after shoving the last piece of pancake into her mouth. After a quick cleanup, they headed upstairs to pull on work clothes and head to the barn to put the final touches on the maze.

* * *

Cassie put the final adjustments on her costume as she gazed into the mirror. She adjusted the black bow in her hair and smoothed out the apron on her Alice in Wonderland costume. Willy stared at her from the bed.

She shot him a glance through the mirror. "You should have come with us. You could have been the Cheshire Cat."

His one eye slowly slid closed, and he let his head fall to the mattress below him.

"I'll take that as a no," Cassie said, adjusting her ribbon one last time before she left the room.

With one hour to go before the maze opened, they'd have just enough time to turn on all the gadgets for the grand opening.

She approached the stairs as Lily emerged from her room.

"Wow," Cassie exclaimed at her mother's costume.

A floor-length green and black dress swished across the floor. A pointy witch's hat topped Lily's blonde hair.

Lily held her arms out to the sides. "What do you think? Do I look like a storybook witch?"

"Yeah! I should have done something more fun like that," Cassie said with a pout.

"I told you Alice was boring."

"She's not *that* boring," Cassie contended as they descended the stairs and she grabbed her keys.

"She's sort of boring. You should have been the Queen. Off with their heads!"

They strode to the Wrangler, climbing inside. Cassie flicked a gaze to the rearview mirror and twisted her bow to the side. "There, now I'm twisted Alice."

Lily chuckled as she tugged on her seatbelt. "Okay, kid, let's do this!"

A grin formed on Cassie's face as she threw the shifter into drive. "Haunted Hay Maze here we go! Let's make a killing!"

Red, yellow, and orange leaves swept past their feet as Cassie and Lily stood at the entrance of the maze. The lighted sign above them pronounced the entrance to the indoor component of the Magical Carnival.

Families wandered through the outdoor portion, formed by hay bales before approaching the barn. The cool breeze sweeping past them sent a shiver up Cassie's spine as they waited for the first patrons to enter.

Mayor Thompson led a large group of people from the exit of the hay maze, marching the group toward them. "Well, ladies! It's here! The big moment!"

Lily and Cassie each offered nervous chuckles. "We certainly hope you enjoy it," Lily said.

"Oh, I'm sure we all will!" Tinsley answered. She turned to the crowd gathering behind her, walking backward up the ramp to the barn door. As she hovered above them, she waved her hands in the air.

"Folks! Folks! Gather around!"

The crowd pressed closer, and a hush fell over the group. Tinsley clasped her hands together in front of her and offered a broad smile as she scanned the group.

"I'm so happy to see so many of you here to celebrate our fall festivities!"

Applause broke out and Tinsley allowed them to continue for a few moments before she waved her hands to hush the crowd again.

"Our little town's Fall Festival has grown leaps and bounds since the first time we offered it way back during my first year as mayor! There's *so* much to enjoy. And this year, I'm proud to present our latest addition by some of our town's newest residents!

"Lily Bennett and Cassie McGuire have spent countless hours putting together this magical maze! And I think it's going to be a hit! Now, before I let you all in, let me remind you to enjoy the apple cider, pumpkin carving, vendor booths, kids' craft tent, and the costume party-slash-dance later tonight!

"And now, without further ado... I give you the Magical Carnival!"

Applause sounded again before Tinsley waved the crowd ahead. They flocked inside in a steady stream as Tinsley greeted several of them.

"Well, ladies," she said as the crowd thinned, "fabulous job as always. I can't wait to see the finished product. If you don't mind, I'm going to duck in!"

"Enjoy!" Cassie called over the heads of the people entering.

They milled around the entrance for several minutes in case there were any issues or malfunctions within the maze. Laughter echoed from inside along with a few shouts of surprise or screams of fake terror.

"I'm going to get a cider," Lily said as the first few people emerged from the exit, clapping their hands with grins spread across their faces.

"I'll join you. I think the maze will be okay for a minute."

"The first few people came out okay and they look pleased, so it seems to be going well!"

"Let's hope there are no malfunctions!" Cassie said as they strode toward the tent serving the spiced cider.

With the warm drinks in their hands, they perched on a hay bale seat and sipped at them. Wyatt wandered over to them in his uniform.

"Hi, ladies," he said, his hands perched on his belt.

"Working tonight, huh?" Lily asked.

"No," Wyatt answered with a crinkled forehead.

Lily studied his uniform as she sipped her cider.

"Do you always come to events in uniform?" Cassie asked.

Wyatt glanced down at his attire before he laughed. "Oh, no. This is my costume!"

Lily coughed as she choked down the apple cider. "You went as a sheriff?"

"Of course not! Don't be ridiculous." He poked a finger at his name tag. "Hopper, see."

"I'm not getting it," Cassie answered. "You're wearing your sheriff's uniform."

Wyatt's eyes slid side to side before he explained. "I'm Police Chief Hopper. From *Stranger Things*. Get it?" He waved a hand at them to dismiss it. "Someone told me I looked like him. I thought it'd be a great idea."

Cassie straightened, an expression of understanding crossing her features as she nodded. "Oh! Oh, I get it, yeah."

"Very clever, Wyatt," Lily said before sipping at her cider again.

"Have you gotten any early feedback on the maze?"

Lily crumpled her plastic cider cup after draining it. "Not yet. We just stepped away as the first people came out."

"I ran into Mayor Thompson on my way over here and she said it was great. I was just heading over there to check it out."

"Well, I hope you enjoy it," Cassie said.

"And I'm glad Tinsley did."

Wyatt pointed a finger gun at them. "She was raving over it. I'm guessing you two will be dreaming up another maze for next year."

"We'll put our thinking caps on," Lily said.

"I've already got ideas for changes," Cassie added.

Wyatt grinned at them before glancing over at the barn. "Well, I guess I'll–"

A blood-curdling scream ripped through the night air, cutting off Wyatt's words.

"Wow," Cassie said as she squashed her cup into a ball and tossed it in the nearby trash can. "That sounded intense."

Lily cocked her head and raised her eyebrows. "No kidding."

"It's probably that stupid clown head you put in there. I told you it was borderline gross."

"It wasn't that sc-" Lily began when a crowd rushed from the barn, streaming from both the entrance and the exit.

Shouts sounded and a few more screams before someone finally explained the cause of the panic.

A woman dressed as a black cat pressed her paw gloves to her face and screamed, "There's a dead body in there!"

CHAPTER 12

*L*ily and Cassie shot to standing, their eyes wide. "What?" Lily questioned.

"Well, yeah," Cassie said. "There's a lot of dead bodies in there. It's a haunted maze."

The woman across the way continued her hysterics as people grouped around her. Others continued to stream from the inside, many of them shouting the same thing.

Tinsley emerged, her face a mask of worry. She scanned the crowd, locking her gaze on Wyatt. She strode across the field toward him.

"Wyatt, we have an emergency," she said.

"Emergency? What's going on?"

Tinsley clenched her jaw. "There's a dead body," she said, pointing discreetly at the barn.

"Surely, there's some mistake," Lily said. "There are a lot of props in there. Maybe someone thought–"

"No," Tinsley said with a flick of her hand to cut Lily's words off, "it's not a prop. It's a dead body. And it's a fairly gruesome scene. It's in the fortune teller's room."

Wyatt swallowed hard and tugged his radio from his "costume," calling for backup.

"This has to be a misunderstanding," Cassie said as Wyatt spoke with his deputy.

"I agree," Lily said. She glanced at Wyatt who spoke a few words into the radio perched on his shoulder. "Come on."

Lily strode toward the maze, leaving the mayor and sheriff behind. Cassie trailed behind her. "Mom," she breathed, "where are you going?"

"I'm going to check this out! This must be a mistake."

"Maybe one of the props got moved," Cassie said as they climbed the ramp to the barn and slipped through the door.

"We'll soon find out," Lily said, expertly navigating through the halls, her witch's costume flowing behind her as she twisted through the maze, the walls billowing behind her.

The two women wound around to the back corner housing the fortune teller's display. Cassie pushed through the beaded curtain cordoning off the square space. Across from the opening, a veiled fortune teller sat behind a round table draped with a purple tablecloth. Her outstretched hands reached for a crystal ball, surrounded by tarot cards.

On the ceiling, stars and moons floated in a mystical display. A new decoration adorned the space. One Lily and Cassie had not been responsible for adding.

Cassie covered her mouth as she stifled a scream. A groan escaped from Lily's lips, and she pressed a hand to her forehead.

Against the barn's back wall, a body lay sprawled. The dead man's mouth gaped open in a silent plea for help. From his slashed throat dripped rivulets of blood.

Cassie and Lily stood in stunned silence, both of them staring at the dead body across the room.

"Th-th-that's not one of our props," Cassie stammered.

"No," Lily said with a sigh. "No, it's not."

Cassie wrapped her arms around her midriff as she stared at the man. A shiver ran up her spine and she shuddered.

Lily slipped her arm around her daughter's shoulders. "Come on, let's tell Wyatt."

Cassie didn't budge, her eyes fixed on the man's face. Her eyebrows knit as she studied him.

"Cass, come on." Lily tugged her away from the gruesome scene and they wound their way through the makeshift halls to the front entrance.

With Tinsley, Wyatt strode to the entrance of the barn, climbing up the ramp. He pulled the door slightly closed. Lily and Cassie joined him as he spun back to face the growing crowd.

"Folks! Our apologies, we've got a bit of a situation. We'll need to close the maze as we check it out. Thank you for your cooperation!"

"Is it true that someone's dead?" a shout rose from the crowd.

"We have no confirmation of anything. But we are asking you to keep back and let us do our work. Thank you!"

"Someone said there's someone gutted in there! What's going on?"

"Yeah, what's going on Sheriff?"

Wyatt held his hands up. "We don't have any information at this time. Now, please, folks, let the deputies through so we can do our job."

Wyatt waved to the two deputies at the rear of the crowd as they fought their way through. The crowd cleared a path for them, and they joined everyone else near the door.

"Secure the exit and make sure everyone's out of there," Wyatt murmured to them, sending them to the other door around the side of the barn.

"There's definitely a body in there," Lily said to him.

His eyes bulged. "You went inside?"

"While you were organizing, we went to check in case it was a mistake. Unfortunately, it wasn't," Lily explained.

Wyatt shook his head and held a hand out in front of him. "All right, well, just stay here now, okay? We'll handle this." He motioned for one of the deputies to follow him inside.

"It's by the fortune teller in the back corner," Cassie said.

"Right," Wyatt answered.

"We'll show you," Lily said.

"No, absolutely not!"

Lily tilted her head and drew her lips into a thin line. "Wyatt, it will be much faster for us to show you where it is."

"It's a crime scene."

"That dozens of people have trampled through at this point."

Wyatt squeezed his lips together and nodded. "All right, fine. Just take me the fastest way and don't go inside the space with the body, okay?"

"Fine," Lily answered, holding up her hands in defeat.

Together, the foursome wound through the maze again with Lily and Cassie in the lead. When they reached the beaded curtains, Lily tugged them back and motioned for Wyatt to enter. With his flashlight shining, he ducked through the makeshift doorway, his beam sweeping the space.

It settled on the body. Under the flashlight's light, the body appeared even more gruesome than in the dimly lit room. His ashy gray skin, blank stare, and gaping mouth created a horrible horror scene.

Lily pursed her lips as she averted her eyes while Cassie scrubbed her face with her hands.

Wyatt radioed to the other deputy. "We've got a crime scene. We're going to need to call forensics."

As he finished his request, flashes of light lit up the space.

Wyatt's eye grew wide, and he waved his hands in front of him. "Hey! What do you think you're doing? Get out of here!"

Three teens scurried from the maze, disappearing around a corner. Wyatt cursed under his breath. "Whittaker, you've got to secure the door. We just had three people in here taking pictures."

The radio crackled to life. "Sorry, Sheriff, they must have been in there before we shut it down."

"Well, we've got to make sure this place is clear. Call Carter and Miller and get them to man the doors so we can do a sweep and make sure no one is in here."

"You got it, Sheriff," Whittaker answered.

Wyatt let his arm fall from the radio and faced Lily and Cassie. "I'm going to have to ask you both to step out."

"We'll take over watching the door so Whittaker can come in and help you clear the place."

"Send him in, but let Carter take over as soon as he gets here."

Lily nodded and wrapped her arm around Cassie, who stood staring at the body again. She led them to the exit, sending the deputy inside as they took over barring the door to any entrants.

"I can't believe this," Cassie mumbled, still staring inside the maze.

"It's not exactly the opening night I envisioned," Lily admitted.

Cassie wrapped her arms around her midriff again, biting her lower lip.

Lily pushed a lock of Cassie's blonde hair over her shoulder. "Cass, you okay?"

Cassie gave her a slow nod in silent response.

"It's okay not to be okay. That was pretty gruesome." Lily paused, awaiting a response. "I'm not certain I'll ever get that image out of my mind. We probably shouldn't have barged in there."

"It's not that," Cassie answered quietly.

Lily furrowed her brow as she stared at her daughter, uncertain of her meaning.

Cassie flicked her gaze to her mother. "Did you look at his face?"

Lily crossed her arms, the crease between her brows deepening. "Yes. It was… disturbing. Cassie, I think dwelling on this isn't a good idea. I know it's hard but I think we should try to–"

"Ladies!" Tinsley interrupted. "*What* is going on in there?" She poked a finger into the barn.

"Wyatt's making sure everyone is out of there before they bring the forensic team in."

Tinsley lowered her eyes, her head shaking. "How could this happen?"

Penny hurried toward them, her eyes wide. "What's going on?"

Tinsley pressed a hand to her forehead. "Oh, it's just awful."

"Everyone's asking what's going on. And if the festival is canceled. Maybe you should–"

"You're absolutely right. I need to make a speech! Have everyone meet in the tent where the dance is being held."

Penny nodded and disappeared, shouting to the first group of people, "Folks! Folks, Mayor Thompson has asked everyone to go to the central tent where she'll make an announcement."

She continued around the field, informing event-goers to gather at the tent. People slowly began to disperse from around the barn, making their way to the tent.

Tinsley pressed a hand against Lily's arm. "Have Wyatt report to me as soon as he has *any* information. I need to go handle the frightened townspeople. Duty calls." She spun on her heel and hurried away, waving people toward the tent as she went.

"At least she's good in a crisis," Lily said as they watched Tinsley trudge toward the tent.

Cassie crossed her arms tightly over her chest, shuddering. Her face pinched with consternation.

Wyatt appeared in the doorway with another man. "Okay, ladies, Sergeant Carter can take over door duties now. Why don't you both head home and get some rest?"

"Are you sure there isn't anything else we need to do?" Lily inquired.

"We'll need you both to come down to the station sometime and get your prints on file. They're likely everywhere in there and forensics will want to be able to distinguish them from any other prints we may find."

Lily blew out a long breath. "There should be no shortage of our prints. I certainly hope that doesn't present a problem."

Wyatt didn't respond directly, a fact that didn't escape Lily. "There's no rush on the prints, though if you have a chance tomorrow…"

Lily offered a tight-lipped smile. "We'll come in tomorrow, no problem. Are you sure there's nothing else we need to do?"

"Not unless you want to listen to Mayor Thompson's speech. We're just waiting on forensics to arrive. Until then, the maze is closed."

Lily and Wyatt said their goodnights and he disappeared into the depths of the maze. "All that work," Lily lamented as she spun to leave.

Cassie remained silent, lost in her own thoughts.

"I suppose at least most of the town got to see it before the body appeared."

They stalked across the field to Cassie's Wrangler and climbed inside. Cassie fired the engine, and they headed back to Whispering Manor. The two tired ladies slogged through the front door, greeted by a one-eyed tuxedo cat.

"I bet you're happy, Willy," Lily said. "We're home much earlier than expected. I know I'm happy! I can't wait to get out of this costume. How about it, Cass? Cuddle up on the couch with a hot chocolate?"

"Sure," Cassie said, already climbing the stairs to her room.

The two women changed out of their costumes and into cozy pajamas. Lily already had the milk heating when Cassie rejoined her downstairs. She poured it into two mugs, topped it with whipped cream and marshmallows, and handed one off to Cassie.

They shuffled into the living room and plopped down on the couch.

"Wanna watch a movie?" Lily asked.

Cassie shook her head as she sipped at her hot chocolate.

"What's wrong, Cass? You were quiet all the way home. I know it was hard to see that body but..."

Cassie shrugged as she scooped a dollop of whipped cream from her mug. "His face."

"I didn't really study it. The scene was pretty gruesome."

Tears welled in Cassie's eyes as she spoke. "He looked like Trevor."

CHAPTER 13

*L*ily coughed, choking on her sip of hot chocolate. "What?"

"He looked like Trevor. Not identical, but similar. His eyes were so much like Trevor's."

Lily bit her lower lip, realizing what upset Cassie about the scene. The man, who Cassie believed bore a resemblance to her recently deceased husband, had probably dredged up lots of painful memories.

"Oh, Cassie, I hadn't noticed," Lily answered as she slipped her arm around her daughter's shoulders. "I didn't look closely since it was so gruesome."

"It's all I could see," Cassie choked out, swallowing down her tears and blinking as she set her mug aside.

Lily pulled her closer, setting her mug down and wrapping both arms around her. "Aw, Cassie. I'm sorry." She paused a moment as she kissed her hair. "You know it wasn't Trevor, though, right? It's just bringing up lots of bad things."

"Things we worked so hard to put behind us only to have it all crop up again with one dead body who probably doesn't look anything like Trevor really. I probably made it all up."

"I doubt you did that. But the shock may have been enough to make you think he looks more like Trevor than he does."

Cassie took a few shaky breaths before blowing out a long one. She flicked at a stray tear that had fallen onto her cheek. "You're probably right. I probably only thought he looked like Trevor."

"Maybe we can ask Wyatt tomorrow. Another look at his face in the cold light of day may settle your nerves."

Cassie guffawed, drawing her chin back to her chest. "You want me to take *another* look at a dead body?"

Lily stroked her hair. "If it'll settle your nerves, yes."

Cassie drew in a deep breath and retrieved her hot chocolate. "Then that's what I'll do. You're probably right. I probably imagined it. It was so dark in there, I couldn't have gotten a good look."

"Trevor didn't have any siblings," Lily answered, settling back with her mug. "So, it couldn't be a brother. Maybe a cousin at best, but I think that's a stretch."

Cassie offered a chuckle at the statement. "Yeah, what are the chances Trevor's distant relative ends up dead in our maze after we move into a new town."

* * *

Lily studied the headline of the morning paper as she retrieved it from the front porch. With a shake of her head, she shuffled back inside in her robe and slippers. She found Cassie in the kitchen, already tugging their waffle maker from a cupboard.

"Waffles, huh?" she asked.

"I need it," Cassie claimed. "Comfort food."

"Did you get any sleep?"

Cassie shoved a lock of hair behind her ear as she shoved

the plug into an outlet. "I did, surprisingly. But I still want waffles. We found a dead body last night."

Lily motioned to the paper with one hand as she retrieved a bowl for the batter with another. "Wait until you see the headline this morning."

Cassie shot her a glance before stalking toward the table and picking up the town's newspaper. Bold black letters announced MAZE MANIA: BODY FOUND IN CARNI-VAL-THEMED HALLOWEEN MAZE

She scanned the article, rolling her eyes. "Oh, boy, they just *had* to mention that it happened in the "newcomers'" contribution to the town's festival."

"At least Tinsley told them we couldn't have done it."

Cassie read the second column, her lips forming a frown as she read the mayor's quote. "I suppose that's a good thing, though I can't believe we're suspected because we built the maze. There were hundreds of people inside."

"We're suspected because we're new."

"And I guess we're always trouble. First the treasure and now this."

Lily chuckled as she poured the batter into the waffle maker and closed it. "We're getting quite the reputation."

"They'll be running us out of town soon."

Lily lifted the lid on the waffle maker. The warm aromatic scent of a freshly cooked Belgian waffle wafted through the room as she pried it from the griddle and slid it onto a plate before pouring in more batter. "I hope not. I like it here."

Cassie carefully filled each pocket of her waffle with maple syrup. "The town, the house, or both?"

"Mmm, both, but I simply adore the house and its location."

Cassie chewed on a piece of her waffle as she considered the answer. "I like living by the sea, too."

"But not the house?" Lily inquired as she settled next to Cassie with her waffle.

"I like the house. I'll like it better when I know it's not haunted."

"It's not haunted. Isn't your little doll still in the same place you left her days ago?"

"She is. Though I still think she could have moved. And now that we're on to her, she'll probably be discreet."

Lily chuckled at the words and rolled her eyes. "I think you're being silly. The house isn't haunted. The doll isn't moving on her own."

"Maybe we should have Ruby come in just in case."

"Tell you what. If that doll moves again on its own, we'll call her. Otherwise, let's just chalk it up to a hazy memory and agree this beautiful old house isn't haunted."

"Okay," Cassie said. "Deal."

The ladies finished their breakfast and parted ways to dress for a trip to the police station. As Cassie pulled a sweater over her head, she pushed the image of the man's startled face from her mind. It had already begun to fade. She felt certain she had imagined his resemblance to Trevor. Likely a remnant from the recent tragedy, her brain had probably concocted the scenario to cope with the shock of seeing a dead body.

She wasn't even sure she'd ask Wyatt to view the body today. Her mind turned back to her ghost downstairs. The doll hadn't moved from its spot since she'd put it there. Perhaps it all had been a fluke. Maybe her mind was overworked from building the maze.

Either way, she hoped both situations resolved themselves. She was ready to slip away into a quiet November, spend her first Thanksgiving in Whispering Manor and prepare for the Christmas holiday.

As a distraction, she imagined decorating a large

Christmas tree in the living room with hot chocolate and *White Christmas* playing in the background. Holiday tunes filled the air as they trimmed the massive tree placed in front of the bay window. Could she convince her mother to get a live tree, or would they use one of the fake trees they had in storage from their previous residences?

She finished tying her shoes and pushed the thought from her mind as she stood and smoothed her jeans. They had plenty of time to decide between now and Christmas, she thought, as she grabbed her purse and slung it over her shoulder.

Emerging from her room, she spotted her mom's door still closed. She descended the stairs, figuring she'd wait by the door. As she waited, she wandered into the living room and stared at the Victorian woman frozen in place.

She chuckled at the doll's face. "And to think I imagined you were Henrietta trying to tell me something."

She stepped into the foyer as her mother's footsteps sounded on the creaky stairs.

"Ready?" she inquired.

"Yep. Gosh, I hope they don't use the ink here still."

"I'm sure everything's digital now. Although, I'm also sure Wyatt won't know how to use the machine."

"I hope Ruby's working," Lily said as she swung the door shut behind her.

Cassie meandered to the Wrangler in their gravel driveway. "Me too, otherwise we may be stuck with the ink."

Lily wrinkled her nose, climbing into the pink car and pulling on her seatbelt. Cassie eased the car onto Ocean Drive and headed for the police station. They arrived within ten minutes and slid to the pavement below before climbing the few stairs up to the door.

Ruby sat behind the desk at the entrance. Her ruby red lips formed a smile as they swept in leaving the cloudy

October day behind. She wiggled her ruby-tipped fingers at them. "Hi, gals!"

"Hi, Ruby," Lily said. "Reporting for fingerprinting."

Ruby arched a perfectly made-up eyebrow at them. "Sheriff told me this morning. What a crazy set of events. Don't worry, though, we'll get you printed and out of here in no time." She offered another smile before she rolled her chair backward several feet and spun to face the back. "Hey, Sheriff! Lily and Cassie are here!"

"Okay, send them back," Wyatt answered.

Ruby rolled her wheeled office chair back to the counter. "You can go ahead back."

"Thanks," Lily said with a nod. They skirted around the desk and disappeared into the hallway leading to the conference room and Wyatt's office.

He emerged from his office looking beleaguered. "Morning," he mumbled as he waved for them to enter the conference room.

"Long night, huh?" Lily asked as she settled into a chair.

"Definitely," Wyatt lamented, plopping into a chair and setting a folder down in front of him. He rubbed his face with his hands before he faced the two women. "I just wanted to explain to you that we're fingerprinting you both since we expect to find your fingerprints within the barn and the crime scene. That does not mean we think you're guilty or that we're ruling you out as the guilty party, either. And you don't have to do this. You're willingly offering us your fingerprints to assist with the investigation, but you are under no obligation at this time to do so. And if you want to consult with an attorney first, that's perfectly fine at this juncture."

Lily guffawed at his speech, offering him an amused grin. "You're joking, right?"

"I'm not," he answered. "I…" His voice trailed off and he

heaved a sigh. "There have been some developments. I... I think it may be best that you consult with someone first before we do anything."

"Are you serious?" Cassie exclaimed. "You really think we need an attorney? We didn't do anything!"

Wyatt remained silent.

Lily drummed her hands on the table, her face filled with consternation. "It bothers me that you're not answering."

Wyatt's gaze fell to the folder in front of him. "I told you, there have been some developments."

"Such as?" Lily asked.

"I'm really not at liberty to say..." Wyatt began.

Lily's eyebrows shot up and her jaw dropped open. "You're not at liberty to say but you're hinting that we're guilty! So, what is it, Wyatt? Do you think we did this?"

"No, no, I–it's– ahh, heck, this is really..." He blew out a long breath as he focused on the manila folder.

"Yeah," Lily said, her head bobbing up and down as her features pinched, "this is really..."

"Insane is what it is," Cassie finished. "We haven't done anything. We're just offering our fingerprints so you can rule them out in the investigation."

"Look, ladies, I don't–I can't–" He sighed and started again. "My hands are tied here."

Lily flung her hands out. "Why? What developments could have made you think we did it? Did you find the murder weapon? Or some evidence that points to us?"

Wyatt shook his head, his lips drawn into a thin line. "No, we ID'ed the victim though."

"And?" Lily inquired. "And the identity makes you think we did it?"

"It's not that it makes me think you did it but... well, you had a connection to the victim. Damnit, Lily, why didn't you say something to me last night?"

Cassie's eyes widened. Perhaps she hadn't been crazy to think he'd resembled Trevor. But Trevor had no family to speak of, so who could it be?

"I have no idea what you're talking about! I don't know the man."

Wyatt flicked his gaze to Cassie, his eyebrows raising to prod a response from her.

"I didn't recognize him either," Cassie said. She had only recognized a resemblance to Trevor, but she'd never seen the man before in her life.

Wyatt's forehead crinkled and he stared down at the folder again. "But then…" His face pinched in confusion.

"Why don't you tell us how you think we know this person and maybe we can sort this all out? It's got to be a simple misunderstanding," Lily suggested.

Wyatt flicked the folder open. Cassie spotted a picture of the deceased man paper clipped to the top of the document. We identified him as Kyle McGuire."

Cassie swallowed hard as he spoke her married last name.

Wyatt flicked his eyes to Cassie. "That's the same as your name."

"Her married name," Lily reminded him.

"Right. So, are you saying you didn't recognize your brother-in-law?"

Cassie's jaw dropped at his words. "Brother-in-law?" she gasped.

"Now, wait just a minute," Lily said, waving a finger in the air. "It's just as I suspected. This is a huge mistake. Trevor didn't have a brother."

"Except he did," Wyatt argued. "Kyle McGuire was Trevor's younger brother."

"No," Cassie murmured as she shook her head in disbelief. "No, that can't be. Mom's right. Trevor didn't have any siblings."

"That's not what the records say," Wyatt answered with a shake of his head.

"Are you joking?" Lily questioned.

Wyatt continued his head shake. "ID came back as Kyle McGuire, born to Jonas and Kendra McGuire on February 17, 1980. Brother Trevor McGuire. Trevor's even listed as his emergency contact with the hospital." Wyatt screwed up his face as he leaned back in his chair. "Are you saying neither of you was aware that Trevor had a younger brother?"

Both women wore masks of shock. "I–I–I had no idea," Cassie stammered. She sucked in a shaky breath, pressing trembling fingers against her forehead.

She shot Wyatt an incredulous glance. "Are you sure?"

He licked his lower lip and gave a slight nod. "Yeah. We're certain. The body we found belonged to one Kyle McGuire. Your deceased husband's brother."

CHAPTER 14

Lily swallowed hard and clapped a hand over Cassie's. "This is, understandably, a shock," she said. "Could you give us a few moments?"

"Sure," Wyatt answered, closing his folder and tapping it against the wooden table. "Just let me know when you're ready to proceed. Either with the prints, or leaving, or whatever."

He tapped the folder on the table again as he stood and hesitated. "Look, Lily, I–"

"It's okay, Wyatt, just give us a minute."

He pursed his lips and nodded again before disappearing from the room, tugging the door partially closed behind him.

Cassie stared blankly ahead at the light oak table, absent-mindedly tracing the wood grain with a shaky finger.

"Cass?" Lily prodded, tucking a lock of hair behind her daughter's ear.

"This can't be right. He's got to have it wrong."

"It sounds like they think it's right. And that they have evidence to corroborate it."

"How?" Cassie exclaimed, tossing her arms in the air. She

leapt from her seat and stalked to the window, wrapping her arms around herself as she stared out.

"I'm not sure," Lily admitted.

"How could Trevor have a brother?" She spun to face her mother. "And how could I not know about it?"

"I'm sure there's some explanation, Cassie," Lily said, rising from the chair and skirting the table to approach her daughter. She grasped her arms and squeezed. "Maybe they were estranged."

"Estranged enough that Trevor never even mentioned him to me? At all? Not even to say he has a brother but they're not speaking?"

"Apparently not, Cass," Lily answered with a sigh.

Cassie shook her head, her gaze falling to the worn carpet on the floor below them. She let out a sharp breath. "Makes me wonder what else Trevor wasn't telling me."

Lily pushed a lock of hair behind Cassie's other ear. "Maybe nothing. Families are tough. Look at Clif and Ri. They were estranged and she never mentioned him."

Cassie lifted her eyes to her mother's face. "Do you think Kyle was a pirate?"

Lily chuckled at the poor attempt at humor and Cassie cracked a smile.

Her smile faded quickly, and she shook her head again. "What news, huh?"

"Yeah, it'll take some time to get over, I think. But in the meantime, we need to decide what we're going to do about these fingerprints."

Cassie shrugged and waved a hand in the air. "Unlike Trevor, I have nothing to hide."

"Are you sure you want to give them your prints? With the odd connection to your late husband, maybe we should rethink."

"I didn't do anything, Mom. And won't we look guilty if we do that?"

Lily pressed her lips together as she considered it. "Maybe. But I don't want to chance doing something wrong in case they try to blame one of us, namely, you."

"Mom!" Cassie shouted. "I'm innocent."

"Yes, I know that! I'm not saying you did it. But given the odd connection, I don't want to make this worse in the event that they try to pin this on you."

"Do you really think Wyatt would do that?"

"No, I don't. But Wyatt may not be the only one involved. Maybe we should talk to an attorney."

Cassie considered her mother's words. "I guess it couldn't hurt but…"

"But?"

"What difference does it make? If they suspect me, they'll arrest me and fingerprint me anyway. At least this way we've cooperated."

Lily held her hands up in defeat. "All right. If you're sure."

"I don't see how it could hurt. They'll get my prints if they want them no matter what."

Lily called out the door to Wyatt. His office chair squeaked as he launched from it and hurried inside. "Hey, listen, I hope you don't think I'm accusing either of you–"

Lily cut him off with a wave of her hands. "No, it's okay. It's just a shock, that's all. We certainly never expected this."

Wyatt shoved his hands in his pockets and nodded. "And I certainly understand if you decide not to go through with providing fingerprints."

"We're going to do that. If we can help with the investigation at all, we'd like to. We don't have anything to hide," Lily answered.

Wyatt bobbed his head up and down as his lips tugged down at the corners. "Of course not." He paused for a moment, and they stood in awkward silence. "Uh, well, why don't you both take a seat and I'll get everything ready, and then we'll get your prints and get you on your way."

"Thanks, Wyatt," Lily said, returning to her seat.

Cassie spun to stare out the window, biting her lower lip as Wyatt left the room.

"Come sit down, Cass," Lily said, patting the chair next to her.

Cassie pulled herself away from the window and skirted the table, plopping into the seat next to her mother.

She sunk her chin into her palm, balancing an elbow on the table's edge. "At least this explains why he reminded me of Trevor."

"Yeah, I guess so," Lily admitted, smoothing down a lock of her daughter's hair.

"So, I'm not going crazy."

"Nah, just the believing in ghosts part is crazy. You were right about this part."

Cassie flicked her gaze sideways, offering her mother a wry grin. "Very funny. And if I'm right about this, maybe I'm right about the ghosts, too."

Lily pressed her lips together in an unimpressed stare. "Let's not get ahead of ourselves. We have no proof of that."

"Yet," Cassie reminded her.

Before Lily could reply, Wyatt knocked on the door jamb. "Okay, we're all ready. Lily, you want to go first?"

"Age before beauty, I guess," Lily said as she rose.

"Or…beauty before beauty," Wyatt stammered in an awkward response as he scratched his head. He chuckled at his own statement, motioning for Lily to follow him.

Cassie sat in the room alone, drumming her fingers against the table as she waited for her mother's return. Her mind raced in hundreds of directions at once, each thought fighting for attention.

Why had Trevor concealed the fact that he had a brother? If the reason was that they were estranged, what happened between them to prompt such animosity? He'd told Cassie he had no family. He had only invited friends to their wedding. Cassie had split her guests, sending some to the groom's side to fill the church.

The sound of Wyatt's voice interrupted her ruminating. "Hey, Ruby!" he called.

"Wow," Cassie murmured, "he really is bad at technology."

She leaned back in her seat, crossing her arms over her chest. Perhaps some clue existed in Trevor's things. She'd put much of it in storage when they'd moved, planning to sort through it at another time when she felt ready. She pondered the best place to begin her search when Lily reappeared at the doorway.

"You're up," she said as she strode to her chair and sank into it. "Don't worry, it's digital. And Ruby makes it quick and painless."

An amused glance crossed Cassie's face. "I heard him call for her."

Lily wiggled her eyebrows as Cassie rounded her chair. "Yep. He is really bad at technology."

Cassie stepped into the hall and hurried to where Wyatt waited for her. "Okay, this should be pretty simple. At least for Ruby."

Cassie chuckled as Ruby clicked a few times on the computer and then instructed Cassie on placing her index finger on the glass panel and rolling it to get the full print.

"Hey, Cassie, I'm really sorry to have sprung this on you. I thought you'd at least know about Trevor having a brother even if you didn't recognize him in the confusion of last night."

"Nope, sorry. I had no idea. I've been going over it again and again in my mind. Quite frankly, I'm shocked. I mean, he didn't have any family at our wedding. I just assumed he had no relatives, certainly not a brother."

"Well, again, I'm sorry to be the one to tell you." Wyatt searched her face for a reaction.

Cassie offered a tentative smile. "Thanks, though it's not your fault."

They finished with the fingerprints and Wyatt offered his thanks for their assistance. "You're free to go. If I have any other questions for you, I'll give you a call or stop by." He paused as though unsure if he should offer any additional comments or not. He chose not to, pressing his lips together in a tight smile.

"Thanks, Wyatt."

Cassie collected her mother from the conference room, and they climbed back into her Jeep.

"Do you mind if we swing by the storage space?" Cassie inquired as she buckled her seatbelt.

"No, but are you sure that's a good idea?"

Cassie fired the engine and tugged the shifter into gear. "What do you mean?"

"I assume you're going to look through Trevor's things. Cass, if he hid this from you, maybe you don't want to know about it. Maybe it's best left buried."

"It's not buried, though, Mom," Cassie said as she swung the car onto the road. "It's lying in the morgue with its throat sliced open."

Lily flicked her eyebrows up and aimed her gaze out the window. Her daughter had a point.

"I just can't believe he kept something this big from me."

"That's what I mean, Cassie. Maybe it's best to just forget it. Trevor is gone. Why dredge all this up? You may never have answers and it may only upset you and the happy memories you have with him."

"I can't forget it. I married this man. And the whole time he had a huge secret."

"I'm not sure a wayward brother is a huge secret."

"He said he was an only child. He said it. Second date while we ate ice cream next to the carousel in the park. He lied. He could have just said I have a brother, it's complicated, we don't speak."

"Maybe he was afraid you'd try to push them to make amends. Who knows why he did it?"

"We may never know, but I have to at least try to find some answers."

"All right. Let's grab some of his stuff and we'll go through it. Maybe we'll find some clue."

Cassie navigated to the storage facility on the outskirts of town, pulling her car off the road and tapping her code into the metal keypad to open the gate. She eased the car through the metal gate and wound through the narrow, paved pathways to the storage unit they'd rented when they'd moved to Hideaway Bay.

Cassie slid her key into the padlock before sliding up the large orange door. They stepped inside the dark space, and she flicked on her flashlight. She swept the beam across the boxes stacked near the front, ignoring the furniture piled in the back.

"Here," she called, finding a box labeled "Trevor's personal effects" in the second stack from the door. "This is probably the best starting place.

Lily scrunched her nose at it. "Of course, it would be buried under two other boxes."

"I'll get the ladder," Cassie said, dragging the metal contraption from the opposite corner and setting it up. She climbed up, tugging one box onto the top step before she handed it off to her mother.

She descended a step and pulled the next one over,

passing it off. Lily set them on a covered armchair nearby. Cassie yanked Trevor's box from the stack.

"Do you want to go through it here?"

Cassie shook her head and hefted the box up onto her hip. "No, I'll take it home. Then I can go over it with a fine-toothed comb. Or put it off some more."

Lily offered Cassie a consoling glance and a rub on her shoulder. "You can just leave this to the police, Cass. You don't have to do anything."

Cassie lifted her shoulders and sighed. "I'll see how I feel when I get home."

Lily closed and locked the storage unit while Cassie shoved the box into the back of the Wrangler. They climbed into the car and drove the short distance to their home.

Cassie lugged the box from the back while Lily unlocked the door after making certain she disabled the alarm system.

They slogged through the front door, finding Willy sitting on the third step. He stared at them with his single eye.

"What's the matter with you, Willy?" Lily asked as she dumped her keys into the bowl on the entryway table. "Cat got your tongue?" She chuckled at her own joke.

"What a terrible pun, Mom," Cassie said, shifting the box from one hip to the other. "What's up, buddy? This isn't like you."

"No, he's normally down here trying to trip me the minute we walk through the door."

"He hasn't budged an inch since we walked in." Cassie set the box on the floor and squatted down, holding her hand out. "Hey, buddy. What's up?"

The cat flicked a gaze upstairs before he leapt to his feet, tail wiggling in the air. He brushed against the railing before he pranced across the step to the opposite side and swiped his face across the baluster.

After a moment, he hopped from his perch and crossed to Cassie, rubbing against her hand with a loud purr.

"Guess he just wasn't that excited to see us," Cassie said, running a hand down his back and up his tail.

"Maybe it was the box. He may have been afraid of that."

"We brought boxes in from the Halloween store and he didn't seem to mind."

"That box may have a stronger scent of a stranger to him."

"Hmm, true," Cassie said as she offered a rueful glance at the box of her dead husband's things. "Well, he seems to be back to normal now."

"Whew," Lily exclaimed. "I've had enough of this day already. I vote we order in and do a movie marathon."

"I agree," Cassie said with a final stroke down Willy's back before she stood and lifted the box, balancing it on her hip.

"I could go for tacos. Should I call Nacho's?"

"Sounds good to me. I'm heading up to change while you call the order in," Cassie said, mounting the first stair.

"I'll call as long as I can pick the movies!" Lily called over her shoulder as she shuffled to the kitchen to retrieve the number.

Cassie smiled and shook her head at her mother's request as she lugged the box up the stairs. Her mind turned to its contents. Did she want to go through it? Did she want to remind herself of everything she'd worked so hard not to remember since it happened?

The dead body in the morgue almost forced her to. She couldn't ignore it. She'd pushed memories of Trevor away since his untimely death. She could. She didn't need to face them. Not yet. At least that's what she told herself. But now, with the body of Trevor's brother almost on her doorstep, she needed answers. She knew her mind wouldn't rest until she got them.

She'd have to be strong and search for clues, even if it

brought up every painful memory of her life with Trevor and how it had been ripped away on one dark, stormy summer night.

She reached her decision as she stepped off the final stair. With her eyes studying the cardboard container in her arms, she swung right toward her bedroom. As she reached the corner of the railing leading to her hall, she stopped dead. Her jaw fell open. Her heart thudded hard against her ribs as her breath caught in her throat.

The box slipped from her hands, thudding to the floor below, its contents rattling around inside. Cassie stood motionless, a chill running up her spine. She pressed her trembling hands to her face as she struggled to catch her breath. In front of her, with an outstretched hand reaching toward the wall, stood the animatronic ghost.

CHAPTER 15

*L*ily's voice floated up the stairs, growing louder with each syllable. "Cassie? Cass? What was that? Are you alright?"

Cassie stared ahead at the ghost woman, unable to voice a response.

"Cassie?" her mother called from the foot of the stairs.

"Uh-uh-up here," Cassie breathed.

Lily pounded up the stairs. "What happened? Is everything okay?"

Cassie spun on her heel and retreated to the top of the stairway. Her pale face, three shades lighter than normal, betrayed her shock. She shook her head at her mother, pressing her lips together in a thin line.

Lily stopped her ascent, staring at her daughter for a moment. She flung her arms out to her sides with an exasperated sigh. "What is it, Cass? What's wrong?"

Cassie sucked in a shaky breath. "I think you'd better see for yourself."

"All right," Lily answered with a shrug and a head shake. "Lead the way."

Cassie motioned for her to follow and strode to where the box still sat on the floor, one corner smashed from the impact of being dropped.

She pointed a trembling finger at the ghost woman ahead and turned to face her mother.

Lily's brow furrowed as her footsteps slowed. She cocked her head, her eyes flicking between the prop and Cassie.

"I didn't move her," Cassie said preemptively. "When we left for the police station, she was in the living room."

Lily stared at the scene for a moment longer before she spoke. "Then…" she began, no other words following.

"How did she get up here?" Cassie shrieked in a frightened voice an octave higher than normal. "That's exactly what I'd like to know!"

"Maybe she's defective and doesn't turn off all the way."

Cassie's eyes shot wide, and her jaw fell open again. "She can't climb stairs, Mom! She rides around on a glorified Roomba!"

"Are you sure you didn't–"

"I'm sure. I'm one hundred percent certain I did not move her upstairs before we left. She was downstairs in the living room in the corner I put her in two nights ago."

Lily swallowed hard and stared ahead at the Victorian ghost. "Then how in heavens did she get up here?"

They stood in silence, each of them staring at the perplexing location of the supposedly inanimate object.

"There has to be–" Lily began, her voice sluggish and low.

"Please don't say a reasonable explanation," Cassie said, cutting her gaze to Lily. "Because there isn't. There is no explanation for why a Halloween prop went from being in the living room corner downstairs to being upstairs in the hall to my bedroom."

"And why here?" Lily questioned, tilting her head as she studied the doll.

"Why anywhere?" Cassie shouted, waving her arm at the doll. "What difference does it make if she was hovering at the top of the stairs or standing there."

"Well, if someone put her there, why pick this spot?"

"Did you turn the alarm on when we left?"

"Yes," Lily said with a nod.

"Then no one put her there. Or the alarm would have gone off! So, it moved up here by itself."

Lily crossed her arms and shook her head. "That's impossible."

"Yet here she is!" Cassie shouted, waving her arms at the doll. "We've both seen it with our own eyes." She huffed and crossed her arms. "I think we should call Ruby."

Lily sighed, her eyes still fixed on the ghost prop frozen across the distance. "Maybe we should." She twisted to face Cassie, wagging a finger at her. "But, Cassie, she may not help. She may be a charlatan."

"Charlatan? Really? Do you think Ruby will just be looking for a payout?"

"No, that's not what I mean. What I mean is she may always 'feel' something. She may assume the house is haunted and feel a presence because she thinks she should."

"I'll take what she says with a grain of salt. I'm not looking for vague feelings, though, I'm looking for answers!"

"I'm not sure you'll find them, Cass."

Cassie frowned, crossing her arms and flicking her gaze to the animatron. "I hope we find something. I'm not sure I can take much more of this phenomenon."

"Ghost or not, I still need to eat. Why don't you text Wyatt while I call for the tacos?"

"Maybe you should get extra orders in case he brings Ruby over. If he offers, I'm accepting. I need to know before I try to sleep in this house tonight."

"I'll order two extra meals. If they don't come over, we'll have extra for later this week."

Cassie nodded as she tugged her phone from her jeans pocket and toggled it open. She eyed the animatron warily as her mother descended the stairs. She expected it to leap at her at any moment, babbling on about the journals it had told her about in her sleep. With her lips pulled into a frown, she inched past the Victorian ghost, breaking into a run after passing it and sprinting the length of the hall to her bedroom. She pushed the door shut behind her and wandered to the bed, sinking onto it.

With her text app open, she typed and retyped a message to Wyatt, unable to settle on the words she wanted. After the oddity with Trevor's brother earlier, she didn't want to sound crazier than she probably already did. What kind of woman didn't know her husband had a brother? She narrowed her eyes at her reflection in the mirror across from her and shook her head at herself.

"Who did you marry, Cassie?"

With a deep inhale, she returned her attention to her phone and tried again with her message, settling on: *Sorry to bother you, I know you have a lot going on with the investigation, but... does your offer for Ruby to stop by the house still stand?*

Cassie blew out a long breath, tapping her fingers against the back of her phone as she bobbed her leg up and down.

Her phone chimed moments later with a response. *Yeah, sure. I'm sure she'd be happy to stop by. I'll ask her. Something happen?*

Cassie stared at the words on the screen. How much should she tell him? Anything? The whole story? Would it be best if Ruby came in without knowing the creepy tale?

Another message popped up as she weighed her response: *Do you need me to come over right away?*

Cassie quickly typed a response. *No, it's not urgent. But, yes, something happened that we can't explain, and we'd like to see if Ruby can offer any insight into what may be happening here.*

Three dots popped on the screen as Wyatt typed a response. Cassie blew out another sigh of relief as she saw the dots appear. At least he wasn't racing over to Whispering Manor, sirens blaring.

I'll talk to Ruby now and let you know. As long as you're sure it's not urgent.

Cassie smiled at the message as she typed back: *Not urgent, just uncanny.*

She clicked off her phone and gave herself another look in the mirror. How would she sleep tonight? Visions of her tying the Victorian prop to a chair danced in her mind. No, she mused, if the spirit of Henrietta lurked inside the doll, she'd just drag the chair with her and then berate Cassie for daring to confine her.

She set her phone on the charger and crossed her room, inching her door open. She peered into the hall. The ghost stood sentinel, its outstretched hand still touching the wall.

Cassie flicked her eyes to the box she'd dropped earlier. She should drag it into her room. She pressed her lips together and pulled the door open fully. Swallowing hard and squaring her shoulders, she strode down the hall and past the ghost. She heaved the box up and, with a wrinkled nose, skirted past the doll again, dumping the box on the hardwood floor of her bedroom.

Across the room, her cell phone's notification light blinked, indicating a new message. Cassie hurried toward it and swiped open her lock screen. A message from Wyatt awaited her. *Ruby said she'd be happy to help if she can. We can drop by in about an hour if that's okay. If not, let me know a good time.*

A smile crept across Cassie's features as her thumbs flew across the virtual keyboard confirming the visit today. She bit her lower lip as she rested her chin on the phone after pressing send. She hoped this meant answers would be forthcoming.

A beep sounded, calling her attention back to the device. A new message from Wyatt popped on her screen, asking if they'd like him to pick up anything for dinner.

Cassie responded: *Mom's got it covered. Tacos from Nacho Average Restaurant. I hope Ruby likes tacos.*

Wyatt's response was immediate: *Ruby loves tacos. She'll be thrilled when I tell her. See you soon.*

Cassie dumped her phone on the charger, noting the time before she stepped into the hallway and peered over the railing. "Mom?"

She received no answer. "Mom!"

With no response, Cassie's mind raced ahead of her. She should be able to hear her call from the kitchen. And she should be done placing the order by now. Did something happen? With her heart in her throat, Cassie swept past the creepy doll and started to descend the stairs.

"Mom!" she shouted again as she hastened down the creaky boards to the floor below. "Mom!"

Cassie rounded the corner, grabbing the railing and spinning herself in a circle to face the kitchen. "Mo–" she began when Lily appeared at the rear of the house, stepping in from the deck.

Cassie blew out a sigh of relief, pressing her hand to her heart. "Oh, there you are."

"Yeah, everything okay?" Lily asked, noting the consternation on Cassie's face. "Did the doll move again? Or talk to you?"

Cassie shook her head as she caught her breath. "No. Wyatt and Ruby are coming in an hour. I called down to let you know and you didn't answer. I thought something happened to you."

"Like what? The ghost got me?"

"No, of course not," Cassie said with a rueful shake of her head. "Like you fell or fainted or something."

"Fell? Cassie, I'm not eighty."

"People in their sixties fall, Mom."

"This lady in her sixties is not frail and does not fall. I'm fine. I just stepped onto the deck to take a call after I ordered the tacos."

Cassie's eyebrows rose to her hairline. "Who called that you had to step out for?"

"Wyatt," Lily said, waving the phone in the air.

Cassie crinkled her brow at the comment, as her mother explained further. "He called in a panic, asking if you were okay. Said you sounded cryptic in your message."

"No, I didn't!" Cassie claimed.

Lily shrugged and wandered toward Cassie. "He wanted to make sure we really were able to wait the hour before he came with Ruby."

Cassie followed her mother to the living room and plopped on the couch next to her. "I told him you ordered tacos. He said Ruby will be thrilled."

Lily aimed the remote at the television and powered it on. "I ordered six."

"Six?"

"After thinking about it, I wanted to have two orders for later this week regardless of whether or not Wyatt and Ruby came over. So, I ordered extra extras."

Cassie eyed the screen as potential titles flew past on the streaming app. "Nacho's is going to think we're huge eaters."

"Oh well. You'll thank me for this later this week."

"I'm sure I will," Cassie said, settling back into the cushions.

Her mother stopped scrolling, dropping her hand to the cushion below her and arching an eyebrow at Cassie.

Cassie stared at the screen for a moment, then shot her mother a glance. "No. Are you serious?"

Lily shrugged as she pressed the center button to select the show. "Just trying to get you prepared for what may happen with Ruby."

On the screen, the silhouette of a gothic house appeared as an actor did a voiceover. With a huff, Cassie fidgeted in her seat, squeezing a throw pillow to her chest. Waves crashed against a rocky shoreline on the television as the decorative font floated around before centering itself on the screen. Cassie shook her head at the white lettering that spelled out the show's name: *Dark Shadows.*

A knock at the door startled both women from the show they watched.

"Has it been an hour already?" Lily inquired as she inched to the cushion's edge and pushed herself up.

"Maybe it's the tacos," Cassie suggested.

Lily shuffled to the door and pulled it open. Wyatt and Ruby stepped inside. Wyatt held two large bags emblamed with a massive red nacho chip and the words *Nacho Average Restaurant.*

"Ran into the delivery guy on the way in and figured we'd just grab the food."

"Oh, great, thanks," Lily said, grabbing a bag from Wyatt. "And thanks for coming."

"Yeah," Cassie said, hovering in the doorway to the living room, her hand on the decorative wooden trim. "Thanks, Ruby. We really appreciate it."

They stood in silence for a moment. With her hands shoved into her jacket pockets, Ruby glanced around the house.

"Ah, well," Lily said, wiggling the bag in the air, "should we eat first?"

"Yeah, that'd be great," Wyatt said. "Unless you'd prefer Ruby to dive right in."

"No, let's eat," Cassie said. "Unless Ruby would prefer not to."

"I'm fine with eating," Ruby said. "And you don't have to walk on eggshells around me. I have some psychic abilities, but I'm not sensing anything that's making me run for the hills right now. I'll let you know if that changes."

Cassie's heart sank at the answer. Perhaps this would solve nothing. Then what would they do? Find another psychic? Have an exorcism? Maybe they did need to watch more *Dark Shadows*, she ruminated as Lily led them down the hall to the kitchen.

She set out four containers of tacos and the complimentary chips and salsa, stowing two meals in the refrigerator for later in the week.

They gathered around the table, diving into their meal.

"So, Ruby," Cassie said, breaking the silence only shattered by the crunching of taco shells moments earlier, "how does this work exactly? I hope that's okay to ask."

Ruby chewed her taco as she nodded. "Yeah, it's fine. Umm, so I'll go around the house and see if I get any feelings or vibes. I may, I may not. It really depends on if the spirit is present where I am. If there's anywhere in particular that you want me to focus on, I can revisit it. Oh, but please don't tell me ahead of time. I don't want it to skew my reading."

"Right, okay, sure. That makes sense."

"Wyatt said you'd been having a few disturbances in the house, though?"

Cassie dipped a chip into the salsa before letting it hover over her plate as she answered. "Yeah, a few different things. We thought the supposed haunting could be attributed to the treasure hunters, but..."

Lily filled in the rest after Cassie's voice trailed off. "Even after that cleared up, we've had some unexplained incidents."

Ruby nodded as she sipped at the soda Lily poured for her before sitting down. "Maybe you should have gotten margaritas. Sounds like you may have needed it." She arched an eyebrow, a coy smile tugging at the corners of her ruby red lips.

Lily chuckled at the statement, shooting a glance at Cassie and then Wyatt. Cassie cracked a smile. "I may be ordering one later. I'm not sure I'll sleep in this house."

"After I tour the place, you can describe them to me. And, you know, if I don't find anything that doesn't mean there's nothing here. I have a few friends who set up all kinds of equipment and monitor for presences and stuff. I'm sure they'd be happy to help out if you'd like."

Lily licked her lips and nodded, her mouth hanging open as she considered the best way to formulate her next words. "I don't mean to be indelicate, but may I ask what you and your friends charge for this?"

"Oh," Ruby said, fluttering her red nails in the air, "I don't charge anything."

"Are you sure?" Lily asked.

"Positive. I have a gift of sorts. It'd be wrong of me to try to use it to make money when people need help."

Lily shot Cassie a glance and Ruby added, "Besides, I got tacos. I can't complain."

"That's a pretty poor offering for us to ask you to roam around our house looking for a creepy ghost."

"The ghost may not be creepy, Cassie," Ruby said with a shrug. "They usually want or need something."

Cassie winced as she closed the lid on her takeout container. "Want something? That sounds creepy."

"It's usually not," Ruby promised.

Cassie wrinkled her nose at the statement, disturbed by

Ruby's nonchalance. "What have the ghosts you've encountered wanted in the past?"

"I've only encountered two scenarios where there have actually been ghosts in the past. Lots of people think they have them, and it turns out to be explainable."

Lily shot Cassie a pointed glance at the words. Cassie pressed her lips together, resisting the urge to roll her eyes at her mother.

Ruby continued, "And in the two I've actually encountered, the first wanted her daughter to know she forgave her and the second wanted a picture album to be found."

"Well," Lily said as she stood and stacked the empty plastic to-go containers, "that sounds innocuous enough. Let's hope ours is as simple *if* there are even any ghosts here."

"And that's a big if," Ruby said.

"What?" Wyatt questioned, his features pulling into an incredulous expression. "You said you never came to Whispering Manor because it was haunted."

"I didn't say because, I said *in case*. Same reason I won't go in the barn. When you're sensitive like me, you can't unsee things."

Cassie waved a trash bag in the air, snapping it a few times to open it. "But if they're usually innocuous, what's to unsee?"

"I don't want to find out in case I run into one that's not."

"I sure hope we're not the reason you come across the first thing you want to unsee," Cassie said with a wince.

Ruby slapped her hands against the table as she rose. "Well, so far, so good. I haven't felt anything evil or odd since I stepped into the house."

Cassie blew out a sigh of relief at the statement. Whatever Ruby found, perhaps it wouldn't be as dire as she suspected.

Lily eyed Ruby and Wyatt. "Should we get started?"

"Sure. Lead the way!" Ruby said, waving her red nails in the air.

"Well, I suppose you've gotten a good feel for the kitchen, so we'll head into the library next," Lily said, leading the foursome into the hall and toward the foyer.

Lily motioned for them to enter the library space at the front of the house. "And then you said to wait to tell you of any incidents until after you've been through the whole house, right?"

"Sure. We can sit down and talk about everything once I've seen all the rooms. I'll let you know if I pick up on anything and you can let me know what's happened to have you call me in to begin with." Ruby flashed a smile with her red lips as she stepped inside the library.

She closed her eyes, inhaling deeply before her eyes shot open. She cocked her head and furrowed her brow. In a moment, she snapped her gaze to the bookshelf housing Henrietta's novels. She narrowed her eyes at it before she swiveled her head to gaze at other parts of the room.

Cassie bit her lower lip as she eyed the scene. Did Ruby sense something? It would fit given this was one of the rooms where an odd occurrence had plagued her.

With a sniff, Ruby nodded her head and said, "Okay, next room."

They worked their way around the house, touring from room-to-room downstairs before mounting the creaky wooden staircase leading upward.

On the top level, they began with Lily's room and made their way through each of the other spaces. Ruby paused several times in different areas, her brow furrowing and her interest piqued.

As they passed down the hall to Cassie's room, their last stop, Ruby ground to a halt, her hands shoved into her back pockets. She wrinkled her nose at the Victorian doll standing against the wall. "What's up with this creepy character?"

"Oh, that's a Halloween prop we found at the store over in Misty Hollow. I thought she looked pretty cool," Cassie said.

"Kind of creepy. Not sure I'd want that thing hanging around my hallways when I'm afraid my house is haunted."

Cassie shot Lily a glance, her features wrinkling. Lily put her arm around her daughter's shoulders and squeezed her closer. "Well, we can discuss that once you've finished with your perusal of the house. Cassie's room awaits!"

"Lead the way," Ruby said with one last glance at the creepy doll.

They led Ruby down the hall to Cassie's bedroom. With her red lips puckered, she stepped over the threshold, her eyes scanning the space.

"Oh, I like your carousel," she said, her ruby red nail tracing one of the horse's backs.

"Thanks," Cassie said as Ruby took another step into the room.

She pressed her lips together and closed her eyes for a moment. After a deep inhale, she opened them and glanced around again.

Cassie's eyes bore into her as she searched her face for even the slightest clue as to what she may or may not perceive.

Across the room, Ruby's eyebrows squashed together for a moment, and she shivered all over. Her eyes shot around the room again before she let out a long breath and offered a tight-lipped smile at Lily & Cassie.

"Okay, I'm all set. Ready to discuss what's been going on here and anything I may have picked up on?"

CHAPTER 16

Lily crossed her arms and shrugged at Ruby, shooting a glance at Cassie. "As ready as we'll ever be, I guess. Should we meet in the kitchen? I ordered dessert from Nacho's."

Wyatt's eyes lit up at the words. "You didn't tell me you had dessert."

Lily flicked her gaze to Wyatt, a playful smile crossing her lips. "Yeah, so you wouldn't eat it before any of us could."

"What is it?" Wyatt questioned as they followed Lily and Cassie from the room and down the stairs. "Please tell me it's their churros."

"And that you got the chocolate sauce," Ruby added.

Lily chuckled, waving a finger in the air as they descended the stairs. "It is churros *and* I got chocolate sauce. I can't even fathom that some people dunk them in fruit-flavored sauce."

"It's disgusting and irresponsible," Ruby said. "Those people are ruining dessert as we know it."

They entered the kitchen and settled in around the table as Lily reheated the churros and warmed the chocolate sauce before setting them out in the middle of the table. The grin on Wyatt's face widened as he snagged a steaming churro from the takeout container and dumped it on his dessert plate.

"Anyone mind if I just dip into the sauce or are we being polite and spooning it onto our plate?" he asked.

"Just dunk it, Wyatt," Ruby said with a grin before she shot a surprised glance at Lily and Cassie. "Oh, unless you're grossed out by it?"

"Nah," Lily answered with a wave of the churro she'd grab. "Dunk away. You can even double-dip. Won't bother me or Cassie."

"Thanks!" Wyatt said, shoving the churro into the chocolate sauce and smothering one end. He leaned forward to bite it before it dripped on his plate.

"So," Cassie said, nibbling on the end of a churro before she flicked her gaze to Ruby, "what did you find?" She scrunched her nose and offered a half-frightened grimace as though she really didn't want to know the answer.

Ruby chewed a bite of her dessert before she answered, setting the stick down on her plate and wiping the sugar from her hands with her napkin. "Well..." She raised her eyebrows as she licked her lips. "I'd say you've got a presence here."

Cassie set her churro down, biting her lower lip as her features twisted into a concerned mask.

"Doesn't seem nefarious. And it seems a little shy. The presence is fleeting in most cases."

"Where did you notice it?" Lily inquired.

"The library. Then again in Cassie's room."

Cassie's pulse quickened at the words. Some spirit haunted her room. She supposed the non-nefarious part was good, but she wasn't sure it mattered. A ghost was hanging around her room. Why? And what if it wasn't quite so benign?

"Was it the same spirit in both places, or are there two?" Wyatt asked as he bit into his second churro.

Ruby pressed her red lips together, sucking in a breath before answering. "I think the same one. I think she was moving around the house. Maybe following us. Or fleeing from us. I'm not sure which. But I got the same vibe both times."

"She?" Cassie said. "It's a woman?"

Ruby's shoulders raised, hitting her large dangling hoops. "Seems feminine to me. She's so fleeting though, it's hard to tell, but I get a girl vibe from her."

Cassie shot her mother a glance, lifting her eyebrows.

"You should tell her," Wyatt said, with a mouthful of churro. "About the stuff that's been happening."

"Well," Lily said, dusting sugar from her hands, "there's no smoking gun here, but… one night I was reading in bed and right in front of my door in the hall, there's a squeaky floorboard. It squeaked. I assumed it was Cassie or Willy."

"Who's Willy?" Ruby interrupted.

"The cat." Wyatt pointed to his eye. "You know, with the one eye."

"Ohhh, right," Ruby said. "Sorry, go on."

"Well, when I got up to check, there was no one there. I didn't think anything of it, but the next morning Cassie told me she had experienced something strange in the library."

All eyes turned to Cassie. She set down her half-eaten churro and recounted the tale of the flying book to her guests.

Ruby nodded as Cassie told the tale. "Okay, that makes sense with the presence I sensed. It was near the bookcase you mentioned."

"And then," Cassie said, pausing to suck in a deep breath,

"I… one night in my sleep, that doll wandered into my room and told me to find some journals. I thought maybe I dreamed it, but she was in a different position the next morning than the one I'd left her in."

"Creepy Victorian lady, you mean?" Ruby questioned.

"Yeah, creepy Victorian lady," Cassie said with a nod.

"Tell them about the time you called me for help."

"I didn't call you for help, you called me. And then I asked for help," Lily corrected. She flicked her gaze to Ruby. "Anyway, one night Cassie and I ended up locked in our rooms at the same time. We chalked it up to the widow's walk door being unlatched and the wind blowing the doors closed. But we both experienced some strange incidents while locked in our rooms."

"Do tell," Ruby said with a wiggle of her eyebrows.

"I had the journal of Henrietta Blanchard," Lily began.

"The one who offed herself from the widow's walk?"

"One and the same," Lily confirmed. "During the windstorm, her journal blew open on my nightstand. It blew to a page containing three words. Time for death."

"Spooky," Ruby said, biting on her red nail.

Wyatt shivered and shook his head. "Still creeps me out."

"Well, here's the creepier part. I searched her journal. Those words aren't in there. I thought maybe I was seeing things. Maybe it was a figment of my imagination. But Cassie said while she was locked in her room, a ghost typed a message to her on her phone. It, too, was gone when we tried to find it."

Ruby's perfectly shaped eyebrows shot up. "The plot thickens."

"And then there's the reason we called you," Cassie said. "And this is the real icing on the proverbial cake."

All eyes turned to Cassie again. "When we left to come into the police station earlier, the creepy Victorian doll was in the living room." She paused, her eyes flicking between Ruby and Wyatt, watching for a reaction as she spoke her next words. "And when we came home, she was upstairs."

Wyatt's eyes widened and he dropped the last bite of his third churro onto his plate. "What? Are you serious?"

Cassie pressed her lips together and nodded. "Yeah."

Lily nodded as she pressed her lips together. "Even I can't explain that one away. The doll is designed to move on its own. You know, it wanders around the house and says random spooky things. But it can't go up steps. There's no way to explain how it got from the living room to the upstairs hallway."

Ruby slapped her hand against the table. "Well, I'd say you've got a bona fide haunting here."

Cassie shook her head. "What should we do?"

"I can give my friends a call," Ruby said, "but that'll just confirm what we already suspect."

"So, there's nothing we can do about this?" Cassie exclaimed, the fear in her voice forcing it an octave higher

"I didn't say that," Ruby answered. "I have a suggestion, but you may not like it."

"Shoot," Lily said.

Ruby adjusted her glasses and flicked her gaze between the two women. "We should have a seance."

Cassie's jaw dropped open at the words. "Are you serious?"

"Yes," Ruby answered. "It's a perfect way to reach out and see if we can determine what this spirit may want. Why it's here or if it'll leave."

Cassie grimaced, shooting a pleading glance at her mother.

"We'll have to think about this," Lily answered.

Wyatt shifted in his seat, the wooden chair creaking under his weight. "You can't do it now anyway."

"Why not?" Ruby asked.

Wyatt searched the air for a moment, his lower lip bobbing up and down. "Well, I'm here."

Ruby screwed up her face, her nose wrinkling in confusion. "So?"

"So, I don't want to be here! No way am I going to sit in a circle and summon a spirit. No way, no how. Uh-uh."

Ruby's eyebrows shot up and an amused grin crossed her face. "Wyatt, you big 'fraidy cat! I never knew you were scared of ghosts!"

"You bet I am! It creeps me out thinking there's a spirit roaming around in here, but to try to talk to it?" He drew his chin back as he straightened in his seat and shook his head, waving his hands in front of him. "No way. Hard pass."

Ruby lifted a shoulder in the air as Wyatt's phone rang. He held a finger up as he tugged it from the holder on his belt.

"Cooper," he said after swiping to accept the call. His face fell and his eyebrows scrunched. "Okay. Yeah. Yeah, I'll be right there."

He ended the call and snapped the phone back into its holster. "Well, sorry to cut this short, though it may be for the best." He shot Ruby a distrustful glance. "I need to get back to the station."

"Oh, sure. Hope everything's okay," Lily said.

"More or less. They found the murder weapon."

Cassie's eyebrows shot up and Lily straightened in her chair. "Oh, good! Maybe this whole thing will wrap up faster than you anticipated!"

"I sure hope so," Wyatt answered her. "Mind if I grab a churro for the road?"

"Go ahead," Lily answered as Wyatt snagged another from the to-go container and dunked it in the chocolate sauce.

"Well, sorry to cut this short, I'd love to talk more about your ghost, but I came with Wyatt."

Cassie shot a glance at her mother before focusing on Ruby. "Oh, well, we could take you home if you'd like to stay and chat longer."

The corners of Ruby's mouth turned down and she eased back into her chair. "If you don't mind, sure. I'm just going to go home to talk to my cat."

"Sure, no problem," Cassie said.

Lily pushed up from her seat. "I'll walk you out, Wyatt."

Wyatt followed her from the kitchen, palming his keys as he approached the door.

"Thanks for bringing Ruby over," Lily said, tugging the door open.

Wyatt flicked his gaze out to the darkening skies. "I'm sorry it wasn't better news."

Lily drummed her palms against her thighs as she sighed. "It's what we expected, I guess. Though I'm still not certain I can get on board with the whole ghost thing."

"How else can you explain the creepy doll moving upstairs?"

Lily shook her head, her eyes floating up to the floor above. "I don't know. I'm starting to wonder if this is another string of break-ins."

"You had the alarm set, right?"

Lily lifted her eyebrows for a moment and nodded. "Yeah, we did. So, theoretically, it should have gone off if someone came in."

"Motion cams would have been triggered by someone moving the doll."

Lily mulled over his statement, squashing her lips together. "Or by the doll moving on its own," she murmured.

Lily tugged her phone from her pocket and toggled it on.

Wyatt hovered over her shoulder, glancing down at her screen. "Checking the feed?"

"Yeah." Lily glanced over her shoulder before pulling up the video of the foyer. "I don't want Cassie to see this."

"She's pretty upset about it, huh?"

"She is. She hates watching scary movies because she can't sleep after. If she sees that doll floating through the halls on camera, she's going to lose it."

Lily tapped around on her phone, pulling up today's video from the on-screen list. "Here goes nothing," she said as she tapped the play button.

After a moment of fiddling, she sped the video to four times the normal speed. Hours ticked by from midnight on until a yawning Cassie sped down the stairs and raced to the kitchen. Moments later an equally sleepy-looking Lily sprinted down the stairs and through the front door, returning with the paper in hand.

The speeded-up versions of the ladies reappeared, heading upstairs in their pajamas. Cassie dashed down the stairs first and hovered on the edge of the camera's viewpoint.

"She must be looking at the doll," Lily said.

A moment later, Lily appeared, and they raced around the foyer before leaving. On-screen, nothing moved outside of the shifting shadows from the sun. The minutes ticked by on the timestamp.

"We came home around three, I think, so we should be close to something happening," Lily said, noting the 1:00 p.m. hour.

As the time stamp approached 1:39, the video feed skipped, turning fuzzy and distorted. The odd display continued until the camera snapped back to normal at 1:43.

"Whoa," Wyatt exclaimed. "What was that?"

A few moments later, Lily and Cassie burst through the

front door. Lily shook her head and paused the video. "Well, the doll's upstairs already, so it happened before this."

"Go back to the weird part where it's fuzzy and the feed is rolling."

Lily nodded as she dragged the slider backward until the timestamp read just before 1:39. She let the video play. After a second, it glitched, the feed turning fuzzy and rolling on the screen. They went back several more times.

Lily knit her brows, narrowing her eyes at a specific spot on the screen. "Did you see that?"

"What?" Wyatt asked.

"Up here, just at the edge of the view near the doorway leading to the living room."

Lily rewound it and let it play again. A flutter of fabric appeared in the doorway just as the camera went haywire. "Did you see it?"

"Yeah, looked like something was moving but then the camera cuts out."

Lily sighed as she clicked off her camera display "Well, outside of a possibly moving piece of something in the doorway, there's nothing definitive."

"No," Wyatt agreed, his hands on his hips. "But the glitchy camera in and of itself is suspect. That has to be when the doll moved."

"So, did someone mess with the feed and move the doll?"

"Or did the doll's ghostly movement interfere with the camera?"

Lily sucked in a breath as she considered admitting they may have a ghost roaming the halls of Whispering Manor. "I don't know, but either way, I'm not showing this to Cassie."

"I won't say anything either," Wyatt promised. "Especially not after the whole Kyle McGuire thing earlier. Gosh, I still feel really bad about that, Lily."

Lily patted his shoulder. "It's okay. She'll be okay."

"But?"

Lily hiked her eyebrows upward, surprised he'd read the unspoken words in her mind. "But she's understandably disturbed by the fact that her husband kept a secret that big from her. And she's determined to try to find the reason or some clue about this brother of his."

Wyatt shook his head and bit his lower lip. "I wouldn't do that. It's probably best if she just lets us handle this."

Lily shrugged her shoulders and flung her arms out as she leaned against the open front door. "I tried to tell her that, but she wants to find answers. I'm a little concerned about what this will do to her memory of Trevor but, then again, what will not knowing do."

"If I come across anything, I'll shoot you a text."

"Thanks, Wyatt, I appreciate that."

"Have a good night," he said, stepping onto the porch. He spun back to face her again. "Oh, and if you need anything, just call."

Lily offered him a tight-lipped smile and a nod as he spun back toward the setting sun and headed for his car. She waved as he pulled away and eased the door shut, leaning against it for a moment. What had the camera caught before it'd glitched? Was it tampered with? Or did a spirit haunt these halls?

And if it was the latter, what were they going to do about it?

CHAPTER 17

Cassie returned her gaze to the blonde sitting across the table from her as her mother and Wyatt shuffled from the room. The lightened tips of her pixie cut were tugged closely around her expertly made-up features.

She offered the woman a lopsided smile. "I really appreciate you coming out to do a walkthrough of the house, Ruby. And thanks for staying."

Ruby's red lips formed a warm smile. "No problem. Like I said, I'm only going home to my cat."

"If he's anything like our Willy, you'll be in for it if you're too late."

"He's a big, lazy lug. I'm not sure he'd drag himself off the couch to notice I'm missing," Ruby said with a chuckle.

Silence fell between them, and Cassie offered an awkward smile. She clasped and unclasped her hands a few times before she spoke again. "So, can you tell me more about this seance you suggested?"

"Oh, sure," Ruby said, her eyes lighting up at the prospect. "It's probably just what you'd imagine. We'd sit in a circle and try to make contact with the spirit world by concentrating, staying quiet, and letting the spirit come to us."

Cassie swallowed hard at the prospect. "My only experience with seances is from watching that old TV show, *Dark Shadows*. I think they had them regularly."

Ruby chuckled as her fingers toyed with the long beaded necklace she wore over her jean jacket. "It's usually a little less dramatic than the ones on TV."

"So, no passing out and speaking in another voice or anything like that?"

Ruby crinkled her nose and shook her head. "Nah. I've never seen anything like that happen. The craziest thing I've ever experienced was communicating through knocks."

"Knocks?"

"Yeah, you know," Ruby said, wrapping her knuckles against the table. "One knock for no, two for yes."

"Oh, right," Cassie said as realization dawned on her.

Lily rejoined them in the kitchen, plopping back into her seat.

"We were just talking about the seance Ruby suggested," Cassie informed her.

"Right," Lily said. "Do you imagine we'd find anything out that way?"

Ruby shrugged her shoulders, her earrings swinging wildly as she wagged her head back and forth. "Hard to say. Your ghost seems shy. But not shy enough that she hasn't been reaching out to you. So, you may get somewhere."

"And you could do it?" Lily inquired.

"I could, yes. I'm not sure we'd get much. You may want someone with a stronger sense or more experience, but if you'd like to just try quickly to see if there's anything you can learn, I'd be happy to serve as the medium."

Lily chewed the inside of her lower lip as she nodded. "How long would you need to prepare?"

"Nothing to prepare, really. I could do it right now if you'd like."

Cassie's eyes widened at the thought. As much as she wanted answers, she wasn't certain how she felt about speaking with a spirit. "Really, Mom?"

Lily shot her daughter a glance. "No time like the present. I don't see why we shouldn't try to get a few answers."

"Didn't you want to think about it?"

"Is there something holding you back?"

Cassie let her gaze fall to the table below, tracing the woodgrain with her fingertip. After a second, she shook her head. "Nothing outside of my own fear."

"Well, if it'll help us solve this or set your mind at ease, I say let's do it. I don't want to send poor Ruby home and then have her traipsing back out here in another day or so."

Cassie squashed her lips together and offered a tentative nod as her leg bobbed up and down under the table.

"I thought you wanted to try it!" Lily exclaimed.

"I do. I just would rather have no ghosts show up. Or a kindly spirit of a gentle librarian who just wants us to read more."

Ruby burst into laughter. "Well, I don't think your spirit is that unkindly. But I do think someone's trying to tell you something."

"Should we try for it here?" Lily asked, patting the tabletop.

Ruby narrowed her eyes and glanced around in thought. "Umm, what about in the library? You said you had an incident in there. And I felt something earlier. It may be an ideal spot to contact your ghost."

"Okay," Lily said with a nod.

They climbed from their seats to head to the room suggested by Ruby. "Oh, you may want to grab your creepy doll friend. If you think she's being used as a conduit. It may help us contact the spirit."

"All right. I'll get her," Cassie agreed. She darted up the stairs and approached the doll, still standing with its fingers grazing the wall. With a frown, she grabbed hold of its waist, wrapping her arm around the Victorian-style dress and tugging it upward. She lumbered down the steps with the doll in tow, finding her mother and Ruby rearranging the library's furniture to create a space for the seance. Lily lit a candle in the middle of the table.

"Should I place her anywhere specific?" Cassie inquired.

"Here, by the table," Ruby said, motioning toward an empty spot at the round table. Cassie stood the doll in the space and slipped into the chair next to her. Her eyes slid sideways in a suspicious glance as her mother doused the lights. Lit only by the flickering flame of candlelight, the doll gained a sinister countenance.

Cassie tore her eyes away from the spooky sight, directing her gaze to her mother, then Ruby. "What now?"

"Everyone put your hands on the table, with your fingers outstretched." Ruby demonstrated by placing both her hands with her fingers wide on the wooden tabletop.

Cassie and Lily both placed their hands in a similar fashion.

Ruby slid one hand toward Cassie, placing it in the middle of the table. "Now, we'll touch hands."

They shifted their hands around until their pinky fingers touched, creating a circle.

"It's important not to break the circle during the séance." Ruby flicked her gaze from mother to daughter. "Are we ready to begin?"

With nods responding to her query, she closed her eyes and sucked in a deep breath. Cassie glanced around the shadows of the room as Ruby called out to the spirits that may be roaming the house.

"We want to speak to you. We want to know why you're here. We want to help you."

The room fell into silence as they awaited some response. They received none. Cassie shifted her gaze to the doll standing at the table next to her. She half-expected it to begin speaking to them. With its arm still outstretched, she stood in eerie silence, her features frozen.

"Spirit that's in this house, can you hear us? If you can communicate to us in some way!" Ruby called, her eyes still squeezed closed.

The flame on the candle flickered. Cassie glanced to her mother, whose eyes scanned the darkened room for any sign of response.

Overhead, thunder rumbled. Lightning lit the darkening sky, illuminating the library. Cassie leapt in her seat, careful to keep her hands plastered on the table and not break the circle. Her eyes widened as another bolt of lightning tore through the sky and thunder rumbled.

Lily firmed her lower lip and offered her daughter a consoling glance and a nod, hoping to assuage her growing fear.

The winds kicked up and the whispering sound that the manor was named for blew through the house. Cassie strained for any sounds of a ghostly message but heard nothing beyond the wailing wind gusts.

Ruby continued her efforts to reach the elusive ghost. "Spirit, you've been using this doll to communicate. Can you use her again?"

Cassie swallowed hard and focused on the doll, her eyes rising to the porcelain face. The flickering candlelight cast harsh shadows across it, making her appear angry. Or perhaps she was angry. Had her expression changed, Cassie wondered?

"Spirit in this house," Ruby called again, "please reach out to us! We want to help."

A large gust of wind whipped past the house, rattling the windows in their frames. Cassie bit her lower lip, sucking in a frightened breath.

Lily pressed her lips together as she glanced around into the shadows, searching for any sign of spirits. "Come on! If you're really here, talk to us!"

On the heel of Lily's demand, thunder boomed overhead. Lightning shot through the sky again, illuminating the doll's face in an unearthly blue-white light. Cassie gulped as the wind whisked past the house again.

The old house groaned as a massive gust slammed against its side. The front door blew open, swinging on its creaky hinges and slamming into the table behind it.

Cassie jumped in her seat as the door wobbled on its hinges. Rain pelted the roof and windows. It pounded against the boards on the front porch.

Lily leapt from her chair and hurried toward the open door. In the darkness, she smacked into the moved coffee table, crying out in pain as she hopped around on one foot, a curse escaping her.

Wind blew through the open door, fluttered the curtains, and whipped their hair around. The Victorian doll's dress quavered before it began to wobble. After a second, it pitched forward, its outstretched fingers reaching out.

The doll twisted toward Cassie and, in slow motion, flopped forward. The plastic fingers raked through her hair as the other hand fell onto her shoulder. Cassie shrieked as the doll fell on top of her. She batted at it to push it away, but the doll clung to her.

"Get off me! Get off me!" she screamed. "Help!"

Ruby rushed around the table and tugged at the doll, but could not pull it back. Another gust of wind blew past them and with it a sound. The rambling whispers the manor was known for turned, in an instant, from unintelligible murmurs to one clear, breathy word: journals.

Cassie's eyes rolled back in her head and her muscles went limp. Her chin lolled to the side as her arms dangled from the chair. A final rumble of thunder rolled overhead, and the winds died down.

Ruby, still tugging at the doll's stiff form, freed it from Cassie's listless body, toppling backward onto her rear as the doll righted herself. Outside the rain ceased, turning into a light drizzle and the door slowly swung closed, its lock clicking quietly shut.

Lily gulped as the house returned to normal. "Quick, get the lights!"

Ruby scrambled to her feet and hurried to the opening of the foyer, flicking the switch and illuminating the space.

Lily hovered over Cassie's slack form, tapping her cheeks lightly. "Cassie! Cassie! Come on, honey, wake up."

"Is she okay?" Ruby asked, hurrying to Lily's side.

Cassie moaned, her head thrashing back and forth before she startled awake, flailing her arms at the two women in front of her.

Lily grabbed her daughter's thrashing arms. "Cass, Cassie, it's okay. It's us."

Cassie's wide eyes flicked between the two women, and she sucked in a few gasping breaths before the rapid rise and fall of her chest eased to slow, steady breaths. "Sorry," she whispered.

"It's okay. You passed out."

Cassie's lips formed a pouty frown, and she studied the blue patterned area rug underneath her. "That doll came right for me and wouldn't let go."

"I think the wind knocked her over, honey," Lily said.

Ruby glanced up at Lily before pressing her lips shut.

Cassie glanced around the room, her eyes focusing on the door beyond it. After a moment, she shook her head. "No. It grabbed me and said journals."

"Well, with the front door blowing open, I think–"

Ruby nudged her glasses higher on her face, then shoved her hands into her back pockets. "I heard it, too." She gave Cassie a comforting nod.

"Yes, I thought I heard a voice, too, but that's why the house is called Whispering Manor. Because it sounds like voices whispering in the wind."

"I didn't *think* I heard it, Mom, I heard it."

"And that doll had a good grip on her," Ruby added. "I couldn't pull it away."

"I think her fingers may have gotten caught in your hair which is probably why." Lily crossed the room and retrieved a few strands of Cassie's hair from the doll's plastic fingers.

Cassie pressed her lips together in a frustrated line. "I just find it odd that during a seance, the door bursts open, the doll grabs hold of me, and someone whispers 'journals.' This cannot be a coincidence."

Lily crossed her arms and sighed. "Maybe not, but it's hardly proof. If the spirit was here, why didn't it answer Ruby?"

"Maybe it did," Ruby said. "Or maybe it answered you when you demanded it answer."

Cassie shot her mother a glance. "You were rather demanding. Maybe that's what caused the door to fly open and the doll to grab me."

Lily offered her companions an unimpressed stare. "The door blew open because a violent storm was raging outside. The doll toppled because of the gust of air blowing around in here. And we probably thought we heard the word journals because that's what we expected to hear given the previous incidents."

Silence fell between them as they all considered the explanation and the odd events that prompted it.

Lily threw her arms out and slapped her sides. "Either way, I don't think we're getting any more answers tonight."

"Probably not," Cassie said. She flicked her gaze to Ruby. "I guess I should take you home."

"Uh, maybe I should drive her home. You just passed out. I'm not sure you should be driving."

"Okay," Cassie agreed. She climbed from her seat and headed for the front door.

"Where are you going? I can take her," Lily said, confusion crossing her features.

Cassie wrinkled her forehead. "I'm not staying here alone after that!"

Lily set her mouth in a mock unimpressed display. "Okay, come on, 'fraidy cat." She grabbed her keys and they headed for her car.

"Sorry, I couldn't get you any more information, ladies," Ruby said as they made the short trip from Whispering Manor to her townhouse.

"Thank you for trying, Ruby," Cassie said from the backseat.

Ruby slid her seatbelt off as Lily eased the car to a stop in the driveway. "No problem. If you'd like to try again in a few days, we can. Maybe we'll pick a day with better weather."

Cassie climbed from the car, switching seats from the back to the front as Ruby stepped toward her front door. "Okay, we'll see how things go after tonight and let you know."

They waited for Ruby to unlock and enter her front door, giving them a wave. Cassie blew out a long breath as Lily backed the car from Ruby's driveway.

She let her head fall back against the headrest. "What a night."

Lily glanced both ways before pulling onto the small street on the edge of town. "Wanna talk about it? Privately?"

Cassie swung her head toward her mother. "You mean, really get it all out without Ruby present?"

"Yeah, that's what I mean."

Cassie glanced out the window, letting out a long breath that fogged the glass as she watched the cute townhouses roll past. "I don't know."

Lily flicked her gaze to her daughter before focusing on the road ahead, swerving the wheel to avoid a huge puddle. "All right, I won't push."

Cassie sank her chin into her palm, puckering her lips before she cocked her head to glance at her mother. "But you'd prefer we discuss it."

"Well, yeah. You passed out, Cassie. Clearly, you were terrified, and I'd like to at least talk about it."

Cassie tossed her hands in the air as they pulled onto Ocean Drive. "I don't know what to think anymore. Maybe you're right and I just think I heard the word journals, but it sure sounded like journals. The whole thing could have been a series of odd chance happenings, or it could have been a spirit trying to tell us something. It's so frustrating!"

"Yes, it could have been. Though the doll moving wasn't." Lily fell silent for a moment, clicking on her turn signal and swinging the car into their driveway. They bounced down the gravel drive, the tires crunching the limestone. She threw the shifter into park and tugged on her emergency brake.

Instead of opening her door after releasing her seat belt, she twisted to face Cassie, putting her hand on Cassie's arm and squeezing. "Cassie, Wyatt and I reviewed the security footage from the house."

Cassie's eyes grew wide, and she squashed her eyebrows

together, her fingers lingering on the door handle. "And? Did you see something?"

Lily shook her head with a rueful glance at the house. "The video glitched for a few minutes. I'm assuming that's when the doll moved. So, there's no way to tell if someone moved the doll or the doll moved itself."

Cassie's shoulders slumped and she let her head thud against the window. "Another dead end."

"I'm afraid so. I wasn't going to tell you, but I thought you should know."

Cassie shoved her door open, and the damp night air rushed inside. "It doesn't really change anything. No new information."

Lily squeezed her arm again in a silent display of support.

"Come on, let's head in. I really want to be in my pajamas."

Cassie slid from the SUV's seat to the gravel below and slogged toward the house.

Lily climbed the stairs ahead of her, turning off their alarm and sliding her key into the lock. The door creaked open, and she motioned for Cassie to precede her.

Cassie shambled through the door, stopping dead just as she passed over the threshold. "Ugh."

"What is it?" Lily questioned, squeezing into the foyer behind her. "Oh."

Cassie sighed and shook her head as Lily winced. Both of them stared at the same object. In the middle of the foyer stood the Victorian doll.

Cassie eyed the doll standing in the middle of the entryway. "This is really getting old."

"Well, there is good news," Lily answered.

Cassie's eyes shot wide as she twisted her neck to gape at her mother, her jaw hanging wide.

Lily shrugged and motioned to the doll. "I'm not sure we can keep chalking this up to chance."

"I would say there are way too many coincidences for that anymore."

"Looks like we may need to have Ruby back in soon. We need to find some answers."

Cassie narrowed her eyes at the doll's porcelain face. "What are you trying to tell us?"

Without warning, the doll lurched forward, its outstretched arms reaching toward Cassie. Cassie's jaw dropped and her eyes widened as her heart pounded against her ribs. "Ahhhhh!" she screamed as she scrambled backward, falling out the door and hitting the porch's wooden floorboards with a thud.

Lily reacted to the falling doll, reaching out and grabbing

it before it could latch on to Cassie. As the doll swooned into her arms, she glanced behind it, an amused expression playing on her features.

The smile on her face broadened and she started to giggle. The giggle turned into a full-blown belly laugh as she stood the doll up again.

The panicked expression still covering Cassie's features turned to annoyance. Her eyebrows knit, and she frowned at her mother. "What's so funny? She almost attacked me again."

"Sure she did," Lily choked out between giggles. She crooked a finger and pointed at something behind the doll.

Cassie craned her neck to glance behind the doll's blue dress. A one-eyed tuxedo cat sashayed from behind it, his tail flicking in the air. After a moment, he spun and paraded back in the opposite direction. The doll pitched forward again as he brushed against it.

"Haunted by my own cat," Cassie groaned as she picked herself up off the porch and dusted off her pants.

Lily covered her mouth as she attempted to reign in her chuckling. "At least this one has a solution."

"That's one incident solved at least."

Lily wrapped an arm around Cassie's shoulders as she swung the door shut. "Come on, let's get into our jammies, and then I'll make you a hot chocolate for your nerves."

They strode to the stairs leading up as Cassie pressed a palm to her cheek. "A hot chocolate for my nerves? What have I become?"

They mounted the stairs in unison and Lily squeezed Cassie's shoulder. "A Victorian lady with a delicate disposition."

"Maybe Henrietta is floating around in my head, giving me the vapors."

"I doubt that."

"Really?" Cassie said as they reached the top of the steps.

"If Henrietta was in your head, you'd be demanding a hot chocolate and stamping your feet if you didn't get it. She was a real handful, remember?"

"Hey, speaking of, maybe she's trying to tell us to read her journal. Maybe she wants us to discover the reason she died."

Lily puckered her lips, her eyes falling to the floorboards below her feet as she raised her eyebrows. "That's not a half-bad theory, Cass. Maybe you're on to something."

"Perhaps you should try reading it tonight."

Lily scrunched her nose at the thought. "Alone? In my bedroom with a ghost running around the house? Pass. We'll read it together while we drink the hot chocolate."

Cassie lifted a shoulder to her ear, her lips forming a grimace. "Too risky. You may spill hot chocolate on it."

"I'll be careful," Lily promised with a roll of her eyes. "Meet you downstairs in ten."

Cassie puckered her lips at the lost battle as she spun toward her room, but continued without complaint, entering her room and tugging off her sweater. Her mind raced through the details of the past few hours.

Their seance had been eventful, but had it been helpful? Had she really heard the word journals? Maybe reading Henrietta's journal and determining the reason she'd killed herself would suffice. Perhaps the ghost wanted people to know her reasoning.

Cassie tugged the plaid long-sleeve t-shirt of her pajamas over her head as she strode to the bathroom. With the cloth covering her eyes, her foot smacked into something. She struggled to stay upright as she freed herself from the shirt.

She glanced down at what she'd kicked. Her heart sank as she studied the cardboard box. Her handwriting in black sharpie read "Trevor's Personal Effects." She swallowed hard as she considered the prospect of going through it.

She wasn't certain which she hated more: reading Henrietta's journal or searching Trevor's things. With a sigh, she figured she could put off searching through the box. She slid on her matching plaid bottoms, shoved her feet into her fluffy moccasin-style slippers, wrapped up in her robe, and headed out of her bedroom.

She met her mother downstairs. Lily stood over the stove, stirring the chocolate-y milk as steam rose from it.

Cassie swung open a cupboard and grabbed a package of cookies. "Did you bring the journal?"

Lily patted her robe pocket. "Got it right here."

"Darn. I was hoping you forgot it."

"No chance."

"Hey, since this is a group effort with Henrietta's journal, can I interest you in a team exercise searching through Trevor's things?"

Lily poured the steaming milk into two mugs, sprayed whipped cream on top, and stuck a pirouette cookie in each. "You know I'll help you."

Cassie offered her mother a tight-lipped smile before they shuffled to the living room and settled on the couch.

Lily took a sip of her hot chocolate, then slid the mug onto her side table. She pulled the journal from her pocket, running her fingers over the worn, brown leather. She licked her lips as she studied it before flicking a gaze at Cassie.

With a wiggle of her eyebrows, she said, "Here we go."

Cassie leaned over her mother's shoulder as she wrapped both hands around her warm mug. Henrietta's stylized handwriting filled the pages.

"Okay, she's just installed the locking mechanism on the bookcase. Let's see what happens next. Oh, by the way," Lily said, as she slid her reading glasses onto the bridge of her nose, "she's not despondent over her husband at all. It's all an act."

. . .

I have ridden on a pirate ship! As I pen these words in the ever-growing morning light, my heart still beats with excitement.

Clifton arrived in the dead of night on his ship, Neptune's Servant. Black sails billowed in the wind as he weighed anchor offshore from Whispering Manor. I awaited him on the beach. He stood in one of the skiffs as his men rowed ashore, their boat laden with treasure.

As he leapt from the wooden conveyance, his tall boots splashing in the water, I studied him. A sword swung from his hips and a tricorn hat perched on his head. A pistol tucked into his belt completed the ensemble.

He grinned at me, offering a greeting.

"I have never seen you in your pirate regalia," I told him.

He gave me a playful bow before motioning toward the ship floating in the waters on the horizon. "I've flown the Jolly Roger for you."

"I noticed."

"And have I struck fear into your heart?" he asked as I perused the trunks being unloaded from the skiff.

With a scoff, I answered, "I am trembling. Though more from the chill in the air than your Jolly Roger."

He smacked his chest with his hand. "A dagger to my heart. There are men who shrink with fear when Neptune's Servant overtakes them."

I arched an eyebrow at him. "I am not so faint of heart."

More boats arrived and Clif's crew busily unloaded the chests before returning to the ship for more. My mind still marvels at the number of items unloaded. Some chests were too large to be slipped through the opening and had to be unloaded piece by piece.

What I assumed to be a jest about sinking his ship proved to be fact. I am surprised Neptune's Servant isn't on the bottom of the ocean with the bounty she carried.

Within the treasure, I found a ruby necklace I quite fancied. When I inquired to Clif about keeping it, he reminded me that I need not ask. Apparently, his offer to share the treasure equally was not in word only, but in deed, as well. I pocketed the lovely item and, even now, it sits on my desk so I may admire it as I pen this entry.

After unloading, Clif convinced me to sail into Hideaway Bay's port aboard his ship. With the Jolly Roger snapping in the wind, we slipped into the dock still under the cover of night.

What a thrilling experience. I wonder if Clif may, at some point, allow me to sail with him on his adventures.

After ogling our fortune again and passing the passcode off to Clif, we discussed our problematic friend, and the reason Clif moved the treasure. Redbeard, Clif's pirate nemesis, has not been in contact, though Clif assured me he continues to search for the treasure.

I worried he may suspect Hideaway Bay as the chosen hiding spot. Clif cleverly picked up on my apprehension, swearing to protect me. To that end, he has promised to leave me with a pistol and train me to use it.

I have felt the weight of it in my hands already earlier. I must say, it is heavier than I imagined, though I felt quite secure holding it. As I practiced my aim, I found myself pondering if I could take a man's life if needed.

I decided the answer is yes. If Clif manages, so, too, shall I.

"Wow," Cassie breathed before taking another sip of her hot chocolate. "What a different life she led."

Lily tugged her glasses from her face and laid them on top of the open journal in her lap. "I told you. It's fascinating to read this. Not only in terms of seeing how a woman lived when they had little rights, but just experiencing through her eyes the crazy adventure of having a pirate for a brother."

"She doesn't seem at all suicidal. In fact, she seems happy, if you could call it that."

"Content, I'd say. She seems like she's finding her path in life."

"And excited to explore the new avenue."

Lily nodded, flicking her eyebrows up. "I can't understand what makes her fling herself from the widow's walk."

"Let's read a little more," Cassie suggested.

An amused smile crossed Lily's lips as she slid her glasses back on. "Read more, huh?"

Cassie shrugged, lifting her mug to her lips. "Okay, okay, it's interesting. You were right." With a roll of her eyes at her mother's amused grin, Cassie leaned over Lily's shoulder to read the next entry.

* * *

A crash startled Lily awake. She leapt, flailing her arms as she attempted to orient herself. She swallowed hard, peeling off her glasses. She sat in the living room. A lone lamp next to her lit the space. Cassie, long since asleep, dozed next to her with Willy curled in the crook of her legs.

They must have fallen asleep while reading Henrietta's journal. Lily winced, rubbing at the crick in her neck as picked the journal up off the area rug near her feet. It must have toppled off her lap and awakened her when it thudded against the thick rug.

She slid her eyes sideways, wondering if she should wake Cassie or leave her to ride the night out on the couch. As she considered the question, she glanced across the room. The sight made her swallow hard.

Her muscles stiffened and her posture went stick-straight. The Victorian doll stood in the doorway to the foyer.

Lily narrowed her eyes at the animatron. "Hello, Ri."

The doll remained silent, staring at them with an outstretched arm.

"I'm starting to think you really are possessed."

"Hmm?" Cassie murmured, fidgeting in her sleep. After a moment, her eyes fluttered open, and she sucked in a breath. With droopy eyelids, she pushed herself up. "Did you say something?"

A chuckle escaped Lily's lips as she eyed Cassie's hair, sticking out at odd angles from her nap on the couch.

"Yes, I did. We must have fallen asleep reading the journal."

Cassie stretched and yawned. "Yeah. And still nothing on why she killed herself. She's only talked about Clif's adventures and their trouble with that Redbeard guy. She didn't even–"

Cassie's voice ceased as she spotted the doll at the door. "Oh, you're kidding. You again?"

"And it wasn't your cat this time." Lily poked a finger toward a sleeping Willy.

Cassie grimaced at the doll. "Maybe she wants us to keep reading."

Lily stifled another yawn. "I'm not sure I'm going to make it."

"Me either," Cassie answered with a stretch. She shot a glance at the doll. "Sorry, Ri, we need a little rest."

"I tried talking to her before. She just stands there like a dummy."

Cassie wrinkled her nose and shot her mother a dubious glance. "Well, she is a doll."

"A haunted one," Lily said, pushing off the cushions to stand and stretching her arms overhead.

"Don't get me started before I try to go back to sleep. I'll never sleep if I'm afraid she's going to fly up the stairs and holler at me again."

Lily chuckled as she crossed the room and shoved the doll from the doorway into the corner. "Come on, let's get some sleep."

They climbed upstairs, going in opposite directions to reach their respective rooms. Lily tossed her robe across the foot of the bed and crawled under the covers. With a satisfied sigh, she stretched out and let the mattress mold to her.

Her mind flitted to the journal she'd placed on her nightstand moments ago. She flicked her gaze to it before returning to stare at the ceiling.

With a grimace, she gave the brown journal another look. Its worn surface reflected the dim moonlight coming through her ocean-facing window.

She shook her head and rolled onto her side, facing away from the small book. "Cassie'll kill me if I read ahead," she murmured.

She squeezed her eyes shut in the hopes of falling asleep.

After a moment, her eyes popped open. She sighed and tugged the covers closer to her. Wind gusted past her window, sounding like the whispering voices for which the house was named.

She stared out the window at the trees limned in moonlight. Their branches didn't move. The whispering wind failed to rustle even one of the few remaining, colored leaves clinging to the branches.

Lily furrowed her brow, propping herself up on an elbow for a better look. The whispering sounded again. Not a twig moved on the tree.

"How is it windy but the trees aren't moving?" Lily questioned aloud.

The whispering noise became clearer, sounding like a woman's voice. "Lilllllly," the lilting voice called to her.

Lily's eyes went wide, and she glanced over her shoulder at her closed bedroom door.

The voice called again. Lily's heart beat faster and she sat up, scanning the room to find the source. The voice seemed to come from everywhere and nowhere at the same time.

"Lilllllllllyyyyyy," the whisper called again.

"What?" Lily answered. "Wh-wh-what do you want?"

"The journals, Lily."

Lily swallowed hard, blood rushing into her ears as her pulse pounded. She flicked her eyes to the brown leather on the night table.

"I'll read it. I promise," she called.

A thud sounded at her bedroom door and Lily issued a startled cry. Her breathing turned ragged, and she stared at the wooden barrier, hoping it kept out whatever spirit sought her in the dead of the night.

Another pound against the door. The articles of clothing hanging on the back shimmied as the door rattled in the jamb. Lily's chest rose and fell in rapid succession.

"Go away!" she yelled.

The thudding quieted and her breathing slowed though her gaze remained fixed on the door. Just as her heart settled to a normal rhythm, it ratcheted back up as the crystal door-knob handle twisted and turned.

Lily gulped as a high-pitched squeal of the old mechanism filled the air. She flung the covers back and raced to her door, spinning the key that sat in the lock. With trembling hands, she shoved a lock of hair from her face as she inched backward, her eyes trained on the door.

The knob stopped spinning. A shadow moved in the pale light that flooded from under the door. The dark spot disappeared after a moment. *Had the spirit left*, Lily wondered?

She eyed the door suspiciously, afraid to unlock it and peek into the hall. She took an unsteady step forward, determined to investigate when she stopped. Her brows knit together, and she stared incredulously at the bottom of the door.

White smoke poured in from under it. Lily sucked in a sharp breath and hurried toward the door. She unlocked it and flung it open, expecting to find a hallway full of smoke or a fire raging.

Only quiet darkness met her gaze. With her heart pounding hard, she sucked in a few breaths, her eyes scanning the hall and peering over the railing to the floor below.

Finding nothing, she eased the door shut and spun to return to her bed. Once again, she stopped dead in her tracks. A wisp of white smoke hovered in front of her. An echoing whisper filled the room. "Journals."

Lily licked her lips as the white smoke wafted in the air. "I'll read it. I promise."

The foggy form shifted shape, becoming more human-like. Lily's eyes bulged as she stared at the ghostly figure. It floated across the room and hovered over her night table. The journal flicked open. Pages fluttered by one after another until the book lay two-thirds of the way open.

The smoky wisp darted back across the room. Lily began to move as though shoved from behind. She gasped in breaths as her feet skidded across the floor. She stretched her arms out in front of her in a desperate attempt to stop her forward progression. It did little good.

She continued her forced flight forward until she crashed into the nightstand. The impact bent her at the hip, and she stared down at the open journal, lit only by moonlight.

Three words were scrawled across the page. *Time for death.*

CHAPTER 19

Cassie left her mother behind at the top of the stairs and shuffled down the hall to her bedroom. With another wide yawn, she stretched and tugged the covers back, setting her knee on the bed, ready to climb between the sheets for the night.

A creaking noise drew her attention to her door. Her heart thudded as she whipped around, expecting to find the Victorian doll standing there.

Instead, a tuxedo cat squeezed through the thin opening and sashayed his way across the room in the moonlight. He leapt onto the bed and curled on his plaid blanket.

With an amused chuckle, Cassie padded back to the door and pushed it closed, latching it this time. She hurried across the room and climbed into bed, pulling the covers over her as she snuggled down into the mattress.

Next to her, the one-eyed cat purred as she settled in next to him. With a deep sigh, she closed her eyes.

Within minutes, they popped open again. She stared at the moonlit ceiling, trying to force her mind away from the details of the ghostly doll's appearance in the living room.

She rolled onto her side and considered sneaking into her mother's room to retrieve the journal and finish reading it.

She sighed and murmured, "Better not. Mom'll kill me if I read it without her."

Glints of moonlight shone through her side window, casting long shadows across the room. One shard of light shone on the box she'd retrieved from storage. Lit like a beacon, she fixed her gaze on the cardboard container. A frown formed on her lips.

She'd have to go through the items. Though she could put the task off until they finished the journal. Appeasing a disturbed spirit was more important, right?

Cassie assured herself it was as she rolled in the opposite direction. She stared out at the moonlit sky as her hand absentmindedly stroked Willy's soft fur. His purring grew louder but he did not stir, one white paw wrapped around his head to cover his eye.

Cassie let her eyes slide shut, but after a moment she fluttered them open again. It was no use. She'd never sleep. The odd encounter with the doll rattled around in her brain, making her uneasy every time she closed her eyes.

With a sigh, she flopped onto her back for a few moments before rising and stalking to the carousel on her dresser. Her fingers found the winding key in the dark and turned it until the little musical device sprang to life. Lights lit and the horses bobbed up and down in a circle. Music floated through the air.

Cassie shambled back to her bed and propped a few pillows up on the headboard. She slid under the covers and leaned back into the pillow wall. She let her head sink back onto the padded headboard as weariness overcame her. Though she was still too restless to sleep, exhaustion coursed through her.

She focused her attention on the dancing carousel across

the room as it spun. The lights blinked on and off once. Cassie cocked her head at the device. It continued to spiral around playing its jaunty music. A glitch, she assumed. Until it happened again.

The lights blinked on and off twice and the music slowed. Cassie's shoulders slumped forward as she wondered what could be wrong with the item. Perhaps the mechanisms were wearing out. She could look at the gears tomorrow.

Her thoughts were interrupted by the whispering wind outside the window. Indistinct voices floated on the breeze. She slid further down, clutching at the duvet and tugging it up over her. With a ghost on the loose, the whispering winds unsettled her more than she already was.

The wind whipped again, spreading the hushed tones of whispers through her room. Cassie's brow furrowed as the whisper sounded more realistic rather than vague.

A woman's voice stood out to her. "Cassssssie," the voice called.

Cassie's eyes widened and her pulse sped up as the voice spoke her name again. She gulped, reaching for her phone and snatching it from the charger. Too afraid to move from her bed, she swiped into her phone app, intent on calling her mother.

The phone nearly flew out of her hands when it started to ring. Her heart thudded against her ribs as she checked the display. It read RESTRICTED.

Cassie flicked a finger across the screen, sending the call to voicemail and fiddling with the touchscreen to return to her contact list. Before she could scroll to her mother's entry, the phone rang again. The RESTRICTED display returned to the screen.

Cassie frowned at it as she swiped to dismiss the call for a second time. Her annoyance grew as she wondered who was calling in the middle of the night.

Cassie tried again to reach her mother. She swiped through her contact list and pressed the green phone icon as quickly as she could. The screen turned black as the call connected. Cassie pressed the phone to her ear and waited.

No trilling filled the air, and she pulled the phone away to check the connection. The phone showed MOM on the display and a connected call. With a wrinkled forehead, Cassie lifted the phone to her ear again.

"Hello?" she inquired.

"Cassie," a raspy voice answered.

"Mom?"

"Cassie," the voice said again.

Cassie's eyes widened as the woman's voice called her name again. It was not her mother's voice.

"Wh-wh-who is this?" Cassie stammered.

"The journals," the voice whispered.

Cassie gripped the phone with white knuckles. "Henrietta?"

The breathy voice repeated its original request. "The journals."

"Okay. I'll read it. But I fell asleep. I'll read it tomorrow."

A click sounded as the call disconnected. Cassie pulled the phone from her ear and stared down at it, swallowing hard. With trembling fingers, she attempted to access her text app, hoping to send a message to her mother since a call seemed problematic.

The message thread with her mom appeared on the screen and Cassie tried to type, but no letters appeared. A bubble containing three dots popped up, indicating her mother was typing a message.

A new text appeared on her screen moments later. It read *Time for death.*

* * *

Lily thrashed her arms wildly, clawing at the air as she shot up to sit. Her heart pounded against her ribs, and she gasped for breath. After a moment, she scanned the room. She sat in her bed. Next to her, the journal lay on her nightstand, still closed. Across the room, her door remained shut. No wisps of smoke or ghostly figures prowled in any corners and no hint of whispering voices filled the air.

Lily sucked in a breath, attempting to steady her racing pulse and pounding heart. She must have fallen asleep and dreamt the entire thing with her ghostly visitor. She flopped back in her bed as she started to calm down.

They really needed to finish reading this journal, she thought, before their lives were consumed with thoughts of Henrietta Nichols Blanchard.

Lily adjusted the covers around her, hoping she could fall asleep again when a shriek tore through the night air. She shot upright again, throwing the covers off and pulling on her robe as she stood.

In bare feet, she ran to her door and flung it open. Her eyes darted around the darkened space, searching for the source of the scream.

"Cassie!" she called into the darkness. Lily tugged her robe around her, tying it shut as her bare feet slapped against the hardwood. She hurried toward Cassie's room, rounding the railing and focusing on Cassie's closed door.

"Cassie!" she called again.

The door whipped open before she reached it. A pale Cassie stuck her head into the hall. "Mom!"

"Cassie! Are you alright? I heard a scream."

"Yeah, I'm okay. I had a nightmare."

Lily breathed out a sigh of relief, pressing a hand to her chest. "I thought something happened."

"Something did. I had a nightmare."

"So did I," Lily confessed. "I woke up just before I heard you shout."

"Sorry, mine was disturbing. What was yours about?"

Lily grabbed her daughter's hand and pulled her down the hall. "Come on, I could use a warm cup of tea."

Cassie followed her, pausing at the top of the stairs as her mother let go of her hand and darted into her bedroom. She returned waving Henrietta's journal in the air and with slippers on her feet. "We may want this."

They descended the stairs, finding the doll awaiting them at the bottom. Cassie frowned at the woman. "She's persistent, I'll give her that."

"Tea first, Ri," Lily said, bypassing her and waving a hand in the air. "I need it after what you pulled."

Cassie's eyebrows arched as she followed her mother to the kitchen. "What Henrietta pulled? Was your dream about Henrietta?"

"It was," Lily answered, tossing the journal on the table and bustling around the kitchen to ready two mugs of English tea.

Cassie froze while tearing open a red packet containing a teabag. Her jaw dropped open and she snapped her eyes to her mother who filled their electric teakettle. "Mine too!"

Lily flicked the switch and set the kettle to heating, spinning to lean against the counter. "You want to go first?"

"Okay. I couldn't sleep, but I must have at some point. I dreamt that I woke up in my room. I wound the carousel but it glitched and stopped playing. Then the whispering winds started, but instead of being indistinct, I heard a voice. It called my name. I grabbed my phone to call you, but I got another call. It said restricted. I couldn't get a call out to you. When I thought I'd managed to do it, someone else answered. The voice said, 'the journals.' After they hung up on me, I tried to text you, but I got a message from you that said, 'time for death.'"

Cassie puckered her lips as she finished and stared at her mother. "Your turn."

The kettled clicked off, and Lily poured the steaming liquid into their mugs as she spoke. "Mine was similar. I woke up in my room. I heard the whispering winds. They called my name. Then someone pounded on my door and tried to get in. Then a bunch of smoke came underneath. I thought there was a fire but when I opened the door there was nothing. When I turned around, there was a ghost or something in front of me. The journal on my nightstand opened and something pushed me toward it. When I got to the journal, three words were written on the page. Time for death."

Cassie sucked in a breath. "This can't be a coincidence."

"Well, it could be," Lily countered. "I told you the story about me looking for that in the journal after seeing it the time we both got locked in."

"But it's not in the journal. And how strange is it that we both had a dream insisting we read the journal? And we both got 'time for death' messages?"

Lily dunked the teabags for a moment before removing them and sipping at the hot liquid after blowing on it.

"We both were reading the journal, maybe our minds are stuck on that and the time for death thing."

"Both at the same time?"

Lily shrugged as she grabbed the journal on her way out of the kitchen. "It's a stretch."

Cassie trailed behind her, sipping the hot tea. "No kidding. That many similarities in the dream makes this less likely a coincidence and more likely..." She paused as she rounded the corner and stared at the doll standing at the foot of the stairs. She poked a finger at it. "Well, and more likely her."

With her free arm, Cassie lifted the doll up and carried it into the living room, setting it down by the couch before she plopped onto it.

"There's one thing I don't understand though," Lily said.

Cassie eyed the ghost-like animatron. "Why she won't just tell us what she wants us to know instead of making us read her journal?"

"No," Lily said with a shake of her head, "you said she told you 'the journals.' She said that to me, too."

"So? She obviously wants us to finish that journal."

Lily waved the journal in the air again. "Why say journals, plural? This is a journal, singular."

"Maybe she did say journal. Maybe we heard wrong, or I recounted it incorrectly."

Lily shook her head as she sipped her tea again. "No. You said journals, not journal. And she said that in my dream, too. I assumed she meant this journal. But now that you said it plural, I recall her saying that too."

Cassie bit her lower lip as she considered it. With a shrug, she answered, "I'm not sure, but I think we need to finish that journal ASAP before either of us loses any more sleep."

"I almost read it when I couldn't sleep, but I thought you'd be mad at me."

Cassie shot her mother an amused glance, the corners of her lips turning upward. "I almost snuck into your room and stole it to read, but I thought you'd be mad."

"Gosh, if one of us would have just said something, maybe we could have avoided our terrifying nightmare."

Cassie flicked her gaze to the Victorian doll. "Well, Ri, will you let us off the hook if we read this?"

The doll stood silent next to her.

"It can't hurt," Lily answered. "And I'd like to know what happened to her even if she isn't haunting us."

"Let's find out," Cassie said, leaning over her mother's shoulder to read the yellowed pages.

Trouble is afoot. Clif has managed to keep the trouble at bay until now. However, as I delivered letters to the post office this morning, a man approached. He introduced himself as Ronan O' Rourke, though his flaming red curls and pointed red beard gave him away immediately to me. The man is the dreaded Redbeard and Clif's nemesis.

He offered his condolences. I, of course, maintained my act as the ever-hopeful wife, telling him my husband was not dead. He attempted to invite himself for tea, but I side-stepped by telling him my afternoon was too full.

I returned home, pondering the ways I could contact Clif and intent on retrieving the pistol he'd left me to protect myself until he arrived. I climbed to my bedroom where I found Clif lurking in the shadows. After I scolded him for startling me, we both blurted out that we have a problem.

Clif asked for my troubling news first. I informed him his pirate brother seemed to have made his way to Hideaway Bay. The report that the man had approached me and even attempted to invite himself to my home angered Clif and he confessed that his problem was the same as mine. He'd heard rumors that Redbeard traveled north and feared he may appear here.

Clif expects trouble to follow and suggested that the man must be removed before any harm comes to me. I appreciated the senti-ment, though I, myself, am quite capable to assist in this respect. I lamented my refusal of his tea request. One dash of poison and we could have been rid of the dastardly man.

Clif would not hear of it. "I handle my own problems, Ri," he told me.

Of course, I balked. "Are we not partners?" I inquired.

"I will not allow my sister to do my dirty work. Besides, it takes the fun out of it, really."

"Fun?" I asked.

"Yes, I shall quite enjoy sinking his ship." He offered me a coy glance when I raised my eyebrows at his response. "It can be quite fun blowing holes into things."

We discussed a plan to lure him to a location where Clif could ensure a victory over him. Our plot involves a fictitious bounty of gemstones arriving via a specific route. The supposed path will allow Clif's ship to lie in wait and overtake Redbeard's vessel.

I do not feel entirely comfortable with the plan, particularly since Clif skimped on the details, claiming it to be his affair. I held back rolling my eyes and allowed him to proceed. He promised to return within a month. I threatened if he did not, I should seek him out and kill him a second time.

He promised victory, flashing me a salute and a grin as he disappeared through my door. As I write, I solidify the memory of his smiling face in my mind as I worry it may be the last image of him I ever see.

"Wow," Cassie breathed, gripping her mug with both hands as she raised it to her lips.

Lily raised her eyebrows as she stared down at the journal. "Reading this, I'd really think her brother's death was what caused her suicide. If you hadn't told me she died before him, I'd have guessed this Redbeard character killed him."

"But we know he doesn't. At least not until after Henrietta throws herself from the balcony."

Both women glanced at the doll, still a silent sentinel next to them.

"Let's press on," Lily said.

Clif has returned to me safe. And he has brought fantastic news. Redbeard will trouble us no further! He has succeeded in removing the man from this earth. He shared with me the details of his rousing battle, and the subsequent sinking of the Scourge of the Seas.

The battle seemed quite epic, and I recorded the details below. They should make a nice addition to my writing!

I wonder if I should, one day, have the rush of sailing the seven seas and engaging in a daring battle! I should think not, though, one never knows what life may hold.

Lily and Cassie scanned over the details of the exciting pirate battle as told by Clifton Nichols to his sister, Henrietta.

"Wow, sounds like a humdinger of a battle," Lily said as they finished the entry.

Cassie sipped at the last of her tea. "No kidding. I can't even imagine this going on. Cannons firing from ship to ship and men swinging across to the other deck."

"It sounds like a movie."

"Yeah, it really does. I wonder how much he embellished and how much was true."

"We may never know."

Cassie slid her empty mug onto the side table. "Well, what we do know is he lived. And Henrietta has no reason, so far, to be despondent enough to throw herself off the widow's walk."

Lily scanned the remaining pages with writing scrawled across them. "Two more entries."

Cassie flicked her eyebrows up. "Let's get to the bottom of this."

Lily nodded and held the journal between them to read the second to last entry.

Clif returned without warning today. When he does that, there is usually a problem. And this is no exception. Redbeard, his cursed enemy, is dead. We thought ourselves rid of the trouble. But a new, more deadly trouble has reared its ugly, red-haired head.

Redbeard's son has threatened Clif. While I thought the threat to be containable, Clif assures me we must take it more seriously than even Redbeard's threats.

Beyond the threat outstanding against my brother, the contemptible man has threatened both me and Carolina. While I can understand his hatred toward me, I cannot understand nor tolerate the threat to my sister.

There is certainly no love lost between Carolina and me, however, I do not wish to see her life snuffed out because of our war with another pirate.

Clif and I have spoken at length on the matter, and I proposed a solution. I do not believe giving the man the treasure he demanded will suffice. Clif agrees. He believes the man's threats to be revenge motivated. The only solution then is to kill him or allow him to kill us.

I, however, have proposed an alternative to both of these. Clif agrees it is risky but is our best course. It ensures Carolina's safety and removes us from danger as well.

I shall not include the details here for fear that we may be found out.

Cassie's shoulders sagged as the entry came to an end. "Really, Ri?"

Lily rubbed her forehead as she turned the page to the final entry. "Oh, she's always this coy."

"I wonder if her plan didn't work out and Pearl was right when she told that story at our store opening. Was she killed?"

"Maybe. Maybe that's what she wants us to know. That she didn't kill herself but that she was murdered."

Cassie arched her eyebrows and leaned closer to the journal. "Let's find out."

Lily offered her a closed mouth smile and a nod as she tugged the book open to the last entry.

The time has come. The situation must be resolved and tonight we will begin resolving it. I am prepared. I realize what I am doing. Clif has asked me more than once if I am certain. I am. His checking on my choice has almost become aggravating.

While I am a woman, and most discount my opinion, I have a mind and I have made it up. I will not be questioned and will not have my decisions reversed. After an impassioned outburst on my part, Clif finally realizes this and has questioned me no further.

So, we shall begin tonight. Everything is readied. Nothing stands in my way.

Tonight, I shall take the first steps in cementing my destiny.

Cassie bit her lower lip as she read the chilling last words penned on the paper.

"She cemented her destiny, all right," Lily said.

Cassie shook her head as she stared up at the doll. "But we still have no idea what happened. No reason for her to kill herself. No inkling that it wasn't suicide, but murder. What was she hoping we'd gain from this?"

Lily scanned the last entry a second time before paging through the rest of the book. "No other entries. That's it." She flicked her gaze to the Victorian doll. "What were you hoping we learned, Ri?"

The doll stood silently, staring ahead with a blank expression.

Cassie sucked in a breath. "Well, we did what she asked. We read the journal. Maybe now she'll allow us to get some sleep."

Lily flipped the book closed and ran a hand over the leather cover. "Maybe."

"Maybe we should get Ruby back to see if she'll be more communicative now that we've read the journal."

"We can try," Lily said. "Maybe this will die down though."

Cassie stood from the couch and grabbed both mugs. "Maybe, though I doubt it. She isn't haunting us for no reason, and we haven't figured anything out yet."

"Here's to hoping we figure it out before we're both sleep-deprived and crazy."

Cassie chuckled as she hovered at the entrance to the living room. She eyed the doll standing across the space. "I guess I'll leave her there."

Lily shot a glance over her shoulder and shrugged. "Don't worry. If she doesn't want to stay there, she'll move herself."

"That's so creepy," Cassie said with a sigh.

"Get some rest, Cass. Try not to think about it." Lily kissed her daughter's forehead before she headed up the steps, leaving Cassie to return the mugs to the kitchen before heading to her bedroom.

* * *

Lily opened her eyes to bright sunshine streaming through her windows. She'd managed to get some sleep after their marathon reading session the previous night. With a yawn, she stretched, and her gaze fell to the leather journal on her nightstand. She reached out and ran her fingers over the worn binding.

They'd finished the journal and still had no idea what drove Henrietta Blanchard to throw herself from the widow's walk. Nor if she had been murdered. They also had no idea why the spirit that seemed to be haunting them insisted they read it.

With a sigh, Lily sat up and pulled her robe around her shoulders before swinging her legs over the edge of the bed. She could use a cup of tea. The limited amount of sleep she'd managed wasn't nearly enough to face the day.

She shuffled across the room and made her way downstairs. With a peek into the living room, she found the Victorian doll still standing where Cassie left her in the wee hours of the morning.

"Maybe finishing the journal was all she wanted," Lily murmured to herself as she crossed the foyer and headed for the kitchen.

She shambled around the space, making a morning cup of hot tea. After retrieving the newspaper from the front porch, she settled on the deck, letting the morning sun warm the cool fall air. She snuggled her robe tighter around her and sipped at the hot liquid in her mug, watching the waves lap against the beach.

With a deep inhale of the crisp seaside air, she pulled the newspaper closer to her and flipped it open to peruse the headlines. The letters at the top of the page caused her heart to skip a beat. Her jaw dropped open as she read them again, certain she had been mistaken on her first round.

Lily gripped the paper and pulled it closer as she read the black letters printed on the page.

LOCAL REALTOR ARRESTED FOR MAZE MURDER

A picture of a stunned Lucy being led away in handcuffs by Wyatt and a deputy followed the bold letters.

"No! This can't be," Lily gasped. "Lucy?"

"Lucy what?" Cassie asked from behind her.

Lily jumped in her seat and swiveled to face her daughter.

Cassie stood in her robe and slippers, a steaming mug clutched in her hands and a messy bun poking from the top of her head.

"Wyatt arrested Lucy for the murder of Trevor's brother."

"What?" Cassie asked, her voice raising an octave as she hurried forward toward the table. She slipped into the seat next to her mother and peered over her shoulder at the newspaper.

The two women scanned the article, detailing the murder and subsequent arrest. Wyatt made no comment to the press further than to say they were still investigating but that Lucy was a person of interest and was brought in for questioning. When pushed by the reporter for details of why the local realtor was being led away in handcuffs if she was merely a person of interest, Wyatt clapped back that he had no comment regarding the ongoing investigation.

"Oh my," Lily murmured as she read the details.

"How could this be? Why arrest Lucy?"

"They must have some evidence," Lily concluded.

"But what?"

Lily stared off at the rolling ocean. "Her prints on the murder weapon?"

Cassie's eyes went wide at the thought. "Oh my gosh, that's right. Wyatt said they found the murder weapon. And then they arrested Lucy. I wonder if her prints were on it."

"I can't believe it. Our realtor… a murderer."

"And the weird connection to Trevor makes it even stranger. What are the odds that the realtor we bought this house from knew Trevor's brother well enough to murder him?"

"I wonder if Wyatt would have any information."

"Doesn't sound like he's talking," Cassie said, tapping her finger against the newspaper next to the "no comment" line.

Lily shrugged her shoulders and sipped her tea. "Not to the press."

Cassie arched an eyebrow at her as she settled back into the deck chair. "Wow. You think he'll slip you some information, huh?"

"Given our connection to the dead man, he might."

Cassie let out a chuckle. "Mom! We have no connection to the dead man."

"You're his sister-in-law. For all we know, you're his closest next-of-kin."

"Yes, he's my brother-in-law. That I didn't know even existed. Our so-called connection is tenuous at best."

Lily lifted a shoulder again, tendrils of hair tickling her skin as the autumn breeze blew off the sea. "If he offers anything, I'll take it. I can't believe Lucy killed him!"

"Why arrest her then?"

"To make things look good. To make sure people think they're making progress on the case."

They settled into silence as both of them considered the latest developments on the case. Cassie flipped the collar of her robe up higher on her neck before sipping her tea. "Did you get any sleep after we finished the journal?"

"I did. Did you?"

"Yes. No nightmares, no interruptions."

"Maybe reading the journal is what she wanted."

Cassie sighed and set down her almost empty mug on the glass table. "I guess that means it's on to the next project. Sorting through Trevor's stuff."

"Maybe you don't have to now."

Cassie stared at the picture of Lucy being hauled away in handcuffs. "I do. Even if Lucy did this, and I'm shocked if she did, I still need answers."

"All right. We'll tackle it together when we get home."

"Okay. I'll drag the box down when we get back from the shop this afternoon and we can go through it."

"Sounds like a plan. Now, I guess we'd better get in gear and get dressed to head in."

Cassie let her head fall back and blew out a long sigh. "Yeah, I guess it's that time."

Reluctantly, they climbed from their chairs and, after a minimal breakfast, trudged up the stairs to dress for the day. Cassie eyed the box of Trevor's things as she pulled on her ballet flats and gave Willy another rub on the head.

"Just a half day today, buddy. I'll be home before you know it!"

With one final pat and one last rueful glance shot to the box, Cassie slung her purse over her shoulder and headed out her door.

Lily waited for her downstairs, peering into the living room. "Still in the same place," she reported as Cassie swung the front door open.

"Good. Maybe one of our problems is solved." Cassie slid her sunglasses on as she stepped into the bright morning.

Within minutes, they were pulling into their usual parking spot behind their Main Street shop, *Buy the Sea*.

Lily slid her seatbelt off and grabbed her purse. "Good thing it's just a half day today. I'm too tired for anything else."

Cassie slid out of the car and shot her mother a glance over the bright pink hood. "Maybe we should stop by the Seaside Cafe on the way home, so we don't have to cook."

Lily poked a finger in Cassie's direction. "Now you're getting smart, kid. And if you don't mind, I'll stop at *Cake my Day* and get some cookies for dessert."

"I don't mind at all," Cassie said with a grin. "Make sure you get some of the oatmeal scotchies. They're my favorite."

"I didn't forget," Lily said, pushing through the shop's backdoor and into the packed storeroom.

Boxes rose from floor to ceiling in some places. Other cartons packed shelves and large decorations stood against the wall.

"How did we accumulate so much stuff in such a small time," Lily asked as she skirted past a stack of bins.

"Good at spending money, I guess," Cassie said with a grin.

"You always had a talent for it," Lily answered with a chuckle as they pushed into the shop. Four women huddled at the register. Silence fell between the group as they entered.

Lily arched an eyebrow at them. "Good morning, ladies. Are we interrupting?"

Chloe grabbed a feather duster and flitted to the shop's front window, waving it over the display. Amber busied herself fiddling with the register.

Genny shoved her hands into her back pockets with a slight shrug, and Meghan bit down on her perfectly lipsticked lip.

"Uhhh, not really," Meghan answered after a moment. "We were just shooting the breeze."

"Shooting the breeze, huh?" Lily asked as she stowed her purse behind the counter and shot a glance at Amber.

"It's just that... well..." Meghan began, her voice trailing off.

"We were hoping someone had more information on what went down with Lucy," Genny admitted. Her eyes flicked to Chloe who continued to dust the displays.

"I'd like to know the same thing," Lily admitted.

All eyes turned to Chloe who concentrated hard on her task.

"That's your cue, Chloe," Meghan prompted her.

Chloe spun on her heel, her eyes wide. "Huh? I mean, why would I know anything?"

Meghan rolled her eyes, the green eye shadow sparkling overtop of them. "Because you're the sheriff's niece, duh."

"So?" Chloe answered, throwing her arms out to the side. "It's not like he calls me to keep me up to date on all the crime around here."

"There isn't any crime around here. This is big news!" Meghan countered. "Are you telling me you haven't talked to Wyatt since he arrested Lucy?"

Chloe pressed her lips together, her face reddening. "Okay, okay!" she exclaimed. "Of course, I talked to him and yes, he told me stuff. But seriously, it can't leave this shop. He'll kill me if I let all the details out!"

"All the details are going to get out anyway," Genny said. "It's Hideaway Bay. Ruby's probably telling everyone she comes across."

"Yeah, just blame Ruby," Meghan said with a shrug.

Chloe rolled her eyes but approached the group, leaning on the counter. "Okay, here's the deal. Uncle Wyatt arrested Lucy because her prints are on the murder weapon."

$\mathcal{M}$eghan's eyes grew wide at Chloe's statement. "What?"

"Are you kidding?" Genny chimed in, adjusting her tortoise-shell glasses.

Amber slammed the cash register drawer shut after counting a stack of fives. "So, did she confess and everything? Why did she do it?"

Chloe shook her head, biting her lower lip. "Oh, no. She says she's innocent. Says she doesn't know how her prints got on that knife."

"But it's her, right? It has to be. Her prints are on the knife," Meghan exclaimed.

Chloe arched her eyebrows, waving the feather duster around as she flicked her gaze around the room. "That's where it gets really interesting."

"What do you mean?" Genny asked.

"I mean," Chloe answered, "Lucy's prints aren't the only ones on that knife."

Amber gripped the counter and leaned toward Chloe. "No way!"

"Way," Chloe said, resting her chin in her palm as she leaned against the counter again.

"Who else's prints were on the knife?" Cassie inquired.

Chloe pursed her lips, an amused expression on her features. "Frida's, Pearl's, and…" She paused, glancing around again. "Mayor Thompson's."

Meghan slapped the counter with her hand. "No! OMG!"

"Mayor Thompson?" Genny shouted, her jaw unhinging.

"None other than Tinsley herself," Chloe said, her chin rising in the air triumphantly.

"So, wait," Lily said, holding up a hand and narrowing her eyes, "why did they arrest Lucy if there are four sets of prints on the knife?"

"Gotta start somewhere," Chloe answered with a shrug.

"And why was she the best place to start?" Lily prodded.

"Because she knew the victim. She dated him."

"No! Jilted lover!" Meghan sang.

"Could be," Meghan said. "Maybe he dumped her, and she got super mad and killed him."

"Or maybe it was something else," Genny suggested with a shrug.

"Such as?" Meghan asked.

"Yeah, what else causes someone to snap and kill their boyfriend?" Amber asked.

"Maybe he attacked her, and she defended herself," Genny answered.

"Then why not say that," Meghan argued. "Uh-uh, no way, she offed him probably because he was a cheating louse or something."

Silence fell between them as each of them mulled over the information. After a moment, Meghan slapped her hand against the counter. "Well, I guess we've solved it. Better get back to *High Grounds* before the afternoon rush hits."

"Yeah, I've left the bakery unattended for too long," Genny agreed. "Thanks for the gossip, ladies!"

Meghan pushed her way through the door, jangling the bell overhead. "Tell your uncle we've solved the case, Chloe."

"I'll let him know. Jilted lover," Chloe called over as she waved the feather duster over the nearest shelf.

Meghan pointed a finger gun at her and winked.

Lily waved a hand at the departing ladies. "Genny, I'll be over before we head home. Save me some scotchies and some of those Spanish cookies."

Genny pointed a finger in the air as she stepped into the autumn sunshine. "You got it, Lil!"

Silence fell over the shop as the two other store owners departed. Chloe shot a few discreet glances at Lily and Cassie but continued her dusting.

"So, did your uncle say anything else?" Lily inquired as she stocked more wooden lighthouses decorated with ghosts and pumpkins.

Chloe shot her a frightened glance, her eyes wide. The door's bell rang, welcoming a new customer into the store and squashing any conversation about the murder investigation.

"Hi, welcome to Buy the Sea!" Chloe exclaimed. "If you need anything, just ask."

A steady stream of customers over the morning prevented any further information from flowing. And as the early afternoon hours ticked by, Lily and Cassie packed up for the day.

They stepped into the warm afternoon sun and meandered down Main Street toward the Seaside Cafe.

"That chicken salad croissant is calling my name," Lily said.

"Mmm, I'm between that and the grilled cheese."

Lily wrinkled her nose and shot her daughter a sideways glance. "You and that grilled cheese."

"I like the pickles and the chips that come with it."

Lily gave her an eye roll as she tugged the door open to the Seaside Cafe and motioned for Cassie to precede her. They settled into a table for two tucked in the corner near a window overlooking the blue bay water. A small sailboat rolled on the waters in the distance under the cloudless sky.

After the waitress took their order and collected their menus, Cassie sank her chin into her palm and focused her gaze on the waters shimmering under the afternoon sun.

Lily rearranged her napkin on her lap. "The grilled cheese, huh?"

Cassie offered a wistful nod.

"Are you sick?"

Cassie's brow furrowed and she flicked her gaze to her mother. "No. Why?"

"You're quiet."

Cassie unfolded her napkin and draped it across her lap. "I'm just curious to know if Chloe knows anything else."

They fell silent as the waitress dropped off two ginger sodas. Lily took a sip before she answered. "Didn't sound like she held back when she spilled the beans about Lucy being the jilted lover of the deceased."

Cassie rolled her eyes as she bobbed her straw up and down in the light amber liquid. "It's odd that she knows all that but that she doesn't know that Kyle was Trevor's brother. My brother-in-law."

Lily squashed her lips together as she nodded slowly. "Ah, I see."

"Come on. She knows all the rest but not that? I'm just waiting to get the weird looks and the whispering every time I walk into a room."

"Look on the bright side," Lily said, leaning back in her chair.

Cassie took a sip of her soda. "What's that?"

"At least your prints weren't on the knife."

The waitress arrived with their orders, setting down a chicken salad croissant with a side salad for Lily and a grilled cheese with chips and bread and butter pickles for Cassie. "Have you heard whose prints *were* on the knife?" the woman inquired.

"We have, yes," Lily said.

"I can't believe Lucy killed him. But I'm not entirely surprised! Anything else I can get you?"

"I think we're good, thanks."

Cassie bit into a pickle as the waitress smiled and spun on her heel, darting across the room to wait on another table. "Ugh. Once the news gets out about my connection, people will have me in a cell next to Lucy."

Lily drizzled dressing on her salad, waving her free hand in the air. "It's a small town. People talk. And everyone knows everything. I think half of what Chloe supposedly knows is from her own imagination."

"So, you think Wyatt didn't tell her anything?"

Lily stabbed a grape tomato with her fork. "Oh, I'm sure he told her the facts. I'm just not sure he told her any more beyond that Lucy had a personal connection to Kyle."

Cassie stared out the window again, her food sitting untouched. "Do you think she knew Trevor?"

"Lucy?"

Cassie eyed her mother and nodded. "Yeah. Do you think she knew Trevor? Do you think she knew us?"

"Does it matter?"

"It matters to me!" Cassie exclaimed, tears welling in her eyes. "I suddenly feel like my husband was a stranger to me. He had a brother I didn't know about. Did other people know? Did Lucy know? And if she did, why did she get to know, and I didn't?"

Lily pressed her lips into a thin line and reached across the table to grasp her daughter's hand. "I don't know, Cass. And I'm sorry this happened, but there must be a reason."

"I have to see her."

Lily snapped her head back. "Who, Lucy?"

Cassie nodded as she flicked away a tear that had fallen to her cheek. "I need to know if she knew."

"You may not get in to see her."

"Can't hurt to ask." Cassie picked up half of her grilled cheese sandwich and took a bite.

"Okay, if you feel you need to see her, we'll go before we go home."

Cassie popped a chip in her mouth. "Thanks, Mom."

Lily offered her a smile before biting into the croissant. "Of course, honey."

A shadow hovered over their table and both women snapped their gaze at the figure approaching.

"Ladies," Wyatt said, tipping his hat.

"Hi, Wyatt. Fancy meeting you here," Lily said with a grin.

"Just stopped in for a late lunch."

"I'll bet you're busy," Cassie said as he hauled a chair over to their table and plopped into it.

"Oh, yeah," he said, pulling his hat off and balancing it on his knee. "Barely pulled myself away to grab some food."

Wyatt flagged the waitress down and ordered a burger to go. "Hope you don't mind me waiting here, but I'm afraid to stand alone."

"Afraid?" Cassie questioned.

Wyatt rubbed the back of his neck. "Yeah. People won't leave me alone. Everyone wants to know everything about this case."

"I'll bet. Especially with the set of suspects you have. I

can't believe Mayor Thompson's not beating down your door to make a statement about her innocence," Lily said as she stabbed at her salad.

Wyatt opened his mouth to respond. He crinkled his brow and shot Lily a confused glance. "How did–" He squeezed his eyes closed and sighed, his head wagging back and forth. "Chloe."

"If you don't want the town to know, maybe you shouldn't tell her all the details of the investigation," Lily suggested with a shrug.

Wyatt waved the comment away. "The whole town will know anyway. Given the set of people whose prints are on the knife, I'm surprised there hasn't been a press conference held yet."

"Did she have an explanation?" Lily questioned.

"Oh, yeah. Said Pearl gave her the knife and asked her to give it to you or Cassie to return to wherever it came from. They figured it was a prop with fake blood on it."

"How did Pearl get it?" Cassie asked.

"Pearl says she got it from Frida, who says she kicked it across the floor while going through the maze and picked it up, assuming it was–"

"A prop, right," Lily said before sipping her soda.

"And Lucy says she didn't do it?" Cassie asked.

"Swears she didn't, but her story's got inconsistencies."

Cassie bit into a chip, wiping her hands on her napkin before she spoke. "Would it be possible for me to see her?"

"What? Why? Look, if you want to get the scoop from her–"

Cassie waved her hand in the air. "No, it's not that. I just… I'd like to know if she knew Trevor. Chloe said she knew Kyle. That she dated him. And I'm wondering…" Cassie's voice trailed off.

"You're wondering if your husband knew her and never told you. Or she knew you," Wyatt said.

"Right," Cassie answered.

The sheriff sucked in a deep breath. "Can it wait until tomorrow? I'd really prefer no visitors until we can sort out a few things."

Cassie nodded in understanding. "Sure. It can wait. I'd just like some answers at some point."

Wyatt nodded his head as he spun his hat in his hands. "How are things at home? With the, ah, you know…" He wiggled his fingers in the air, his mouth forming an "o" as he imitated a haunting spirit.

Cassie's eyebrows lifted for a moment before she answered. "We may have made some progress on that front."

Wyatt cocked his head, flicking his gaze from Cassie to Lily.

"We finished Henrietta's journal last night. So far, no new incidents with our spirit," Lily answered.

"That's good. How long of a streak?"

Cassie blew out an amused breath. "Only hours, but our animated ghost hasn't moved, and we actually got some sleep after we finished, so things are looking good."

Wyatt dug into his breast pocket and pulled out a scrap of paper, sliding it onto the table. "On that note, Ruby asked me to pass her cell phone number along in case you need it. She said to call or text anytime."

Cassie grabbed the paper, waving it in the air as she polished off her sandwich before sliding it into her purse. "Thanks."

"I'm hoping we don't have to bother her at all. Maybe Henrietta just wanted us to read her journal."

Wyatt crinkled his brow and scratched his head. "Why did she kill herself?"

Lily shrugged as she wiped the corners of her mouth. "Never said."

"She really didn't seem suicidal in her last entries. But Pearl suggested someone murdered her, and I'm wondering if that was true."

"Another murder, huh? Please don't mention it to anyone. I'm not sure this town can take any more murders right now."

Lily chuckled at his statement as the waitress dropped a take-out bag off with Wyatt, patting his arm. "I put an extra slice of pie in there for you. I'll bet you could use it. You look thinner. This investigation is really taking a toll."

"Thanks, Susie, I appreciate that," Wyatt said with a smile. Susie flitted away and he turned to face Lily and Cassie. "Okay, maybe murder's not so bad."

"It did score you an extra slice of pie," Cassie admitted with a grin.

"For all that weight you lost in the last two days," Lily added, an amused smile playing on her features.

The trio stood as Lily laid a few bills on the table. "I probably did. Two days of being pestered by Tinsley and–"

A shout across the room interrupted his statement. One of the patrons waved frantically at the television mounted in the corner of the room. The waitress raced toward it, emphatically pressing a remote control as she aimed it at the device.

The volume rose and a familiar voice filled the air. Mayor Tinsley Thompson stood behind a podium, a bevy of microphones surrounding her.

With a grim expression, she let her eyes rise to the camera and began reading from her note cards. "Citizens of Hideaway Bay, it is with a solemn heart that I address you this evening. As most of you know, our tiny town experienced a horrible tragedy at our annual Halloween event.

"Our sheriff, Wyatt Cooper, has been working nonstop to identify the culprit and bring them to justice. Many of you are also aware that an arrest has been made in the case already.

"I am not here to comment on that arrest or the ongoing investigation into the murder. But I am here to address one fact unearthed as part of Sheriff Cooper's work to unmask the perpetrator of this heinous crime.

"During the investigation, forensics revealed my fingerprints were found on the murder weapon."

"Ugh," Wyatt groaned as he rubbed his eyes and shook his head.

Gasps rang out throughout the restaurant and, on-screen, Tinsley paused as reporters glanced at each other with shocked expressions or eyebrows raised.

She nodded before she continued. "Yes. I, too, was shocked when I learned this, but there is a reasonable explanation. Another reveler at the festival handed me the knife. I assumed it was a prop from the maze. I hoped to return it to its correct place, not realizing it had played a part in the night's tragedy.

"As your mayor, I felt it was my duty to inform you of my involvement and give you my solemn word that I played no part in the tragic events of Friday night. Rest assured that I am cooperating with the police in every respect to help them as much as I can. I thank you for your time and understanding and let us all support our local law enforcement as they wade through the details of this case in their valiant efforts to remove crime from our normally safe streets. Thank you."

With a nod, she grabbed her notecards as a flurry of activity erupted behind the podium. Reporters frantically hollered in an attempt to ask follow-up questions. An assistant from the Mayor's office waved a hand at the camera. "No questions. There will be no questions or further statements."

She escorted Mayor Thompson from the room as the questions continued to fly. The feed cut to the local news reporter who raised a microphone to her mouth, a surprised yet solemn expression on her youthful features.

"Well, there you have it, folks. Mayor Tinsley Thompson admits her fingerprints are on the murder weapon found at the scene of Friday night's crime. Local law enforcement have made an arrest, but, as we reported earlier, continue to be baffled by this grisly murder in our normally quiet hamlet."

"Seriously? Baffled is hardly the word I'd use," Wyatt said with a wrinkled nose.

Lily patted him on the shoulder. "Don't sweat it, Wyatt, they just like a good story."

"I wish they didn't have to drag my name through the mud to get it."

"The focus will be on Mayor Thompson now," Cassie said, waving her arm around at the cafe patrons who whispered among themselves about the latest announcement by their town's mayor.

Wyatt sighed, grasping his to-go bag tighter in his hand. "Well, I guess I'd better get back to being baffled."

"Good luck," Lily said as he stuck his hat on his head and strode across the room, avoiding conversation with anyone.

The women ambled from the restaurant, waving to Wyatt as he pulled away in the police car before they retraced their steps toward their shop. After a quick stop in the bakery for their cookie order, they piled into Cassie's Wrangler and headed for Whispering Manor.

"That mayor of ours is really something, huh?" Lily said as she slid out of the car with her two boxes of cookies.

"Well, I guess she's doomed either way she goes. She

either admits it and is honest and called dramatic or she doesn't say anything and when it comes out, everyone accuses her of hiding it."

They climbed the porch stairs in tandem. "Either way she plays it, someone won't be happy. That's the way of the world."

Cassie nodded as she switched off the alarm system and slipped her key inside the door.

"I suddenly don't feel at all like going through Trevor's things. I'd rather park myself on the couch, find a good movie and eat these cookies."

"Well, it is our dinner, so I suppose we should throw a hot chocolate in on that deal. For the protein," Lily said with a wink.

A grin crossed Cassie's face as she swung the door open and entered the foyer. The smile quickly faded, and she came to a dead stop. Lily plowed into the back of her, crushing the box of cookies between them.

"Cassie!" Lily complained before she spotted the reason for Cassie's hesitance. "Oh." Her shoulders drooped and she frowned at the scene in the foyer.

The Victorian doll stood with her outstretched arm, reaching toward them. Willy stood next to her, his tail wrapped around her dress. He offered a meow at their entrance, brushing against the doll as though she'd kept him company.

"So much for that problem being solved. Looks like Ri moved herself to the door to wait for us," Cassie said.

Lily lifted her shoulders as she stared at the doll. "Maybe Willy turned her Roomba on, and she just wandered out here by pure coincidence."

Cassie shot her an incredulous glance. "And what? Her battery died at this exact moment?" Cassie bent over and tugged up the doll's skirt. "Nope. The switch is in the off position. So, Willy didn't flip her on. She came here of her own volition."

Lily arched an eyebrow at the doll. "Well, I'll be darned if I know what she wants now. We read her journal. There's nothing more we can do."

"Maybe we ought to have Ruby over again."

Lily pursed her lips as she slid the smashed cookie boxes onto the foyer table. "Let's talk about it over our hot chocolate."

"After I slip into my jammies."

"I wouldn't have it any other way. And, hey, don't dally. I'm always stuck making the hot chocolate."

"I don't dally!" Cassie claimed as she darted up the steps. "I can't help that I'm not as fast as you."

"Right," Lily said, trailing behind her. "Sure. I can just see you slowly pulling on those cat slippers as you watch the time tick by, wondering if you waited long enough for me to have already warmed the milk."

"I'll hurry," Cassie said with a roll of her eyes before she turned right at the top of the stairs and wandered along the railing to her bedroom.

Willy trailed behind her, but stopped short, not following her into her room. Cassie hurried around, whipping off her clothes and throwing on her pajamas. Her eyes fell on the box of Trevor's personal items as she pulled on her fuzzy slippers. She shook her head at it, not wanting to get lost in thought and miss out on the milk warming.

She wrapped her robe around her and tied it as she strolled down the hall. Willy sat facing a corner, his tail swishing across the hardwood.

"What'd you find, buddy?" Cassie asked.

The cat stared up at the wall, leaping onto his hind legs and batting at it.

"I don't see anything," Cassie said. The cat descended to

his hind legs slowly, his eyes fixed on the empty spot on the mint-colored wall.

The cat mewed, his tail swishing again. Cassie rubbed his head, eliciting a purr. "Come on. We'll get your dish before we start that milk warming."

The cat left the wall behind in favor of food, trailing behind Cassie as she descended the stairs and skirted past the doll standing at the bottom, giving it the evil eye.

With Willy in tow, she hurried down the hall to the kitchen. After dumping a can of cat food into his red bowl and placing it on his mat, he dove in, devouring the food before Cassie even set a pot of milk on the stove.

He stalked across toward the table, sprawling on the rug underneath to clean himself. Cassie smiled at him as she gave the milk a stir before crossing to the cupboard to retrieve mugs. She swung the door open, blocking her view of the kitchen entrance.

"Looks like Mom's the one dallying today, Willy!" Cassie called as she rose to her tiptoes to grab the large mugs from the top of the cupboard.

With two cups in hand, she lowered herself and swung the cupboard closed. Her eyes widened as she spotted the Victorian doll hovering in the entryway.

"Hello," the doll said.

One mug slipped from Cassie's fingers, smashing into the tiled floor and shattering as Cassie jumped, a yelp escaping her lips. She stared wide-eyed at the doll.

Lily's voice called down the hall "What are you do–" Her words stopped when she spotted the doll. "I see she's on the move again."

Cassie's features pinched as she nodded. "And she's talking."

Lily's eyebrows raised and she slid her eyes sideways to the doll. "She's talking?"

"She said hello." Cassie's eyes fell to the floor and a frown formed on her face. "And that's when I dropped the mug and broke it. Ohhh."

"Don't worry about that," Lily said, hurrying past the doll and into the kitchen to help Cassie clean up the mess.

"Oh, the milk!" Cassie shouted as she grabbed several of the larger pieces, then dropped them on the counter. She turned down the stove as she stirred the steaming milk.

Lily bent on one knee, sweeping the remaining shards of

the mug into a dustpan. "Remind me next time not to make you hurry down here."

"It was her fault!" Cassie exclaimed. "Besides, you should've known better. Remember Christmas dinner?"

Lily rose and crossed to the trash compactor, shaking the pieces into it. "I do. And those soppy brownies. And the salmon burgers you tried to make that were awful."

"I'm not domestic," Cassie said, stirring the hot chocolate mix into the milk as she eyed the doll. "I really think we need to call Ruby."

Lily pulled another mug from the cupboard, then stuck a hand on her hip and stared at the doll across the room. "Well, Henrietta, if you've got something to say, say it."

The doll stood silent, her outstretched hand reaching toward them.

Lily arched an eyebrow at her. "Come on! Don't be shy."

Cassie's gaze flicked between the doll and her mother. "Maybe you shouldn't provoke her."

"Provoke her? She hasn't said two words and if she's going to keep jetting around the house, I'd like to just have this out."

Cassie poured milk into the mugs on the counter, side-eying the doll, and whispered to her mother, "I'm not so sure I want to have it out with a woman who guarded a treasure with a gun."

Lily motioned at the inanimate doll across the room. "She doesn't have a gun now, Cass!"

Cassie sprayed whipped cream onto the steaming chocolate drink. "I'm going to text Ruby when we sit down. She's obviously trying to communicate something to us."

"Or drive us batty," Lily added as they carried their mugs to the living room, squeezing past the doll in the doorway.

They plopped onto the couch with the two boxes of cookies spread between them after Cassie dumped the large chunks of mug in the trash on the porch and retrieved her phone and Ruby's number. Cassie balanced her mug in one hand as she pulled her phone from her pocket with the other, swiping into her text app.

She tapped in Ruby's number, saving it into her contacts before opening a text message to her.

"What are you saying to her?" Lily asked as she scanned the list of movies on their streaming app.

Cassie read her message as she typed it. "Hi, Ruby. Thanks for sending your number. Just in the nick of time. We're still having some strange incidents. It seems like that doll we have is trying to communicate with us. She followed me into the kitchen and said hello, but won't say anything else. She's trying to communicate, but not having much luck. Can you help? Sorry for the long message."

Cassie's thumb hovered over the send button as she pressed her lips together, wondering if she should send it. With a deep inhale, she tapped the arrow and sent the message on its way.

Lily waved the remote at the television, silently asking for approval of the movie she selected.

Cassie groaned, shooting her a glance. "You're kidding, right?"

"I thought it was appropriate," Lily answered with a shrug, selecting the movie to play.

The opening scene of *The Haunting* played.

"You just love to torture me," Cassie said as she slouched in her seat.

Minutes into the movie, her phone chimed. "It's Ruby," Cassie said, sitting up straighter.

Lily paused the movie. "What'd she say?"

"She said she agrees the spirit is trying to contact us. And that we should try to help her do that."

"Help her how?"

Cassie set her mug on the side table, her thumbs flying across her virtual keyboard. "I'm asking her that now. Maybe another seance?"

"Are you certain you heard her say hello? Could you have thought you heard it?"

Cassie shot her mother a narrow-eyed glance. "She said hello! I heard it. I–"

A whirring noise interrupted her statement. Their attention turned to the foyer where a flutter of blue fabric floated around the corner before the Victorian doll came into full view. It glided two feet into the room before winding to a stop. "Hello."

Cassie snapped her head toward her mother. "Told you."

Lily eyed the doll standing across the room. "Hello."

Cassie slid her eyes back and forth between her mother and the doll as the two stared at each other.

The chime of Cassie's phone sent her leaping, and she blew out a quick breath as her heart skipped a beat. "It's Ruby. She says we can try another seance, but she can't come tonight. In the meantime, we can try making it easier for her to communicate by bringing something she is familiar with closer to her and trying to make a letter board that she can use to spell things if she can't speak."

"Like a ouija board?"

Cassie shrugged as she typed a response. "I guess."

"Well, I assume this is Henrietta. So, the personal thing would be her journal. Oh!" Lily exclaimed, snapping her fingers in the air. "I wonder if *that's* what she meant! Maybe she didn't want us to read the journal. Maybe she wanted us to give it back to her."

"You mean give it to the doll."

"Well, I assume she's hanging out inside the doll, so technically giving it to the doll is giving it to her."

Cassie pursed her lips and set her phone on the arm of

the sofa. "Okay, I'll go get the journal. You stay here with the creepy doll."

"Thanks a lot, Cass!" Lily shouted over her shoulder as Cassie leapt from her seat and darted from the room, using the back entrance rather than pass by the doll.

She returned her gaze to the Victorian woman across the room. "We're getting your journal, Ri."

No response came from the life-sized animatron.

Lily's eyes flicked to a round portrait hanging over the room's fireplace then back to the doll. "That doll really does resemble you. Is that why you picked it?"

Cassie's footsteps clamored down the stairs, announcing her return. She darted into the room through the back entrance again a moment later, waving the brown journal in the air. "Got it."

"Okay, give it to her."

Cassie winced and wrinkled her nose, shoving the journal toward her mother. "You give it to her."

Lily offered her an annoyed glance. "Why should I do it?"

"She's your friend."

"She isn't my friend! I don't even know the woman."

Cassie shook the journal at her mother again. "You read her journal!"

"And you're the one she's haunting. I think it should come from you."

Cassie let her arm drop and her shoulders slumped. "Fine."

She stomped across the room, slowing as she approached the doll. With pursed lips, she delicately placed the brown leather book onto the outstretched arm of the doll. It wobbled there for a moment before flopping to the floor below with a thud.

Lily pushed herself to stand with a sigh. "Oh, Cassie, you've got to move her arm."

"You move her arm! What if I hurt her!"

"She's dead. You can't hurt her much more than she already is," Lily said as she swiped the book from the hardwood. She carefully placed it in the hand closest to the doll, then bent the outstretched arm to hold the book close to her chest.

"There," she said with a nod of her head after a few more adjustments to make sure the book didn't topple again. "Okay, there's your journal, Ri. Is that what you wanted?"

The doll stood silent for a moment, stoically clutching the book against her blue dress.

Lily's lips formed a mouth shrug, and she cocked her head. "Maybe that did it."

"Yeah, she–"

The whirring noise sounded again, and the doll spun before lurching forward. She continued toward the fireplace, then spun and retreated toward the window.

Lily tugged Cassie back a few steps as their eyes followed the doll's pacing back and forth

Cassie's fingers clamped onto her mother's arm and she whispered, "What's she–"

The doll spun again, and the journal launched from her arms, flying across the room and landing with a loud slap against the floor's slats. It slid toward the fireplace, coming to a stop near the bricks.

"Journals. Journals. Journals," the doll repeated over and over.

"We just gave you your journal!" Cassie cried.

Lily cocked her head as the doll continued her back-and-forth trek across the room, repeating the same word over and over.

"Wait, she's saying journals, not journal."

Cassie's face turned into a mask of confusion, and she glanced at her mother.

"Plural. More than one journal."

"There are no other journals!" Cassie said. "That's it. She said she started it at the beginning and obviously the last entry is just before her death. There can't be more journals."

The spirit's incessant babbling changed from repeating one word to a series of three. "Find the journals. Find the journals."

Lily waved a hand toward the doll. "Find the journals. See. It's not that one. She's talking about something else. There must be other journals she wants us to find."

The doll stopped on a dime, spinning to face them. "Yes."

"This is getting creepy," Cassie said as the doll responded to Lily.

Lily nodded at the doll before grabbing Cassie's hand and pulling her toward the foyer. "Come on, let's look in the library. Maybe we missed something in there."

Cassie crinkled her nose, offering the doll the evil eye as they passed her on a mission to search the library. A glance over her shoulder as she crossed the foyer made her eyes go wide. The doll followed behind them.

"She's following us," Cassie whispered.

"Good. Maybe she can help us find whatever it is she wants."

The doll stopped in front of the stairs, not continuing past them as Cassie and Lily stepped into the library. "She stopped."

Lily scanned the shelves that filled two walls of the room. "Maybe she ran out of energy. I'll start on this end. You start over there."

Cassie nodded in the direction of her mother's pointed finger and crossed to the shelves hiding the secret passage. She scanned the books in search of handwritten journals. Across the room, Lily tugged books from the shelf, searching behind them for other hidden books.

"What if they were in the treasure horde?" Cassie asked as she shifted a few tomes around on the shelf.

"We could email the museum and ask them, I guess, though I don't remember anyone mentioning that when they announced the find."

They continued pulling books from the shelves in search of the missing journals their ghost sought.

A voice sounded behind them. "Nitwits."

Startled, the books Cassie held in her hands flew into the air, toppling to the floor below. Both women spun to face the doll, now standing in the doorway.

"Did… did she just call us nitwits?" Cassie asked.

The doll spun and charged toward the stairs.

Lily crossed to the foyer entrance. "I think she's trying to tell us something."

Cassie followed her mother, hovering in the doorway as they watched the doll.

She came to a stop at the stairs, turning to face them. "There."

"Where?" Cassie asked.

The doll spun in circles. "Upstairs. Upstairs. Upstairs."

"That's definitely Henrietta. No doubt," Lily murmured to Cassie before raising her voice. "Okay, Ri, we get it."

The doll ceased her motion and stared up the steps.

With a deep sigh, Lily crossed to the stairs and climbed up two before she slowed and twisted to stare at Cassie. "Well, come on!"

Cassie's shoulders slumped and she let her arms fall limply to her sides as she shuffled across the foyer. "I can't believe we're listening to a doll."

"You're the first one who insisted the doll was trying to tell us something," Lily said, climbing two more stairs before stopping again. She waved a finger at the Victorian woman's likeness. "Better take her with us. We may need her."

Cassie huffed as she retreated back down the steps and stood next to the doll. She eyed it suspiciously before wrapping her arm around the waist and heaving it upward. She trudged up the stairs with the doll in hand. "You made it up these steps once, Ri. Couldn't you have floated up?"

She finished her comment as she set the doll on the landing at the top. As the doll's base hit the floorboard, she spun, her hand smacking Cassie in the cheek.

"Ouch!" Cassie shouted, pressing a palm against her skin, an incredulous expression on her features.

Lily pushed one of the drawers closed on the table in the hall leading to Cassie's room, resting a flashlight on her shoulder. "What?"

"She slapped me!"

Lily cocked her head, her eyebrows scrunching as she smirked. "She's a doll."

"She's a spirit inside a doll! And she cracked me across the cheek because I asked her why she couldn't float up the stairs like she did the last time."

"Maybe you shouldn't provoke her," Lily said with a smirk.

Cassie offered her mother an unimpressed glance.

Lily scanned the space. "Where should we start?"

Cassie poked her thumb at the doll. "Why don't you ask Bride of Chucky over here?"

"You're going to earn yourself another slap on the face with that kind of talk," Lily answered before turning her attention to the doll. "All right, Henrietta. Now where?"

The doll stood silent, staring blankly ahead.

"Well?" Cassie inquired. She poked at the doll's shoulder. The action elicited no response.

"Doesn't look like she's talking."

"No. I guess she zapped all her energy with that slap."

Lily offered a shrug. "Well, I guess we can check a few

places up here and see what we find. But without her help, we may come up empty."

Cassie nodded in agreement as she scanned the space at the top of the stairs.

"I wonder which bedroom was hers. That may help," Lily said, her gaze flicking to the doll again.

Cassie eyed the animatron, too. "Maybe if I get her journal again, it'll energize her. She went nuts after we gave her that."

"Doesn't hurt to try."

With a nod, Cassie skipped down the stairs to retrieve the discarded journal. After climbing back to the second floor, she placed it in the doll's arms. Both women stared expectantly at the object.

After a moment, Cassie flung her hands in the air. "Nothing."

"She must be done for the night."

Cassie rolled her eyes. "Yeah, until she trundles into one of our bedrooms while we're trying to sleep."

Lily took another glance around the space. "I guess we can–"

A scraping noise cut off her words.

Cassie's eyes went wide. "What was that?" she whispered.

"I don't know," Lily answered, wandering to the top of the stairs and glancing down them. "Sounded like it came from down there."

"Yeah, out on the porch," Cassie agreed.

"Maybe an animal," Lily suggested. "Raccoon or something."

"I'd better go check that it's not digging through the trashcan on the side of the house."

Cassie hopped down the stairs and crossed to the foyer, pulling open the front door. She stepped onto the porch, glancing toward the corner as she stepped out.

A shadow from around the corner moved, one far bigger than a raccoon.

Cassie took two steps down the porch when footsteps sounded on the floorboards. A dark figure charged toward her, a box in hand.

The hooded individual barreled into her, knocking her backward as they fled past and pounded down the stairs. Cassie fell hard onto her backside, her arm breaking her fall.

CHAPTER 23

"Hey!" Cassie shouted after the fleeing individual.

"Cassie!" Lily shrieked from the doorway. She hurried toward her downed daughter, crouching to wrap her arms around her. "What happened?"

"Someone was going through our trash! They grabbed that box of stuff I tossed out earlier this week and ran. They knocked me over when they raced out of here."

"Did you see who it was?"

"No," Cassie said with a shake of her head as she struggled to stand up. "They had a hood on, and it covered most of their face."

"Are you okay?" Lily asked, helping Cassie to stand.

"Yeah, I'm fine. I just jammed my shoulder when I landed. A few ibuprofen should fix me up though."

"Are you sure? We can run to the urgent care if you sprained something or hit your head."

Cassie brushed off her pants where she'd landed and shook her head again. "No, I didn't hit my head. I'm fine."

Lily grabbed her hand and tugged her back inside the house. "I'm calling Wyatt."

Cassie let out a disgusted sigh. "I really thought we were done with all these prowler types when we found the treasure."

"Me too. Then again, I thought we were done with our haunting also and that turned out to be false."

"It's like the first month here all over again," Cassie said as her mother tapped around on her cell phone before pressing it to her ear. "Sit down, Cass. Do you want me to get the ibuprofen?"

Cassie shook her head as she collapsed onto the couch. "I'll get it later."

Lily nodded before directing her attention to the phone call. "Hey, it's Lily. Sorry to call, I know you've got your hands full, but we just had someone picking through our trash." She paused for a moment. "Yeah, they knocked Cassie over running away."

Another pause before she answered, "I don't know but if you have some time, that'd be fine… Okay, thanks."

Lily pulled the phone from her ear and tossed it on the couch cushion before plopping next to it. "Wyatt said he'll come over and check it out."

"I'm not sure there's much to check out," Cassie answered, slouching further down the thick cushion.

"He'll know better than us, I guess."

"Well, unless this case baffles him, too," Cassie said with a grin.

"Don't let him hear you say that. It's the first thing he said when I mentioned him having his hands full."

Within minutes, the red and blue lights of a police cruiser flashed through the window. Lily waited at the door, welcoming the sheriff into Whispering Manor on police business for the umpteenth time.

"Hey, Lily," he said with a wince. "More trouble, huh?"

"Yeah, more trouble. I thought we were done with all this."

"You said they were going through your trash?"

"Yeah, it's here on the side porch," Lily said, motioning for him to follow her out the door and around the corner. "Cassie said they took a box of stuff she'd thrown out earlier this week."

"Anything important? Documents with sensitive information or anything like that?"

"I don't think so. We can ask her to be sure."

Wyatt shone his flashlight around the trash can in search of anything that may point to the ransacker's identity. He clicked it off after a moment. "I don't see any scraps of fabric or buttons we could use to identify them. We can try for prints, but it may be a lost cause."

Lily crossed her arms and shot him a weak smile. "Sorry to give you another baffling case."

He rolled his eyes and shook his head. "Don't remind mc. The entire situation with Kyle McGuire has taken a real turn for the worse."

"Want to talk about it?"

Wyatt stowed his flashlight on his belt and put his hands on his hips. "I probably shouldn't discuss an ongoing case, but..."

"But?"

"I could be persuaded to let a few details slip for one of those cookies you bought from Cake my Day earlier."

Lily smirked at him as she motioned for him to follow her. "Come on. We have a few left."

She led him into the foyer. The Victorian doll loomed at the top of the stairs. Wyatt's gaze hovered on it for a moment before he slid his eyes sideways to Lily. "How's the whole ghost situation going?"

"Don't ask." She wandered into the living room, finding Cassie with her fluffy slippers propped on the coffee table.

"Hey, Cassie," Wyatt said as he plopped into an armchair. "How are you feeling? Didn't get hurt, did you?"

"No, I'm okay, thanks. I just can't believe we've got another prowler."

Lily pulled open a box of cookies, grabbed a cookie, then slid them toward him. Wyatt helped himself, biting into one before he spoke again.

"Was there anything sensitive in the box that was taken?"

Cassie pulled a cookie from the box, setting it on a napkin as she broke off a corner. "No. Just a few old knickknacks. Oh, and the big shards of that mug I broke earlier when Henrietta scared me."

"Henrietta?" Wyatt questioned with a mouthful of cookie. "Like the ghost?"

"One and the same," Cassie said.

"She's talking now," Lily added. "Not very much, but enough to have scared the daylights out of Cassie."

Wyatt glanced toward the foyer and bit his lower lip. "Does she give you any warning when she's about to jump out at you and talk?"

Lily shook her head as she polished off her cookie. "Not really, why?"

"I'd rather not be here when she starts talking again."

"You're as big a scaredy cat as Cassie, Wyatt!"

"And I'm not ashamed to admit it," he said with a grin.

"All right, well you've heard our sordid story with the trash picker and the ghost. Now, what's this about the case taking a turn for the worse?"

Cassie leaned forward, shooting an inquisitive glance in Wyatt's direction. "Was there a break?"

"Nope, that's just it. No breaks. Nothing. Nothing even makes sense."

"What do you mean?" Lily asked, settling into the couch cushions.

"We arrested Lucy only because of her personal connection to Kyle. She says she didn't do it. And she has no idea how the prints got on that knife. Says she hasn't seen Kyle in over a year, didn't know he was even in town, and when they did date, it wasn't for very long."

Cassie kicked her feet onto the coffee table as she considered his story. "So, she hasn't admitted to touching the knife yet?"

"Nope, says she never touched it."

Lily leaned forward to grab another cookie before pulling her legs underneath her. "Wait, Frida said she picked the knife up off the floor."

Wyatt nodded and pointed a finger at Lily. "Right."

"And she gave it to Pearl."

"Correct, who gave it to Tinsley who says she set it down somewhere in one of the displays."

Cassie traced the rim of her mug absentmindedly as she thought through the scenario. "Okay, so their story makes sense. Maybe Lucy picked up the knife from where Tinsley set it down."

"Why not say that?" Lily countered.

Cassie shrugged. "Afraid it implicates her somehow?"

Wyatt shook his head, cutting off any further surmising on their part. "Some of the prints were overlapped. Lucy's prints were underneath Frida's and Tinsley's."

Cassie snapped her gaze to Wyatt as he snagged another cookie from the box. "Which means she touched it first."

"And that she could have killed Kyle, tossed the knife away, and got out of dodge."

"Bingo," Wyatt said. "But her story never changes, and we can't catch a break on implicating her or anyone else."

They fell into silence for a few moments as they contemplated the situation. Wyatt grabbed another cookie, waving it at Cassie. "Hey, Cass, I'm really sorry to bring this up, but are you sure there's nothing you remember about this guy, Kyle? Anything. Even the slightest mention."

Cassie shook her head, fighting back tears. "Trevor never even mentioned having a brother. I'm still in shock and I've been going over and over everything in my mind, searching for even the slightest clue that he was keeping something from me." She shoved her hands between her knees and shrugged. "I've got nothing. I'm sorry."

Wyatt shook his head. "You don't need to apologize. I'm sure this was a shock to you. I'm just grasping at anything that may give me some information to solve this. Before the media accuses me of being a bumbling idiot again."

"They didn't really say that," Lily countered.

Wyatt threw his hands in the air, letting them flop down against the chair's arms. "They will. When Lucy's lawyer points out my case has more holes than Swiss cheese. If only there was some way–"

A noise over their heads made him stop. His eyes grew wide, and he shot a glance at Lily and Cassie. "What is that?"

The rumbling noise continued, growing louder before it sounded as though it was right on top of them.

"You don't think…" Cassie started as her eyes rose to the ceiling.

Lily set aside the throw pillow she'd been clutching during the conversation. "Only one way to find out."

With her eyes trained on the ceiling above, Lily rose from her seat and tiptoed across the room, peering out into the foyer and up the stairs. After a moment, she crept further over.

"She's gone!" she called from the foot of the stairs.

"Henrietta?" Cassie asked, leaping from her seat on the couch.

"The ghost?" Wyatt asked, wide-eyed as he launched out of his chair.

"Yeah, the ghost, Henrietta," Lily confirmed as they joined her in the foyer. She waved a hand upstairs. "See?"

"Sounded like she was right above us," Wyatt said.

Cassie gulped and her nose wrinkled. "Which means she's running around in my room."

"Maybe we should go see what she wants," Lily suggested.

Cassie made a face at her mother, her fingers wrapping in a white-knuckled grip around the banister. "You go. She likes you better."

"That's ridiculous," Lily answered with a roll of her eyes. "If she's in your room, it's you she wants."

"Maybe she got lost," Cassie suggested.

"In her own house? Doubtful."

Cassie shook her head, her fingers tightening on the wood. "I'm not going up there alone!"

"I'll go with you."

"Well, I guess you two ladies have this under control," Wyatt said. "I probably should go."

Lily arched an eyebrow at him. "You don't want to see her in action?"

"Uhhh," Wyatt murmured before his lips formed a frown and he shook his head as he backed to the door. "Nah. I might frighten her."

He continued his trek backward, bumping into the front door and feeling behind him for the handle. He swung it open and backed through. "Take care now."

With that, he pulled the door shut behind him, disappearing from view. Moments later, they heard the engine rev on his cruiser and the gravel crunched as he pulled away.

"What a fraidy-cat," Lily said with a shake of her head.

"Yeah, I'm not far behind him. What's she doing up there?"

"Only one way to know." Lily grabbed Cassie's hand and tugged her up the stairs. Cassie trailed behind her mother, glancing through the railing as they ascended to the second floor.

A flash of blue fabric passed inside her door before disappearing from her sight. They arrived at the top of the stairs and navigated around the railing and down the gallery hall to her bedroom.

The doll circled around inside, pacing back and forth at the foot of the bed.

Cassie and Lily hovered inside the doorway for a moment before Lily spoke. "Something on your mind, Henrietta?"

The doll stopped at the mention of her name.

"It is Henrietta we're speaking with, correct?" Lily questioned.

"Ri," the doll answered, still clutching her journal in her arms.

"Ri," Lily repeated. "I like that nickname."

Cassie scrunched her face, shooting her mother a glance. "Are you trying to be her best friend or find out what she's doing in here?"

"A little friendliness never hurt, right, Ri?"

The doll resumed her pacing, trundling back and forth over the throw rug.

Lily eyed the moving target. "Is there a reason you're in here? Is the journal you want us to find in here?"

The doll continued her back and forth. "The key."

Cassie squashed her eyebrows together as she shoved her hands in her pockets. "The key? What do you mean? Is this room the key to finding the journals?"

The doll spun in a tight circle and trundled back toward them. "The key. The key. The key."

Cassie pursed her lips as the doll's frustrated voice repeated the same phrase over and over. "This is impossible."

The doll's mantra changed. "Help. Help. Help."

Lily stepped into the room and held her hands out in front of her, stopping the doll's progress. "All right, Ri. We're going to get you some help. Maybe then you'll be able to communicate more effectively with us. Until then, how about if you get some rest?"

The doll did not respond. Lily twisted and shot a glance at Cassie over her shoulder. "Maybe we should put her in the hall for the night."

Cassie eyed the doll disdainfully. "Maybe we should lock her in the basement for the night. I don't want her creeping around while I'm trying to sleep!"

The doll broke free from Lily's grip and raced toward Cassie. Cassie shielded herself, throwing both arms up in front of her. "Sorry! I'm sorry!"

The doll stopped short of ramming into her, the brown curls bouncing as she came to an abrupt halt. "Help."

"We'll get you help, Ri," Lily said, patting the doll's shoulder. "But you may need to be patient."

"Help," the doll said again.

"I know. Patience isn't your strong suit. But you'll need to give us some time. In the meantime, how about letting us get a good night's sleep?"

The doll did not respond. Lily flashed crossed fingers at Cassie before she lifted the doll from the floor and carried it into the hallway. "I'll clean up downstairs and then I'm going to try to get some sleep."

Cassie followed her mother down the stairs. "Let's hope a certain someone lets us."

* * *

A creaking noise woke Lily from a restless sleep. Her eyelids fluttered open, and she stared into the darkened room as she listened. Another groan echoed through the air.

She closed her eyes for a second, assuming it was Cassie. Her eyes snapped open a moment later. What was Cassie doing up at two in the morning? Was it the ghost doll?

Wearily, Lily tossed back the covers and slid her feet into her slippers, pulling her robe over her. She tugged her door open, her heart skipping a beat. She stumbled back a few steps as she came face to face with the doll.

"Help," the doll said.

CHAPTER 24

*L*ily stared at the doll standing in front of her as she tied her belt around her, securing her robe tighter. "What's wrong? Is it Cassie? Did something happen?"

Lily scanned the landing behind the ghost. Downstairs, a light bobbed around. Unless Cassie was carrying a flashlight around in the library, it wasn't Cassie downstairs.

"Help," the doll repeated.

The light stopped moving, pointing toward the foyer.

"Shh," Lily said, placing a finger to her lips. She stood frozen in silence as the light shone into the foyer. After a moment, it moved again.

Lily's eyes grew to the size of saucers as a hooded figure emerged from the library. Her pulse quickened and blood rushed into her ears.

The light swept up the staircase. Lily grabbed the doll and pulled it inside, easing her door closed.

The first stair groaned under the weight of the intruder.

She sucked in a breath as she slowly turned the key to

lock her door before rushing across the room and swiping her phone from the charger.

"Help. Cassie," the doll said.

"I'm trying," Lily whispered. "Keep your voice down!"

Her hands shook as she swiped into her phone and scrolled through her contacts, pressing to initiate a call.

The line trilled on the other end a few times. Lily bounced up and down on her toes. "Come on, come on. Pick up."

A scraping noise sounded on the other end of the line as the staircase offered another creak.

"Lily?" Wyatt's tired voice asked. "You okay?"

"No. There's someone in the house."

Another rustling noise sounded as Wyatt spoke again, the sleep in his voice replaced by shock. "What? Are you safe? Can you get out of the house?"

Panic filled Lily's voice as reality set in. She ran her fingers through her hair, trying to steady her voice. "I can't. He's on the stairs. I'm locked in my bedroom, but I can't get to Cassie."

"I'm on my way. I want you to hang up and call 9-1-1. Stay on the line with them until someone gets there."

Lily bobbed her head up and down as she answered. "Okay."

The line disconnected, and Lily pulled the phone from her ear. She licked her lips as she tried to steady her hand and dial the emergency number. Another creak caused tears to well in her eyes.

The line trilled again, and she pressed the phone to her ear.

"9-1-1, what is your emergency?"

"This is Lily Bennett, I'm at 101 Ocean Drive. There's an intruder in my house."

"I'm dispatching units to you now. Are you safe?"

"Yes, right now I am."

"Are you able to get out of the house?"

"No," Lily moaned. "I'm not. He's on the stairs and I'm upstairs. I locked my door, but my daughter is across the house, and I can't warn her."

"Units are two minutes from your home, ma'am, and I'm going to stay on the line until they arrive and secure the premises."

Lily nodded, biting her lower lip as a tear fell onto her cheek. A siren rang out in the night air and the footsteps creeping up the stairs ceased.

Lily tiptoed to her door, easing the key backward to unlock it. She inched the door open, peering into the hall. No light shone up the stairs.

She pulled the door open wider and stuck her head out. A scan of the staircase showed no one. She tiptoed further out, her trembling hand wrapping around the banister as she crept toward the staircase and peered downstairs.

The front door stood wide open. Lily's heart hammered in her chest as she backed away from the railing and dashed down the hall, rounding the corner and racing toward Cassie's room.

She reached the closed door and twisted the doorknob, throwing it open. "Cassie!" she hissed into the darkness.

The lump in the bed with the covers pulled up to her ear squirmed. Lily pushed the door closed and hurried across the room, shaking her daughter's shoulders.

"Cassie, wake up!"

Cassie's eyes fluttered open, and her brow creased. She clutched at her duvet and pushed herself up onto her elbow. "Mom? What's wrong?"

Lily gasped out a response between ragged breaths. "There was someone in the house. I'm not sure if they're gone or not, but–"

A loud banging caused them both to jump.

"Hideaway Bay Sheriff's Department. Is there anyone inside?"

"Yes!" Lily's voice called out. "We're upstairs."

Footsteps pounded up the stairs as Lily hurried to the door and peered out a small crack. An officer, his weapon and flashlight drawn, searched the darkened space.

Lily swung the door open and stuck her head out. "We're in here."

The officer hurried toward them, squeezing inside Cassie's room and closing the door behind them. "We'll wait in here for the all-clear. Are you both all right?"

"Yes, we're fine. Just a little scared."

Cassie finished tying her robe around her and wrapped her arm around her mother's waist. Lily pulled her daughter closer as the officer with them radioed to his partner.

After a few tense moments, his radio crackled to life. "We're all clear. Sheriff Cooper is here, asking to see the residents."

"Ten-four. I've got both of them with me. I'll escort them down now."

The young officer twisted to face them, offering a weak smile. "Should be all safe now, ladies." He swung the door open and motioned for them to precede him.

Lights blazed in the house and the front door still stood open. Alternating blue and red lights bathed the front porch as they made their way down the stairs.

Wyatt stood at the open door, speaking to another officer. His untied boots and untucked shirttails suggested the haste with which he'd dressed. He caught sight of Lily and Cassie being led down the stairs.

"Lily! Cassie! Are you alright?"

"We're fine," Lily answered with her arms still around Cassie.

"I didn't even know what was happening. I slept through it," Cassie admitted.

"Did you get a good look at the intruder? Can you give us a description?"

Lily slid a piece of hair behind her ear as she shook her head. "Not really. It was dark. He had a hoodie on."

"He? So, you think this was a male?" Wyatt waved the other officer over toward them. "Get this down."

"I would assume a he based on how the figure moved, the bulk under the sweatshirt. But I never saw the face."

The officer jotted down a few notes as Wyatt continued to question Lily. "Was he short, tall? Skinny, heavy? Anything you can tell us may help."

"Uh, I'd say he was medium build, a bit on the stockier side, not tall and thin. Average height. Black hoodie, jeans, and heavy shoes."

Wyatt cocked his head. "Heavy shoes?"

"Yeah, like boots or something with thick soles. Just based on the sound they made when he was walking, even though he was trying to be quiet."

Wyatt placed his hand on Lily's shoulder and patted it. The officer jotted a few more notes. "Okay, great. That's good."

"Wow, I can't believe you caught all that, Mom," Cassie said, snaking an arm around her mother's waist and squeezing. "You must have been so scared."

Lily nodded as she blew out a sigh. "I could use a cup of tea. Anyone else?"

"I'm good, thanks, ma'am," the officer said as he flipped his notebook closed. "We're going to head out unless there's anything else." He flicked his gaze to Wyatt.

"No, get on that description back at the station and see what you can find."

"I don't think we'll come up with much on something this vague, Sheriff."

"I don't want to hear your excuses. I want to see results. Now, find me a perp."

The man shoved the notebook into his pocket with a curt nod. "I'll get on it."

The two officers skirted past them and headed out the door. Wyatt pushed it shut with a long sigh. "I'll take you up on that offer for that cup of tea if you don't mind."

Lily nodded and started toward the kitchen before she doubled back. "Ugh, wait. Henrietta's still upstairs in my room."

"Ahhhhh," Wyatt said, his eyes wide as they slid side to side, "like, the ghost?"

"Yes, the ghost. She warned me about the intruder."

Cassie's jaw dropped, and her chin dipped to her chest. "Seriously?"

"Yes. When I heard the noise, I opened the door, and she was standing there. Cassie, would you mind running up to get her? I don't want her alone up there."

Cassie's jaw remained agape. "Are-are you serious? You don't want her alone?"

"Yes! That poor ghost was scared, too, and very concerned about you. She kept saying 'help Cassie.' The least you can do is go up and get her so she's not alone."

Wyatt raised his hand in the air before speaking. "I was kind of on Cassie's side on this. Leave her up there."

"This isn't a vote. Go get her," Lily said with a huff, waving her arm up the stairs.

"Okay, okay," Cassie agreed, darting past Lily up the steps.

She reached the top and hovered in the doorway to her mother's room for a moment. The Victorian doll stood a few steps away with her back to her.

Cassie firmed her jaw as she stepped inside the room and approached the doll. "Hi, Ri. I came to get you."

The doll stood silent, and Cassie slipped an arm around her waist and lifted her up, carrying her down the stairs and into the kitchen. She set the doll next to the table before retrieving teabags for the mugs Lily set out.

Wyatt eyed the haunted animatron sideways, his arms crossed over his chest tightly as he frowned at it.

Lily filled the electric tea kettle and turned it on, glancing at the silent doll. "Cassie's okay, Ri. See?" She stroked Cassie's hair and shot a smile at the doll.

Wyatt's eyes widened as he stared at the doll, then flicked his gaze to Lily. "Does she normally talk back?"

The kettle's blue light clicked off. Lily lifted it from the base and poured steaming water into each mug. "Sometimes. She's not really communicative yet. I'm not sure if she can't talk more or won't talk more."

"Did you ask Ruby about it?'

"I did. She's going to come back out to see if she can help whenever she gets the chance," Cassie said as she settled into the chair next to Wyatt with her steaming mug.

Lily set a mug down in front of the sheriff before easing into the chair next to the doll.

"She ought to come out right away!" Wyatt exclaimed. "Do you have any cookies?"

Lily shot him an unimpressed stare as she slid the bakery box across the table. "Is that the only reason you stayed?"

Wyatt pulled one from the white box and bit into it. "Part of it." He waved the cookie in the air. "Anyway, when is Ruby coming?"

"I'm not sure," Cassie admitted. "Though it would be great if she could say more than only the few words she says now."

"What does she say?"

"Journals, mostly. Oh, and then something about a key," Lily answered.

"Yeah," Cassie confirmed. "That and called us nitwits."

Wyatt stared at Cassie for a breath, his brows pinching together. "Are you serious?"

"Yes. She asked us to find journals and we went into the library to look, and she called us nitwits before she told us to look upstairs."

Wyatt's eyebrow arched and he shot a glance at the Victorian woman standing at the table. "I think I'd get rid of that doll."

Cassie opened her mouth to answer, but the whirring sound of the doll's base cut her off. The animatron sped toward Wyatt, stopping short in front of him. He leaned back in his chair, stretching away from the doll as it approached, his eyes wide.

"Help," the doll said.

Cassie pulled a cookie from the box. "Uh-oh. You made her mad."

Wyatt's wide eyes darted around the room. "Seriously?"

"Yeah, you're lucky she didn't smack you across the face like she did to me when I told her to carry herself up the stairs."

Wyatt's face twisted into a mask of fear, his lips forming an open-mouthed grimace. "She hit you?"

Cassie offered him a slow nod as she chewed her cookie.

"That hasn't been proven, but her hand did crack Cassie across the cheek," Lily said. "You may want to apologize to her."

Wyatt wrinkled his nose and glanced up at the doll. "Sorry." He leaned forward toward Lily and lowered his voice. "Still, I think I'd–" He swiped a finger across his throat and thumbed toward the doll.

Lily shook her head. "I'm not going to do that. This was

her house before it was ours. I'm not going to throw the poor woman out of her house! You heard her. She needs help."

The comment prompted the doll to spin away from Wyatt and begin pacing the floor behind Cassie. "Help Cassie. The key."

Fear shone on Wyatt's features as his eyes followed the doll's movements. "Wait, is she asking Cassie to help her or saying she wants to help Cassie?"

Cassie shrugged her shoulders as she sipped the warm liquid. "That's why we need Ruby. She just speaks in these clipped phrases. I have no idea what the key is or how it helps me."

"Help Wyatt. The key."

"That's new," Lily said. "Now she's talking about you."

"Great," Wyatt grumbled. "Now I'm all over her radar."

"No wonder. You tried to get rid of her," Lily said with a shrug, biting into her cookie.

"How can you be so calm about this?" Wyatt asked.

Cassie threw her arms in the air. "How are you getting off scot-free? You tried to off her and now she wants to help you. I asked her to climb the stairs on her own and got slapped!"

Lily waved her hands in the air. "Okay, wait. We have to figure out what key she's trying to tell us about. She's mentioned it in conjunction with both of your names now. Which is odd. How does the key apply to both of you?"

Wyatt licked his lips as he considered it. He reached for his belt and tugged a large keyring from it, tossing it on the table. "I've got a lot of keys. Are any of these what you're looking for?"

"The key. The key."

Cassie crossed her arms over her chest and slouched in her chair. "It's like an ornery parrot."

The doll's hand flung out and smacked into the back of her head before continuing along its path.

"Ow!" Cassie exclaimed, straightening and rubbing the back of her head. "Did you see that?"

Wyatt's jaw dropped open. "I saw it. I still can't believe it. She hates you."

"She does," Cassie said with a pout.

"The key," the doll repeated as she trundled across the room toward Lily.

"Yes, Ri, we've got that part. What key? Where? How does it help Cassie and Wyatt?"

Wyatt tugged his phone from his pants pocket. "I'm calling Ruby. This is crazy."

"It's the middle of the night!" Lily said.

"And you've got a crazed doll possessed by a spirit attacking Cassie. We need help!"

"How are you getting away with saying this and not getting smacked?" Cassie inquired. "Can she only hear us?"

"She heard him talking before," Lily reminded her as Wyatt threw his phone down on the table.

"No answer!"

"It's the middle of the night. What did you expect?" Lily questioned. "We've got to figure out what she's talking about ourselves."

Cassie tapped her fingernails against the side of her mug. "What key could she be talking about?"

Lily rubbed a finger along her jawline. "That helps both you and Wyatt." She shook her head and flung her arms in the air. "I don't know. We need another way to attack this."

Wyatt picked up his phone and tapped around on it. "I'll call Ruby again."

Lily waved for him to stop. "No, let the poor woman sleep. Besides, there's no guarantee that'll help. It would be nice if she was more communicative, but this is what we're working with right now."

Wyatt set the phone on the table. "So, what do you suggest? Oh, maybe if I leave, she'll talk more."

Cassie drained the last sip of her tea and collected the empty mugs from the table, ambling to the sink with them. "Trying to get away, huh?"

"Honestly, it makes me uncomfortable."

Lily wagged a finger at him. "You're part of this. She said, 'Help Wyatt.'"

"I still don't understand what she meant. That she's going to help me or that I should help her?"

"Either way, she mentioned your name. You're staying." Lily drummed her fingers on the table. "I wonder if we move her from room to room if she'll give us a clue."

Cassie finished rinsing the last mug and set it in the dish drainer, grabbing a towel to dry her hands. "It's worth a shot. She seems to react to certain things."

Lily stood from her chair and eyed the doll. "Okay, Ri, let's see if we can figure out how you'd like to help."

CHAPTER 25

Cassie let her hip rest against the counter as she studied the doll across the room. "Maybe we should start upstairs. She didn't seem interested in the library the last time we were in there."

Lily poked a finger in Cassie's direction. "Good idea. Let's take her upstairs. We'll start in my bedroom and work our way around. Though she didn't mention anything to me when she charged in when the prowler was here."

"Can't hurt to try." Cassie snaked her arm around the doll's waist and lifted her from the floor. The quartet paraded to the foyer and climbed the stairs, veering left to Lily's room.

Cassie set the doll down inside the doorway.

"Okay, Ri. Anything in here?" Lily asked.

The doll stood silent, staring ahead with no comment.

Cassie threw her arms out to the sides. "I guess it's not in here. Should we move to another room?"

"I guess so," Lily said. "We'll try Susan's old bedroom next."

Wyatt crinkled his nose as Cassie hefted the doll up and

carried her down the hall to the next bedroom. "Susan, like Susan Davies?"

"Yes," Lily said. "We found her bedroom closed off. It's cleared out now, but it was sad seeing all her things left behind."

The grimace on Wyatt's lips intensified as they approached the room. "This night gets worse and worse. I'll stay out here if you don't mind."

Lily rolled her eyes at him as she passed into the empty room. "Geez, you're worse than Cassie."

Cassie set the doll down on the hardwood floor and flicked on the light switch. "How about this room, Ri? Is the key in here?"

The doll did not move or answer.

"Another strikeout," Cassie said, her voice echoing in the empty room.

"Moving on," Lily announced as they exited the bedroom and moved to the next space, a spare bedroom in the same hall.

Cassie set the doll down near the antique tallboy dresser and put her hands on her hips.

"Is it here, Ri?" Lily questioned.

No answer.

"Maybe she left," Wyatt said, hope in his voice.

"There are still a few more rooms to go," Lily answered.

Cassie collected the doll and they moved to the next bedroom with no luck. With a sigh, Cassie dragged the animatron from the room. "Only my room left."

Lily flashed her crossed fingers as they strode down the hall toward the front of the house. Cassie ducked into her bedroom with the doll in tow first, followed by Lily and Wyatt. Willy lounged on the bed, the excitement of earlier in the evening no longer a concern. He lazily opened his one eye as they trudged inside, offering a wide yawn.

"Okay, Ri, last room upstairs. Is this where the key is?" Lily questioned.

All eyes fell to the doll whose silent blank stare gave away nothing.

Cassie's shoulders sagged. "Well, so much for that idea. That didn't seem to help."

"I think she left," Wyatt said. "Which is fine by me. Maybe you'll have more luck when Ruby tries. Schedule it for a time when I can't be here."

Lily crossed her arms and eyed him. "Did you say a time when you *can't* be here?"

"Yep," he confirmed. "I'd prefer not to be around when the ghost is wandering through the house. You can tell me later what key she wanted you to find."

Lily sighed and tossed a lock of hair over her shoulder. "I really thought this would work. Oh well, I suppose we should let you head home and get some sleep."

Wyatt shuffled to the door. "Thanks for the tea. I hope you ladies are able to get some sleep with all the ex–"

"The key!" the doll exclaimed.

Everyone swung to face her, and Lily rushed toward her. "Is the key here? Is it in this room?"

"Find the key. Help Wyatt. Help Cassie."

"Yes," Lily said, her head bobbing up and down, "yes, we want to find the key. But we don't know where to look."

The doll did not answer.

"Okay, everyone spread out and start searching for a key," Lily suggested.

Willy propped himself up on one arm, eyeing the chaos of the search. Wyatt glanced around on the top of Cassie's dresser.

Cassie dug into her purse and pulled out a set of keys. "Here are my keys. Is this it?" She jangled them in front of the doll with her eyebrows raised. No answer.

Lily tugged drawers open on the dresser, shifting contents around inside. "Maybe there's something in one of the dresser drawers left over from a previous occupant."

The now-familiar whirring noise filled the air as the doll trundled across the room. She headed for the tall dresser near the bathroom door. As she barreled toward the bathroom door, she knocked into the storage box containing Trevor's personal items.

The doll stopped, bouncing backward a few inches.

"Shoot," Cassie mumbled as she hurried forward and tugged the box out of the way.

The doll stood unmoving.

"Go ahead, Ri. I moved it." Cassie waved the doll forward. The doll did not budge.

Cassie heaved a sigh and rolled her eyes. "Great. She ran into the box and now she's stuck again."

The doll spun and lunged forward again, smacking into the box before bouncing back a few inches.

"Ugh!" Cassie groaned. "I just moved that so you could go, and you turn around and run into it again!"

The doll darted forward again, hitting the box, and moving it several inches toward Cassie.

"Wait, I'll move it."

"Wait!" Lily exclaimed, holding her hand in the air.

"What?" Cassie asked.

Lily cocked her head, her eyes on the box. "I—I think she's trying to tell us the key is in the box."

The doll whirled in a circle and faced Lily. "The key."

Cassie's eyes widened and she stared down at the box by her feet. Her forehead crinkled as she gave it an incredulous look. "The key to helping me and Wyatt is in Trevor's stuff?"

Cassie dropped to her knees and tugged the box's top open. She rifled around inside the cardboard container in search of any keys. With a confused expression, she shrugged, glancing up at the room's other two living occupants. "There's nothing in here."

"Really?" Lily inquired, making her way over. She plopped on the edge of the bed and peered into the box. After rooting around through a few things, she raised her eyes to the doll. "Are you sure, Ri?"

With a sigh, Cassie collapsed onto her heels and began removing items, setting them on the floor around her.

"Check inside the valet box."

"He didn't keep keys in there," Cassie said as she pulled open the drawer and shuffled the items around inside. "A pair of cufflinks and a few old driver's licenses."

She slid up the miniature roll-top concealing a cubby. "And a picture of us at the park. No key."

She set it aside and moved on, pulling out a worn ball cap. Tears welled in her eyes as she rubbed a finger along the brim. She sniffled and set it aside, mumbling an apology as she grabbed the corner of the box and turned it upside down.

With a shake, she announced, "Empty. No key."

She set the box down and glanced at the doll, who had spun to face them as they worked. "What gives, Ri?"

The doll wheeled toward Cassie, who scrambled back on all fours away from it, shielding her head from an anticipated smack. Instead, the doll stopped short near the array of items spread across the floor.

The brown leather journal clattered to the floor as the doll's arms moved of their own volition, stretching out over the scattered items. The valet rose in the air, bobbing around clumsily.

Cassie's eyes grew wide, and her jaw fell open. Willy's ears flattened against his head, and he slinked off the bed, hiding underneath it. Wyatt stumbled backward, slipping behind the open door and using it as a shield, peering around it with eyes as big as saucers.

"Mom, look out!" Cassie shouted as the wooden valet rose toward the woman.

The drawer slid open and flew across the room, smacking off the dresser and clattering to the floor below. The contents sprawled across the hardwood as it landed face down. The valet crashed back to the floor, splintering into pieces as it hit.

"Oh my goodness, Cassie, look!" Lily exclaimed, pointing a trembling finger at the upturned drawer.

"The key," the doll whispered, sounding winded. "Help."

Cassie crawled onto her hands and knees and clamored toward the small drawer. A silver key was taped to the underside. She ripped it away from the wood, holding it up in the air, her face a mask of surprise. A smile spread across her lips, and she glanced at her mother, then the doll.

Lily bit her lower lip and stood, patting the doll's shoulder. "Yes, you did help, Ri. You did it. You found the key."

Cassie climbed to her feet, the key still clutched in her hand. "Thank you, Ri."

She swiped the journal from the floor and pressed it against the doll's chest, bending her arms back to hold it. "Here's your journal back. You did a good job. Now, can you tell us how it helps us?"

"Cassie!" Lily said, patting the doll on the shoulder again. "That took a toll on her. I bet she's tired."

Wyatt crept from behind the door, his eyes still wide. "Is she done? Is it over?" he whispered.

"Yeah, I think that effort just about finished her for a bit," Lily answered. "Why don't we head downstairs and take a closer look at this key?"

Cassie closed her fingers around the key. "Sounds good. Do you want me to take–" She nudged her head toward the doll and raised her eyebrows.

Lily nodded at her. "Yeah, I'm sure she'd like to be involved."

Wyatt wrinkled his nose as Cassie lifted the doll and carried her from the room. "I hope we can get you to a point where you can move around on your own, Ri. That would make things much easier."

"I wouldn't be hoping for that," Wyatt murmured as he trailed behind her. "That whole thing was creepy. I don't know how you're going to stay in this house after tonight."

"It's not that creepy," Lily contended, leading the way to the kitchen. "The woman's spirit is stuck here, that's all. And she's not harmful. In fact, she's going out of her way to help."

Lily meandered to the sink and filled the electric teakettle again. "Anyone else want more tea? I do."

"Me," Cassie chimed in.

"Me," the doll parroted.

Cassie snapped her gaze toward her, her eyebrows raised high before she shot her mother a glance.

"Okay, three teas. How about it, Wyatt?" Lily set the kettle on its base without skipping a beat.

"Any chance of a coffee?" Wyatt inquired as he slumped into a kitchen chair.

Lily pulled down the canister of coffee from the cupboard. "Sure. Tea for three and one coffee."

Cassie wandered to the counter, setting out three mugs and spooning sugar into two. She set the other mug in front of Wyatt along with the sugar bowl. "Cream?"

"Yeah, thanks," he said.

Lily filled the coffee pot with water and a few scoops of the aromatic grounds. "Cass, you forgot a mug."

Cassie slowly swung the refrigerator door closed with the creamer in her hand. "Are-are you serious? I'm really supposed to get a mug for the doll?"

"Yes, Ri wants tea. I think she deserves it, don't you?"

Cassie squashed her lips together as she pulled another mug down from the cupboard and set it on the counter.

"Cream and sugar," the doll announced.

Cassie shot her mother a sideways glance before she dumped two teaspoons of sugar into the mug. The teakettle clicked off and Lily poured steaming water into the mugs while Cassie grabbed the quickly filling coffee pot and poured Wyatt a cup.

Cassie bit her lower lip as she returned the coffee pot to the coffee maker and eyed the three mugs of tea. "What am I supposed to do with hers?"

"Put cream in it and give it to her," Lily said, lifting her mug from the counter and shuffling to her seat at the table.

Cassie poured a bit of cream and stirred it before inching the mug toward the doll at the corner of the table.

"If she starts drinking that, I'm out of here," Wyatt said.

They sat in silence for a moment before Lily said, "All right, let's take a look at this key."

Cassie dug it from within her robe's pocket and set the silver item in the center of the table. Wyatt snatched it, holding it in the air as he studied it.

"Does it say anything?" Cassie asked.

"Do not duplicate," Wyatt read. "And a number."

"Like a phone number?" Cassie asked, craning her neck for a look.

"No, just a string of numbers." Wyatt passed the key over to Cassie.

Lily waved her hand in the air, curling her fingers toward her palm. "Let me see it."

Cassie slid the key across the tabletop to her mother. Lily dug her glasses from her robe's pocket and slid them onto the bridge of her nose before eying the key.

"Looks like a safe deposit box key. Those usually can't be duplicated."

"You're right," Wyatt answered.

Cassie wrapped her hands around her mug before taking a sip. "What's the number mean? The box it belongs to? Trevor never said anything about a safe deposit box to me."

Lily pulled her phone from her pocket and tapped around on it. "Says here safe deposit keys often have the routing number of the bank printed on them."

"How long are routing numbers?" Cassie inquired.

After a few taps on her phone, Lily reported, "Nine digits."

"And how long is our number?" Wyatt asked between sips of coffee.

Lily squinted at the silver key, her finger tapping along as she counted. "Nine."

"So, this could be a safe deposit box key," Cassie said. "Can we reverse search the routing number to find the bank?"

Lily tapped around on her phone again. "Yep. Here's a website for that."

"Well, input the number and see what it says!" Cassie exclaimed.

Lily held one hand in the air as she typed with the other. "Okay, okay. Give me a second."

She gave one final tap then stared at the output, a frown on her face. "No results found."

Cassie slumped in her seat as she tapped on her mug with her fingernails. "Maybe it's not a safe deposit box key then."

"Oh, wait," Lily said, squinting her eyes, "is this a six or an eight? I can't see it."

She slid the key toward Cassie. "The third digit? It's a six."

"Ah, that may be the problem. I put an eight. Sorry, my glasses need glasses." She adjusted the number in her search and tried again.

"Did it work?" Cassie inquired, peering over at her mother's screen.

"Yes. I got a result."

"Where is it?" Wyatt asked.

Lily tapped on her screen. "Let me see. It's loading." Her jaw dropped open and she glanced up at Cassie and Wyatt.

"What is it?" Cassie asked.

"It's for a bank called First Federal Savings and Loan over in Misty Hollow."

Cassie cocked her head at the location. "The neighboring town? Trevor had a safe deposit box in the town neighboring this one?"

"Well, someone did," Lily said.

Cassie let her fist slam onto the table, rattling the mugs. "Trevor did. No one else had a safe deposit box and taped the key to the bottom of Trevor's valet drawer. I certainly didn't and the only other people with access to our house was you and dad. Unless someone broke in and left it there for safe-keeping, Trevor had a safe deposit box."

Cassie stared straight ahead for a few seconds before a sharp laugh escaped her. "Another thing he kept from me."

"Could have been his brother's and he hid the key for him," Lily said.

"Either way, he kept it from me." She shook her head as she drummed her fingers against the tabletop. "What time does the bank open tomorrow?"

"Ten," Lily reported after consulting her phone.

Cassie swiped the key from the table and eyed it. "I'm going there tomorrow at ten and opening that box."

CHAPTER 26

Cassie twirled the key in her hands, staring at it.

Lily shot Wyatt a glance, licking her lips before she turned her attention to Cassie. "Cass, I'm not certain that's a good idea."

"Why not?" Cassie snapped.

"We have no idea why he may have had that box. Are you sure you want to know? It may change the way you remember him. And he's not here to defend himself."

Cassie ground her teeth together, flexing her jaw. "I have to know."

"Uh, sorry to interrupt here, but I'd also like to know," Wyatt said.

Both women turned their attention to Wyatt who shrugged as he took another sip of his coffee. "Well, I mean Trevor is related to my vic. I'd like to know if there's anything related to Kyle McGuire in that box."

Cassie arched an eyebrow at him before she returned to tracing the woodgrain on the table.

Lily furrowed her brow, glancing up at the doll standing next to her. "I wonder…"

"Wonder what?" Cassie asked.

"Ri said help Cassie, help Wyatt. I wonder if there is something related to your case."

Cassie smacked her hand against the table as she stood and collected her empty tea mug. "That settles it, then. We have to go tomorrow and see what's in the box. Ready or not."

"Maybe I should go with you in my official capacity in case there is something in there related to my case."

Cassie nodded as she rinsed the teacup. "Okay, sure. Might be nice to have the moral support, too."

Lily rose and delivered her teacup to the sink. "Well, I was going to go for moral support."

"Of course," Cassie said as she washed and rinsed the mug, "but the more the merrier. I'll take the support wherever I can get it. Moral and legal."

Wyatt nodded as he stood and handed his empty mug off. "Should we meet here around nine-thirty? We can go in my car."

"Sounds good," Cassie said. With a deep inhale, she added, "Tomorrow we start unraveling the secrets Trevor hid from me."

"We'll figure it out. Try to get some rest, ladies."

"Thanks, Wyatt. And thanks for racing over here with that intruder. Gosh, I hope that's the end of the excitement around here."

Wyatt's eyes slid to the doll standing near the table. "I doubt that with the, ah, new houseguest, but hopefully no new live occupants."

Lily offered him an amused smile as Cassie meandered to the table for the last mug to wash. She stopped dead before she reached the table, her eyes going wide.

"What's wrong, Cass?" Lily questioned.

Cassie spun to face them, her lips moving but no sound

coming out for a moment. "She drank the tea!"

Lily skirted around Wyatt and pushed past Cassie, her eyes bulging as she stared into the empty tea mug.

"Aaaaand that's my cue to leave," Wyatt said. "Told you I'd skedaddle if she drank the tea." He hastened past the room's two living occupants and into the foyer. The front door slammed moments later.

"Wow," Lily said.

"Yeah, no kidding. I never expected her to drink it."

"No, I meant Wyatt. He really is a scaredy cat."

The two ladies chuckled over Wyatt's fear of ghosts as Cassie washed the last mug before they climbed the stairs to head to bed after Cassie tucked Henrietta away in the library.

Cassie pulled her door shut, her fingertips lingering on the knob for a few moments. She shuffled toward the bed and plopped on the edge. Trevor's things were still spread in an array on the floor. With her foot, she slid several of the wayward items into a pile, vowing to clean it up tomorrow.

She slid under the covers, shimmying toward the middle of the bed as far as a sprawled Willy would allow. As the room plunged into darkness after she flicked the lamp off, she stared at the shadows. The chunky forms of Trevor's belongings filled her field of vision.

Questions shot through her mind. What would she find in the safe deposit box? What had Trevor hidden from her? And why? The last question burned the largest hole in her brain and her heart. Why had her husband lied to her?

A tear slid from the corner of her eye, dripping onto her pillow. She sniffled and wiped it away, rolling onto her back in favor of staring at the ceiling.

She pushed the memories of Trevor and the curiosity over what she may find in the bank's deposit box from her thoughts, trying to focus on something else that may allow her to fall asleep.

Her mind turned to the way they found the key. Visions of the valet rising from the floor at the doll's behest danced through her memory. The rumors about Whispering Manor had been correct. The house was haunted. And the ghost had found a new home in her doll.

How would they move forward from here? And what would their lives look like now?

* * *

Lily's eyelids fluttered open as rays of the bright morning sun shone through her ocean-facing windows.

"Oh, I need to get room darkening blinds," she lamented as she squeezed her eyes closed and stretched.

She sat up, opening her eyes. She clutched at her blankets, tugging them higher as she spotted the sight at the end of her bed.

The Victorian doll stood at the foot of her bed. "Help Cassie."

Lily blew out a long breath as she pulled her robe around her shoulders and swung her legs over the bed. "Good morning, Ri. Would you mind letting me get out of bed and get some breakfast first before any requests today?"

Lily shoved her feet into her slippers before shuffling into her en-suite bathroom.

The doll rolled behind her. "Help me."

Lily turned on the water, testing the temperature with her fingers. "Help you? What do you need help with? Do you need more tea?"

"Help me. The journals."

She splashed water on her face, reaching blindly for her cleanser and gently scrubbing her skin with it and rinsing it away before she whipped the towel from the ring hanging next to the sink. She blotted the water from her skin and glanced in the mirror, grimacing at the dark circles under her eyes.

"Right, the journals. We haven't found them yet. But we will. I promise." Lily spun to face the doll. "Right after we get a full night's sleep."

The doll stood staring into the bathroom as Lily slathered lotion on her face and brushed her hair. She stepped toward the bedroom, blocked from leaving by the doll. She picked up the doll and stepped into the bedroom, setting it down a few steps away.

"If you're going to stick around, we really need to have a conversation about privacy, Ri," Lily called over her shoulder as she pulled open her door and stepped into the hall.

Cassie's door remained closed, so she shuffled downstairs and into the kitchen. She sank to her knees, pulling open the cupboard and shifting things around until she retrieved the waffle maker.

She plugged it in, painted some oil onto the griddle, and turned it on to heat. Within a few minutes, she had Belgian waffle batter ready to pour. After testing the heat, she poured the first waffle onto the iron and closed the lid, letting it cook.

Cassie shuffled in as steam rose from the waffle maker, yawning and offering a sleepy "good morning."

"Good morning, hun, did you get any sleep?"

Cassie covered another big yawn as she slumped onto a kitchen chair. "A little. You?"

"I got some." Lily lifted the lid of the waffle iron, peering inside before she shut it again. "I had a visitor this morning."

Cassie shot her mother an unimpressed glance. "Are you kidding?"

"Nope," Lily said as she freed the golden-brown waffle from the iron and slid it onto a plate, waving it in the air toward Cassie.

Cassie stood and grabbed the proffered plate, retrieving the maple syrup from the hot water bath Lily set it in earlier. "Same visitor or a new one?"

"Same one. Standing at the foot of my bed when I woke up."

Cassie let her head fall between her shoulders with a groan. "Now what?"

"Well, she started out talking about helping you again."

Cassie drowned one wedge of her waffle in syrup before slicing into it.

Lily tapped her fingers on the counter as she waited for her waffle to cook. "And then she asked me to help her."

"Help her with what?" Cassie asked as she waited for the syrup to drip from her next bite of waffle.

Lily lifted the lid on the waffle iron and pried the waffle loose. "The journals."

"Oh, right. The journals. We still haven't found them."

"Nope," Lily said, sliding into her seat and drizzling syrup on her golden brown breakfast.

"Well, at least she's bugging you about them now instead of me." Cassie offered her mother a playful smile and a wink. "She likes you."

Lily shot her a glance. "I'm the only one who's nice to her."

"I'm not mean to her!" Cassie cried defensively.

"You could be nicer."

Cassie shook her head, reaching for the syrup to add more to her next quarter. "Nah. I don't think it's that at all. I think she's jealous of me."

"Oh? Jealous, huh? Thinks blondes have more fun?"

"Not of my looks," Cassie said.

Lily sawed off another piece of waffle and slid it around in the pool of syrup on her plate. "Of what then?"

"My mother."

Lily lifted her eyebrows in response as she chewed. She poked her fork toward her chest. "Me?"

Cassie nodded and jabbed a finger in her direction. "You. I think she wishes she had you as a mother. Remember she didn't get along with her mother."

Lily considered it for a moment before she shrugged. "Well, that's too bad. I'm already someone else's mom. And I told her we'd help her with the journals after we figured this thing out with Trevor and got a good night's sleep."

"Bet she loved that."

"She stopped talking to me," Lily said with a chuckle.

Cassie finished her waffle and dumped her plate in the dishwasher. "Sounds about right. Maybe she thinks now that she's helped us, we should help her."

"Could be. Maybe we'll take a look around after the bank trip today. Depending on how we feel."

Cassie glanced at the clock on the microwave. "Speaking of, I guess we'd better get ready. Wyatt will be here soon."

Lily nodded and collected her plate and fork from the table, placing them in the dishwasher before they shuffled upstairs to dress for the trip.

As Cassie slid her feet into her ballet flats, her stomach rolled with anticipation. What would she find in the safe deposit box? With the answer looming in the near future, she wondered if she truly wanted to know.

Her mother's voice stopped her rambling thoughts. "Wyatt's here!"

"Okay!" Cassie called back as she stood from the bed and grabbed her purse. "Coming!"

She gave Willy a pat on the head as he lounged across her dresser, promising him she'd be back soon, and darted from the room, hopping down the stairs.

Lily swung the door open, finding Wyatt sitting in the

porch glider nearest the door. "Good morning, ladies. Get any sleep?"

"A little," Lily said.

"Had a patrol car watch the house last night and they said no further disturbances."

"We didn't hear anything," Lily said as they stepped onto the porch and she swung the door closed, locking it and arming the alarm system.

"Except Ri bugging Mom this morning about helping her."

"Persistent, huh?" Wyatt tugged his phone from his pocket and checked the display. "Still didn't hear back from Ruby. She should be on her way into the office by now."

Wyatt stood from his spot on the wicker glider. "Speaking of, would you mind stopping by the police station before we head to the bank?"

Lily shot a glance at Cassie with a shrug. "No, why?"

Wyatt heaved a sigh. "Lucy's asking to see Cassie. She won't say anything to us outside of she didn't do it, but this morning she asked to talk to Cassie."

Cassie swallowed hard, her stomach somersaulting again. All eyes turned to her, and she flicked her gaze between Lily and Wyatt. With a meek nod, she answered, "Okay."

Wyatt motioned for them to precede him off the porch to his waiting car.

"I thought you didn't want her to see anyone until you sorted some things out?" Lily asked as she slipped into the passenger's seat.

"Well," Wyatt said, climbing behind the wheel and firing the engine, "I didn't, but we're not getting anywhere with her. She's got a bail hearing set up this afternoon. I'm not going to be able to hold her any longer even with the charge." He flicked his eyes over his shoulder to Cassie in the back-seat. "Maybe you can get something out of her."

Cassie settled back into her seat, tugging at the seatbelt at her neck. Already nervous about what she may learn from Lucy, she now added the worry of trying to elicit information from the woman about a crime she claimed she didn't commit.

"I hope I don't say anything wrong," Cassie murmured.

"You want me to go in with you, honey?" Lily asked, twisting to glance at Cassie in the backseat.

"Maybe," Cassie said with a wrinkled nose.

"You can't say anything wrong, Cassie," Wyatt assured her. "Sorry, I didn't mean to put pressure on you like that. I just meant maybe she'd open up to you. Woman to woman or something. Sorry, that was sexist." Wyatt wrinkled his nose and shook his head, wincing. "Maybe she'll say something that'll help clear this up."

Cassie forced a smile on her face and nodded. "I hope she can clear a few things up on my end, too. Though I'm almost afraid of what she'll tell me."

Lily squeezed her lips together and reached into the backseat for Cassie's hand. She squeezed it in a silent display of support.

"Sorry, I just can't believe Trevor lied to me like this. And with every secret I uncover, I'm even further astounded instead of less so."

Wyatt flicked a gaze in his mirror. "I can't imagine what this must be like. Sorry, Cassie."

Cassie nodded at him, still clinging to her mother's hand as she sucked in a deep breath, trying to quell the surge of her emotions.

Wyatt swung his car into the Hideaway Bay Police Department's lot and slid it into the parking space marked for the Sheriff.

Lily swung her door open inches from the front door leading inside. "Wow, what a great parking space."

"I know the Sheriff," Wyatt said with a grin.

Even Cassie cracked a smile at his terrible joke as she climbed from the car and stared up at the nondescript brick building. She swallowed hard as she followed her mother and Wyatt inside. Ruby's desk still sat empty, with her chair neatly tucked under the desk and a ruby-red sweater draped around the back.

Wyatt bypassed the reception area, pushing open the door to the conference room and motioning for Lily and Cassie to enter.

"If you wouldn't mind waiting in here for a few minutes while I get Lucy from lock-up. There's tea and coffee if you can figure out the machine and donuts."

"Thanks," Lily said as he nodded and left them to settle into the chairs around the table.

Lily grabbed Cassie's hand as she traced the wood grain pattern, her leg bobbing up and down under the table. She pushed a lock of hair over her daughter's shoulder. "You okay?"

Cassie shot her a fleeting glance. "I can't wait until this is over."

"What are you afraid she'll say?"

"I don't know," Cassie said, flinging her hands upward before she drew them together, wringing them on the table-top. "That's just it, I guess. I don't know what to expect. Did she know him? Did she know him well? Were they…"

"What?"

"Involved," Cassie choked out. "Were they involved? Did she date Trevor? Did she have an affair with Trevor?"

Lily rubbed her daughter's back, unable to provide any consoling words at the moment. "It'll be over soon, honey."

Cassie nodded and slicked her hair behind her ears.

A moment later, Wyatt knocked at the door. "She's ready. I have her in an interrogation room."

Both women rose from their seats.

Wyatt held his hand out in front of him. "Ah, she asked for Cassie only."

"Oh," Lily said, drawing her chin to her chest in surprise before she shot a glance at Cassie. "Cass?"

Cassie sucked in a shaky breath. "Okay."

"Listen, we will be right in the next room. We can hear everything you say, so if you need someone in there just yell, okay? We'll be right behind the glass."

Cassie offered a tentative nod and a brief smile as he led them from the room, threading through the tight corridors to another hallway with four doors. He opened the first and motioned for Lily to enter a darkened room. A large window looked into another room. Cassie spotted Lucy huddled over a white table, handcuffs still around her wrists.

Wyatt led Cassie to the next door down the hall and opened it. "Good luck," he said with a nod.

Cassie brushed past him and into the brightly lit and sparsely furnished room. She sucked in a deep breath as Lucy flicked her gaze up at her and offered a hopeful, but apologetic smile. The woman tugged at the sleeves of her teal hoodie as Cassie dragged the metal chair from under the table and sat down across from her.

"Hey, Cassie, thanks for seeing me."

Cassie's heart pounded in her chest as she offered a tight-lipped smile and slouched in the slick metal chair.

The handcuffs rattled as Lucy lifted her chained hands to slick a piece of blonde hair behind her ear. "Umm, listen, I know it's weird that I asked to see you, but…"

"No, it's okay," Cassie interrupted. "I…I actually wanted to see you, too."

"You did?" Lucy asked. "I didn't do it, Cassie. I didn't kill Kyle. You have to believe me!"

CHAPTER 27

Wyatt stood with a finger tapping his lips as he eyed the first bits of the exchange between Lucy and Cassie. Next to him, Lily placed a hand against the glass as she offered her daughter support from a distance.

After the first few moments, Wyatt flung a hand in the air. "See, there she goes. What did she drag Cassie down here for just to tell her she's innocent? That's all she'll say."

"Something is very odd here. And I find myself wondering the same things that I think have been keeping Cassie up at night. Did she know Trevor? How well? And did she know us when she sold us Whispering Manor?"

Wyatt leaned against the wall next to the two-way mirror and sucked in a deep breath. "A week ago, I would have said no. But this whole investigation has me questioning everything."

"I hope Lucy can give Cassie some answers before Cassie goes crazy wondering just how many lies Trevor told."

They returned their attention to the conversation unfolding in the room next door.

"I don't know what to believe anymore, Lucy," Cassie admitted with a sigh.

"I didn't do this, Cassie. I didn't."

Cassie's chest heaved a few times as she focused on twisting a string from her striped shirt around between her thumb and index finger. "Why did you want to see me?"

"Because I need your help."

Lily's eyebrows rose to her hairline, and she pressed a hand to her chest. "Need her help? I can't imagine how Cassie'll react to that."

Cassie snapped her head up, a confused expression clouding her features. "What?"

Lucy's eyes pleaded with her as she repeated her statement. "I need your help."

"How could I possibly help you, Lucy? I know less than you do, obviously."

"You were married to Kyle's brother. You have to know something."

Cassie's features turned stony, and her jaw flexed as she fought through the emotions of the statement. "I was married to Trevor, yes. But I had no idea he had a brother. I'm the one who should be asking you for help."

"What do you mean?" Lucy inquired.

"Did you know me when I came to Hideaway Bay? Did you know who I was?"

Lucy licked her lips, dropping her gaze to the shiny metal table between them.

"Did you?" Cassie said, slamming her hand on the table with her voice raised.

Wyatt flicked his gaze to Lily. "You want me to go get her?"

Lily's focus remained on the scene unfolding, but she shook her head. "No. Let her get it out. She needs answers."

Lucy pursed her lips and shook her head. "No, I didn't

know you. I didn't even know Trevor was married. But when Kyle showed up again a few weeks ago and started talking about his brother being dead and a plane crash… I put the pieces together."

Cassie swallowed hard at the admission. She blinked back the tears forming in her eyes and pressed forward. "So, you knew Trevor?"

"Yeah, I knew him," Lucy admitted.

Cassie let her eyes float up to the ceiling as she processed the news.

"I swear, Cassie, I didn't know about you. I would have said something when we met. I didn't know–"

"Did you sleep with him?"

"Uh-oh," Wyatt said, wincing and shooting another glance at Lily.

Lily held up a hand. "Let her work through it. She has to know."

Lucy sat in stunned silence for another moment, her eyes wide before her head began to wag back and forth. "No, of course not."

"Well, you said you didn't know he was married."

"That doesn't mean I was sleeping with him! I–" Lucy waved her cuffed hands in front of her as if to clear the air and tried again. "Look, I knew Kyle. We dated for a little bit way back when and whenever he'd come into town, we'd catch up. That's it. I didn't sleep with either of them. I only knew Trevor because I met him a few times with Kyle."

"Whew, dodged a bullet there," Wyatt said after Lucy's confession.

In the interrogation room, Cassie's brow furrowed at the statements. "So, you were casual acquaintances with Trevor?"

"Yes. We saw each other a few times here and there. I didn't even know Kyle that well."

"But whenever he came into town, you'd catch up. You knew him well enough to see him every time he was here."

"Yeah, he usually just wanted a place to crash or something."

"And this last time he came into town?"

Lucy shrugged, the handcuffs scraping against the metal table. "He was strange. Distracted, odd. Scared."

"Scared of what?"

"I don't know. Something or someone. He told me about Trevor's plane crash. Said he needed help."

"And did you help him?"

"I gave him some money. I thought he left town. Then he turned up dead. But I didn't kill him."

Cassie bit her lower lip as she considered the information. "I still don't understand why you asked to see me. How can I help you prove you didn't do it?"

"Someone killed Kyle, Cassie. Someone was after him."

"Why?"

"I don't know. But I always had the sense that he and Trevor were involved in something."

"What?" Cassie asked, her eyes going wide.

"I don't know what. Something dangerous. Something people would kill them over."

Cassie huffed out a sharp laugh. "What makes you think I'd believe you?"

"Cassie," Lucy said, heaving a sigh, "why did Trevor lie to you? And to me? The few times I met him, he never mentioned a wife, never wore a ring, and when I asked Kyle anything about him, he wouldn't say much. Just that Trevor was his brother, and they were involved in some kind of business together."

Cassie fluttered her eyelashes as she worked through the allegations. After a moment, she licked her lips. "Okay, even if you're right, how can I help you? You just said Trevor lied to me. He obviously kept a good bit of his life hidden from me. I don't know anything."

"There has to be something!" Lucy cried, flinging her hands at Cassie. "Some little clue, a hint or something. Anything. Please."

Cassie remained quiet for a moment before she spoke again. "There may be one thing."

The door burst open to the room and Wyatt hovered inside the doorway. "Time's up."

"Just another minute, please, Wyatt," Lucy said.

"Nope, sorry," he said in a deep voice. "Can't do it. Rules are rules. Come on, Cassie. I've got to get the prisoner back to lock-up." He waved for Cassie to leave the room.

"Uh," Cassie stammered, "s-sure."

"No, Cassie, wait!"

"I'll do what I can," Cassie said with a nod. She squeezed past Wyatt into the hall where her mother waited for her.

"Let's wait in the car," Lily said as Wyatt entered the room and tugged Lucy to her feet. She rubbed Cassie's back as she led her to the front of the office. They passed Ruby's still empty chair and pushed into the fall sunshine.

After climbing into the car, Lily spun to face Cassie. "Feel better or worse?"

Cassie lifted her shoulders in a shrug as she shook her head. "I'm not sure. In some ways, better in other ways, worse. Why did Wyatt interrupt us?"

"He didn't want you telling her about the safe deposit box. He wasn't sure it was a good idea, and I trusted his judgment."

"Oh," Cassie murmured, tracing a seam on her jeans.

"Cass, are you okay?"

Cassie flicked her gaze up to meet her mother's eyes. She gave a slight nod. "Yeah, I'm all right. That was probably smart of Wyatt to stop me from spilling the beans."

"We have no idea what is in that safe deposit box, but I wouldn't say anything to Lucy yet."

Cassie fidgeted in her seat. "Do you think she's right?"

"About Trevor being involved in something?" Lily asked as she scanned the front door for a sign of Wyatt.

"Yeah."

"I don't know, Cass. It doesn't seem like Trevor. At least not the Trevor we knew."

Cassie studied the trees waving in the breeze on the building's side. "But did we know the real Trevor?"

"I guess we'll find out soon," Lily answered as Wyatt emerged into the sunshine and hopped down the steps, skirting the car and sliding behind the wheel.

"Sorry for the delay. I wanted to check in on your intruder investigation."

"Anything on that?" Lily asked as Wyatt fired the engine.

He backed the car from the space and pulled out, heading for the neighboring town of Misty Hollow. "Nothing. I'm not surprised. We don't have very many leads."

Lily rested her elbow on the car door, her index finger rubbing her lips. "I wonder if this is connected to Trevor somehow."

"The intruder?" Cassie asked, stretching her seatbelt as she leaned forward.

Lily twisted to glance at her. "Yeah. It just seems weird that this happened shortly after this murder."

Cassie settled back in the seat, her forehead wrinkling with worry as she watched the autumn-colored trees whip past her window.

"I'd think it has to do with that treasure. People wondering if there's anything else hidden in there. You said he came from the library, right?"

"Yes. He came out of the library," Lily confirmed. "And I'm not sure that's the case. We haven't had a disturbance in a while. And it's just strange that it's out of the blue suddenly."

Wyatt shrugged as they passed the sign welcoming them to Misty Hollow. "Not out of the blue for Whispering Manor."

Lily crinkled her forehead, staring at nothing for a moment. "Or is it out of the blue?"

"That's what I'm saying. It's not for that house. All those disturbances for all those years were treasure hunters. Or at least one in particular."

"Or Ri," Cassie called from the backseat.

Lily shook her head. "No, that's not what I meant. The other day I swear I saw someone lurking around in the trees at the edge of the property. I'm wondering if they're connected."

"What?" Cassie exclaimed.

Wyatt swerved as he shot a glance at Lily. "Are you saying you saw someone before the break-in last night and you never reported it?"

"I didn't think anything of it. And I *thought* I saw someone. I wasn't sure. But now I'm wondering if someone has been casing the house."

The conversation ended as Wyatt pulled into the First Federal Savings and Loan. Cassie eyed the small brick building with its white gabled roof. What secrets did it hold, she wondered? She'd soon find out.

She sucked in a deep breath as she followed her mother and Wyatt into the lobby. Wyatt asked about opening a safe deposit box and they were led to a bank associate sitting within a glass cubicle.

"Good morning," the perky blonde said with a broad smile. "I understand you'd like to access your safe deposit box."

"Actually," Cassie said, easing into the scratchy fabric seat between the plastic arms, "it's my late husband's safe deposit box. I'd like to access it and remove any items inside, and close the account."

The woman gave her a consoling glance. "I am very sorry for your loss and of course, we can assist you with that. I'll need to see your ID and a death certificate for your husband." She tapped around on her keyboard as Cassie opened her purse.

"Of course. Here is my license and I also have my marriage license and Trevor's death certificate here." Lily rubbed her daughter's arm as she passed over the documents.

The woman glanced at each of them before tapping around on the keyboard again. "Thank you, Mrs. McGuire. If you'll follow me to the vault, I'll have someone come down with the bank's key to open the box."

Cassie collected the documents and stuffed them back in her purse as she stood. "Thank you."

"Do you want us to wait here?" Lily questioned.

"No, I'd like you both to go, if that's okay." Cassie shot a questioning glance at Wyatt as she took a step on her wobbly legs.

"Sure, honey," Lily said, slipping an arm around her shoulders.

Wyatt nodded and offered an "Of course" as he trailed behind them.

The blonde shot a glance over her shoulder and smiled as they followed her down a set of stairs and into a large room lined with safe deposit boxes on three sides. Cassie sank onto a chair in front of a large rectangular table in the center of the room.

"I'll have Mark come right down with that key," the woman said before disappearing from their sight.

Silence pervaded the small room as they waited for the bank key to arrive. Within moments, a dark-haired man in a black suit appeared with a key in his hand. He glanced at a sticky note in his left hand before offering a smile to the room's occupants. "We're opening box 338 today?"

Cassie nodded and rose to follow the man to the box. She inserted the key she'd dug from her purse and turned it before the man did the same. He swung the door open and pulled the metal box from within, carrying it to the table and easing it onto the top.

"I'll give you some privacy," he said, stepping from the room and pulling a curtain across the door.

Cassie stared down at the silver box, contrasted against the black table. She bit her lower lip as she pondered the contents. A tear slipped to her cheek, and she flicked it away. "Guess we may as well get it over with."

"Take your time, Cass," Lily said as she rubbed her shoulders.

With a trembling hand, Cassie flicked the box's lid open on its hinge. Her brow furrowed as she stared at the contents inside. Various items lay piled inside the box including wads of cash, a flash drive, and several passports. On top of them, a black handgun gleamed under the fluorescent lights.

She snapped her gaze up to Wyatt who pulled a handkerchief from his pocket.

He wrapped the white fabric around the handle of the weapon and lifted it from the box. "I'll handle that if that's okay."

Cassie nodded as she stared at the remaining contents.

Wyatt slid the clip from the gun and peered inside. "It's loaded."

Cassie sank into the chair as she pondered why Trevor had a loaded gun in a safe deposit box in a seaside town. She lifted one of the passports from inside and flicked it open. A picture of Trevor stared back at her. She read the name listed next to it. James Winston.

Her brow pinched together as she pulled another passport from the box. She flipped it open to find the same picture of Trevor with another name next to it. This one read Phillip Canton.

Cassie sucked in a breath as she reached for another passport book and found yet another picture of Trevor with yet another name.

"These are all of Trevor. But none of these are his name. Or his real name. Unless Trevor wasn't his real name."

Cassie stared down at the items sprawled in front of her and the stacks of hundreds still in the box. "What were you into, Trevor?"

* * *

Cassie shielded her eyes against the bright sun as they stepped from within the muted bank's lights. She shuffled to the car, clutching her purse tightly against her chest.

Wyatt aimed the car for Hideaway Bay, leaving the town of Misty Hollow behind. "Listen, Cassie, I'm going to do some digging on this as soon as we get back, okay?"

"Thanks, Wyatt," Cassie said, her gaze never leaving the passing scenery.

"There's got to be an explanation for this," he murmured.

"Maybe Lucy was right. Trevor was involved in something with Kyle."

Wyatt glanced over his shoulder at her as they waited at a red light. "We'll look into it. Anything we find, I'll let you know right away."

"Thanks," Cassie repeated. She blew out a long breath. "Although I'm not sure I want to know."

"It may not be anything, Cassie," Lily said.

"And it may be that my entire marriage was a lie."

"Let's not jump to any conclusions until Wyatt's done some digging," Lily answered.

"I guess this is what Ri meant when she said help Wyatt. Maybe this will help your investigation into Kyle's death."

Wyatt raised his eyebrows, an expression of understanding crossed his face. "Oh, maybe! Maybe that's what she meant."

He swung the car onto Ocean Drive as silence fell between them. Cassie stared out the window at the seaside homes dotting the oceanfront. The rambling form of Whispering Manor appeared on the horizon and Wyatt swung the car into the gravel drive.

The car stopped short, still a good distance from the house. Wyatt's hand fumbled around in search of his phone in the car's cupholder as he stared straight ahead, his eyes wide.

"What did you–" Lily started, glancing up at him as she dug through her purse for the keys.

"Oh my gosh!" Cassie exclaimed as she spotted the source of Wyatt's concern.

Wyatt pressed a button on his phone and raised it to his ear. "I need two units immediately to Whispering Manor. There's been another break-in."

CHAPTER 28

*L*ily pressed her nose against the glass as she watched Wyatt creep toward their open front door with his gun at the ready.

"I can't believe this," Cassie said from the seat behind her. "Why didn't the alarm go off?"

Wyatt disappeared into the house and Lily let out a sigh. "No idea. I hope no one's in there."

"Why?" Cassie asked, her voice incredulous. "I'd rather they get caught!"

"I'd rather Wyatt not risk his life doing it."

Cassie clamped her mouth closed and patted her mother's shoulder. "I'm sure he'll be okay. He's trained for this."

"And he's worked in a sleepy town with no trouble for decades. Until we showed up."

Seconds later, two police cruisers barreled down the driveway, running into the grass on either side as they skirted around Wyatt's car. Uniformed officers raced from the vehicles, hurrying into the house with guns drawn.

Lily bit her thumbnail as they waited for ten tense minutes for someone to emerge from the house. Finally,

Wyatt trudged out with one of his deputies. She blew out a sigh of relief.

"I guess they didn't find anyone," Cassie noted.

"Doesn't look like it unless they've still got them inside."

Wyatt motioned for them to exit the car. Lily pushed her door open, swinging her purse onto her shoulder as she and Cassie closed the distance to the house and climbed the stairs onto the porch.

"House is clear. No one inside," Wyatt informed them as they gathered outside the front door.

"Any trace of them? How bad is it?"

"No trace of the perp. Looks like a few things are out of place in there, but no real damage." Wyatt pressed his lips into a thin line as he flicked his gaze between the two of them.

"What?" Lily asked, reading the consternation on his features.

"I think they were after something."

Cassie put her hands on her hips. "After what?"

"Did you move Trevor's personal effects last night after I left?"

Cassie's head waggled back and forth as confusion crossed her face. "No."

Wyatt squeezed his jaw closed again. "I'm sorry to tell you this, but they're gone."

Cassie's shoulders slid down her back as she tensed. "What? They took Trevor's stuff?" Tears filled her eyes as she stared into the house where the other officers finished their work.

"Sorry, Cassie. They took everything. Box and all."

Cassie fluttered her eyelashes as she considered the statement, tears welling in her eyes. Lily wrapped an arm around her and squeezed her shoulders. "It's okay, Cass. That wasn't Trevor. Just some stuff he left behind, okay?"

Cassie bobbed her head up and down without answering.

"Umm, listen the guys are probably done, so we can head in and sit down. They're just trying to pull some prints, but I doubt they left any behind."

Lily squeezed Cassie's shoulder again and tugged her toward the door. She led her into the living room, and they collapsed onto the couch together. Wyatt followed them in, perching in an armchair next to the couch.

"So, the alarm system was off when we came in, meaning the perp found a way to disarm it. We can check your video footage, but I'm assuming he or she disarmed it before they entered to avoid showing up on any cameras."

Lily sank her head into her palm. "What's the use in having the damn thing if someone can disarm it and waltz right in here?"

Wyatt licked his lips as he nodded his head. "I understand your frustration, Lily, I do. But this could be a helpful clue."

"How?"

"Well, the perp either knows you and can disarm your alarm or has familiarity with alarm systems. Either way, this was no quick score. Someone didn't just bust through your front door trying to find something of value. They were here for a reason, and they were smart about it."

Lily shook her head and sighed. "So, what do we do now?"

"Well, I'm going to have a patrol car out here twenty-four, seven to start with. This guy isn't a quitter, and I don't want him coming back. Especially while you two are here alone."

"Do you think he will?" Cassie asked, speaking up for the first time since entering the house.

"I think he may after he realizes you still have what he's after."

Cassie arched an eyebrow at Wyatt. "Which is?"

"I'd bet it was the safe deposit key."

Cassie shook her head. "I'm glad you're taking the stuff from inside that box into evidence."

Wyatt firmed his lower lip and nodded at her. "We'll get some answers. And I'm going to alert the bank. If anyone else tries to access that safe deposit box, I want to be notified."

One of the uniformed officers knocked on the doorjamb leading to the living room. "All finished, boss."

Wyatt twisted to speak to him. "All right, you can head out. Let me know if anything comes up from what you process. Tell Patterson to stay behind. We're keeping an officer at the house twenty-four, seven until further notice."

"Yes, sir," the man said with a curt nod before he disappeared through the front door, pulling it shut behind him.

Wyatt faced the women again. "Do you want me to stay?"

"No, I think we're fine," Lily said with a wave of her hand. "You go home and enjoy your day off."

"You sure?"

"Yeah," she said, rising from the couch. "I'll walk you out."

They shuffled to the front door and Wyatt peeked over Lily's head before he faced her again. "She gonna be okay?"

Lily glanced over her shoulder as she leaned against the doorjamb. Cassie curled on the couch, absentmindedly running her hand down her tuxedo cat's back after he'd crawled from under the couch to greet her. "Yeah, I think so. She just needs some time."

"Are you going to be okay? This would unnerve anyone."

"Yeah. They'd be really stupid to try something again with a police officer right outside."

Wyatt nodded his head at the statement before he placed a hand on Lily's shoulder. "If you need anything, call, okay?"

"I will. And thanks for everything today."

"You're sure you don't want me to stay?" he asked as he stepped onto the porch.

Lily shot another glance at Cassie in the living room. "Yeah, I think we need some girl time."

Wyatt offered her a tight-lipped nod. "Call if you need me."

"I will," Lily said as he stepped off the porch. She swung the door shut as he stopped to have a few words with his deputy and shuffled back into the living room, collapsing on the couch with a deep sigh.

She rubbed her forehead with her fingertips and reached over to stroke Cassie's leg. "How are you holding up?"

Cassie shrugged, tears threatening. "I don't know what to think."

"Want me to make you a hot chocolate?"

A tear spilled to Cassie's cheek, and she offered a quiet chuckle. "I'm not going to say no," she said with a sniffle.

Lily giggled and smiled at her as she stood and rubbed Cassie's head. "I'll be right–"

A loud thud sounded overhead and both women raised their eyes to the ceiling. Another bang followed.

"What was that?" Cassie whispered.

"Willy?" Lily answered.

"He's right here," Cassie said, leaping to her feet with the cat in her arms.

Lily slid her gaze sideways before rolling her eyes back up to the ceiling as another thud sounded. "So, who's up there?"

Cassie's heart beat hard in her chest as she shot a panicked glance at her mother. "Should I go get the deputy outside?"

"They just cleared the house. There can't be anyone up there."

Another thud echoed. "Obviously someone is up there, Mom."

Lily licked her lips and strode to the foyer, peering up the steps.

"Mom!" Cassie called in a lowered voice. "What are you doing? Let's go get the police!"

Lily waved the statement away and stepped up onto the first step. "I'm coming up with the police! Better come out now!"

Cassie followed behind her, setting Willy on his cat tree before she crossed the foyer and mounted the stairs.

"Sounds like it's coming from my room," Lily said, tapping a finger in the direction of her door.

They slinked up the stairs and over to Lily's open bedroom door. Lily scanned the interior, finding nothing.

Another thump sounded from across the space.

"The closet," Cassie whispered.

Lily nodded her head in a silent response as she snuck across the floorboards, wrapping her fingers around the doorknob. She flicked a glance at Cassie before she whipped the door open.

A pale face emerged from within the clothes, uttering one word. "Help."

Lily pressed her lips together, putting a hand on her hip. She shot another glance at Cassie. "It's Ri. Come out of there, would you? You scared us half to death. We thought the robber was still in here."

The doll trundled out into the bedroom. "Man. Gun. Hide."

"Yeah, I get it. Someone broke in and stole a few things."

Still hovering in the doorway, Cassie crinkled her forehead as she shoved her hands into her pockets. "He had a gun?"

"Gun," the doll repeated.

Cassie's jaw flexed as she parsed through the doll's simple statements.

"I don't think he'd have hurt you. I'm not even sure he could have," Lily said, patting the doll's shoulder. "Although

I guess if he shot you, maybe you couldn't talk to us anymore."

Cassie bit her lower lip as she crossed to the doll. "I think we need to get Ruby here right away."

"Why?" Lily questioned.

"She was here when the intruder broke in. She can identify him. She's a witness."

Lily's eyebrows shot up on her forehead and she flicked her gaze to the doll. "Oh, I hadn't thought of that. But you did see him, didn't you?"

"Man. Gun."

Lily nodded her head at the statement. "We'll need a little more than that, but you're right, Cassie. She may be able to identify the robber."

Lily pulled her cell phone from her pocket and tapped around.

"Are you calling Ruby?"

"No, I'm texting Wyatt. He can have Ruby get in touch with us. But I think he should know we have a witness."

Her thumbs flew across the phone before she shoved it back into her pocket. "Okay. Now, about that hot chocolate."

Before they could leave the room, the doll darted across it, zipping into the hall.

Cassie twisted to follow her flight from the room. "Wow. I wonder if she wants a cup, too."

Lily shrugged as she crossed the room, following behind the doll, with Cassie trailing behind her. They found the Victorian animatron on the opposite side of the staircase, facing the wall. Next to her, Willy peered at the wall, his tail swishing against the floor.

"Glitch?" Cassie asked.

"Maybe she likes to chase bugs like your cat," Lily suggested.

The doll whipped around to face them. "Help."

"What do you want help with?" Cassie asked. "Do you want to come downstairs for a hot chocolate?"

"Help!" the doll insisted.

"Umm, yeah, you can help us, though I think we're going to need some help so you can say a few more words before we can get anything meaningful."

Willy leapt up at the wall, batting it with his paw before he settled back to his haunches.

"Help me," the doll said.

Cassie glanced at Lily with a shrug. "What is she talking about?"

"Help you how, Ri?" Lily asked.

"The journals. Help me."

Cassie heaved a sigh. "She's after the journals again. Look, Ri, we'd love to help you but we have no idea where they are. If you could–"

The doll spun around to face the wall again. "The journals."

Lily cocked her head and stared at the blank space. Both the doll and the cat seemed intrigued by the empty wall. "I think she is telling us where they are. I think they're inside that wall."

Cassie stared at the mint green paint. "Like behind it?"

"That's not the first time she's been at that wall."

"No, you're right. The night she was wandering around she kept ramming into it. I wonder if there's a compartment or something."

"There's only one way to find out."

"Look for a trigger?" Cassie said, scanning the wall for something that may open a secret panel.

"No, I'm going to break down the wall," Lily answered.

"What? Mom, are you kidding?"

Lily shuffled to the wall and ran her hand along it. I don't feel any panels or anything. I doubt there's a trigger to open something like there was in Susan's room." She glanced around the surrounding area. "There's not even a trigger here."

"Okay, then we break down the wall, I guess. I'll get a hammer from my toolkit."

Lily nodded as she squatted next to the cat and continued to eye the surface. Cassie retrieved her pink-handled hammer and plopped onto the floor next to her mother.

"Where do you want me to start?"

Lily glanced at the doll hovering above them. "Where should we open the wall, Ri?"

The doll stared ahead, silent and motionless. Cassie huffed out a sigh and pressed the hammer head against the wall, glancing at the doll. "Here?"

No response. She pressed her lips together, moving the hammer to another spot. "How about here?"

Nothing.

"Try tapping on it," Lily suggested. "See if it sounds hollow or not."

Cassie climbed to her knees and tapped a few places along the wall until she hit a spot that made a dull thudding sound when tapped. She raised her eyebrows and glanced at her mother, her lips curling into a slight smile.

Lily cocked her head and motioned for Cassie to give it a smack with the hammer.

"Here goes nothing," Cassie said with a sigh.

CHAPTER 29

Cassie lined up the hammer and swung, knocking a hole into the painted surface. It crumbled away, leaving dust and debris on the floor below.

Cassie gave it a few more taps, widening the hole until she could wiggle her fingers inside. She pried a few pieces of the plaster loose and tugged her cell phone from her pocket, toggling on the flashlight. She shined it inside the small opening.

"Anything?"

"I can't see anything yet. I need a bigger hole."

She pounded away, knocking more pieces of the wall away until something caught her eye. After wiping her dusty hands against her jeans, she lifted the cell phone's flashlight and peered inside. "There's something in here!"

"What is it? Journals?" Lily asked.

"No," Cassie said with a shake of her head. She stuck her hand inside up to her shoulder as she bit her lower lip, her forehead crinkling in concentration. She felt around blindly until her fingers grazed a wooden object.

She grabbed hold of it and hauled it upward, wiggling it

out of the hole. A thick layer of dust covered the top of the wooden box. Cassie blew it off, coughing as dust billowed into the air before she set it down between them.

Lily studied the container, her fingers grazing the clasp holding it shut.

"Should we open it?" Cassie asked.

Lily nodded in response to her question. "Do you want to do the honors or me?"

Cassie poked a finger at Lily. "You do it. You've been with her since the start, reading her journal."

"Hope this is what you're looking for, Ri," Lily said as she swung the latch up and tugged open the top.

Cassie peered over her shoulder at the contents. Four small black books lined the inside. Atop them sat a pearl necklace and a ruby necklace.

"Wow," Cassie breathed as she stared at the large teardrop ruby as she lifted it from the box. Lily pulled one of the black books from inside, thumbing through it as the spine cracked in protest.

Cassie pulled her attention away from the necklace and glanced at the pages as they flew by while absentmindedly stroking Willy's soft fur. "Are these the journals, Ri?"

Lily glanced up at the doll for confirmation.

"The journals," she said.

Cassie grinned at Lily. "We found them!"

"Yes," Lily said, returning her attention to the yellowed pages. "But why did she want us to?"

"Maybe they're hers. Maybe they explain why she–" Cassie shot a glance at the doll before continuing. "–you know."

Lily pulled a second book open and studied a few pages. "No."

"What do you mean?"

"This isn't her handwriting."

Cassie's brow furrowed and she shook her head. "So, then why did she want us to find them?"

"Read," the doll said.

Lily collected the remaining journals from the box along with the pearl necklace before closing it. She eyed the hole in the wall. "We're going to need to fix that."

"Yeah, I'll have to run to the hardware store for some supplies," Cassie said as she climbed to her feet.

"Help me up first," Lily requested, reaching her hands up to Cassie. "It's terrible getting old. I do not recommend it."

"I'll clean this up first and then head over for the stuff I need to fix it. Oh, what should we do with these necklaces?"

"Ri," Lily said to the doll, dangling one of the necklaces from her fingers, "do you want these?"

The doll spun to face them. "Keep."

"Maybe she wants to wear them," Cassie offered. "Maybe that will help her communicate."

Lily unclasped the pearl necklace. "We can give it a try."

Cassie wound it around the doll's neck and fastened it. "Pretty," she said, eyeing the pearls atop the blue fabric before she added the ruby necklace. "How's that?"

The doll stood motionless. Lily shrugged at it as she collected the journals from the floor. "Well, I guess I'll check these out and see if I can figure out whose they are and what order to read them in."

"Sounds like a great rainy day afternoon project," Cassie said, waving a finger to the darkening skies visible through the large second-story window above the front door. "Do you want Ri downstairs with you?"

"Maybe. Perhaps something I read will trigger a response."

"I'll take her down now and grab the shop vac."

Cassie lifted the doll and lugged her downstairs, setting

her in the library near the window seat before she retrieved the shop vac.

"Looks like I'll have quite a show," Lily said as Cassie rolled the round item to the stairs. She settled into the window seat with the stack of journals and a cup of hot tea. The doll stood motionless at her side.

Thunder rumbled overhead and a flash of lightning raced across the darkened sky. "Have fun," Cassie said with a grin before hefting the vacuum onto her hip and climbing the stairs.

Lily settled back against the pillows and stared outside for a few moments. Wind tossed the fall leaves around, tearing many from the limbs and scattering them in wet clumps on the ground.

With a deep inhale, she stared at the black-bound books next to her. She pulled the first onto her lap and flicked open the front cover. No names covered the pages.

The date on the first entry read May 18, 1803. The year after Henrietta's death, Lily recalled. This definitely was not written by Henrietta. She skimmed the first few words, her brow furrowing. It spoke about traveling and studying local culture.

The writing appeared feminine, though she couldn't be sure. The journal must have belonged to a woman. Perhaps the second mistress of Whispering Manor. But why would Henrietta want her to discover journals from another occupant?

Lily set it aside in favor of checking the others for names and dates to establish an order. She opened the next on the stack, its spine creaking with effort as she stretched it open. No name. The date on the first entry read July 24, 1803.

The whir of the shop vac drowned out most other noise as she set the second book aside without scanning any further, assuming it wouldn't aid in her quest to find the owner and was not the first in the series.

As she pulled the third book open, her breath caught in her throat. The name inscribed on the interior of the cover read Carolina Nichols Johnson. Lily scrunched her forehead as she recalled the name Carolina appearing in Henrietta's journals.

She snapped her gaze up to the silent doll in front of her. "Were these your sister's journals?"

The doll did not respond, standing sentinel near her feet. Another boom of thunder sounded, shaking the house as Lily checked the date on the first entry.

March 14, 1803

Today, I travel with my husband, James, south into the jungles. James intends to study the Mayan ruins and search for clues conquistadors may have missed to the vast legendary treasures the lost kingdom supposedly held.

Before our departure, one of James's colleagues uttered several nasty comments during a send-off get-together hosted by the department at his university. "Treasure hunters," he called us. Seeking to gain fame and fortune. Just like your brother, he spat at me, waving a finger in my face.

I must admit, I grow weary of the accusations against my deceased brother. The poor man met a watery grave and even after his death, cannot escape the vicious rumors that followed him throughout his life.

. . .

Lily arched an eyebrow at the words as the vacuum noise died down upstairs. "So, this is your sister," she said to her quiet companion. "And she really didn't believe Clif was a pirate, huh?"

"Read," the doll answered.

"Okay, okay," Lily said, holding a hand up. "I'll keep reading."

She pulled open the same journal to continue perusing Carolina's first entry.

"No," the doll burst out.

Her arm rose slowly and hovered over Lily's lap. The journal clattered to the floor, and another rose in the air.

Lily grabbed hold of it as it floated in front of her. "Why would you want me to read this one?"

"Read," the doll insisted.

"Okay, okay," Lily repeated, pulling open the journal she'd set aside moments ago. She stared at the date marked July 24, 1803, before she read the first sentence.

Today we climbed to the top of

The paper fluttered, blowing over to the second page of the book.

"Hey!" Lily complained with a huff. "You wanted me to read this and now you're blowing the pages around."

"Read."

"I'm trying to read it. You keep turning the pages. Stop it."

"Read. August 31."

Lily shot the doll a curious glance as she paged through the book in search of an entry marked with the given date.

"Okay, here it is. August 31." Lily flicked her gaze up to the doll before she read the entry.

.   .   .

August 31, 1803

Our camp is in turmoil. Our small party has been captured by pirates.

"Whoa! Your sister was captured by pirates? Your family really does not have the best luck, do they?"

"Read."

Lily squashed her lips together and settled into the seat as thunder rumbled again.

They marched into the camp, holding us all at gunpoint or the tips of their swords. In some instances, both. One of them requested to know the leader of our party. James shoved me behind him and stepped forward, taking responsibility. The man smacked him hard against the jaw, dropping him to his knees.

Within moments, his hands and legs were bound, and he was strung up in a nearby tree, hanging from his bound wrists. The rest of us were herded into one of the tents, bound and gagged. I feared for my life and my pride as one of the sailors, smelling of liquor and sweat, leaned close to me and sniffed at me as though he was an animal on the hunt.

I imagined the terrible things a band of men may do to a woman they held captive, and a tear rolled down my cheek. Just then, the flap of the tent flicked open, and the man pulled away from me, standing at attention. I expected the captain to enter moments later.

A figure stood limned in the moonlight outside the darkened tent. A lantern flared to life and was shoved in our faces as the figure leaned forward to peer inside.

When the light came close to me, I shrank away, but one of the men grasped my arm roughly and tugged me closer. I could swear the figure stiffened, the feather in his cap wiggling as his posture straightened. The flap dropped closed and the figure disappeared.

We waited almost twenty minutes huddled in fear and trembling before the man who struck James pushed into the tent. "Bring the woman," his gruff voice said.

I was hauled to my feet and shoved from the tent. Tears streamed down my cheeks as I assumed the worst, girding myself for what I expected to be a humiliating and painful experience.

They paraded me into the temple near which we'd made camp. Torches burned brightly as I was led down a corridor and into a large chamber. Two figures stood at the back, hidden in the shadows.

"Here she is," the man who struck James said to them as he shoved me forward. I kept my chin tucked to my chest, unwilling to raise my eyes to them.

"Light," a voice echoed in the chamber. A torch was passed to my captor, and he shoved it close to me.

I shied away from it, but he grabbed my arm and shook me as another squashed my cheeks in his grimy hands and turned my face toward the light. A gasp sounded from across the room.

The two figures fidgeted in the darkness, their shadows shifting.

"Carolina," one said.

My brow furrowed, questioning how this savage man knew my name. Perhaps James had offered it to him. Or he had beaten it from him. I struggled to firm my lower lip as the man crossed closer to me. My trembling body threatened to collapse, but the strong grip of the sailor kept me upright.

"Please, sir," I said, sounding more pitiful than I had hoped as he hovered over me.

A finger touched my chin, and I shrank away, but the other

sailor held me firm. The finger grazed me again, tipping my head upward. My eyes were the last to move. As I licked my lips, I slowly slid them upward, my heart seizing in my chest as the flaming torch flickered against the man's features.

"Carolina," he repeated, a grin spreading across his face.

Another sob escaped me, and a tear fell to my cheek as confusion coursed through my body. "Clif?" I questioned.

His grin broadened as I pondered if a ghost stood in front of me. Had even Davy Jones spat Clif back and forced him to live or had the reports of his death been a mistake?

"And that's not all," Clif said, waving behind him.

The other figure approached, stalking forward with an odd gait, the reason for which was revealed as light lit them.

My eyes bulged from my head as I recognized the feminine form and delicate features. I gasped in a breath. "Henrietta?"

Clif wiggled his eyebrows at me, the grin still affixed to his face.

"No," I said with a shake of my head. "No, it cannot be. You're dead. You're both dead."

"Mere trickery. Rather an excellent plan on Ri's part. As you can see, we remain very much alive."

Lily's eyebrows arched upward, and her jaw fell open. She snapped her gaze up to the doll in front of her. "You didn't die! Either of you. You faked your deaths!"

CHAPTER 30

Cassie flicked the switch on the shop vac, wrangling the thick hose with its flat attachment around to reach the floor and sucking up the pieces of plaster scattered across the hardwood. The loud appliance hummed in her ear as she sucked up the dust along the edge of the baseboard.

She dropped the hose and studied the hole, wondering if anything else hid behind the house's walls. She pulled her phone from her back pocket and shined the light inside, finding only a mess.

After removing a few more pieces of the wall, she fed the extracted bits into the shop vac and stuck the hose inside the wall to suck up any debris.

She flicked off the loud canister vac and wound up the cord, hoisting the round drum high and hauling it downstairs. Wind whipped outside, bending tree branches to their breaking point.

Cassie shuffled back in through the foyer, glancing at her mom in the library. She read one of the journals, the book propped against her bent knees. She grabbed her keys from the bowl on the table, hoping to make it to the hardware store and back before the rain started.

She swung the front door open. A package sat on the doormat with a pile of mail underneath it. Their mail carrier's jacket blew in the wind as he hurried toward his mail truck, offering a wave to the officer in the parked police car.

Cassie collected the package and pieces of mail as a deluge poured from the sky. Rain battered the house, pounding against the roof and siding.

She retreated inside, pushing the door closed and tossing her keys into the bowl.

"So much for the hardware store," she muttered as she flipped through the correspondence. She set aside a few bills before she got to a white envelope with a handwritten address.

The salutation made her pause, her muscles stiffening and her forehead wrinkling.

"The widows," she whispered aloud. "What is this?"

Fury burned through her as she read the words again and wondered what sorry excuse for a human considered that greeting appropriate. She flipped open the envelope and ripped the letter from the inside, shaking it open.

In the center of the page, black block letters spelled out a simple, single-sentence message.

Your husbands' deaths weren't an accident, they were murdered.

Cassie's knees wobbled as she read the words and heat washed over her body. The other pieces of mail fell from her hands, sprawling across the foyer's parquet floor. Her senses dulled as blood rushed in her ears and her heart pounded in her chest.

She pressed a shaky hand to her lips, her eyes welling with tears. She sucked in a deep breath, trying to steady her nerves.

"Mom!" she called in a shaky voice.

"Cassie!" her mother's voice answered, filled with excitement.

"Mom!"

"Cassie!"

Lily appeared at the entrance to the library, her eyes wide and the corners of her lips curled into a partial smile. It faded quickly as she spotted the upset on her daughter's face.

"Cass? Is something wrong?"

Without a word, Cassie handed the paper to her mother. Lily scanned the page, her eyebrows raising as she read the words.

"Where did this come from?"

"It was in the mail," Cassie explained, her voice still shaky. "Addressed to 'The Widows.'" She flipped the envelope over and glanced at the corner. "Hand delivered. No postmark on it."

Lily stared at the paper again before shaking her head, her forehead wrinkling in confusion. "Murdered?"

"Yep. Just like you're going to be," a new male voice said.

Lily and Cassie snapped their eyes in the direction of the voice. A burly man in a dark hoodie strode toward them from the sliding door at the rear of the house. Cassie swallowed hard as she stared at the black gun pointed their way.

Lily backed a few steps away from the library toward Cassie, placing herself between the man and her daughter. "If it's money you're after, there some in my sock drawer upstairs. Take it and go."

The man smirked at her, scoffing before he answered with a shake of his head. "I'm not after your money."

"Then what?" Lily demanded. "The treasure is all gone. It's been gone for months."

The man screwed up his face. "What?"

"The pirate treasure buried in the house. It's been cleared out by the university cataloging it. It's all gone. There's nothing more here for you."

The man scoffed again. "I'm not after some treasure. I'm after the key."

Lily stuck her hands behind her, inching Cassie back a few steps. "Key? What key?"

"The key to the safe deposit box. It wasn't in Richie's stuff. And we want it."

Cassie's brow furrowed as the man spoke. "Richie?" she questioned.

The man's lips twisted into a patronizing grin. "I think you knew him as Trevor."

The words stung her as she faced the realization that she knew far less about her so-called husband than she realized. She licked her lips and opened her mouth to answer.

Lily beat her to it. "It's upstairs. We have to get it."

The man wiggled the gun at them. "No, no. Let blondie run up. Let's you and I get cozy in the living room, huh, grandma?"

"Grandma?" Lily questioned him as he approached her with the gun. "Just who do you think you're calling a grandma?"

"Take it easy, lady," the man said, grabbing her by the arm and dragging her toward the living room. "No need to get your knickers in a twist. But you aren't exactly young anymore."

Lily narrowed her eyes at him as he dragged her away.

"Wait!" Cassie shouted before they reached the other room.

Lily spun to face her, giving a slight shake of her head.

Cassie eyed her before flicking her gaze back to the man. "I–I put the key away. Actually, that's not true. I threw it across my room in a fit of rage. It may take me a few minutes to find it and dig it out. I think it went behind my dresser."

"Well, I'd suggest you hurry. I don't have all day. And neither does Mommy Dearest." He leveled the gun at Lily's head.

"Okay, just take it easy. I just don't want you to think I'm trying to pull something. I'll get the key and you can have it. No problem. I don't want it. And I don't want to know what Trevor was involved in."

He waggled the gun toward the stairs. "Hop to it, sister."

Cassie gave a nervous nod before she hurried up the stairs, shooting a pained glance at her mother.

"Oh, just a minute," the man yelled as she neared the top.

Cassie froze and spun to face him.

"Your phone. Toss it down here."

Cassie squeezed her eyes closed as she pulled the phone from her back pocket and tossed it to the man. He caught it one-handed, offering a snide "thanks" before he waved Lily into the living room.

She strode in with her hands raised. "Take a seat," the man growled, tossing Cassie's phone on the cushion of the armchair.

Lily sank onto the sofa, her hands still raised. "So, you knew Trevor, huh?"

The man paced the floor of the living room, glancing up as Cassie's footsteps wandered around above them.

"Did you know his brother, Kyle?"

The man shot a sideways glance at Lily. "Lady, do you think I'm an idiot?"

Lily shrugged her shoulders before she lowered her hands to her lap. "I didn't say that. I wasn't aware being involved with Trevor or Kyle made you an idiot."

"I know what you're trying to do. You want some bleeding-heart confession about my misdeeds. You're not getting it."

"So, you didn't kill Kyle?"

"You got a big mouth, Mama. All right, if it makes you feel any better, yeah, I killed him. And as soon as I get that key, I'm going to kill you."

Cassie's footsteps creaked on the stairs and the man rushed back over to the foyer, his gun trained on her as she descended.

"There may be a problem," Cassie said.

"Oh? I don't like problems."

Cassie froze on the stairs and blew out a breath, trying to formulate the words to tell him she did not have the key. She bit her lower lip, the pained expression returning to her face.

A knock on the front door interrupted any further conversation. The man's muscles stiffened, and he glanced out the window next to the door.

A curse slipped between his lips, and he waved Lily toward him. "It's that cop. Get rid of him."

He grabbed Cassie's wrist and tugged her down the stairs, wrapping his arm around her neck and pressing the gun to her temple. "Try anything funny and little blondie's brains will be all over this floor."

The man dragged Cassie back a few steps, disappearing behind the stairs.

Lily nodded and tugged her tunic further down around her waist. She blew out a nervous breath before she slid the chain lock onto the door and tugged it open.

Wyatt started toward the opening door before stopping abruptly. He stared in with a wrinkled forehead at Lily.

"Hey, Wyatt, now's not a great time."

"I got your message about the ghost doll seeing something. I brought Ruby." Ruby popped her head around

Wyatt and waved. "I thought we could get something out of her."

Lily glanced over her shoulder and shook her head. "Yeah, the thing is, Cassie's having a really tough time. I don't think she could take visitors at the moment. Could you come back later?"

"Uhhh," Wyatt said, glancing behind Lily before he returned his gaze to her, "sure."

"Thanks," Lily said as she started to push the door closed.

She met with resistance as Wyatt placed his hand against it. "Are you sure everything's okay, Lily?"

Lily sucked in a deep breath, forcing a smile onto her lips. "Yeah. Everything's fine. It's just Cassie. She's really upset."

Wyatt nodded, his hands falling to his hips. "Okay. Well, if you need anything, just call or text."

"Will do. Thanks." She pushed the door closed and leaned against it, blowing out a long breath. She tugged the baseball bat from the umbrella stand next to the door, hiding it discreetly behind her.

"Good work, Mom," the man said, shuffling back toward them with Cassie still in his grasp. He shoved her forward and she stumbled toward Lily before regaining her balance and spinning to face him. "Now, what's all this about a problem?"

"Cassie, don't," Lily cautioned.

"Mom, we don't have another choice."

"Cassie–" Lily warned again, gripping her arm.

"We don't have the key," Cassie choked out.

The man cocked his head, the gun wavering in his hand. "What?"

"We don't have it," Cassie repeated. "I lied earlier. I–I panicked, and I lied. I turned it in to the bank earlier today."

The man's face contorted into a mask of rage. He gripped the sides of his head as he roared with anger. He recovered slightly and leveled the gun at them again. "I want what was in the box."

Cassie squashed her lips together as she shook her head, holding her shaky hands out in front of her. "The money I can get you, but I don't have it on me and–"

"I already told you I don't want the money. I want the flash drive."

Cassie gasped in a breath, her mind searching for a solution. Could she locate another flash drive fast enough to pass it off to him? Would it matter? He'd likely kill them, especially if he thought they had seen any evidence of wrongdoing on the flash drive.

Before Cassie could answer, a new voice entered the conversation. The whirring of the doll's base echoed in the room. "Stop. Now."

The man twisted to glance behind him, swinging the gun toward the new voice. His eyes widened as he stared at the doll behind him. "What the hell?"

Before he could swing around toward them again, Lily shoved Cassie to the side and raised the bat. She cracked the man's shoulder as she swung it down. He cried out in pain, stumbling a few steps, but keeping hold of the gun.

Lily raised the bat again and swung down against his wrist. He issued a sharp cry and the gun clattered to the floor. Cassie raced across the space, kicking it away.

The man grasped at his wrist, turning toward Lily, his features twisted into a mask of anger. He lunged toward Lily. "You stupid bi–"

"I wouldn't do that," Wyatt said, emerging from behind the stairs, his gun trained on the man. "Get your hands up and don't you move."

The man twisted to face him, noting the weapon, and raised his hands overhead as Lily and Cassie backed away.

Lily offered him a satisfied glance. "Now, who are you calling grandma?"

"You two okay?" Wyatt asked as he approached the man, instructing him to kneel and then lay flat.

"Yeah, we're okay," Lily said, her breathing still shaky. "Thanks for the save."

Wyatt tugged his cell phone from his pocket, keeping the gun trained on the man, and dialed a number. "Perp's been contained. Send in a unit to get him out of here."

"He killed Kyle," Lily said. "Lucy was telling the truth. She's innocent."

"And I'm betting he's your prowler, too," Wyatt responded as officers flooded into the house from the back.

One of them secured the man, handcuffing his hands behind his back before two officers hauled him to his feet.

"And maybe he's behind this?" Cassie asked, swiping the letter from where it had fallen when they'd been taken hostage. She passed it to Wyatt who scanned it.

"When did you receive this?"

"Today. In the mail. No postmark, though."

"Why would he send that message and then storm in here?" Lily questioned.

Wyatt studied it for another moment. "My best guess is, he didn't. There must be more going on here."

"There is," Cassie answered. "He was after that flash drive you took into evidence. Something must be on it. Something incriminating."

"Something that got Trevor and Blake murdered," Lily added.

Wyatt waved the paper in the air. "We're going to look into this and find out."

"So are we," Lily said with a nod. "This isn't over. Not by a longshot."

EPILOGUE

"So, Clif and Ri didn't die on the dates listed?" Cassie asked as she bobbed her teabag up and down in her mug.

"Nope. That's what I was coming to tell you when all heck broke loose, and that idiot held us at gunpoint."

"And the journals," she said, sliding into the deck chair next to Lily, "belong to Henrietta's sister?"

Lily nodded as she sipped at her hot tea, staring out over the waves as they pounded the beach. "Yep. Her husband was an academic, and they traveled to Central America where they happened to be taken hostage by a group of pirates. Who turned out to be her illustrious brother and sister."

"Hmm," Cassie said before sipping at the steaming liquid.

Lily patted the journals stacked on the table. "I can't wait to read these. Particularly, the ones after she realizes Henrietta is alive. I wonder if she kept in touch or not."

"We should try to find some information about them. There has to be something we can track down about their lives after their supposed deaths."

"May be difficult," Lily said, glancing over at her daugh-

325

ter. "And we do have our hands full with investigating the note we received."

Cassie squashed her lips together and wrinkled her nose. "Somehow I think I'd rather chase pirates than find out what Trevor got himself into that got both him and dad killed."

Lily patted her hand and squeezed it. "Then we'll do both. A little of each to balance things out."

Cassie smiled at her mother. "Sounds like a plan."

She spent a minute in silent contemplation before she spoke again. "Speaking of our little trouble, how did Wyatt know to come in? We could hear everything you said and nothing tipped us off. Did you give him a note or a signal?"

Lily raised her eyebrows and shook her head. "Nope. I asked him how he knew."

"And?"

Lily flicked her gaze to Cassie before reaching to her side. Her fingers closed around the arm of the haunted doll. "Our dear Ri tipped him off. She ran onto the porch and told him there was a man with a gun and we needed help."

Cassie raised her eyes to the animatron that now housed the spirit of Henrietta Nichols Blanchard. "Wow. Thanks, Ri. You probably saved our lives!"

The doll spun toward them. "You're welcome."

Lily settled back into her seat as the three women, two living and one not, enjoyed the waning warmth of a sunny fall day. "Life is sure going to be interesting around here."

* * *

Look for Book 3 in the Lily & Cassie by the Sea Mysteries series in 2024! Until then, if you love a good cozy, try *Moving is Murder*, Book 1 in the Middle Age is Murder Series.

A NOTE FROM THE AUTHOR

Dear Reader,

Thank you for reading this book!

I hope you enjoyed reading this book as much as I did writing it! If you loved it, please consider leaving a review and help get the book into the hands of other interested readers.

Book 3 in this series is coming soon. In the meantime, check out *Moving is Murder* or *Murder of Pearl* for more fabulous mysteries with mature heroines!

If you'd like to stay up to date with all my news, be the first to find out about new releases first, sales and get free offers, join the Nellie H. Steele's Mystery Readers' Group! Or sign up for my newsletter now!

All the best, Nellie

OTHER SERIES BY NELLIE H. STEELE

Cozy Mystery Series

Cate Kensie Mysteries
Lily & Cassie by the Sea Mysteries
Pearl Party Mysteries
Middle Age is Murder Cozy Mysteries

Supernatural Suspense/Urban Fantasy

Shadow Slayers Stories
Duchess of Blackmoore Mysteries

Adventure

Maggie Edwards Adventures
Clif & Ri on the Sea

www.ingramcontent.com/pod-product-compliance
Lightning Source LLC
Chambersburg PA
CBHW060857210726
48293CB00006B/1847